RETURN TO THE WILD

OTHER ADVENTURES OF THE MACNAUGHTON BROTHERS

Back to the Bush: Another Year in the Wild
'Witty and hilarious, *Back to the Bush* captures life in a game lodge brilliantly. I could not put it down!'
– NICKY RATTRAY

'*Back to the Bush* is just as readable and entertaining, if not more so, than *A Year in the Wild*. It is filled with pathos and bathos and much to make you chuckle, laugh out loud, and even shed a tear or two. There is an unexpected twist in this riotous read.'
– BRIAN JOSS, *Constantiaberg Bulletin*

A Year in the Wild: A Riotous Novel
'There's family conflict, romance, funny anecdotes, poaching and all kinds of intrigue – in other words, something for everyone.'
– KAY-ANN VAN ROOYEN, *GO!*

'It's both delicious and deliciously funny. It draws easy-to-imagine pictures of madness and mayhem; hilarity and horror. And it gives the most fascinating insights into what goes on behind the posh scenes of larney lodges.'
– TIFFANY MARKMAN, Women24

'*A Year in the Wild* is more than an amusing and entertaining account of game lodge goings on; it is also a coming-of-age tale of two brothers who explore life, love, lust and loss.'
– CHRIS ROCHE, Wilderness Safaris

RETURN TO THE WILD

A Novel

Yet Another Year in the Wild

JAMES HENDRY

MACMILLAN

First published in 2022 by Pan Macmillan South Africa
Private Bag X19
Northlands
2116
Johannesburg
South Africa

www.panmacmillan.co.za

ISBN 978-1-77010-806-6
e-ISBN 978-1-77010-807-3

Editing by Nicola Rijsdijk
Proofreading by Sean Fraser
Design and typesetting by Nyx Design
Cover design by publicide
Front cover photograph by James Hendry

Printed by **novus print**, a division of Novus Holdings

For my precious wife Kirsten with whom I fell in love
surrounded by the wilderness

INTRODUCTION

It is four and a half years since the start of Angus MacNaughton's last year in the wild. Much has happened since last we heard from him in the wake of his ascension to the exalted position of head ranger at Sasekile Private Game Reserve.

1

The rain battered against the window, borne on an incessant north-west wind that seemed to have been blowing for at least three months. I stared into the grey gloom. A pine tree waved in the gale, buffeted by rain that came in horizontal needles sharper than those it tore from the tree.

It was impossible to be warm in this weather. I had heard of 'cold seeping into bones', of course, but assumed it applied to winters in the vicinity of the poles – certainly not in the Fair Cape.

Fair Cape, my arse.

The only reason I was looking out at the miserable conifer was because the contents of the small room was so deeply unappealing. I returned my attention to Gareth Watkins, aged seven, just in time to see a shiny globule of snot fall from his left nostril onto the front of his guitar. The mucus slid down inexorably towards the sound hole, whence it disappeared. Gareth Watkins seemed not to notice the emptying of his befouled sinuses onto the cheap instrument, for he continued trying to play 'Mary had a little lamb' – three notes the obviously cretinous child had been attempting to master for three months.

'Watkins,' I said, 'you seem to be leaking.'

The boy looked up, his blue blazer (the cost of which exceeded my pathetic wages by an order of magnitude) covered in food and scuffs.

'Huh?' he grunted, sniffed, and then wiped his nose, adding a slimy green stripe to the right sleeve.

'Never mind,' I replied. 'Time's up – go back to class. I'd tell you to practise but that would be like prevailing upon this northwester to cease.'

'Huh?'

'Go away, Watkins.'

The boy opened the door and mooched out, replaced with a frigid gust from the corridor. I rose, shut the door and slumped back onto my chair.

How the hell had it come to this? How had I sunk so low? Not that I thought teaching was, in any way, an inferior occupation – quite to the contrary. I had huge admiration bordering on jealousy for my more skilled colleagues. But I, Angus MacNaughton, simply did not have the patience for or love of humanity to be teaching its growing members. My occupation as a guitar teacher to the ungrateful children of the rich at this massively pretentious Cape Town private school was borne of the greatest instinct: survival. I had no money, and being skint in Western society means dying of cold and starvation. Poverty in Cape Town means dying of cold, starvation *and* loneliness – Capetonians being famously insular (also conceited, xenophobic and possessed of absurd delusions of their social worth).

Three and a half years previously I had made the move to the Cape in need of a change of scenery – I had left the bush to make a fresh start in what had recently been voted the 'world's most beautiful city'. As I sat there in the guitar room, the incessant bloody wind flinging water at the panes, I had cause to wonder how it had come to this.

2

For many people, the thought of living in Cape Town is deeply appealing – it certainly was for me. Table Mountain, two oceans (in popular lore if not actual fact), the winelands on your doorstep, art, sophistication, gastronomy (is that really the best word for it?), national parks, Robben Island (now an attraction, not a prison) ...

On arrival, I stepped from the plane and was hit in the face by a wind fiercer than a lion charge. This explained the number of passengers awkwardly clutching leaking paper bags. Still, I was in Cape Town – the weather is not perfect anywhere, is it?

Luggage? None. Ever again. The last I saw of my bag was when I bade it a fond adieu in Johannesburg. It contained all of my clothes, bar the pair of shorts and T-shirt I was wearing. (I should have had a jersey for the plane – why do airlines insist on trying to cryogenically preserve their passengers?) Thankfully, I had told the unimpressed flight attendant at check-in that there were greater chances of my parting with my own head than with my guitar.

So I emerged from the airport armed with a guitar and a small knapsack containing a book, a laptop and a pair of earphones. Thus equipped, I met my aunt Kay, who observed my approach with one eyebrow cocked. She and my uncle George had agreed to take me in for a few days – it would have been longer, but they were inconveniently emigrating from the world's greatest city a week after my arrival.

Through the use of George and Kay's stone-age Wi-Fi and Gumtree, I managed to source a room to live in. My dear mother had warned me to consider the wind when seeking accommodation, saying, 'Angus, whatever you do, don't find a place on the town side of the mountain – try to find a spot in Newlands. At least it's vaguely sheltered from that dreadful southeaster.' Despite her propensity for hyperbole, I decided to take her advice. I found a charming garden cottage at the end of an extensive property about a block from Kirstenbosch Gardens and arranged a viewing.

When I rang the doorbell of my potential new landlords, there was an explosion of barking from two obviously immense hounds.

'Good morning,' I said as the heavy oak door to the palatial schloss opened to reveal stately white-and-black chequered tiles. Staircases rose on either side of the space, which centred on a massive rosewood table bowing under the weight of the biggest flower arrangement outside of a funeral I had ever seen.

'Good morning?' said Mrs Clarice van der Veen, flanked by two enormous, slavering Alsatians. They growled, displaying their impressive weapons, and Mrs Van der Veen made no move to quiet them.

'You must be Mrs Van der Veen,' I said, trying not to look the curs in the eye. 'Apologies for my tardiness – I couldn't find the address in Bishopscourt. According to my Google maps, this street is in Newlands.'

'Oh!' she exclaimed as though I'd poked her in the eye. 'No, we are definitely in Bishopscourt.' I was about to apologise for this dastardly error when she continued, 'And it's Van der Veen, not *Fan der Feean*.'

'Right,' I said. An awkward silence followed.

I was standing beneath a portico between two cherub-topiaried hedges, wearing my only garments, which were starting to look like I'd been wearing them for three days – which I had. I was also sweating heavily – the only transport available to me on this scorching day being Uncle George's rusting bicycle (my credit card had bounced on hailing an Uber). On my feet were slops and I held my baseball cap in supplication beneath my chin. It became apparent that to Clarice van der Veen, aged roughly 55, I resembled a beggar poised to ask for bread or taxi fare.

'Can I help you?' she demanded presently. The growling ratcheted up a notch.

She was dressed immaculately in a floral summer dress, low-heeled pink pumps, an intimidatingly complex coiffure, two pearl earrings and about four kilometres of the same around her neck. Other than that, it was difficult to tell what Mrs Van der Veen actually looked like, such was the volume of makeup on her face. The immobility of her forehead spoke of Botox.

'Um, yes, sorry,' I said. 'I am Angus MacNaughton. We spoke on the phone yesterday evening about the flatlet you have for rent?'

'Oh ... yes ... um ...'

It looked like she was about to tell me the cottage was no longer available, so I said, 'Mrs Van der Veen, my luggage was lost by the airline the day before yesterday – please excuse my appearance.'

'Oh ... quite ... yes ... Eh ... You'd better come in then.' Finally she addressed her hounds: 'Hansel, Gretel, quiet. Kitchen.'

They obeyed instantly and disappeared into the house.

And so I was granted access to the hallway. The pale-yellow walls were festooned with oils of the family's ancestors, the dogs' predecessors and, if my limited knowledge of art is to be believed, an Irma Stern of a morose-looking man of Middle Eastern descent.

'Who is it?' bellowed a man from a room to the right of the hall. A newspaper rustled.

'It is the potential lodger, Boris.'

'Bring him in here and let me get a look at him!'

'Boris would like to meet you,' said Clarice, perhaps thinking I was deaf.

'Indeed,' I replied.

The lady of the house led me through wooden double doors into a study the likes of which I would one day like to spend my resting hours. Floor-to-ceiling wooden shelves were mostly filled with books but for deeper shelves on which rested bits of no-doubt expensive art, the centrepiece a disturbing bronze therianthrope (in this case, a man's bottom half with a lion's head). To the right of the door, enormous French windows opened onto the garden beyond, a gentle breeze carrying in the scent of summer flowers ...

On a leather chair facing the open window sat a man enveloped in a cloud of cigar smoke.

Boris van der Veen was huge – overweight, tall and dressed in a red paisley robe, his feet up on a scuffed foot stool. His head was covered in long, unkempt and thinning grey hair. One of his fingers tapped viciously into a tablet, sending little clouds of cigar ash onto his newspaper.

'Egads, man, are you a tramp?' He peered at me from bloodshot eyes above his reading glasses.

'No, just a game ranger, which is financially the same as a tramp,' I replied.

This elicited a bellow of laughter from the chubby face. Boris took a sip from the cognac glass at his side (it was a Wednesday morning, 10h30).

'I think you can stay,' he said. 'Cognac?'

'Um, no, thank you.'

'That's a Dylan Lewis.' Boris followed my gaze, which was on the bronze therianthrope. 'Very fashionable these days.' He took a pull on his cigar. 'Fucking terrifying if you ask me!' He laughed again. 'This is what happens when you get married, see – your wife buys fashionable art and makes you live with the stuff.'

'Boris, I am sure this man ... um ... What's your name again?'

'Angus,' I replied.

'Angus!' boomed Boris. 'Had a friend called Angus once – offed himself with a shotgun a few years ago.' He roared with laughter. 'You're not about to off yourself with a shotgun, are you, Angus?'

'Oh, Boris,' said Clarice, her immobile forehead doing its best to frown.

'Don't want to be cleaning bits of you off the ceiling!' Boris began coughing as his laughter rose to fever pitch, the cigar-holding hand slapping on his thigh sending ash in all directions.

Clarice looked at me as Boris cleared his throat with cognac.

'I suppose you can stay then.'

So it was that I took up residence in Bishopscourt (actually Newlands) for the next three and a half years. An unconventional mentor, Boris was the sort of person who lived entirely by his own code and the older he became, the less of a jot he gave for convention or what anyone else thought. He was almost certainly an alcoholic, but this appeared to have more to do with his attempts to emulate Winston Churchill than actual addiction. Champagne at lunch every day, whisky most other times of the day and, oddly, cognac with his morning news on about five different devices and the newspapers – every day.

The acre on which the Van der Veen schloss spread would have made my mother salivate. Flowerbeds bursting with colour were interspersed with water features and little rockeries. The cottage itself looked like something out of a fairy tale. An exuberant vine grew over a pergola providing shade to the narrow porch on which rested a wrought-iron table and two chairs.

As I signed the lease, Clarice explained the rules.

'No parties of any kind, no loud music, no cooking spicy food in the house and as few disturbances as possible at the main house – Boris and I are very busy people. You would use the garden gate entrance.'

I nearly said, 'The tradesman's entrance?' but managed to stop myself.

'Oh, and no more than three guests at a time.' She looked at me as if this might scare me off.

'That all sounds just fine.'

In time I would discover the implausibility of finding more than three Capetonians friendly enough to visit.

On my first morning, I woke to another glorious summer's day and pulled back the curtains from the French doors leading onto the veranda. Bleary-eyed, I was about to open the door when I noticed Hansel and Gretel staring up at me. For a moment I thought I'd be stuck inside, but then I noticed their wagging tails. As I opened the door, they burst in – the first and only Capetonian friends to visit.

By 06h00, I was on the little veranda with a cup of coffee and a tennis biscuit. The sun warmed the left of my face and to my right the slopes of Kirstenbosch and Skeleton Gorge rose steeply into the blue. In the massive oak tree that shaded my cottage, a grey squirrel went about its morning business, chattering and then playing catch with an enemy or prospective lover – likely the latter, given the size of his scrotum. The idiot squirrel made a dash for the next tree, and the dogs in their wild enthusiasm sent my (thankfully empty) coffee cup flying.

On the lawn, an olive thrush foraged for breakfast and in the vine above me a Cape robin sang for the morning. I felt thoroughly satisfied with my new home. It was just what I needed: a place unfamiliar yet beautiful, and a new start in a different career that didn't involve the dread of meeting new guests every day and the endless stream of employees coming to me in my capacity as head ranger to tell me of their 'problems' (99 per cent of which I could not have cared less about).

In an attempt to hold on to this positive mood, I decided to climb the mountain.

Thirty minutes later I was at the base of Skeleton Gorge, the precipitous path leading up into the shade of the Afromontane forest of yellowwood, stinkwood and many other species I didn't recognise. Unfamiliar birdsong accompanied me; in the background, water burbled over moss- and lichen-covered rocks. My walk was arrested briefly by a pair of olive woodpeckers foraging in the mossy boughs of an ancient yellowwood. A little while later, I cleared the treeline onto the plateau of the mountain proper. Here, the intimidating diversity of the fynbos spread in all directions – proteas being the only plants I could identify.

I turned to face the risen sun and the splendid view. I could see all the way to False Bay and then to the Cape Fold Mountains that barricade the Cape from the rest of Africa. By then, the sun was baking the mountaintop but for a breeze – or, more accurately, a stiff wind. For the moment, the moving air was cooling as I ran past the reservoirs to the mountain's western slopes. There I stopped to marvel at the majesty of the Atlantic as Camps Bay slowly came to life below. Heading south, the wind dropped the lower the path wound and I eventually fetched up on Constantia Nek – leaving me with a long run home along the road. I had no water with me, and when I returned at about 10h30 I was exhausted but deeply satisfied.

That evening, I was about to make myself some scrambled eggs for supper when there was a knock on the open door.

'Boy!' yelled Boris from my veranda. It took me a second to realise I was being addressed. 'Boy!' he bellowed again.

I emerged from the kitchen, a tea towel in my hand.

'Are you addressing me?' I asked.

'Of course!' he shouted. 'Ha – you haven't offed yourself yet? Good show. Good show!' Boris was leaning on the door frame, a massive tumbler of Scotch in hand and dressed in a navy-blue velvet dinner jacket.

'What are you doing for dinner? Hot date? Dirty call girl coming over for some rumpy-pumpy, hey? Ha ha, those were the days!'

'Um, no, I was going to make some eggs and read a book.'

'Eggs and a book? Egads, man, are you planning on boring yourself into an early grave?' He didn't wait for an answer. 'No, we've had a cancellation for our dinner party – you'll have to fill in. Where's your DJ?'

'Boris, I don't even own a suit, let alone a dinner jacket.'

'Sweet Jesus in heaven!' He looked genuinely shocked. 'You don't own a suit? Next you'll be telling me you don't smoke cigars!'

I was so baffled that I just stared at my new landlord.

'Fuck me, you don't smoke cigars!' He took a deep swig. 'Well, Harry has a few suits and things in his cupboard. I'll get you one – be back in five minutes. Have a shower in the meantime – guests arrive in ten.'

Harry, I found out from one of the guests some hours later, was Boris's (but not Clarice's) estranged son. From what I could work out, he was about 35 and worked as a recording engineer somewhere in the Caribbean – he hadn't been home for a decade or so. He and Boris had fallen out when the younger had swindled his father into funding his travels to various drug hotspots around the equator.

That evening was the first of many that saw me in the company of Cape Town's insufferably snobbish and self-obsessed well-to-do. Still, the soirees provided some entertainment, free booze, good food and, in one case, a nocturnal visit from a recently single woman about ten years my senior. A vigorous (violent?) two-week affair had culminated in her flinging a glass vase at my head and banishing me from her swanky Constantia home when I suggested that I 'wasn't ready for commitment' – my escape down the driveway on George's old bicycle made all the more awkward by her jeering fourteen- and sixteen-year-old daughters.

I had come to Cape Town with the promise of work from a wildlife film company. The company died a year after I joined, which wasn't my fault. Well, not only my fault. But this had left me rather desperate for an income just as I enrolled for a master's degree in Development Studies at the University of Cape Town. While I completed the degree in the requisite time, it qualified me for nothing except further study – indeed, a drunk ditch-digger would be imminently more employable.

So it was that I had persuaded the Prelate's College to take me on as a part-time guitar teacher, and there I remained some three years later.

My reminiscence was disturbed by a banging on the locked door of the teaching room. Max Philamore-Stravinsky, aged nine, waited to come out of the cold. His mother, doing her best to inject her offspring with the same sense of entitlement she so enjoyed, had arranged a meeting with the headmaster post the lesson to discuss her son's progress (or astonishing lack thereof). Once the gormless child had finished hacking at his poor instrument for 30 minutes, I wandered over to the office.

'Warren,' the mother began, her manner with the headmaster indicating a familiarity not entirely appropriate, 'Max doesn't seem to be making any progress with his guitar playing.' She sipped her tea, leaving a red stain on the cup, and my jaw clenched involuntarily. 'I would like to explore the reasons for this and seek a solution for the way forward.'

The head, Mr Warren Sergeant, always desperate to ingratiate himself with the wealthy parents, tossed me under the bus: 'Well, eh, Mr MacNaughton is perhaps best placed to give an explanation.'

I ran my tongue over my teeth, uncrossed my legs and sat forward in the uncomfortable antique chair.

'Madam,' I began, 'I'd like to begin by asking how many times a week your son practises his instrument.'

Perhaps my tone was a little harsh because the head interjected immediately.

'Now, Mr MacNaughton, let's keep things civil!'

An awkward silence compelled the mother to respond.

'He's a very busy child,' she snapped, 'an excellent sportsman and with his academics there is little time for guitar.'

'Ah,' I nodded.

'But that is not what I pay for! I pay for you to teach him the guitar, and after two years I'd have expected that he could play some songs – you know, classics like "Sweet Caroline" or ... "Kaptein (Span die seile)".'

'Well, we have a few problems then,' I explained. 'When you signed up young Max for *classical* guitar, I fear you misunderstood what that meant.'

She looked baffled.

'I, without success admittedly, have been trying valiantly to provide Max with the scaffold on which he might build a repertoire extending to Dowland, Bach, Sor and Tárrega.'

'Mr MacNaughton –' the head tried to interject.

I lifted my hand. 'Hang on a second, Warren. Let's be honest here, madam. Max cannot exactly be described as a natural – in fact, he has an ear for music roughly equal to that of the chair I'm sitting on. Regardless, he could learn to hammer out a few tunes ... but only if he practises. Not with all the talent in the world will he master anything if his guitar remains in its bag all week.'

Mrs Philamore-Stravinsky's pursed lips had turned an unattractive shade of purple. I thought it best to drive my point home before either she or the head could recover themselves.

'Might I suggest that if my methods are insufficient to miraculously infuse Max with music, you find him another teacher? I shall make absolutely no attempt to stop you.'

I didn't wait for a response before standing to leave.

'This has been most illuminating,' I said as I walked out.

Fifteen minutes later, the HR manager (a bony spinster aged at least 105) called me to the office and instructed me to sign a warning letter.

Clearly the obsequious head had not found the testicles to hand it to me himself.

Notwithstanding that distasteful episode, this story is not a treatise on the merits, perceived or real, of Capetonians. It is ostensibly a tale of the African wilderness and so there we must return in order to find out how I happened upon life in the Cape in the first place.

3

My third year in the wild began with my being elevated to the position of head ranger at the esteemed Sasekile Game Reserve, a role that ended prematurely in the eyes of some (me) but not others (everyone else). In order for me to explain how I came to swap the glorious Lowveld for the fickle Cape, we must travel back some four and a half years.

I suppose my fall from grace was inevitable.

When I ascended to the lofty designation of head ranger, everyone who knew me feared it wouldn't last. We (I include myself here) were simply relieved that for the next while I would be able to support myself and learn the skill of leadership. My mother, father and sister could sleep easy for a few months knowing that when my name appeared on their phone screens it was most likely for a chat rather than the announcement of another self-inflicted tragedy.

While the salary, given the shit I had to put up with, was by no means adequate, I was able to buy a car (a working-order Mazda Drifter), settle a few debts and even start saving a little. I felt satisfied that my career was on the up. I was in a meaningful relationship with a stable woman (Allegra), who actually enjoyed my quirks.

On my promotion, I was handed the keys to the head ranger's digs – salubrious bush accommodations with a large bedroom, a loft for another bed or storage and a small open-plan kitchen-dining area. It was cosy and big enough for two, which meant that Allegra packed up her pokey little staff room and shacked up with me. I thought this an excellent idea.

Julia, my ever-wiser sister, cautioned me.

'Angus, you're not exactly good at compromise – are you sure you're ready to live with someone?'

'Julia, I am 28 years old – if I was a caveman, I'd be a grandfather by now. It'll be fine.' My flippancy didn't convince either of us.

It came out over a Sunday lunch while I was on leave a few weeks later. Allegra was down in KwaZulu with her family, and I was in Johannesburg with mine. The mood on the hot late-January afternoon was festive (my father being famously generous with his cellar). Unusually, both Hugh and I were on leave, and Hugh's girlfriend, Simone, was there too. Halfway through Great-aunt Jill's Marie-biscuit pudding, our grandfather, the Major – still fighting off death with a medically inexplicable will – said to my father:

'When's that oddball son of yours going to get a girl? Eh?'

'He's got a girlfriend now, Dad,' said my mother.

'Does he? Where? Don't believe it for a second – boy's a pooftah, always has been.' The Major had never liked me for reasons, until right then, unknown. He adored Hugh and seemed ambivalent to Julia (and most things female). My grandfather's insults, from the vicious to the deranged, no longer worried me in the slightest. Simone, however, is a champion of the downtrodden and rode to my defence.

'Mr Henderson,' she began, 'Angus not only has a girlfriend, they've moved in together!'

This brought proceedings around the table to an abrupt halt, and it was at this point that I realised my parents had no idea that my little brother had also been living in sin for at least a year.

'Oh God, Simone,' whispered Hugh, turning pale.

'He's *what*?' My mother glared at Simone as though she'd slighted the good name of the family (questionable).

'Well ... I ... eh,' Simone stammered.

Hugh looked like he might be about to speak or vomit, I couldn't tell which.

'Yes, Allegra has moved into my new house with me,' I explained.

'Oh my God,' exploded my mother. 'What on earth will her parents say – have you been married in some sort of Shangane ceremony that you think this is appropriate? Do her parents know?'

'Yes, Mother, her parents know – and unlike some members of the extended MacNaughton/Henderson clan, they no longer dwell in the nineteenth century. This is an excellent pudding as usual, GAJ,' I added casually.

'Oh, Angus,' said my mother. 'Really, what a thing to say!'

'Well, maybe we need to move a little with the times,' suggested cousin Al. She and her beau, Barry, had recently shacked up in a Melville flatlet – also secretly.

'The Lord doesn't move with the times!' Pius Uncle Ant.

'Been to a public pooftah-stoning lately, Ant?' Me again.

'Angus!' My mortified mother.

'I wish there was some respect for those of us who believe.' The squeaky voice of 22-year-old cousin Olivia.

My brother stared at his plate.

The palest pallor around the table belonged to Andy, my age. He had just confessed to Julia (who'd immediately told me) that he had a new boyfriend.

'Coffee and croquet!' announced my father, standing.

'Croquet's for pooftahs,' growled the Major.

'Dad!' My mother.

I never actually invited Allegra to come and live with me; it just sort of happened. She'd spent a few nights with me after I moved in and then it didn't make much sense for me to have all that space with nothing but a shelf full of books and some old uniform to fill it. One morning after breakfast I found her in the room with Isaac Masuku, junior maintenance lackey.

'... and maybe some of that grey paint from Kingfisher Camp on the bathroom door. Would that be okay?' She looked up at me as though it was the most normal thing in the world for her to be decorating my domicile.

'It is no problem,' said Isaac. 'Avuxeni, Angustah,' he greeted me, replaced his ridiculous hat – it had no crown and its fraying edges rendered it useless for the purposes of sun protection – and wandered into the January heat.

'So, Angus MacNaughton,' said Allegra, 'I thought I'd move in.' She shrugged. 'If it's a disaster, I can always ask for my old room back.'

I noticed that the enormous wardrobe which had hitherto contained two shelves of my uniform and my impressive collection of holey under-wear suddenly looked rather full.

Her little blue teddy lay on the right-hand side of the bed.

I wasn't really sure how to take this new development. Aged 28, I was hardly too young to be shacking up with someone. I suppose the thing that should have struck me most about the new arrangement was that I hadn't even considered it until just then.

'I'm sure it will be fine ... um ... no, good!' I said, smiling.

'Are you sure? I should have checked with you.'

'No,' I shrugged, 'it'll be fun.' I walked over, put my arms around her firm waist and kissed her full lips. She was a good four or five inches shorter than me. I rested my nose on her straight blue-black hair and inhaled. She always smelt vaguely of lavender – the oil she used most for her massages. Her strong hands kneaded the flesh around my shoulder blades.

'You're always so tight up here. Is anything particular worrying you, Angus MacNaughton?'

'Not at all.'

And so we settled into a life of cohabitation that suited me fairly well. Allegra was considerate, and my slight fear that I'd find myself lacking for alone time was ill-founded. Lodge life dictated that we were seldom off at the same time. During the middle of the day when I didn't have admin to do, she'd be pressing the flesh (firm and foul) of the guests. I had time to play my guitar, do my exercises and read. At night, she often hosted in the camps, and I often had to sit with guests for dinner. The upshot was that we had no time to get in each other's way.

The only complaint she had was that I spent too long on the throne.

'What are you doing in there?' she asked one late morning when I'd just returned for an emergency 11h00 consideration of the *National Geographic*. She had half an hour free and had decided to spend it with me.

'Do you really want to know?' I asked, closing an article on the Dogon people of Mali.

'Well, considering how long you've been in there, I might have to book you an appointment with a gastroenterologist.' She sounded amused.

'Allegra, all around the world the *National Geographic* is read by patient poopers – in fact, without us I strongly suspect that the National Geographic Society would fall into financial ruin.'

'Angus MacNaughton, I don't want to talk about this any more ... ever.'

'Fair enough – I'll be out in a second.'

I consider my knowledge of human physiology to be basic but thorough, however I swear that in the time that Allegra and I were involved, I never once had cause to think that her bowels worked at all. This suited me just fine but must have been mighty uncomfortable for her.

My new job as head ranger meant that I was no longer required to constantly drive guests – I had various administrative tasks that mercifully precluded this. On our very first morning together, Allegra and I began a routine that we followed religiously.

I woke just before dawn and quietly went to the bathroom for a quick cold shower – a morning ritual I had decided was essential for righting my body for the day ahead. As I dried, I'd hear a grinding noise from the kitchenette. When I emerged in a towel, there Allegra would be, a towelling gown covering her silky negligee, grinding coffee beans.

'I confess I've become a coffee snob,' she admitted the first day, pouring the grinds into the stainless-steel plunger. She pulled a tin from a cupboard above the kettle and placed two rusks on a plate. I watched her arrange the plunger, rusks and two delicate cups and saucers on a little wooden tray.

'Where did that all come from?' I asked.

'What ... the coffee stuff?'

'No, the world's magnificent biodiversity – yes, the coffee stuff.'

She half-smiled. 'I brought it from home – something about coffee in bone china in the morning.' She lifted the tray. 'Come, let's have it outside.'

She'd arranged two old wicker chairs and a table on our tiny veranda. As I sat down I noticed four pots of aloes had miraculously appeared on the low wall on which we rested our feet.

The sky brightened slowly and a white-browed robin-chat began to sing in the Cape honeysuckle hedge separating us from our neighbours. Up in the jackalberry that shaded us, a red-chested cuckoo joined the dawn chorus and a hippo grunted in the Tsessebe River beyond.

I sipped the steaming black brew.

'I told you it was good out of a cup like this,' she said.

'I'm not sure it's the cup, but it's delicious.' I dipped the homemade rusk and took a bite.

A leopard saw echoed through the riverine forest. I looked at Allegra as she daintily sipped her coffee and thought of the home she'd created for us. She'd gone to extraordinary lengths to make our little pad comfortable and beautiful. The walls were freshly painted – not by her, but on her instruction to the recalcitrant maintenance team – and were hung with monochromatic wildlife prints on canvas. The little kitchen cupboard was stocked with rusks, coffee, tea, nuts and two bottles of good Scotch.

I felt a welling of affection. 'Thank you for making this home for us,' I said. 'I'm sorry I haven't said it before. It's beautiful.'

'It's a pleasure.' She smiled. 'I'm glad you like it.'

When I'd finished, I stood and kissed Allegra on her lavender hair.

'I had better get going.'

Our hands lingered in a squeeze.

'I love you,' she whispered as I departed.

4

My eleven months as the head ranger at famed Sasekile Private Game Reserve were a mixed bag.

The job could not be described as daunting from a cerebral perspective. It included allocating new guests to rangers, maintaining the rifle registry, managing the rangers' and trackers' leave cycles (so that the lodge had sufficient staff), going on the odd drive with the other rangers to make sure they weren't telling fibs, conducting the weekly field-team meetings and training new rangers. I was also supposed to be in charge of making sure the game-drive Land Rovers were all in running order.

This last thing was ridiculous for me to be doing – akin to putting me in charge of cardiothoracic surgery at a hospital. I remain utterly confused by the workings of the internal combustion engine, so on my first day in charge, I handed over the Land Rover element of the job to Sipho, who'd been servicing cars since his days in nappies – his father was a keen amateur racing driver. This did not necessarily qualify him, but the lack of skill demonstrated by the workshop duo of Oscar (aged well north of 70) and Douglas (aged somewhere south of 25) could only be improved by Sipho's incessant enthusiasm to 'tune the motors'.

It's almost impossible to define what makes a good leader – though a casual glance at the self-help section in any book store will reveal hundreds of different approaches. I have come to the conclusion that no one really knows the secret to inspiring and cajoling your fellow man; it's easier to list the characteristics that make a poor leader, and as my year in charge progressed I came to appreciate the number of these embedded in my nature. To be fair, my studies of inspirational leadership techniques were lacking, as I'd always done my best to avoid and irritate anyone in authority.

Though I had no real point of reference, I'd often wondered what it would have been like if I, like my paternal grandfather, had ended up a captain in the trenches circa 1916. What role would I have played? Could I have held a company together in the face of those horrendous odds? Would my men have followed me blindly over the top or ignored my orders completely?

After my experience as the head ranger of Sasekile, I'm still not sure.

I was voted into the position and so, unlike an appointee, I had a mandate from the team. Of course, when they'd voted me in, it was on a wave of emotion and goodwill following the tumultuous events of the previous year that culminated in the near death-by-buffalo of my sister, Julia, and her beau, Alistair 'The Legend' Jones. None of the team had any actual experience of me as a leader.

I tackled my new job with great enthusiasm. It was the first position of leadership I'd ever occupied and given that this is a (relatively) honest reflection on this period of my life, it is beholden on me to confess that leading other human beings did not come naturally. The position did not come with any courses, advice or mentorship in the art of leadership. On the day that my predecessor Carrie left, I was immediately expected to fill her shoes with equal success.

Every Tuesday morning there was a trackers' meeting. The tracking team didn't have a head tracker as such, but seniority was derived from a complicated and completely subjective combination of age, skill and length of service. I could not fathom how it worked but was sufficiently aware to know that meddling in the complexities of Shangane leadership was well beyond my skills. My role at trackers' meetings was thus, to a large extent, that of minute-taker and in some cases I might be asked to arbitrate a conflict.

The first meeting saw the arrival of a new tracker – though 'tracker' is a very generous term for Mishak Sithole of Huntington Village. I had a vague knowledge of Mishak as a member of the ineffectual security team that supposedly patrolled the grounds of the lodge at night, though as far as I could make out the team slept more than lions. Over the course of a decade, Mishak had unsuccessfully cajoled Sasekile's general manager, PJ Woodstock, with requests, demands and entreaties to become a tracker, and as soon as I became the head ranger, Mishak came to see me.

Some people have an appalling sense of timing – always where you least want to see them – and Mishak was one such person. Every day at around 14h00 I retreated to the sanctum of my bathroom with a *National Geographic* or *Time* magazine. This, as the business of the year and demands on my time became increasingly barbaric, was a precious escape. Mishak conspired, consciously or unconsciously, to ruin it with astounding regularity.

So it was on New Year's Day, when I left the rangers' room in the stupefying heat of the early afternoon. The excesses of the previous evening promised a productive session in The Sanctum. As I sat down with a satisfied sigh, there was a knock at the main door. At first I ignored it, assuming the visitor would see through the glass into the main room and decide no one was present. I opened my magazine to an article on snow leopards in the Hindu Kush.

Knock, knock, knock – more urgent this time.

I looked at the main picture feeling a deep sense of foreboding.

Knock, knock, knock, knock – the glass threatened to crack.

'Angoos!'

I recognised the voice of Mishak Sithole – a man whom I had less desire to see than an infected pustule on my undercarriage. Mishak's voice had a distinctive timbre – a low-frequency whine with a serrated edge. He seldom shouted but his natural resonance pierced time, distance and concrete, driving through the skull and planting a scalding seed of discomfort in the midbrain.

Perhaps, thought I stupidly, there was an emergency.

'What?' I shouted.

'I need speak you,' he lowed. And then the words that would haunt me again and again over the coming year: 'I got problem!'

'Well, as you might gather, I am currently indisposed!'

Silence.

'On the toilet!' To allay confusion.

More silence. He'd gone.

No, he hadn't. The door opened and heavy footsteps sounded in the room.

'I am on the bloody toilet!' I yelled. 'Is there an emergency?'

'I wait. I got problem.' I heard the bedsprings creak as Mishak made himself at home.

'Mishak, go away and see me in the rangers' room at three o'clock – I'm on the toilet ... the loo ... having a dump ... prairie-dogging, etcetera.'

'I am showering at three clock,' he declared as one might an immutable fact of the universe.

'Well, I'm pooing *now!*'

'I wait.'

One feels a sense of vulnerability on the throne when being observed or listened to. I slapped the magazine onto the floor and completed the bare minimum of what was needed, the peace of The Sanctum irretrievably destroyed.

Two minutes later, I emerged to find Mishak spread-eagled on my (and soon to be Allegra's) bed. He was wearing ancient, torn and paint-bespattered dungarees and a pair of safety boots. Mishak stood about five feet ten inches and weighed around eighty kilos. He wasn't fat, but he was out of shape – unsurprising, given his koala-like levels of activity.

'It's good bed.' He sat up.

'Mishak, why are you here?'

'How are you, I'm fine,' he declared.

'I'm struggling to care,' I replied. 'Now what do you want?'

'I am a great tracker.'

'I see. And how do you know this?'

'I follow the cows when I am small in my village.'

'Mishak, you know a tracker actually has to work quite hard: cleaning the car, fetching the cooler boxes, practising shooting and, most disturbing for a man of your energy-conserving ways, walking in the bush

… often for hours at a time.'

'I am very much physically fit,' he delivered with a confidence that beggared belief. But as the new head ranger I figured that I owed him a fair hearing.

'I am not discussing this here and now. Come and see me in the rangers' room at three o'clock.'

'I am sho–'

'You'll have to find another time for your afternoon toilet … As will I.'

He stared at me for a while and then mooched out of my room without another word. I immediately went to see PJ.

'Oh, for God's sake' –PJ's head banged onto his desk – 'Mishak's been on and on at me for a hundred years about being a tracker. I'm so sick of it. You'll have to interview him. Thankfully there are no positions available so it's just a formality.'

This utterance, of course, jinxed the tracking team. Within a week we were two trackers down. One-eyed Joe, who'd lost his eye in a shebeen fight many years previously, was arrested for cattle rustling while on leave. His culpability was never tested in court but the elders of his village near Phalaborwa gave him 24 hours to clear off or face the barrel of a Russian pistol belonging to the headman. I assume the threat was genuine for two reasons: first, the headman went by the name Makarov Mathebula and second, Joe disappeared to Johannesburg.

Then Albert 'Michelin' Mkansi, aged 62, had to retire hurriedly on account of a severe heart condition and diabetes. He claimed his woes were not the fault of his regime of two litres of Creme Soda a day and refined carbohydrates by the tonne. Rather, he deduced, he had been bewitched by a jealous neighbour who he claimed to know but refused to reveal, stating, 'I will wait for the right time.'

The lodge was full, which meant we needed a tracker posthaste. On the evening in question, the only staff member not on shift was Mishak.

'Mishak,' I said, 'this is a temporary arrangement for just three days until we can interview other potential candidates.'

'Yes, of course,' he lowed, his fingers clasped together in front of his chest like an evil wizard.

A week later, Mishak was formally employed as Sasekile's newest tracker – unsurprising, in the end, since he was the only one to apply for the position. This was largely because of his lineage. For various complicated reasons that I shall not go into here, in rural areas South Africa's constitutional democracy exists side by side with a feudal system of primogeniture. Mishak belonged to the 'ruling' (in his words, 'royal') family of Huntington Village. Most of the security team, I subsequently discovered, came from the same village and didn't dare apply for the job in case they should incur the wrath of royal Mishak (and his large and threatening family).

Other than that, the year trucked along without incident. The team and systems I'd inherited from Carrie were well oiled and professional. I tweaked one or two things, trained a few new rangers and – with the exception of losing my temper a few times with various members of my team, which resulted in my being forced to attend an anger-management course – all was going swimmingly.

Incidentally, the anger-management course was the result of an altercation with Mishak.

Every time he saw me, he brought a litany of complaints – his back was sore, he needed extra leave, he didn't want to drive Germans, he didn't like his ranger, his dog was eaten by a snake so he had to go home for three days ... and on and on it went. I snapped one day when he arrived in my room (again as I sat on the loo). He simply walked in and lowed at me, 'Angus, I want a new ranger, my ranger is a racist, he is not sharing his tips.'

'Mishak, your ranger is Sipho – in case it has escaped your notice, he is a black Shangane man like you.'

'His mother is a Pedi.'

'Go away, Mishak.'

'He does not share tips fifty-fifty!'

The unwritten rule was that rangers and trackers were supposed to share their tips equally, even if the guests gave more to the ranger. If Sipho had been holding some back, I couldn't have blamed him.

5

In my experience, nothing good lasts; the universe will always conspire to defecate on a person (me especially). In my case, the universe had diarrhoea towards the end of my year as head ranger. It was as if the cosmos's bowels had failed to void for eleven months until, two days after my birthday, it took a giant, cosmic laxative.

The first thing to happen was a soul-eviscerating chat with Allegra. We'd been having increasingly frequent 'chats' over the previous six weeks or so. They began with her asking, possibly not unreasonably, why I had not expressed my affection with the words 'I love you', this despite her having used such for almost ten months. I fobbed her off the first time, saying it was an awkward time for me, that I'd only ever said it once to a person and she had died ... I felt a bit bad invoking Anna's death, like I had cheapened it in some way, but I hoped that perhaps its invocation would shut down the subject. It did – for about a week.

Of course, these things are never as complicated as we human beings like to make them out. As with all emotional cowards (that is just about all humans), I did spectacular mental gymnastics to justify my actions: I was still traumatised by Anna's death two years previously; I wasn't ready to commit; I did love her but I just struggled to say it; the words themselves were twee; my job was too stressful, etcetera. All absolute crap.

In hindsight, the reason for my failure to tell Allegra of my undying devotion was simple: I didn't say I loved her because I didn't love her. There was nothing wrong with her; in fact, just about everything seemed to be right about her. She was a beautiful person in body and mind, but I didn't miss her when we were apart. It was nice to see her again after some time away, but when you describe a reunion as 'nice' then you're not describing head-over-heels, arrow-through-the heart levels of desire. It had nothing to do with her. Trouble was, from Anna I knew what that kind of love was, and being with Allegra didn't feel remotely the same. In truth, I didn't expect to ever feel the same aching depth of affection for another human being. And I sure as hell never wanted to feel the same complete and profound despair as I had in the wake of Anna's death from that fateful snakebite.

So there it was. More or less each week, Allegra would raise the subject – normally in the precoital boudoir, which, naturally, murdered any mood that may have led to the removal of her negligee.

After six weeks, things had become so awkward that I was actively avoiding her. Camp managers were astounded at my sudden willingness to sit with guests until late into the night. Normally I'd have sat my guests down at their table while other groups were still enjoying their post-game-drive drinks, and then chivvied the butlers to serve us immediately.

My record, achieved during my first year in the wild, was a Spanish family who spoke no English. I'd had them in and out of the boma in 30 minutes – before any other group had even had starters. My head hit my pillow at 20h00. A brilliant performance.

My brother, String Bean, who was managing Tamboti Camp at the time, had found me at breakfast the next day. He was in something of a froth.

'Angus, what the hell were you doing last night?'

I'd regarded him in confusion and taken mouthful of muesli. 'Hello, String Bean. Phew, I mean, if you must ask, Anna was wearing a new black nighty so –'

He'd cut me off.

'I've no desire to hear about your bloody ... eh ... exploits in the bedroom! I'm talking about the fact that your guests were back in their rooms even before the turndowns had been done! I mean, Francina was still closing the mosquito nets in one suite when Javier and Lola arrived in their room at twenty to eight! They're *Spanish*, for God's sake! They normally eat at *ten*!'

'Well, that probably isn't good for the digestion,' I'd offered.

'I don't give a shit what effect you think Iberian culture has on the digestion. When a distressed guest comes to me to ask why they have to eat dinner so early, *then* I give a shit!' He was shouting.

'How on earth did they ask you that? They don't speak English ...' I'd chewed thoughtfully, '... do they?'

My brother's mouth had adopted the shape of a cat's sphincter.

'They *do* fucking speak English!' he'd yelled. 'How have you taken them on two game drives and not realised that they speak English?!' His face was puce, spittle flying from his mouth. I found this amusing and began to giggle. 'It's not fucking funny!' he'd yelled.

I became more conscientious after that but had, until the awkward period with Allegra, never once been the last to leave the boma. By October of my year as head ranger, however, I was regularly seen asking guests if they'd like to try another bottle of wine or sample a new single malt. Many of the camp managers were now complaining that I was causing unnecessary delays at dinner, which ill-disposed me to the kitchen staff and butlers.

Then I'd arrive home late, normally quite sozzled, hoping Allegra would be fast asleep. Sometimes she was, but it's difficult to be quiet while drunk in the dark, and I'd always knock over something or other, or smash my shin on the heavy wooden box that lived at the base of our bed. My loudly whispered expletives would, inevitably, wake up my unhappy partner.

One evening, six weeks into my avoidance regime, she woke up when I tripped on the metal kitchen dustbin. I was well oiled, partly because my guests were an irritating group of Texans – three couples, the men of whom did nothing but mouth off about how many animals they'd shot and tell extraordinarily exaggerated stories of their courage. Sasekile was their only non-lethal stop on a tour of South Africa's backwater hunting farms of the sort characterised by red-meat diets, brandied bellies and attitudes towards darker races unmodified since the early 1800s.

The metal dustbin flew across the room and clattered into the cupboard under the sink. I swore loudly as I collected my shin on the wooden bed box. Allegra sat up with a start and turned on the light. She ran a hand through her tousled dark hair and looked at me. I knew this was the moment we were going to have the discussion I'd been avoiding for six weeks. She looked sad, angry and irritated, all at once.

'Angus,' she began, 'are you drunk?'

'Sorry about the bin – rough night. Go back to sleep.'

'Are you avoiding me?' Her dark-blue eyes bore into my face. I evaded her gaze by looking at the nasty wound on my right shin.

'I ... um ... no ... just ... eh ... busy.'

'No, you're avoiding me. Why?' Her eyes became glassy.

I felt my stomach lurch. The sensation dropped to my toes.

'I'm ... not ... I ... just.'

She sniffed and a tear escaped down her cheek.

'Please don't lie to me – it's not fair.' She wiped her eyes and her pretty face hardened.

I sighed and sat down on the bed box, wondering where I'd sleep the rest of the night. Despite the booze, I was fairly sure that this conversation was going to return me to bachelorhood. Drunken emotional coward that I was, I couldn't lie to this woman any longer. I really didn't deserve her kindness or patience. The room began to spin.

'This ... isn't working,' I said, and forced the bile back down.

'No shit!' she snapped. 'I want to know *why*! I've done *everything* to make this work! I've changed my schedule to fit in with you. I've made this a home for us. I've been patient with your moods and your temper. I've loved you as much as I can! *Why* isn't it working?' Liquid was fair spurting from her eyes by this stage.

I wanted to be anywhere else or dead.

'It's not you ...' I began.

'If you say, "it's not you, it's me", I swear I'll break something over your head!'

'No, I mean, you've done everything to make this work. I just ... I don't know. I guess I can't commit,' I offered.

'Can't *commit*? What the fuck does that mean?' She never swore. 'Do you want to go and sow your wild oats? See other people? Play the field? I mean, what the hell? You're nearly 30 years old!'

'It's not like that. I don't want to ... sow any oats – I just ... um ...' What I was about to say would really hurt her.

'It's just *what*?!' She wiped her nose with a tissue and glared at me.

I sighed and looked at her.

'I'm sorry,' I said, 'but I'm just not in love with you.'

The next minute or so passed in slow motion, like those scenes in a movie when something too fast to be perceived by the naked eye is slowed right down – a bomb going off, for example. In this case, Allegra – normally the picture of calm – was the bomb. She emerged from the bed in one movement, was suddenly at my side and her right hand, palm open, slammed into the side of my head. The booze, surprise and surreality of the moment made me topple off the box and onto the floor – where she kicked me once in the guts.

'How can you say that to someone? Who *says* that to someone!'

'I'm sorry, it's just ... the truth,' I gasped. 'I owe you the truth.'

'You owed me that long ago! Not ten months after I fell in love with you!'

I rose onto my hands and knees.

'Should I have lied?' A part of me was genuinely curious – the drunk part, probably.

She kicked me again in the stomach and I rolled onto the floor.

'Get out!' she screamed. 'Get the fuck out right now!'

I managed to stand and stagger to the door.

'Angus?'

I turned to face her. She was heaving with sobs.

'Why did you do this to me? You could have ended it long before it came to this!' She slumped onto the bed.

'I'm so, so –'

'Just get out, please, and leave me alone.'

I staggered out and was immediately sick into a plumbago bush. I could have gone to String Bean and Simone's place – my brother would have felt compelled to take me in (well, his girlfriend would have) – or O'Reilly's, since the chef was always ready with a sympathetic ear and bottle of red to share, but I really didn't want to explain myself. I headed for the one place I knew would be unoccupied: the Bat Cave.

Naturally enough, I didn't sleep much that night. I felt truly dreadful. Allegra's reaction indicated the depth of pain I'd subjected her to, and that disturbed me deeply. As I drifted in and out of restless sleep, I couldn't figure out what else I could have said.

So it was that when I met the Texans the next morning on the Main Camp deck, I was not in a particularly jocular mood. I retreated to have a cup of coffee in the corner, still brooding over the night's events and dressed in the previous day's khakis.

'Angus!' It was Jeff, perpetually full of gormless good cheer. 'Where you gonna go this morning? So lekker to drive with you out of Main again ...' The unintentional rhyme put him off his stride. He stared off into the Tsessebe River as his cortex reset itself. 'You gonna try for that male leopard off Sable Clearings? I am. He was stalking an imp last night.'

I sighed. 'Yup, probably.'

'Okay, cool, my guests are ready, I'll see you out there ... um ... boss!' Jeff still didn't really know how to address me.

A few minutes later, the animal-slaying Texans were ready for their drive. I knew this because they'd gathered up their camouflage jackets and mightily expensive binoculars. I put down my cup and followed them to the vehicle.

All six were dressed in their hunting fatigues – American hunting fatigues, so they looked like a badly painted boreal forest drifting in the wind. I waited in silence as they tried to haul their over-nourished physiques into the Land Rover.

In these situations, it's awkward trying to help. Some people with, shall we say, less-than-athletic builds will ask for assistance and make light of it, which can be quite amusing. Some are very upfront about their physical limitations and give enough warning to request the mounting block – of which there's only one in the whole camp. This bunch, however, were under the gross misapprehension that they were limber as an Olympic gymnastics team.

'Can I have the mounting block sent around?' I asked in the politest possible way.

'We're fine,' wheezed Jeremy 'Buck' Flint III, as he hauled his vast bulk into the back row. The suspension groaned as he slumped into his seat, face red with effort. Eventually five of them had huffed, groaned and gasped themselves into place as Elvis, the tracker, and I looked on. Elvis kept his eyes on the floor, trying not to seem amused. Then it was the turn of Rhonda Donaldson, aged roughly 65, mass approaching that of a black rhino.

She gripped the frame of the first row of seats and began to haul herself up. Except that she somehow got both feet on the running board, hands around the frame above, and there she hung, unable to overcome the force of gravity.

'Ahm gonna need a bit a help,' she gasped. 'Hurt my knee in a lacrosse game.'

It was patently clear that Rhonda hadn't played any form of sport for some decades. Elvis and I were thus faced with the unenviable task of boosting this woman into her place. In these situations, the only thing that provides purchase for such a boost is the buttocks. These were low to the ground, however, given the way she was hanging like a baleen windsurfer trying to dip her bum in the water.

I just looked, not knowing what bit of her to touch first. Elvis had no such qualms. He grabbed her belt and hauled up. Rhonda gasped. Elvis had underestimated his task but realised that if he let go, she'd lose her grip on the frame and find herself sprawled in the dust of the now long-empty car park. It is awkward placing your hands on the corpulent buttocks of a Texan woman while her husband is watching, trying not to have a heart attack after his own epic exertions, but there was no other option. I squatted below the massive rear end, put one hand on each cheek and began to push with all my might. My hands all but disappeared up to the wrists in the astonishingly thick blubber.

We almost had her up when she released an almighty flatulence. This was too much. Elvis sputtered, lost his grip and released the belt. I, being directly in the jet of foul gas, collapsed. Rhonda came down on top of me, and ended up sitting on my chest, apparently oblivious to her human cushion.

'Why'doo let me go?' she wailed.

Elvis, normally as demonstrative as a leadwood stump, took in the scene and lost control. He began to guffaw in great belly laughs – to which Jack Donaldson took great umbrage.

'Why you laffen, boy?' he yelled at Elvis.

'Get off me!' I shouted at Rhonda. 'I can't breathe!'

She began to squirm off.

'I asked, why you laffen, boy?' repeated Jack.

Elvis had no idea it was he that was being addressed.

'Don't you dare call him that,' I snapped, pointing a finger at Jack as I stood.

Jack Donaldson, oil mogul, was not used to being addressed in such a manner.

'I paid for this! I'll talk to y'all any goddamn way I please! You threw my wife in the dirt!'

My lack of sleep, the beastly Texans, a killer hangover and the emotions of the night before overwhelmed me. 'I did not throw your wife in the dirt. She farted in my face, and I was unable to squat her mass on my own!' I was shouting. 'I asked if you wanted the mounting block, and you refused.'

'Don't you shout at me! I'll come down there and teach you Africans a bit of Texan respect!'

'I'd like to see that,' I said, squaring up.

True to his word, Jack Donaldson clambered down from his seat and towered over me. He pointed a finger two inches from the bridge of my nose.

'You'd best apologise or there's gonna be some hurt here,' he growled.

Elvis, knowing my temper, attempted to wedge himself between us, but Jack Donaldson was having none of it. He put both hands on Elvis's chest and pushed hard. This was bad enough, but what he said next pre-cipitated the end of my time at Sasekile.

'You stay outta this, boy – no coloured man's gonna tell me what to do!'

The colour I saw at this point was red.

My right fist came up from my hip and caught Jack Donaldson be-tween his top lip and nose. Blood exploded from his schnoz and he bel-lowed. The pain in my hand made me stagger backwards – the Texan's large incisor was in fact a cap, and such was the angle of my attack that the crown came away from its moorings and embedded in the webbing between my ring and middle fingers. I pulled the tooth out of my flesh and looked up.

'Eish, Angus,' Elvis sucked in air, knowing the consequences of what I'd done.

The rest of the Texans were now oozing out of the Land Rover like a group of camouflaged blancmanges. Rhonda waddled over to her hus-band wailing.

'Look what you done to Jack! Look what you done to Jack!'

'I think this is yours,' I said, proffering the ivory cap.

'You gonna pay for this! We're gonna sue!' yelled Jeremy 'Buck' Flint III.

I flicked the tooth at him and turned away, beginning to feel a vice grip closing around me. Punching a guest, no matter the excuse, was not going to be tolerated. Refusing to take him on a drive would have been entirely justifiable, but violence wasn't.

My time in the wild was up, and I knew it.

I walked over to PJ's office, stopping only to vomit with emotion in a guarri bush.

The general manager had just sat down with his morning coffee – he liked to take half an hour of quiet time between 06h00 and 06h30 to read the news and gather his thoughts for the day. His face dropped when he saw me walking towards the office, blood oozing from my hand.

'Morning, Angus,' he said, his face alarmed. 'What's happened?'

I explained, honestly.

'Oh my God,' he said, head in his hands.

'I know it is untenable for me to keep my job,' I offered. 'I'll be gone by the end of the day. I'm so sorry. This time I really am – I just lost my temper ... again. I know there's no excuse and I don't offer one.'

'Right,' he said sadly, 'I guess that's it. How very sad.' He stood up. 'I'd better go and see to the guests. They'll be leaving today. I wouldn't have them stay here but as you say, you can't either – the precedent would not fly.' He walked out of the office.

I trooped back to Allegra and my home.

She was just making coffee when I walked in. Her face was all puffy with crying but she was calm.

'What happened?' she said.

'I punched a guest,' I replied. 'I'm leaving.'

I pulled my bag from the cupboard and explained what had happened while I packed. It took about 30 minutes to put my meagre belongings into a few bags and boxes and carry them out to my little bakkie.

When I returned inside for the final check, Allegra was sitting on the end of the bed, sipping her coffee, eyes full of tears.

'I'm so sorry,' I said, 'about everything.'

She just looked straight ahead.

A few minutes later, as I drove out of the lodge, it was my tears that were flowing.

6

And so back to the pokey guitar-teaching room, almost four years after what I came to refer to as the Allegra-Texan Debacle, where the Cape winter storm was battering the window with renewed enthusiasm. I held my warning letter from the headmaster and considered the regal gold-and-navy logo depicting an Anglican mitre. I then tore it into 24 neat pieces. The warning from the Prelate's College HR department had done nothing to dampen my spirits. The weekend ahead promised to be a good one – away from Cape Town and into the crisp winter of the Drakensberg for a special occasion.

On Saturday, String Bean was to wed the fair and saintly Simone, and I was to play the role of groomsman.

The spot the couple had chosen for the event was a boutique lodge in a valley near Bergville. I knew the place – Hlolela Mountain Lodge – from a two-week stint working as a guide during my second year in the wild. It was owned by my ex-(not-on-speaking-terms)-girlfriend Allegra's aunt and uncle. I hoped there wouldn't be any awkwardness given the demise of our relationship almost four years previously.

I flew from Cape Town to Durban and then hired a car. My continued pathetic financial situation necessitated my hiring a vehicle from an outfit called 'Carfords Cheap Rentals', which, after unsuccessfully investigating the row of car-hire places, I discovered was situated outside the airport perimeter, in a 20-by-20-metre dusty lot excised (almost certainly illegally) from a sugarcane field. The depot, if I can call it that, consisted of a battered prefab building that smelt strongly of mould and

35

stale French fries. Just outside, the company's assets – all three of them – lounged in various states of disrepair.

The owner/manager/general factotum was seated behind an old school desk, picking his teeth with a metal spike. I knocked on the door, but the smell precluded entry.

'Good day,' I said. 'I think I have a booking with you.'

To his credit, the man, though dishevelled and smelling strongly of moonshine, smiled, whipped his feet off the desk, popped the spike into a top pocket and clapped his hands.

'Ah, Mr MacNaughton I presume! Welcome to Carfords! Can I offer you refreshment?' He indicated an old booze crate on which a tea station rested.

I looked at the kettle, discoloured with age, and the mugs, discoloured with use.

'No, thank you. I think I'll just get going,' I replied.

'Good, good, no problem. I am Albert Govender and this is my business.' He said this with such pride, I almost felt impressed.

A few minutes later, I departed in a Toyota Yaris that had obviously experienced a catastrophic accident during its illustrious career. This was evidenced by the fact that the back wheels did not follow the line of the front ones.

And so I drove into the valley five hours later, a loud, whining rattle announcing my arrival at Hlolela Mountain Lodge.

The sun was just sinking over the mountains silhouetted against the carmine sky. The tips of the tall red thatching grass glowed copper in the embers of the day.

And preparations were well under way.

The first person I saw was String Bean. Many are the tales told by grooms of their brides-to-be turning into harpies during the process of planning the 'most important day' of their lives. (Obviously this is ridiculous. The most important days of your life must surely be the day you are born, without which you cannot have life, and the day you die, after which there is no life.) In the case of Simone, a calmer, sweeter, more happy-go-lucky bride you could not hope to find. It was my brother who'd turned into a harpy-with-the-Y-chromosome.

As I pulled up to the entrance, Hugh was gesticulating towards a group of people erecting a marquee on the lawns in front of the lodge. The woman with whom he was remonstrating looked alarmed as she scribbled notes on a clipboard.

The Yaris ground to a noisy halt in front of them and belched an acrid cloud. I wound down the window.

'Hello, String Bean!' I said.

He looked over the Yaris, mouth pinched in disgust.

'Angus, please park this ... *thing* ... somewhere far from where any of my guests will see it.' He turned back to the harassed-looking woman I took to be the wedding planner. 'I don't care how you do it, but you'd better get enough – it's going to be freezing on Saturday night and braziers will set the whole place on fire! Are you hoping to incinerate my guests?'

'No, I, just thought –' she began.

'Well, try not to think. Just do. I will do the thinking,' he continued.

I drove off to hide the car.

That Thursday night was a family affair in the lodge dining room. There was a roaring fire in the old stone fireplace. Julia was on good form, as was her now live-in boyfriend, Alistair 'The Legend' Jones. My father and mother were extremely excited by their youngest's wedding – the former relaxed and happy to have his family around him and the latter in a panic over, well, everything. But that was normal. The Major took to the brandy at around 17h00 and didn't make it to dinner – he simply snored loudly on an armchair in front of the fire, muttering with each exhalation.

The next day we all worked like slaves – but for the Major, of course, who sat in a chair on the veranda, blanket over his lap, mouthing off at anyone who walked past him, and making lewd remarks to the bride. He'd always been rather fond of her.

'Hmm, hello, girlie,' he said to her at around 10h00 as I was carrying the thousandth load of chairs past him to the marquee. 'Come and sit on my lap for a few minutes – let's have a chat about breeding!' Then he saw me. 'Stop malingering, you wastrel!' he shouted. 'You've always been a lazy pooftah – now get on with it, bit of physical labour'll man you up!'

That afternoon, I was enjoying the winter sun, lining the walkway between the marquee and the lodge with brown bags and candles, when the cake arrived. Chantelle (wedding planner) walked onto the veranda with furrowed brow. SB was coming from the other direction, looking at his giant new smartphone, forehead equally wrinkled.

'Angus, don't shirk on filling those bags – they must be half full or they'll collapse. Those two must be redone.' He didn't look at me, and carried on walking.

'Yes, my lord.' I bowed deeply before shooting the bird at him.

'Don't call me that,' he snapped.

'Um, Mr MacNaughton?' This was Chantelle hailing her employer.

Hugh looked up. 'Yes?'

'The, um, cake is here.' Her tone indicated fear and trepidation, so I knew there was going to be entertainment. My next area was outside the main entrance, so I dragged my wheelbarrow-full of brown bags, sand and candles up onto the veranda and followed them inside to the lodge's dining room.

There, on a table, sat the construction.

String Bean's jaw began moving furiously from side to side. His ears reddened, nostrils flared and his breath became audible. He opened his mouth, then closed it again with a squeak.

Behind the table stood a woman of staggering corpulence, her attitude indicating a strange detachment. She reached into the pocket over her pendulous left breast and pulled out an e-cigarette. She vaped lazily and exhaled. The reason for the impasse was, of course, the confectionery resting on the table between them.

Now, in my brother's defence, the cake could not have been what he'd expected – unless he'd ordered a piece of abstract art listing heavily to starboard. The second layer had sunk into the base layer on one side, cracking the white icing to reveal the chocolate inner. The second layer's icing had similarly succumbed to strain, but more uniformly, such that it appeared to be diffusing into the third layer. This layer's main flaw, however, was the fact that it was emerald green.

'You didn't tell me the road was so bad,' said the huge woman, her tone accusatory rather than apologetic.

With that, String Bean exploded.

'I didn't tell you the road was bad?' he yelled. 'What the fu–... hell has that to do with anything? Why does the top layer look like a sinking St Patrick's day celebration? This is completely unusable – you've destroyed my wedding!'

I thought it unwise to point out that it wasn't only *his* wedding.

'Well, you still have to pay me,' said the woman, blowing the vapour towards the stunning view of the Amphitheatre.

'Pay you?' Hugh hit the table; the cake jolted. '*Pay* you!' He slammed his fists into the table again. This proved too much for the confectionary. The base layer subsided entirely on one side and the whole edifice toppled over onto the table.

'Now look what you have done!' yelled the woman.

'What's going on here?' Anthony, the proprietor, emerged from the kitchen. Then he saw the 'cake' on the table. 'Oh ...' He wiped his hands on a dish cloth.

I walked up to the table, took a chunk of the base layer and bit into it. A stunned silence observed me. I masticated the piece thoroughly and then screwed up my nose.

'This,' I declared, holding up the remaining piece and looking around dramatically, 'was made with margarine! It is not fit for human consumption.'

With that, I returned to my wheelbarrow and departed via the main entrance. The eruption that followed dimmed as I exited into the gorgeous mountain air, tinged with the smell of wood smoke.

I was thoroughly exhausted by the time the rehearsal came about that evening. String Bean's best man and four other groomsmen were friends of his from school – corporate types with vastly inflated senses of their value to the universe. The sort who thought their obscene salaries in some way mirrored their intelligence. Men's men of the most putrid, back-thumping, let's-down-a-beer-at-the-nineteenth-hole type. And far too busy to arrive in time to do any heavy (or light) lifting.

I met them in the garden gazebo under which the nuptials were to take place – the last to arrive.

'Angus, you're late,' greeted my dear brother. 'The sunset cocktails need to happen at *sunset*, not midnight. Please tell me you're planning to change before the cocktails?'

His friends glared at me. I was rather sweaty, but that was hardly my fault.

Before I could punch String Bean in the face, the Major came tottering onto the scene, leaning heavily on his walking stick.

'What's going on here?' he bellowed.

'It's time for the rehearsal, Grandad,' explained Julia, taking him by the hand and ushering him to a chair in the congregation.

'Rehearsal? For what? Haven't been in a play since my time at Eagle's Cross. Played a damn fine Shylock, you know – he's a Jew, if you can believe it!'

'Oh, Dad, not this again.' Our mother approached carrying a basket of greenery, but her father was just getting into this stride.

'You should have seen what I got up to with Portia in the wings! Filthy girl she was – filthy. Ha!'

'Oh my God,' said our mother, looking around to see who was listening. (It was everyone.)

'The Lord forgive you,' said his son, pious Uncle Ant.

The extended MacNaughton clan contained in its ranks a number of religious zealots. Our mother vacillated between bouts of godly dedication and lapses of months without a Sunday visit. Her brother and his family, however, did not miss a service and belonged to some newfangled, wave-your-hands-in-the-air church that conducted its business from a giant warehouse. They'd convinced Hugh that their pastor was the man to officiate – a fellow with greasy hair and a great love of himself (and presumably of the Lord as well). He was dressed in a swanky black suit with a shocking-pink shirt, matching pocket square and no tie.

From then on, the rehearsal proceeded without incident. Pastor

Nick, apparently a man without surname, thoroughly enjoyed his time in the limelight, prayed for guidance at various intervals and said, 'Aymen' and 'Praise the Lord' a great deal.

I made the cocktail party just after the sun went down, having showered and dressed in some slacks and a tweed sports jacket I'd found at a Salvation Army store. I picked up a margarita and downed it. Then took another and stepped out onto the lawn overlooking a large dam that reflected the pink sky and silhouetted mountains.

'Well, don't you clean up good,' said a voice behind me.

I turned to see Kerry, one-time trainee chef at Sasekile. She was wearing a green dress with a cashmere (or a cheaper equivalent) shawl around her shoulders. Her wavy red hair was free and splashed onto her shoulders. The soft evening light bathed her slim figure. I hadn't seen her for a few years – we'd lost touch following the end of her internship.

'Yes, I know how to shower,' I replied. 'Well done for cracking the nod.'

'Well, if you made it onto the list, it's a surprise Robert Mugabe wasn't invited.'

'That's quite funny,' I said. 'Let us stroll.'

There was a fishing jetty that extended out into the dam, and we wandered onto it past groups of people enjoying the evening. We settled down on the end of the planking and laughed at reminiscences of the madness of Sasekile.

'I haven't even asked where you are working now,' I said as dark descended.

'I'm at a boutique hotel near Plettenberg Bay – The Fairchild. It's a gorgeous place. Very larney,' she answered. 'You still in Cape Town?'

'For the moment. Frankly I can't stand the place – the wind never stops and the people are vile. I haven't made one friend in three years!'

'I'm sure that's because of all Capetonians and not you.' She laughed.

'Married with kids?' I asked.

She swung her face to me, shocked. 'Oh, you're joking.'

A wood owl called from a stand of yellowwood trees behind the lodge, and a trout broke the still surface of the water. The air was crisp, cold and clear. I looked at my watch, disappointed by the passing of time.

'I need to get everyone in to eat now,' I said quietly, 'or I'll be in trouble ... *again*. Are you staying here?'

'No, I'm staying just down the road, at the backpackers.'

She looked up at the twinkling stars and we sat for another minute or two before I heard Hugh: 'Where the hell is Angus? He's supposed to be getting people to the braai! He's probably violating one of the bridesmaids in a thicket!'

'Oh, Hugh, what a dreadful thing to say!' my mother replied from the other end of the jetty. 'And please don't shout, even if it's true.'

The next morning dawned bright and cold.

I rose with the sun, put on some warm kit and went for a glorious run in the mountains behind the lodge. The smell of the dry grass, the dust and the wood smoke from fires warming the Zulu homesteads in the valley filled me with a sense of peace. It's relaxing to run in nature without having to look behind every bush for a murderous buffalo. As I crested the ridge behind the lodge, a herd of eland started and then trotted off down the eastern slope, their clicking limbs making them sound like a herd of arthritis. On my way back to the lodge, I found a leopard track perfectly formed in the clay on the banks of a little stream. I stopped to examine the track and sipped the frigid, clear mountain water.

The lodge was just stirring when I returned. The smell of breakfast wafted from the kitchen, steam streaming out of the extractor outlet. I greeted a gardener who was sweeping the front entrance and then went to my little garden suite to change. The fact that I had my own room at all was something of a miracle. My brother had wanted to give it to one of the other groomsmen so that they wouldn't have to share.

'You'll have to stay with the folks,' Hugh had declared in Kenton the previous Christmas as we sat around discussing the wedding for the umpteenth time. 'I need that room for Hollingsworth. There'll be a few single ladies at the wedding – he might need some privacy.'

I'd drained my gin but before I could tell SB to get stuffed, my father had interjected.

'That's preposterous! Hollingsworth's horniness has nothing to do with your mother, your brother or me.'

'Oh, goodness!' gasped our mother.

'Angus is your brother and a groomsman, so he'll be on his own and that's the final word.'

We remain slightly afraid of our father when he becomes shouty, so that was that.

Finally, the event was upon us. Everyone was beautifully turned out and on time. Julia and our mother had created a gorgeous-looking cake for one-tenth of the price of the Emerald Tower of Pisa and, naturally, the candles in brown bags were perfectly filled and spaced out, waiting to be lit when darkness fell. It became a slightly cloudy as the day progressed, but this did little to dampen everyone's spirits.

At 14h55, the groomsmen and groom made their way down to the gazebo from where we'd dressed in one of the garden suites. String Bean's mates were wandering about in their khaki suits with no ties ('bush-chic' being the theme), drinking beer and or whisky and making obvious jokes about what SB was likely to get up to that night. If I knew anything about my brother, I figured there would be no getting up of any kind post the party.

At 15h05, Pastor Nick told the DJ to stop with the incessant Pachelbel's Canon and led the congregation and groomsmen in a sonorous prayer. Everyone bowed their heads except me. I was looking at the sky, which was clouding over with alarming speed.

'... and so, dear Lord Father God, we praise you for this day. Hallelujah, aymen!' finished Pastor Nick.

'Praise the Lord,' muttered Uncle Ant and cousin Kathy, raising their hands to the ominous-looking heavens.

'Where's the barman?' shouted the Major.

At 15h10, as Simone's father stood to attention at the gazebo entrance, a jingling of bells could be heard coming from behind the lodge. A cart drawn by two horses emerged from the rear of the furthest stone cottage and trundled down towards the lawn. On the back, the bride and her bridesmaids bounced along in their finery.

The cart was driven by Anthony. It soon became clear that while he ran a successful lodge, driving horse-drawn wagons was not high on the man's skill set. As the first peel of thunder came over the western mountains, the two horses took fright and shifted from a docile walk to a spritely trot. There were a few alarmed mutters from the congregation and the DJ, anticipating a faster arrival, began to play Simone's song – some dreadful ditty by a faux-folk group (I forget which, but no doubt the sort with bad beards, checked shirts and man buns).

What the DJ did not predict was Anthony's inability to stop the horses. As they came down the lawn at increasing speed, squeaks of alarm could be heard from the gaggle of women on the back of the cart, my sister among them, and as they passed the start of the aisle, the back wheel hit a rock. Four bouquets flew into the air as the bridesmaids prioritised their own safety over that of their flowers.

Another thunderclap combined with the squealing bridesmaids drove the horses from a trot to a canter and with that all decorum evaporated. The women started screaming, hanging on like grim death as their transport lurched away from the wedding space and disappeared over the lip of the hill whereupon perched the lodge. For a moment there was silence as the congregants tried to process what we had just witnessed. Then, the absurdity of the situation became too much. I began to laugh.

'Oh my God,' said Hugh, now the colour of snow.

'Oh, fuck,' said The Legend.

We took off at a run, tearing up the aisle and heading for the southeastern section of the lodge. When we crested the ridge, all we could see was dust rising from behind a copse and as we hared down the hill as fast as our dress shoes allowed, I began to worry. Through the trees, the sound of panicked voices grew.

We arrived to find six young women and an elderly man standing around the wagon, sans its left rear wheel, the axle jammed up against a yellowwood tree. The horses were nowhere to be seen.

'I'm so sorry, I just, I just ... well, I don't know what ... I'm so sorry,'

Anthony was saying desperately.

No one was seriously hurt, though the same could not be said for the bridal party's outfits. Simone's white dress had a nasty tear down the back, and blood had seeped through the fabric from a superficial scratch. The front of the garment looked like it had been used to sweep the forest floor and her veil was fluttering in the breeze, four trees back. The bride's hair had come loose from its moorings and the mad rush down the hill had turned her coiffure into Einstein with bed hair.

'Don't worry – we can fix this,' Julia said hopefully.

It was then that the heavens opened.

The Legend and I helped the bridesmaids and bride to find their shoes and then together we trudged up the hill in the rain, Anthony leaning heavily on The Legend for support. We reached halfway up and saw Hugh standing at the top, sopping wet, flanked by our father and one of the groomsmen. When he saw his bride, he came running down the slope, tripped, rolled, stood again and continued without skipping a beat. He took Simone in his arms and the two of them clung to each other as thunder rolled afresh and the rain increased in intensity. Tears rolled down their faces and mixed with the rain and dust, their expressions turning from desperation to joy.

Pastor Nick presided over an altogether less elegant, but more heartfelt and wetter ceremony than anyone could have anticipated.

Two other notable things happened at this event.

At about 22h00, when the pudding was cleared and the dancing well underway, I went to the bar to fetch my umpteenth Scotch. There I found PJ Woodstock, Sasekile's general manager, and the same PJ who had overseen my exit, and Hugh in animated conversation, eight sheets to the wind.

'What-ho,' I said, sipping from my latest glass.

My eye was drawn to Kerry, who was dancing in a group close to the bar. Inhibitions banished, her hips swung from side to side in time with some hideous pop tune.

'Angus,' PJ leant forward conspiratorially, 'your brother and I have been *talking*.' He touched his nose, eyes flicking from side to side.

'I see,' I said, seeing only the disco lights silhouetting Kerry's profile.

'Yes,' said Hugh, also leaning in. 'We've been *talking*!'

'Ah, good, well done,' I said, making a move towards the dance floor.

'Do you want to know what we were talking *about*?' said PJ, grabbing my shirt sleeve.

'Eh, okay,' I said. Kerry turned her back to the lights, caught my eye and smiled.

'Let *me* tell him,' said Hugh, his teeth purple from wine.

'Yes, good idea,' said PJ.

They both looked at me.

'Well?' I said urgently. Gareth Hollingsworth had sidled up to Kerry, his arms out, vast pecs jiggling.

'News is,' said Hugh, 'that I'm going to be the new GM at Sasekile.'

He and PJ looked at each other and giggled.

'Yes,' said PJ. 'I'm going to build a new lodge for the Hogans in Kenya.' He again looked from side to side and touched his nose. '*Big* secret.'

'Well, that's, um, wonderful for you both,' I said. I felt a strange mixture of pride and jealousy for my brother. 'Congratulations.' I turned to leave – Hollingsworth was gyrating his lascivious hips at Kerry.

'Wait!' Hugh lunged for my elbow. 'That's not what we wanted to say. Well, it is but there's more.' They both stared meaningfully at me.

'Yes? I'm listening. Could we hurry this along slightly?' Hollingsworth had placed a hand on Kerry's waist.

'Well, thing is, we need to train up six new rangers,' said PJ.

'We're building a new camp, see,' said Hugh.

'Current crop are, well, you know ...' PJ was at a slight loss.

'Training is not their strong point – great guys, obviously, and we're so busy with the camps that they don't have time for training ...' Hugh explained.

'Oh,' I said. They seemed oblivious to the fact that the best man was re-enacting the raunchiest scenes from *Dirty Dancing* on Kerry, who was not objecting.

'Well, do you want to come and train the new guys?' said PJ.

This drew my attention entirely away from Kerry and Hollingsworth.

'What?' I was gobsmacked.

'Do you want to come and train the new rangers?'

'You mean move back to Sasekile, train new rangers and not have to guide guests?'

'Well, yes, exactly,' said PJ. 'But you'd have to start within two weeks.'

Snapshots of Philamore-Stravinsky, the foul Cape weather and miserable Capetonians flashed through my mind.

'I'll be there in a week.' I downed my Scotch, slammed the glass onto the bar. 'This is most excellent news.' I kissed them once each on the cheek and turned to the dance floor.

Kerry and Hollingsworth were still at it as Britney Spears was replaced with "Every Breath You Take" by The Police. Full of drink and joy, I walked over, grabbed Kerry by the hand and pulled her forcibly away from the best man.

'Hey!' he said, but it was too late for him.

'Be gone, Hollingsworth,' I said.

Kerry giggled as my left arm slipped round her waist and I pulled her tight to me. We moved at half speed to the music, the scent of her hair mingling with that of her subtle perfume. She put her arms on my shoulders and rested her forehead on mine (we were the same height). As the song ended, I took her by the hand and drew her out into the night. We walked wordlessly to the end of the wooden jetty. The sky had cleared and a three-quarter moon reflected on the still surface. A wood owl called some way down the valley as our lips met.

After a few minutes of what may have been considered an indecent display of public affection, we moved our faces apart.

'Why did we never do that before?' she asked.

'I have no idea,' I replied. 'But I would strongly suggest we do it again, vigorously and possibly in my cottage, and possibly for the whole night.'

She laughed as I led her off the jetty.

The next morning, as the sun's early rays shone through the window, I woke, slightly confused and with a sore head. Kerry, her back to me, was fast asleep. I lifted the covers briefly – no, it hadn't just been a pleasant dream. I settled the covers gently down and slid out of the bed to make some coffee. She woke as I poured the water into a plunger.

'Why did we never do that before?' she said, sitting up, carefully pulling the bedclothes around her.

I shook my head.

'Timing, probably – I don't know.'

I handed her a mug of coffee. She took a sip and then picked up her phone from the bedside table. 'Shit, I have to be out of here in the next half an hour. I've got to be back in Plett by this evening.'

'No time for a repeat performance?'

'Not this time,' she replied.

'Ah, so there could be another time?'

'I'm sort of seeing someone.'

'Oh, right,' I said, deflated. 'How seriously?'

'Seriously enough for me to feel a bit guilty. But you know me – it's always complicated.'

And five minutes later she left.

7

After the joyous occasion of SB's (or should I say Simone's) wedding, I returned to Cape Town to pack. I would have happily not returned, but my small collection of belongings needed fetching and I still had to formally resign my exalted position of guitar teacher to the ungrateful children of the rich – a task I relished.

I drove into the school on an unusually fine July morning, the wind and sideways rain having taken a day off. I parked the objectionable Golf I'd acquired in the interim under a plane tree whose leaves littered the ground beneath. Knowing what I was about to do, seeing light at the end of this particular self-inflicted tunnel, gave me a great sense of serenity.

I had a lesson commencing in the next five minutes, but for all I cared, the deficient and dense Max Philamore-Stravinsky could sit and pick his nose outside my teaching room (as opposed to picking his nose inside my teaching room). I bypassed the music block and headed for the junior-school administration block – more precisely for the office of Warren Sergeant, headmaster and spineless eel. I walked past his secretary and straight for the closed door.

'Excuse me,' she said in her affected Cape Town voice – a voice that indicated she felt that I, as a part-time guitar teacher, was the lowest form of life imaginable. 'Where are you going?'

'Madam, I have no need for your assistance this morning,' I replied, wafting one hand at her and putting the other on Warren's door handle.

'You can't go –'

'Oh, but I shall.' I turned the handle.

Warren Sergeant was a little taken aback at my appearance, as was the mother he was entertaining – although it took her a little longer than him to register the disturbance. He was sitting behind his desk, wide-eyed and nigh on slavering while she leant over it, her bosoms threatening to emerge from a low-cut, silky red blouse.

'Now, Mr Sergeant,' she was saying, 'you know that Peter has always wanted to be a prefect, and he –'

'Good morning, Wazza,' I said jovially. 'I do apologise for interrupting what is clearly an important meeting.'

Peter's mother stood up, flustered, and swiped a loose strand of hair behind her ear.

'Mr MacNaughton, what ... eh ... are ... um ... You can't just ... um ... This isn't really ... But ...' the head trailed off.

'Fear not, Wazza,' I said airily. 'How you conduct relations with prospective prefects' mothers is none of my concern. You'll be pleased to hear that I am here to tender my resignation.'

He gawped as I placed an envelope on a spot on his desk hitherto occupied by the enhanced left bosom of Peter's mother.

'I'm sure at this point there should be some sort of conversation in which you wish me luck in my future endeavours and I thank you for this institution's boundless magnanimity in allowing a pauper such as myself to sully its hallowed halls. I think we should skip all that, and I'll let you get back to your, um, meeting.' I nodded to Peter's mother, who had turned the colour of her blouse. 'My apologies, madam, for the disturbance. And may I just say that I hope Peter doesn't learn his moral character from anyone in this room.'

In theory I had to give half a term's notice but my little visit to Wazza was calculated to negate this – I knew he would soon send a minion to instruct me to vacate the premises immediately.

So next I went into the office section of the music block and knocked on the open door of Mr George Pemberly, long-suffering director of music. I wouldn't say my relationship with Mr Pemberly was one of warmth, but there was a mutual respect borne of the solidarity that comes with trying to bludgeon notes through impervious skulls. Mr Pemberly had the advantage of teaching the high-school kids who'd actually *chosen* to take music, and he conducted the choir – gone were the days that he taught juniors about Mary's bloody lamb.

He looked up from his desk and scowled slightly.

'Why do you look so happy? Good wedding? Get laid?' he asked as I sat down on the wooden chair he used for interviews.

'Morning, George. Yes, good wedding, thank you, and while it is not something we should be discussing, I was accompanied to my chambers by a woman, who showed me a rollicking, if slightly terrifying, good time.'

'Oh God, that's enough. I don't suppose the reason you're here delaying the teaching of' – he checked his handwritten timetable – 'young Philamore-Stravinsky is to boast about your sexual exploits?'

'Right again, George.' I sighed and couldn't help but smile. 'I have some devastating news for you and the school community at large. I have just handed in my resignation to Warren. The manner in which I did so will, I suspect, result in my being asked – nay, instructed – to leave the property immediately.'

'Oh for fu– Where am I supposed to find another guitar teacher by the end of the day?'

'George, your fears are unfounded – I have already found someone for you.' I took a piece of paper from my pocket and handed it to the director. 'Here is the name and number of a young, enthusiastic and very skilled guitarist I heard playing in Kommetjie last week. He's looking for a teaching job and is expecting your call.'

We shook hands.

'Well, I wish you luck, Angus – I didn't think this teaching thing was for you but some of your pupils seemed to like you for some reason.'

'Thanks, George. I appreciate the opportunity and tolerance you've extended me.'

I knew this would most likely be the last time I saw George Pemberly. Sometimes when I leave a place or a person, I have a feeling that there is unfinished business. That was how I'd felt when I'd left Sasekile three and a half years previously.

It is not how I felt on departing the Prelate's College for Young Men.

Five minutes later, Max Philamore-Stravinsky was attempting to explain to me how it was that his guitar neck was no longer attached to its body. There was a single knock at the door and a security guard walked in. I'd been expecting this.

I stood, picked up my jersey and said, 'Goodbye, Max. You can explain all this to the next saint who'll be punished with your skills.'

The security guard, possibly expecting some resistance said, 'You, Angus MacNaughton, you need to leave –' He was halfway through his speech when my Golf sputtered to life and I sped off down the driveway towards the mountain for the final time.

Back in Bishopscourt (aka Newlands), I was quite sad to bid Boris and Clarice adieu. They'd been good to me in their way, didn't bother about notice for the flat and told me not to worry about paying the final month's rent. Boris took me to the airport in his Rolls.

'Good luck, Gussy,' he said as I shouldered my bag. 'You're an odd sort for sure, but I have no claim to normality!' He clapped me on the back. 'Stay in touch – I don't say that lightly. Very good decision this – to head back to the game reserve, I mean. Let's face it, you weren't exactly achieving greatness here.'

'I will do, thank you, Boris. And thank you for everything – I'll stay in touch'

We shook hands and I disappeared into the bowels of the Cape Town International Airport.

All in all, it took me precisely 48 hours to pack up my life in the Cape and find myself sipping tea on my parents' sofa in Johannesburg, the Major snoring next to me in his chair, passing wind with eye-watering ferocity and Trubshaw doing much the same at my feet.

'Oh, Angus, I hope you never have to go back to that school – what if you need a job there again one day? You should never burn bridges.' My mother poured a dollop of milk into her cup.

'Your son is a professional bridge-burner.' My father came into the sitting room having just taken off his work clothes.

'He's your son too!'

'Yes, well, sometimes I don't like to admit that.'

'Oh – what a dreadful thing to say.' Mother placed a teacup in front of Father and offered him a piece of homemade shortbread.

'At least he's stopped trying to make excuses and making out that it can't possibly be his fault.'

This was a compliment of sorts from my father.

'Perhaps this new gig will suit me better,' I said.

'We can but hope.' He sounded depressed. 'I fear that reporting to Hugh is going to make that a vain hope, but ... one should never give up.'

An awkward silence ensued, shattered by a colossal flatulence from the Major, which woke him up.

'What did you say?' he shouted at me.

'Nothing, Grandpater.' I tried not to laugh.

'Well, that's typical. Bloody pooftah you are – I've always said so.'

'That you have,' I replied, 'and I thank you.'

'When do you leave?' asked my father.

'Day after tomorrow.'

'How are you getting there?'

'There's a shuttle from the airport to Hoedspruit – I've booked a butt-numbing seat on that.'

My father rose to light the fire as the Major passed out again.

I spent the next day sorting out my affairs and making sure I had some appropriate clobber for the bush. After three and a half years away, I needed a few replacements. There were updated field guides, I had no suitable bush shoes and my backpack wasn't up to the rigours of the wild. At Hyde Park shopping centre I wandered past the offensively priced clothing in stores nobody ever seemed to frequent and a large jewellery store with prices I couldn't fathom. I bought a new bird book, an insect field guide, some science literature and an updated tree book. That almost depleted my pathetic savings account.

Then I went into Cape Union Mart and found a pair of leather bush shoes – non-suede veldskoen.

'Tell me, Jayden,' I said to the shop assistant who was eagerly trying to convince me that a GPS/torch combo was just the thing I needed, 'how is it that a shoe that I suspect was pretty similar to what Moses wore to lead the Israelites from Egypt – namely, a leather upper and rubberish sole – can cost nigh on a thousand rand? Is there something very special about them? Do *they* have a built-in GPS? Bluetooth?'

Jayden, unused to sarcasm and not being blessed with the intellect of Erwin Schrödinger, looked stunned.

'Not to worry,' I said, 'just ring up the shoes, please. I'll use my sextant to navigate – and no, I don't need to buy a new sextant.'

'We don't sell, um, sss–, eh, sextants here, sir.' Clearly words that included the letters 's', 'e', and 'x' in close proximity made Jayden nervous.

'How odd. Never mind – like I say, I have one at home.'

My final stop after being fleeced for the shoes was the liquor store. I had enough money left for a good bottle of Talisker, which I intended to take to Anna's tree and enjoy as soon as I arrived at Sasekile.

The next morning, before setting off for the shuttle station at the airport, I had coffee with Mum and Dad. For my mother, it was like the first time I'd left home. She fussed, worried and ran through endless checklists of things I needed (and definitely did not need).

'Have you got your shaving kit?'

'Yes, Mother.'

'Your toothbrush ... and some extra toothpaste?'

'Yes, Mother.'

'What about your binoculars? You don't want to leave them behind.'

'Those too, Mother.'

'And your pyjamas?'

'I don't sleep in pyjamas, Mum.'

'What?' Scandalised. 'What do you sleep in?'

'Nothing.'

'Oh, Angus – what if there's a fire or some sort of emergency?'

'Are *your* pyjamas fireproof?'

My father snorted his coffee out of his nose.

'Angus, you know what I mean!'

And so it went for 20 minutes until my father decided it was time to leave. He had kindly offered to take me to the Gautrain. And so, after a tearful farewell, I left home and headed for the Lowveld once more.

The shuttle was an experience I hope never to repeat – indeed, I resolved to rather take on crippling debt by buying a car than end up travelling on that godforsaken rattletrap ever again. (Boris and I had agreed that the dilapidated Golf I'd owned in Cape Town would be best left on the side of the road with the keys in it, such was its condition.)

The shuttle was full – all thirteen seats were to have buttocks on them for the six hours it took to arrive in Hoedspruit. On seeing the collection of ticket holders waiting at the bus stop, however, I had serious qualms about the minibus's ability to convey the combined mass as far as Benoni, let alone the Lowveld.

To start, huddled to the side of a gaggle of excitable foreigners was a couple pushing 80. Each with a small suitcase and plastic bag of what turned out to be padkos (road food), they looked genuinely afraid. Their contribution to the mass of the vehicle was negligible.

The bulk – and 'bulk' is a good word – of the passengers were travelling as a group. They had just landed in South Africa and were deeply excited – unless the energy they radiated could be attributed to the refined sugar they were imbibing in the form of cream donuts and jumbo iced coffees. These five men and five women hailed from Minneapolis, Minnesota, in the good old US of A. How do I know this? Well, because they were wearing shirts advertising the fact. Not only were they from Minneapolis, they belonged to the same Calvary Baptist Church, which had decided that South Africa was in need of spiritual revival.

Missionaries. Big ones.

I always imagined missionaries to be ascetic types, nigh on starving and dressed in rags because they'd given all their possessions to the less fortunate. There weren't nothing ascetic about this bunch. They were covered in a layer of adipose tissue that would have seen a grizzly bear through a record-length winter, and they were guzzling at a rate that suggested the donuts were to be their last meal. The piles of luggage indicated quite a lot more than sack cloth would be worn.

I did my level best to become invisible. I don't like talking to strangers at the best of times and I really detest talking to people who, after over-friendly preliminaries, will ask me about my relationship with the Lord – or more accurately, *their* Lord – in the confines of an overstuffed minibus with no means of escape. My musings over the differences between the missionaries and the original apostles ended with the arrival of the driver, a man of pallid, off-green complexion. He was dressed in a pair of khaki shorts, a checked shirt and those dreadful boots made for people too lazy to tie their laces – the ones with elastic about the ankles. He was pitting hard under the arms and from beneath his heavily gelled but thinning combover.

'Morning, morning, morning!' he shouted, holding a clipboard.

I shall not bore you with his introduction speech save to say that the man had dreams of being a tour guide and made the most of his captive audience while extolling the virtues of South Africa and sharing his love of her three Cs: 'cultures, cuisines and conservations'.

Eventually we loaded our luggage and were invited to board the bus. One minute later, I was squashed against a window while a baleen missionary tried to get comfortable in a seat designed for an emaciated toddler. When she had settled, she, as I knew she must, turned to me.

'Well, hello there! I'm Carly-Sue. How are you?'

I had a brainwave. Possibly the greatest idea of my life hitherto. I shrugged my shoulders.

'Angikhulumi isiLungu,' I said apologetically.

'What's that you say?' She looked confused, her smile flagging. I stared blankly at her. 'You don't speak English? Is that your problem?'

I nearly replied, 'No, it's your problem,' but realised this would ruin my ruse.

In the manner of people who cannot comprehend a world in which English is not the only language, she tried again by shouting.

'ME CARLY-ANNE. THESE' – she gestured about her – 'MY FRIENDS. WE FROM THE UNITED STATES ON A MISSION FOR THE LORD.'

I shrugged again. 'Anginandaba, nibuyephi. Angifuni 'kukhuluma nani.'

'I don't think he speaks English,' said a genius in the back seat.

'Oh,' said a deflated (emotionally – most definitely not physically) Carly-Sue.

And so the bus set off with me pinioned in my place and the missionaries singing religious songs more or less from the time we left the airport until we reached Hoedspruit.

After about two hours I managed to shut out the sound, and when we turned off the main highway onto the Dullstroom road, the landscape began to sooth me. The view of highland grasslands, rocky outcrops and trout dams helped dull the noise. Then, some hours later, we passed through the Strydom Tunnel, and the majesty of the Lowveld stretched out in front of us. It reminded me of the first time Hugh and I had beheld the same view, bickering as we were, on our way to start work at fabled Sasekile – he as an assistant camp manager, me as the lowest form of lodge life, the trainee ranger. Gosh, how we had despised each other

That all seemed like a very long time ago. I wished I could share it with him now rather than with the singing, eating and – in at least two cases – vomiting crusaders.

Half an hour later we pulled into a shopping centre in Hoedspruit. The minibus disgorged its passengers and there, under a marula tree, with a massive smile on his face, was Bertie Mathonsi. He was a sight for sore eyes. I elbowed through the evangelical flesh to get to him.

'Ungooooos!' yelled Bertie. 'It is the best great to see you!' He refused to shake my hand, insisting on giving me a big hug.

'And you too, Bertrum.'

'Yoh, you have got thin!' he admonished.

'No lodge food,' I replied.

'Your bags?'

'In the bus.'

We walked back through the missionaries, who were staring at me, agog.

'You speak English?' said Carly-Sue as I took my guitar from the trailer.

'Indeed, madam, I do,' I replied, 'which is not to say I use it all the time.'

I pitied whichever village was about to receive the crusaders. Not so much because they'd defile some indigenous religious practice – those have already withstood almost 400 years of Western religion, and a gaggle of Minnesotan Baptists wasn't going to change that. Rather, I feared that the already imperilled food security of Gazankhulu was about to be placed under even greater strain.

These thoughts quickly faded along with the numbness of my left buttock as Bertie conveyed us towards Sasekile in the lodge's spanky new Land Rover Discovery – business was booming. Bertie was no longer part of the conservation team but was now heading up the lodge's community-development arm. All of the lodges in the area had some sort of outreach/development/stave-off-land-invasion programme – call it what you will. Sasekile's version, with Bertie in charge, at least had someone from the area running things and making recommendations.

The dubious settlement of Hoedspruit receded behind us and after 90 minutes we were on the final stretch to Sasekile. The same road that Hugh and I – about to kill each other – had driven some six and a half years previously.

As we drove into the reserve, I went through the Latin names of the trees, making sure I could remember them. The bushwillow leaves were gold with their remaining foliage, the long dry grass a burnished copper. There must have been excellent rains the previous season because the sward was thick and luxuriant – something that would prove a challenge should a fire sweep through the area in hot weather.

For me, it is always the smell of a place that immediately alters my mood. Just then, the scent of the lowveld winter filled me with a sense of homecoming tinged with painful memory – dry grass, dust, soft spice from the fallen leaves, a hint of woodsmoke from the villages beyond the fence.

8

It is difficult to describe my feelings as Bertie turned the final bend and I saw the rear of the lodge – the staff village, stores, kitchens, laundry and office. People bustled about their days beneath the clear sky – the Sasekile machine in calm motion. Although the lodge had modernised substantially since my last visit, it still felt so familiar.

'We go see PJ first,' Bertie said.

My brother and his new wife were still on honeymoon in the Seychelles (one of the advantages of being the general manager of a place like Sasekile being the reciprocal stays at swanky places at no cost). For the moment, while SB was away, PJ remained general manager while packing up for his Kenyan adventure.

I remained unsure about working under my brother – in fact, two tiers beneath him. I'd actually be reporting directly to the head ranger, a chap I'd never met before.

Bertie pulled up outside the office area. A new herb garden, rockery and bird bath occupied the space between the office and the rangers' room. It was neat, tidy and organised – precisely as designed, since guests regularly came through here on their way to see the new 'traditional Shangane market' in the staff village.

I climbed out of the car, closed my eyes and took a moment to absorb being back. Then we walked through the little garden and I poked my head into the main office.

PJ was on the phone.

'... I am not concerned about your Chinese suppliers' shortages. I paid you a deposit for those lanterns and I expect delivery by the latest tomorrow, or you can expect a legal missive!' He slammed down the phone and looked up. His face twisted into a smile.

'Well, well, well, look at this,' he said standing.

We shook hands across his desk and he indicated a chair in the corner. I pulled it over and sat down.

'So, Angus, how does it feel to be back?'

'I'm not really sure how to express it – it feels rather like coming home, actually.'

He nodded sagely. One of the things I liked about PJ was that he felt no need to make small talk.

'So, this is a good-news/bad-news chat. I'm not sure any of us really remember the conversation we had last weekend at the wedding, and I suspect other than all agreeing it was a good idea for you to come back and train the new squad, the detail got lost in that bottle of Highland Park – so we'll rehash things now.'

'It's a little blurry,' I admitted.

'And my head has still not quite recovered.' PJ rubbed his eyes. 'Anyway, the good news is that we're expanding and consolidating the lodge, which you may remember from our conversation. Business is good and the time is right. We're bashing through the oldest Main Camp rooms to make suites and then adding another three – same number of beds, but quite an operation. Then the new camp, Hogan – a legacy for our employers – is under construction between Main and Kingfisher camps. The idea is to make this the most exclusive, modern – you get the idea – camp in Africa.'

'Every brochure I read these days says they have the most exclusive camp in Africa,' I said.

'Yes, well, Hogan will be the most exclusive, prestigious, blah blah, until our neighbours put up a fancier one. Point is, it's three rooms, all offering a private Land Rover – hence the need for extra guides. But there is an extra motive for Nicolette Hogan. She wants Sasekile to be named "Best Hotel in the World" by Condé Nast at the end of the year. The format of the competition has changed somewhat and Nicolette has managed to convince them to come and do the assessment here, do their deliberations and make the announcement of the winner during a live broadcast from the brand-new Hogan Camp deck.'

'This is starting to ring a bell.' I frowned, trying to bring forth the data from the recesses of my brain. 'Dare I ask for the bad news?'

'You'll get it regardless. Thing is, we've had to knock down those appalling wattle-and-daub houses in the staff village and there are others badly in need of repair. So we find ourselves short of staff accommodation.'

'I think I can see where this is heading,' I said.

'Yes, you started in the Bat Cave and there is a certain amount of symmetry in your returning there. Spare a thought for your charges – they'll be in tents and I'm afraid they'll have to share your bathroom.'

'Good God, all of us in one bathroom?'

'You could always have them dig a latrine, military style – but I'll leave that up to you.'

'How many trainees are there?' I asked.

'Eight will arrive and we need six, so you can get rid of two during the course of the training.'

'So I need to make six guides?'

'Ideally, yes – please try and accept that some will be very different from you and that doesn't make them bad people or, for that matter, bad rangers.'

'Where is Jeff these days?' I asked.

'Jeff, apart from being so excited at your return that we had to give him a Valium, moved out of the BC about a year ago and no one has been there since,' replied PJ. 'And by that I mean *literally* no one has been to see the place. I have no idea what state it's in.'

'When do my charges arrive?' I asked.

'Three days' time – I've had the tents, disassembled beds and a few trestle tables dumped at the BC in the meantime but when, where or how they are set up is up to you – we are simply too busy with the rebuild and our high occupancies to be worried about trainee rangers. In short, you have four months to get these guys up and running. You'll be on your own, and how you do it is up to you. As I say, we simply won't have the time to check on you.'

'Okay,' I said warily. 'I'll do my best.'

'Oh, and that reminds me, the head ranger is a chap called Bradley Pringle – he started about a year ago. Married to Kelly-Anne, one of the camp managers. Frankly, the position of head ranger has not been easy to fill since your departure – which, I might add, came sooner than anyone expected.'

'Yes, well, I'm sorry about that.' I looked at the floor, feeling ashamed.

'Water under the bridge. Bradley's in because at 35 he's the oldest member of the team. But he's probably rather too nice and not very disciplined. He's driving tonight but you can find him tomorrow and introduce yourself.'

'That I shall do.'

'Then, you need to understand that there is a bit of resentment in the team that we've brought someone in from outside to do the training. Mark and Jason both feel that *they* should be doing the training. They've sort of handled it with Bradley for the last two years and we've got by, but their approach seems to have little structure and training new rangers has so far taken seven months.'

'Seven months?!'

'Yes, and while taking a game drive is important, I think you'll agree it's not rocket science. One of your charges – Donald Schultz – has already been training under them for the best part of a year.'

'And the others?' I asked.

'I'll email you the details of your crew, but I need to tell you about one of them. Our great patron has suggested – no, *insisted* – that we take some guy he found surfing on the Wild Coast.'

'Ah,' I said. PJ need not have said another thing. I knew whoever this person was, they'd be a disaster. Dennis Hogan had made a lot of money but was widely rumoured never to have actually been on a game drive. It was his stable and intimidating wife, Nicolette, who had steered Sasekile to its prestigious reputation. PJ's agitation was probably justified.

I rose to leave.

'Angus?' said PJ.

'Yes, boss,'

'Good luck. We're counting on you – this is important.'

'Yes, boss.'

'Oh, one more thing. The Hogans are in camp – might be a good idea to make an appearance in the Main Camp boma this evening to say hello.'

'Yes, boss.'

'And by "might be a good idea", I mean pitch up at seven o'clock in the nearest thing you have to number ones.'

'Yes, boss.'

A few minutes later I was standing in the dust outside the Bat Cave. The place looked worse than it had at my first sight of it six and a half years previously. Without continuous occupation, it had fallen to ruin – not that it was ever much more than that.

One difference since I'd lived there was the addition of a corrugated-iron veranda roof that extended along the full length of the little building. It was not constructed by anyone who'd have been employed at Giza, however; it looked as if it might collapse at the merest zephyr. A beam from its roof, rotten through, blocked the door. The floor was mere ground, out of which grew a number of vicious pioneer plants.

Long grass surrounded the building and a *Jasminum* creeper was attempting an invasion through a broken glass pane. One thing that hadn't changed was the smell – the stink of bat guano was as nasally eviscerating as ever. A pile of tents, folded canvas cupboards and rusted trestle tables leant on a knobthorn nearby.

Despite the state of the place, I felt inspired by the task of creating a bush university entirely of my own design. I was so pleased not to be dealing with 'I've got problem' or 'I need leave' or 'Why must I drive the Germans; they never tip?' or 'How come I can't have a new Land Rover?' or 'Why should I clean my rifle every day?' on and on and on … Also, I'd not have to drive any guests.

I stashed my bags and guitar in the shade and set off for the maintenance shed. I had no idea who was in charge these days, so I knocked on the door and stepped in. The place was relatively clean but there wasn't a soul in sight. I knew from conversations with SB that the lodge had been through a succession of bad to appalling maintenance managers. As Nicolette Hogan once said to me: 'Angus, no maintenance manager in any hotel has ever won employee of the month.'

Finding the tools unguarded, I walked in, found a broom, rake, spade, panga, hammer, bag of nails, pot of white paint and brush, and returned to the BC. I suspected that whoever the maintenance manager was, he was going to take exception to my thieving, but it worried me not.

I spent the rest of the afternoon trying as much as possible to improve the BC without bulldozing it and starting again. I chopped off the branches that scraped the top of the roof and marked out an area where the trainees would set up their tents – four in all, two residents each. As I swept the veranda, dusted the rooms, removed the creepers, cleaned the windows and repositioned the veranda roof beams so that they might actually support the roof, my body began to relax.

The old, familiar sounds and smells of the bush began to seep into me – the drying grass, the dust, the hint of elephant dung and, every so often, the wet smell of the river. Though, of course, my nose had to separate all this from the intensity of the ever-present bat-shit stink. As the shadows lengthened, the birds began their winter-afternoon chorus. A white-browed scrub robin whistled in a spike-thorn behind the BC, a flock of red-billed buffalo weavers squabbled as they returned to their nest – perfectly placed in the knobthorn for a view of the winter sunset. I even heard a leopard calling down in the river and imagined him sauntering across the rocks and creeping through the reeds.

The biodiversity inside the building was equally impressive. There was a great scuttling noise as I entered the tiny bedroom for the first time. Puffs of dust rose off the ground, the resting place of recently departed creatures. Footprints in the muck indicated an enthusiastically breeding community of murids, so I cautiously looked under the bed. The rodents had shredded a sheet and made themselves a warren of nests surrounded by dung pellets. I had no desire to stick my hand into the mess so I prodded it with the broom handle.

There is something primal about being charged by a lion or an elephant. Most humans freeze. It's a quirk of human evolution that when facing a charge by rodent, I know no one who will not engage in the most ungraceful and undignified evasive action. So it was that when four tiny mice of indeterminate taxonomy exploded from the shredded sheet in my direction (there was no other direction), I jerked back, screeching, and slammed the back of my head on the bed.

'Fuuuuuck!' I yelled, jumping onto the bed and hitting the top of my head on the ceiling – which set off the bat colony just as the angrily squeaking rodents, slipping and skidding, emerged from underneath the bed, saw me, did a 180 and charged back to their nest.

As the dust settled, I looked up to find two eyes observing me. Above the window just below the pelmet was an airbrick. Poking its head from the bottom-right corner, roughly a metre from my nose, was a boomslang. The venomous creature eyed me with relaxed disinterest. While not, as far as I am aware, partial to bats, the snake would have been amply fed by the tropical house geckos that occupied various parts of the chipped walls, and probably also the foam-nest frogs that I'd seen in the bathroom.

I decided the snake could stay for the time being, but the mice would have to go. Steeling myself, I climbed off the bed and slowly flipped it sideways to expose the nest, which I then began to sweep towards the door. There was some enraged squeaking from the centre of the shredded sheet and three mice broke cover. I was ready for them this time, and with some fast broom work managed to shepherd them out of the door and onto the veranda.

Of course the main reason any animal builds a nest is so that its babies have a safe, warm place to grow. My sweeping and tipping had revealed a clump of pink, naked, nose-twitching chipolatas – the offspring of at least one of the adults now outside, and apparently frantic about the state of their genetic legacy. I felt sorry for the minute things and managed to find an old box to put them into. This I left under a small guarri bush just off the veranda – hoping that the parents would return to the sound and smell of their babies before the boomslang did.

By the time dusk fell, ye olde Bat Cave looked much better than it had. I would have one room – the tiny space I'd occupied as a trainee. What the hell the previous occupant had done there was difficult to imagine, but all around the bed was a line of thick dirt that could only have come from his head and/or feet – so I painted the walls. The ceiling still bowed under the weight of the bat turds, but my maintenance skills were insufficient to fix that. I decided that the other room – about the same size as mine and in which I happened to know that Jeff had had sex with Melitha – could be where the trainees stored their kit. On the 'veranda', such as it was, I put up the three rusty trestle tables so that the trainees could do their book work and written tests. The tents they could set up themselves.

I sat down on one of the rickety chairs and looked out into the coming night. I felt happy and, as much as someone of my disposition can, inspired and excited by the tasks that lay ahead.

At 18h00 I made my way to the Avuxeni Eatery, where I knew there would be some familiar faces and quite a few new ones. Some distance before from the split-pole fence that surrounded the eatery, I heard very loud shouting. My ears had just discovered the maintenance manager.

'Who the *fok* does come into my stores and just takes stuff? Who the *fok* does that? Whoever does that doesn't know who the fok I am. That's fokken stealing, and you know I'm a believer in a eye for a eye. Sorry, ladies, I know it's not good to vloek like that in front of you.'

I poked my head around the fence and peered into the eatery, which had remained largely unchanged but for the addition of a weatherproof ping-pong table. The man doing the yelling was a massive brute, except that his head seemed to have ceased growing many years before the body beneath it. The noggin was covered in thinning dark hair in what is best described as a spike-over. The wispy productions of the remaining active follicles had been gelled or greased (difficult to say which) into an arrangement that attempted to mask the onset of male-pattern baldness. He looked like a porcupine that had lost eight out of ten quills.

He was railing at Hilda – she of the burgeoning metabolic syndrome

I already knew from the finance office. If anything, her moustache had become more exuberant. The two of them were sitting at the far end of the table. The fellow calmed down after a while and tucked into a massive plate of meat. Just meat. Oh, and chutney. Meat and chutney.

A loud cry from behind me followed by a winding slap on the back ended my considerations of fessing up to my crime.

'Aaaargh! My God, de rumours were troo! Angus fekkin MacNaughton, well, dat's a sight for sore oiys! I can't believe you're back. Fek me, dat's wonderful!' My old friend O'Reilly was beside himself as he dragged me into the eatery. Everyone stopped their chatting and eating and looked up. 'Everyone! Look what Oi found! Can ya fekkin believe it – here's old Angus MacNaughton, back in de bush.'

O'Reilly then set about introducing me to the new staff – all the rangers and trackers were out on drive but some camp managers, chefs, massage therapists and receptionists were having a quick bite before the guests arrived back. The executive chef dragged me around the table to every single place and gave a brief CV of each new person.

I knew very few. Two of the three I did know rushed over immediately. September slapped me on the back so hard that I choked.

'Ah! Angus,' he said. 'Yoh, you are back. We don't think we see you again, but it is good!' He embraced me in a bearhug before returning to his massive plate of stir-fry.

Melissa was next.

'Oh, Anguth!' she exclaimed. 'I knew you'd be back – you jutht had to! Thith ith your thpiritual home and your thpirit mutht have been calling to you!'

'Hello, Melissa,' I replied, accepting the very wet kiss she proffered (although I managed to take the brunt of it on my cheek). 'Well, I'm certainly back – spirit guide or no.'

Candice, the receptionist with a nasal Brakpan twang and brain that functioned with the speed of frozen treacle, was on leave, replaced by Rhirandzu from Hluvukani Village, aged roughly 25.

'Dis is Rhirandzu, de backup receptionist – mooch better dan dat moronic girl wid de big tits.'

Rhirandzu and I shook hands and O'Reilly moved on.

'Oh, and dees two young beauties are me trainee chefs!' O'Reilly indicated two rather harassed-looking people wolfing down some stir-fry. One was a man, for a change – a plump fellow with red cheeks. It seemed to me that there wasn't an angle on his person; every part of him was smooth and rounded. I doubt he'd ever picked up a razor.

'Yes, hello. Well, it's n-n-n-nice to, um … How do you do?' he stuttered. 'I'm S-S-Sam.' He stood, frantically wiping his clammy hands on his top, but his substantial thigh met with the table top and his Coke tipped over onto the table in front of him. 'Oh, well, um, oh,' he said as we moved on to the girl, who'd picked up her plate with great prescience before the Coke had spilt. She extended a sure right hand and shook mine.

'I'm Hayley,' she said. She was short, with piercing blue eyes and strawberry-blonde hair. Her substantial bust nearly hit me in the face as she avoided her colleague's clumsiness – something she was clearly used to. 'Chef has told us much about you – I'm not sure how much of it could be true.'

'Don't believe anything this batshit-mad Munsterman tells you – unless it's to do with cooking, then you might like to pay attention.'

She smiled.

Next to Hayley was a woman with thick black hair, light-brown eyes, full lips and a left ear festooned in gold jewellery; a person of Indian extraction wasn't a common sight at Sasekile. She and a brunette with a tight bun, green eyes and severe face looked up as O'Reilly addressed them.

'And dees two – sweet Lord in heaven, have ya ever seen sooch concentrated byooty?'

Both of the women glared at me and O'Reilly.

'Dis one wit de bun is Claire, massage terrapist. Hands of a goddess and heart of a granite boulder.'

'Pleased to meet you,' said Claire in a manner that indicated she really couldn't have cared less.

'And dis raven-haired magnificence is Mayan.'

'Good evening.' The woman held out a hand, tipped with red finger-nails and liberally decorated with rings of various description. I shook it and smiled. There followed a slightly awkward silence.

'Mayan is from India,' said O'Reilly.

'Oh,' I replied, 'here I was thinking she was an Aboriginal Australian.'

Claire looked at me impassively but I noted a flash of annoyance from Mayan before she turned back to her salad.

Finally we arrived at the end of the table, where Hilda and her large friend were consuming the best part of a fattened steer. O'Reilly seemed fearful of the fellow, who towered over both of us as he stood, proffering a meaty hand.

'Aangenaam,' he said. 'Ek is Francois.'

'Riperile,' I replied. 'Vito ra mina hi Angus.'

Francois just stared at me, so I took the opportunity to grab his hand and shake it, hoping that the element of surprise would allow me to extract my own hand before it was crushed like a beetle. Then I turned to Hilda.

'Lovely to see you again, Hilda.' I smiled. 'No doubt you're as keen to reignite our relationship as I am.'

'Fokken Angus MacNaughton,' she muttered.

I had a quick supper in O'Reilly's company before making for the boma to meet the Hogans. Once there, the first person to arrest my movement was Incredible, erstwhile Tamboti Camp butler now operating out of Main Camp.

'Ah! Angus, yes, you are back. Why are you back?'

'Hello, Incredible. I am fine, thank you and you?'

'Of course!'

'Excellent.'

'Good!' He ran off in the direction of the kitchen.

I turned and wandered over to the bar, behind which stood a rather striking woman of about my height, with dark, straight hair cascading onto her shoulders. Her face was perfectly but subtly made up. An imperious nose, thin mouth and light-brown eyes beneath giraffe-length eyelashes regarded me. I was being appraised.

'Hello?' she said, slightly confused. She knew I wasn't a guest – she'd have checked me in – but she obviously didn't know I was staff.

'Hello,' I replied. She cocked her head quizzically. 'I'm Angus Mac-Naughton.'

The change in her demeanour was quite startling.

'Oh. The ranger trainer,' she said, the pretty face disdainful. 'I'm Kelly-Anne – Main Camp manager. If you'll excuse me, I need to check on the guests. Phanuel will get you a drink.' She left with a curt nod.

I was sipping on an Ardbeg (which I told Phanuel to put on the staff-welfare account) when Dennis Hogan, billionaire Australian proprietor, sauntered in looking like he owned the place – which of course he did.

He was dressed in a pale-blue silk shirt and white-linen trousers, his feet enveloped in some handmade calfskin loafers. The full head of curly grey hair was tamed by something fragrant. He wafted over to the bar and ordered a Windhoek draft.

'Engus, thet's ya name, ain't it?' He always checked, despite having met me at least 20 times.

'Hello, Dennis. Indeed, yes – same as always,' I replied.

He clearly had no idea that I'd been absent from his property for the last three and a half years.

'Well, Engus – I've decided to take up sirffing. Ya know whoi?'

'I can't begin to imagine.'

'I'll tell ya.'

'No doubt.'

'I need ta reconnect with the irth – find me troo nature.' And then the clanger: 'While I still hev me youth.'

'Youth?!' I stared at the leathery visage in front me, but before Dennis could explain where he found such vestiges, he beheld Kelly-Anne, who was tending to a German family. Being a deplorable old lecher, he made for her like a dog catching the scent of heat.

My attention was then drawn to the boma entrance. Nicolette Hogan swept in – the kind of woman that owned a space just by being in it. She wasn't a small human, but it wasn't that so much as the confident authority she radiated. She was dressed in bush-chic khaki trousers and a white shirt-jersey combination with a leopard-print scarf around her neck. Her hair was held rather severely in place by an invisible force.

Nicolette's ability to notice detail was utterly astounding. When she was around, staff would check and recheck their respective stations, but she always spotted something out of place – and had only to look at whatever it was to have the situation rectified.

She now cast her eye over the boma buffet, and there was an almost imperceptible tightening of her mouth. Her eye caught Kelly-Anne, who was giggling at something Dennis was whispering in her ear. Drawn by the irresistible force of Nicolette's gaze, the Main Camp manager looked up and paled as the owner summoned her with a tiny nod to where she stood framed by the blazing torches on either side of the boma entrance. Dennis pretended to be examining the contents of a strelitzia bush in a pot behind them.

I looked over at the buffet arrangement. To my eye, everything looked perfect. I was too far away to hear the conversation but there was no mistaking Kelly-Anne's abject body language as she nodded and apologised, before making for the buffet, summoning two butlers as she went.

Nicolette then spotted me and the corners of her mouth turned up slightly as she walked over to the bar. A glass landed next to me. Not needing to be asked, Phanuel placed Nicolette's standard champagne pre-dinner drink on the counter.

'Well, well, Angus MacNaughton. It is something of a surprise to see you back here.'

I stood upright and held out my hand.

'Hello, Nicolette. I'm probably as surprised as anyone. It's lovely to be back.'

She took my hand. 'I'm sure it is – Sasekile is hardly purgatory.'

'Quite the opposite.' I thought it best to be as ingratiating as possible.

'I must say, I hope PJ and Hugh have made the right decision. The new rangers need to be from the top drawer. This lodge, with Hogan Camp as its flag, *will* be voted Condé Nast's best this year. I hope you are the right person to train the new group. Are you the right person?' Her emerald eyes drilled into me.

'Yes, I think I am the right person. I shall give it my all, I assure you.'

'And you think you can cope working under your brother? Let's just say that if one of you needs to go because of some fraternal conflict, it will not be Hugh. He has done an immense amount for Sasekile in the last five years.'

'That's high praise,' I said. 'No, I don't think I'm going to have a problem with Hugh in his exalted position – I'll keep my head down.'

'Good to hear.' She indicated a huddle of four middle-aged men and women speaking animatedly near the fire. 'You see that group? That's the Condé Nast inspection group. They're considering hosting their end-of-year conference here. They will be returning in December, and they will be guided by the Lowveld's best ranging team. Do you understand what I mean?'

'Indeed I do.'

'Excellent. Have a good evening.' Nicolette departed to do her rounds of the boma.

I returned to the BC as the winter night became chilly and lay awake for a long time listening to the quiet bush. The sound of a few crickets was punctuated every so often by a grunting hippo and once, far in the distance, a lion.

My body began to smile as the peaceful sleep of the wilderness slowly took me.

9

The next day, I continued my Bat Cave clean-up. Then, not wishing to engage Francois but also rather sadistically wanting to see if he'd have another outburst, I left the stuff I'd borrowed in a pile outside the maintenance store when everyone else was at the morning meeting. The roar that emanated from the maintenance shed as I sat down to breakfast sent up a flutter of startled Egyptian geese from the dam in front of camp.

The next thing on my agenda was to make sure our little university had some form of Internet connection. I had only four months to get the new recruits up to speed and on the road – no mean feat – so while there was no need for us to stream high-definition video, I wanted the trainees to have access to every possible resource. When I'd departed, the idea that Sasekile needed an IT manager was utterly ridiculous. Now, one of the most common questions asked by guests was if there was Wi-Fi in their rooms – they apparently needed to be on Facebook while watching the meandering river below their luxurious suites.

So it was that I headed for the offices, where there was a small annex occupied by Bertie, now in his community-development capacity, and the IT guy. When I entered, Bertie was tapping away at a spreadsheet. His corner of the room was neat and dust free, and the only thing on his desk not perpendicular or parallel was his notebook, open on the list of 'Today's goals'.

The desk against the opposite wall looked like the remnants of a children's party in a dump for discarded technology after a dust storm.

On the desk, under the desk, on the floor around the desk and on the chair lay discarded packets of sweets and chips, keyboards, mice (the tech kind – although possibly also the mammal kind), wires, connectors and tools.

'Morning, Bertrum,' I said.

'Hello, yes, and good day.' He looked up from his keyboard and then screwed up his nose. 'There is still a lot of bats in your house.'

'Yes, Bertrum, there are more bats than when I left. There are also mice, geckos, God knows how many snakes snuffling about trying to eat them, and at least three foam-nest frogs aestivating in the bathroom. I'm happy it is winter because there are no insects yet.'

Bertie smiled.

'Bertrum, I am looking for the man in charge of Information Technology.'

'The what?'

'The chap who fixes computers and sorts out the Internet.'

'Oh, Craig? Yes, Craig ... is supposed to be here but normally he is not on time.'

At that moment, Craig arrived. More accurately, he tripped on the stair of the annex and fell into the room. I sidestepped so instead of me breaking his fall, a combination of concrete floor and his office chair arrested his gravity-assisted entrance. He stood as fast as he had fallen and gazed about as though beholding his desk for the first time. Then he looked at Bertie and finally at me.

Craig January was tall – at least six feet and four inches. The arrangement on his head was the most impressive part of him by far. It looked like a giant golden sea sponge had taken up residence on his scalp. The exuberant Afro (for want of a better term) was parted slightly in the centre such that a narrow valley with precipitous sides lead away from the middle of his forehead. On his nose he wore a pair of square spectacles with tortoiseshell frames and glass thicker than bulletproof. He wore a blue-and-green checked shirt, buttoned to the neck, and a pair of black jeans at least two sizes too big. On his feet were sandals. He said nothing as Bertie and I regarded him.

Eventually, I elbowed Bertie on the shoulder.

'Oh, yes,' he said. 'Avuxeni, Craig – this is Angus.'

'Hi, Craig.' I offered my hand but he recoiled slightly and looked from my face to my hand three or four times in quick succession. Then he extended his own hand like the pope might when offering his ring to be kissed. Slowly he brought it down to where mine was waiting. Then, quite suddenly, he touched my hand in the manner one might use to check if the stove is on. A smile spread over his face, lips parting to reveal a mouthful of large white teeth but for a missing right canine.

'Oh,' he said as if coming to a profound realisation. He turned with great speed, brushed the flotsam from his chair to the ground, sat down and began tapping ferociously at his computer without another word.

I looked at Bertie, who shrugged his shoulders.

'Craig,' I said. 'Um, could I ask you something, please?'

The tapping continued. Bertie gave me a thumbs-up.

'I need Internet at the Bat Cave – you know where that is?'

'Mmmmmm,' Craig replied, tapping away. He reached for an open packet of cheese puffs, extracted a fist full of the disgusting things and stuffed them in his mouth.

'Do you think you might manage it by tomorrow? The trainees are coming in then.'

'Mmmmmm.' Craig turned to face me, lips covered in orange powder. He scowled and lifted his finger, then pointed at nothing in particular. 'Mmmmmm,' he said, nodding. 'Today.' The chair swung back around and the hand withdrew another pile of tartrazine and MSG, much of which was soon transferred to the keyboard.

Bertie gave another thumbs-up and mouthed, 'He will fix.'

At around 09h30, I went to the rangers' room to find Bradley Pringle, head ranger, and introduce myself to the rest of the ranging team, some of whom I already knew quite well. No one was back from drive yet, so I walked into the room and gazed about – not without a sense of horror. The place I left had been clean, neat and filled with books, magazines, insect cases and bleached bits of skeleton from various expired animals.

Now it looked like a hand grenade had exploded in the distant past and that people had simply lived around the carnage ever since.

Every surface was covered in dust, the old coffee table listed to port and the shelves of natural-history artefacts were littered with clothes, old rags, a (mercifully unused) condom and bits of paper. The surface of my old desk was strewn with pamphlets and three used coffee cups – one of them filled with cigarette ends. I patted the back of the sagging sofa and then coughed as a cloud of dust enveloped my head.

'Angus!'

I spun round to find Elvis, and we beamed at each other.

'Avuxeni, General Elvis!' I said as he thundered over and threw his massive arms around me. I imagine the feeling was much the same as being set upon by a Kodiak bear, such was Elvis's size – his hug squeezed the air from my lungs and then he slapped my back, leaving me slightly winded.

'You are back!' He appraised me. 'Eish, but you are thin – I see you are not married yet.'

'No, I'm not married.' I laughed. 'And you are *not* thin.'

Elvis laughed. 'No, I'm married – two times!' He clapped me once more on the back and then disappeared outside as the post-game-drive bustle started in earnest.

Rangers and trackers were arriving, some contemplative, some chatting about natural history and others describing the morning's heroics.

'Jissus, bru, in the wine cellar?' exclaimed a stocky blond fellow in his early twenties. A lopsided name badge indicated his name was Sean.

'Ja, on that carpet next to the Shiraz – and she was wild.' A tall, well-built chap with dark-blond hair, of a similar age. Johnno, according to his badge.

'She's a cracker, bru – nice job. Those tits! Throw me your key – I've lost mine.'

'That's why I keep mine under the elie leg.' Johnno-the-Casanova removed a rifle-safe key from behind a cobwebbed giraffe femur I'd collected four years previously, and tossed it to the stocky one. 'Tonight I'm going for a repeat performance.'

'It's a giraffe femur,' I said, apparently invisible against the back of the sofa.

'Huh?' Johnno swung to face me.

'Angus Mac as he lives and breathes!' Brandon stepped through the door, walked over and shook my hand with enthusiastic vigour. 'Good to see you again!' He looked slightly ashamed as he indicated the room. 'Not quite the same as when you left,' he muttered.

Brandon was followed closely by Sipho and Jabu – Sipho having retained the figure of a god, muscles rippling under his clothes, while Jabu had clearly taken to double helpings of the evening puddings.

We exchanged pleasantries as the newer-new rangers put away their rifles. I noticed only one person took the time to give his rifle a once-over before slamming it back into the safe – Jeff.

Ah, Jeff – my one-time partner in the BC, mentee, lover of Melitha, man with cranium filled with scrambled eggs and the only person ever to consider me a hero. He took a cloth and ran it carefully over the whole weapon before removing the bolt and peering down the barrel. He then took a ram rod with a piece of cloth attached to it and ran it through the barrel a few times before re-examining and then replacing the bolt. Only then did he look up and notice me.

'Hello, Jeffrey,' I said.

The effect was amusing and disturbing in equal measure. Jeff's mouth began to quiver as tears welled. He sniffed once, took a step forward, tripped over his bag and sprawled on the dusty floor. From his prone position he lifted his arm towards me, and extended his hand.

'Wow, welcome back hey, but, wow, geewiz, wow – Angus is back!'

I shook his hand and it then seemed to occur to him that lying on the floor wasn't the most dignified way of greeting a person, so he stood, shook my hand again, hugged me and then remembered he was holding a rifle.

'Oh, not good safety!' he said and turned to place it in the safe, which he left wide open – not that anyone else had bothered to close it.

Not one person signed the rifle register.

It was then that a harassed-looking fellow – mousy hair all over the place, face covered with an inaccurate stubble – stepped into the room, dropped his rifle on the ground, picked it up, took out the rounds and then shoved the weapon into the safe. Also not bothering to close it. He saw me and smiled warmly.

'You must be Angus MacNaughton – nice to meet you. I'm Brad, the, um … head ranger.' Brad seemed slightly ashamed of his designation.

'How do you do?' I shook his hand.

'Yes, very well, um – do you have everything you need? Can I help you with anything?'

It was clear from the state of the rangers' room, the bags under Brad's warm eyes and the way his team was tossing their high-calibre hunting rifles about that asking him for anything would be unwise.

'No, thank you,' I replied. 'I have everything under control for now.'

True to his word – and it was just the *one* word – Craig arrived around 15h00 as I was applying paint to what would be the university's storeroom. He walked in, looked around, coughed and walked out again. I followed him onto the veranda. Saying nothing, he examined the roof, moving his arms about as if conducting a large orchestra, and then departed.

Thirty minutes later he returned with a ladder, an aluminium pole and a box of tools.

'Can I help you?' I offered. He scowled. 'I could hold the ladder or something?'

'Hmmmmm. No,' he concluded firmly.

I shrugged and returned to my painting. I saw Craig five minutes later when he entered the Bat Cave storeroom via the ceiling. The chaos this precipitated should not be underestimated. I was putting the final touches to the paint job when the rending of rusted corrugated iron arrested my attention. I looked up as a timber cracked and Craig plunged through the asbestos ceiling, landing, mercifully for him, on the remaining bed (which he went through as well). This was disturbing enough, but worse was the resultant raining excrement of the roof's residents.

Then, suddenly, the room was filled with a cloud of squeaking, furious bats and I began flailing about as they flew into my head and chest. One of them attached itself to my hair; three or four took up a post on my shirt. Every breath came with a mouthful of acrid guano dust. I made for the door, smashed my head on the frame, fell on my backside and then crawled from the room, hordes of bats and decades of their shit close behind. On the veranda I gasped for clean air and my attachments made off into the trees.

Five seconds later, Craig emerged. His golden Afro had ensnared two bats and the IT manager seemed not to notice the blood pumping from a nasty wound on his forehead. No, Craig was rubbing frantically at a stain on the front of his obviously treasured blue-and-green checked shirt.

'Craig,' I said, with no response. 'Craig!'

He looked up quizzically.

'Craig, you have a massive gash on your head and God knows what sort of infection you'll get if you don't go and have it cleaned up.' As I stood, the squeaking bats in his hair managed to escape.

'But my shirt,' said Craig.

'Come,' I commanded, grabbing him by the arm and helping him to his feet.

A few minutes later, I had handed Craig over to Bertie, who took care of the first aid – the IT manager would need stitches. In PJ's office I explained that the maintenance crew would need to visit the Bat Cave with all haste, and PJ agreed to sort something out.

10

There was nothing further I could do that afternoon so I returned to my room, collected my precious bottle of Talisker, my binoculars and a backpack, and headed into the bush on foot. I had one destination in mind.

It had been more than three and a half years since I last visited the mahogany where Anna and I had spent so much of our short, precious time together. Our special place. The human psyche is odd the way it remembers some things and tries to forget others. I had a few mental pictures of Anna, but it was an effort to remember all the times we'd shared. I had a notebook in which I'd written down everything we'd done lest I forget – and, naturally, that had contributed to the demise of my relationship with Allegra. The only things about Allegra I've ever committed to writing are the things you've already read – and the odd birthday card, of course.

I headed west out of camp through the evergreen forest lining the Tsessebe River. The shadows were lengthening and, well cognisant of the fact that my time away had dulled my senses, I made a conscious effort to look around, listen for signs of animal life and reacquaint myself with the distinctive smells of the bush – especially those that might indicate an animal not partial to close human proximity. I reminded myself that anything that whiffed of dairy was likely to indicate the presence of a buffalo, probably the greatest danger I might face on my stroll.

No buffalo materialised but just before I arrived at Anna's tree, I heard a branch crack about 50 metres ahead. I tossed a few dry leaves into the air to check the wind. What little movement there was blew into my face, so the elephant wouldn't smell me. I edged slowly forward, watching where I stepped on the winter leaves and twigs that had been scattered about the ground.

About 20 metres from the mahogany, a smell somewhere between honey, old leather and rotting apricots assailed my nostrils, and a parting in the vegetation revealed a monstrous elephant bull. Viscous urine dripped from his penis sheath covering the insides of his back legs – the bull was in full musth. He'd already pulled down a huge branch and made a perfunctory effort to feed on the leaves, but, as I watched, he reached back up into the mahogany, wrapped his trunk around another limb and began to tug.

I'd possibly spent too long away from the wild to appreciate the idiocy of my next action. Enraged that he would treat our special tree with such wasteful disdain, I came out from my hiding place and clapped my hands.

'Hey!' I shouted. 'Piss off and find something else to eat!'

It can be amusing to see such an awkward animal startle. The bull swung round, head up, and nearly fell on his backside as he caught one of his back legs on the big branch he'd just discarded.

'Hey!' I shouted again, brimming with confidence at his fright. 'Bugger off!'

The elephant's fright took all of three seconds to turn. He bellowed at me, dropped his head and came. I can say with absolute certainty that had it not been for the thick riverine vegetation, my remains would currently be part of the southern bank of the Tsessebe River.

The human body is pathetically inadequate when faced with a threat from any wild creature larger than a squirrel. The human brain is quite exceptional, however. In a split second I had dropped my bag and was running down the bank, reasoning that my two legs would be steadier on the slope than the elephant's lumbering four. Just 20 metres behind me, the bull thundered and crashed through the vegetation.

Use the thick bush and change direction, is what came into my head. To the left, a gap appeared in a spike-thorn thicket and I dived through, rolled once, stood and carried on running parallel with the river. The elephant screamed as he tried to swing his 6-tonne bulk 90 degrees. I felt vaguely sorry for the spike-thorn, which then bore the brunt of the pachyderm's rage – not that I was going to hang around. After 20 metres or so I turned back up a steep part of the bank and ran into a guarri thicket.

By this stage I was gaining ground, the elephant's thundering footsteps receding slightly as he searched for me. While the human brain is quick, it is not without flaw: I had failed to consider the risk of charging headlong through a thicket on the banks of the river. Buffalo bulls like these thickets, but I don't think the one onto whose horns I nearly ran even registered my presence before I was gone. Meanwhile the elephant, using a combination of his sensitive senses of smell and hearing, was still heading towards me. I changed direction again, now heading for Anna's tree from the opposite direction.

If I'd felt slightly guilty about the eviscerated spike-thorn, I felt a deep pang of regret for the buffalo. Having been rudely awakened by my appearance, he was perfectly placed for the elephant to vent his frustrations. I arrived back at the mahogany to the mixed fanfare of bellowing buffalo and trumpeting elephant. Having climbed into the boughs, I peered out of the thinning foliage in time to see the buffalo explode from the guarri thicket, bellowing mightily, and head for the clearing south of the river. Hot on his heels, the elephant had apparently forgotten me entirely – content to pursue the hapless bovid.

My heart rate was somewhere north of 280 beats per minute, my breath coming in ragged gasps as waves of relief washed over me. I slowly climbed back down the tree to retrieve my bag. Thankfully, the fall and the elephant had not damaged the bottle of Talisker. That said, the glass I'd brought had shattered and one shard cut deep into my left middle finger. Still, not the worst injury considering what might have been.

Back in the branches, a view of the setting sun twinkling through the leaves, I uncorked the bottle and took a sip. Probably best that I'd been complacent on my own rather than with eight trainees. The calming elixir infused my being and I sighed with satisfaction before pouring a measure onto the branches for Anna.

For the umpteenth time I thought about all the things she'd asked of me before she died. How she'd pleaded with me to view the world in a positive light, to allow myself to love. I remembered how she didn't sweat the small things – the sorts of things that frustrated and enraged me. I promised myself that I'd be better, that I'd be tolerant of other people's foibles, accept those things out of my control without emotional outbursts. This seemed particularly important given the task that was to commence the following day.

As the sun touched the horizon, I climbed from the arms of the great mahogany. I took out my knife and quickly re-scraped the little giraffe I'd carved into the trunk in Anna's honour. Finally, I poured two tots of Talisker into the soil beneath the giraffe, and made for home.

My original suspicions about Francois, combined with the no-doubt sterling report of my character he'd received from Hilda, meant that the BC remained in much the same state as I'd left it. The storeroom's fresh paint was coated in bat guano, roof dust and shards of ceiling board. Jupiter could be seen smiling down through the recently installed skylight. The door to my room had been open during Craig's gravity-assisted entrance, and my worldly possessions were thus covered in a fine, stinking dust. I was so affected by the atmosphere of the afternoon that instead of swearing loudly, I simply squeezed the bridge of my nose very hard for about a minute and then made my way to the Avuxeni Eatery in the hopes of some scoff and a conversation with Francois.

He was there with a large flock of roast chickens on his plate, their skeletons being rapidly separated from the flesh. Four or five other members of staff sat around the outdoor table chatting but the behemoth maintenance man was alone at the table's head.

'Good evening, Francois,' I began. 'I trust your day has been joyous?'

He grunted and pushed the fat end of a drumstick through his beard. It disappeared into a space where his mouth lived.

'Why, yes, thank you, I had a fantastic day, apart from the fact that my accommodation and that of the eight trainees arriving tomorrow no longer has a functioning roof. PJ was supposed to tell you about this. I shall have to admonish him for being a slaggard.'

The chewing continued with no further sound.

'Francois, do you think you might be able to fix the roof of the Bat Cave before lunch tomorrow?'

Another limb disappeared into the hedge. There was a sucking noise as the jaws moved and then the bone reappeared entirely free of flesh. Slowly the eyes turned to regard me. 'Ja. I'll see what my team can do. But I'm very busy.'

The desire to give him a sarcastic retort was tempered by my desperate need for a roof.

I sighed. 'Thank you, that would be great,' I managed before heading inside the eatery to find what scraps Francois had left for the rest of us.

I could have gone to PJ to plead my case about the roof, but he was harassed enough. The building contractors had threatened to strike if they weren't given danger pay – some union official had spotted an elephant across the river and this had precipitated a demand for increased cash. I decided that Jacob 'Spear of the Lowveld' Mkhonto was an infinitely better bet than Francois. So, after a vegetarian dinner – all meat being in Francois's alimentary canal – I headed up to the staff village.

Jacob was a big, powerful man in his mid-fifties. 'Big' is generally a poor adjective, but there really isn't a better one to describe Jacob – big voice, big bones, big muscles, big beard, big chest. Big. Jacob lived in a secluded section shaded by a massive marula tree. His little hut was next to an exuberant vegetable patch surrounded by a wire cage to prevent it being pillaged by baboons. He always sat outside his room on a stool made from wood scraps. I found him there, in front of a little fire, staring into the flames.

'Riperile, Jacob.'

He looked up and smiled slightly (for Jacob, this is the equivalent of being hugged with desperate fondness). 'Ah, Angus,' he said.

I sat down on an upturned crate and we exchanged pleasantries. All members of his team were doing okay but for Dorcas – one of the astoundingly powerful women in his bush-clearing squad. She had apparently died of a 'long illness' a year previously after being 'bewitched by her husband's girlfriend'.

I then asked Jacob if he and his team might have time to look at the roof of the BC come the early morning.

'Six o'clock, we are there,' he said.

This was great news and a little while later I climbed into bed, the acrid guano dust on my tongue (and every surface in the BC).

Jacob, Nhlanhla and the rest of the team turned up just as the dawn was beginning to show in the east. They brought tools, a few sheets of corrugated iron, a tin of paint and a sheet of modern ceiling material (given asbestos's nasty habit of causing cancer). I did not ask where the stuff came from – I suspected the building site of the new camp and a storeroom Francois might have thought more secure than it was.

With cajoling from Jacob, we – the crew and I – managed to have the place fixed up by 07h00. It was a remarkable achievement, all the more so because it had begun in the dark – which was clever, given that most of the bats were out. I felt deeply grateful when the conservation team departed to commence the day's labours for which they were actually paid.

Craig arrived a little after that, and he was quite a sight. It was a cold morning, what with it being the middle of winter, and Craig was dressed for it – like a fashion-blind yeti. Over his Afro was a multicoloured woolly hat I could quite easily have used as a jersey. His forehead sported a massive sticking plaster, beneath which a little blood had seeped and crusted. His jacket was a jarring combination of pink, turquoise and black parachute material of sufficient quantity to make an actual parachute. His legs were covered in thermal pseudo-tartan trousers, massive around the buttocks but revealing the ankles. His feet – well, they were covered in pink socks and slippers.

He nodded at me vaguely and set to work with his ladder. This time I insisted on helping – I held the ladder and handed him tools, which he asked for by pointing and grunting. By 08h00 the mast was up, the Wi-Fi router was in the storeroom and my computer was downloading emails.

'Thank you very much, Craig,' I said.

He cocked his head and raised his left index finger. There he paused for an awkward moment. 'Good,' he seemed to agree with himself before disappearing back towards the lodge.

The university was almost ready, but I needed one more thing before it could be a fully functioning place of learning: coffee.

There was a little shortcut through the bush that led to the back of the kitchen, and I spent a pleasant ten minutes looking at two grey-headed bush shrikes calling to each other as they foraged among the thinning combretum leaves. The path emerged into the shade of a blue sweetberry bush underneath which stood a rickety table and chairs – a spot where the kitchen staff came to have their tea, coffee or cigarettes during the day. From the kitchen came the usual sound of organised pandemonium as preparation for breakfast neared completion.

'Rufina, Oi told ya ta use less oil on dees fritters! Oi'll have ta give dis one to Douglas in the workshop to grease up a wheel!' O'Reilly was yelling at one of the chefs from beside a stove top. He moved over to the serving counter where a plate of eggs Florentine awaited some final garnishing. 'Oh, my Munster soul – where's dat tub o' no-good lard? Sam!'

Sam, the terrified trainee chef, appeared from the scullery carrying a tiny spoon. 'Y-y-y-yes, Ch-chef?'

O'Reilly, on seeing Sam about to lose his bowels, looked down and bit hard on his lip.

'Sam, dis asparagus looks awful – quickly do some more. And tink about it loik dis – asparagus is loik a man's langer. It's fekkin useless wilted!'

Sam went a shade of lobster.

Eventually, O'Reilly noticed me observing proceedings from the side door. He shook his head and looked to the sky.

'He'll get dere in de end,' he said. 'What can Oi do for ya, Angus?'

'Morning, Chef. I wondered if you had an old kettle, some mugs and a coffee plunger at hand?'

'Oi'll see what Oi can do,' he promised with a smile.

About an hour later, Sam and Hayley arrived at the BC not with a plunger and a few mugs but with an old bar fridge, a kettle, a plunger, a bag of ground coffee, milk, sugar, an assortment of teas and a bucket of rusks. I had them deliver it to the recently repaired storeroom. Sam stared about the place goggle-eyed.

'Y-y-y you live here?'

'You should have seen it two days ago.'

'Where are they all going to sleep?' Hayley cast about her.

'In the tents over there.' I pointed at the pile of canvas and poles.

'Yoh – okay,' she said. 'Even *our* rooms are bigger than this!'

'And probably substantially less stinky too.'

'Not when Sam takes off his shoes.'

Sam went bright red again. 'Y-y-yes, b-but I g-got some of that … um … p-p-powder s-s-stuff.'

There was an awkward silence as Sam looked from Hayley to me and then at his shoes.

'Good. Well, thanks for bringing over the stuff– drop by for tea any time, etcetera!' I offered.

'Might do that,' Hayley said, and the chefs departed along the short cut.

I brewed some coffee, set up my computer, connected to Craig's speedy Internet and downloaded my emails – the trainees were arriving that evening and I still had no idea who I was supposed to be training. There were few mails of interest, just a letter from the Prelate's School for Boys with my final payslip – unsurprisingly, it did not come with a bonus for my years of dedicated service.

There was also a letter from PJ with the CVs of the eight trainees.

I've come to realise that a CV can be absolute fiction or perfect truth, and it's difficult to tell the difference. That said, you can glean from a CV certain things about a person's impression of themselves. The Curriculum Vitae of one Jerome le Roux indicated a man with whom I was going to struggle.

The first full page of the document was his picture. Not a passport photo, but a super-sized shot of a young man posing in khaki bush attire, looking wistfully into the distance. Quite what distance I am not sure, because it was clearly taken in a studio. He was a bulky fellow, and had made this obvious by wearing a T-shirt with a plunging neckline that revealed the tops of impressive and hairless pectoral muscles. I have no idea if there's an official name for his coiffure, but I'd describe it as a Viking undercut: the hair long on top while the back and sides were almost bald.

The face was covered in a perfectly shaped beard – thin about the cheeks and progressively thicker and pointier towards the chin. But the most amazing part of the ensemble was the pants. These looked like khaki jodhpurs made for a child a quarter of Jerome's size (my nether regions thanked me with a stab of sympathetic pain). His ankles were exposed, the feet dressed in a pair of suede veldskoen with green laces.

The written part of Jerome's CV began with a letter that I include here for its entertainment value:

Dear Sasekile,

I am Jerome le Roux and this letter will explain why the Sasekile and me are a perfect match!

First, my personality! I am a outgoing, friendly, funny and loyal guy! Guests will really appreciate my ability to engage with them and take their every need extremely seriously. To be 100% honest, I am a happy freak and people just can't help being happy around me!

Secondly, I have the world's biggest passion for the bush! The bush has been my passion since my Oupa (rest his soul in Heaven) took me to the Kruger when I was four years old! I am very knowledgeable about wildlife!

Thirdly, I am blessed with a natural physique of strength! This combined with my personality makes me a great leader. I was a prefect at school and the guys loved me – not boasting or anything just saying so you know.

Fourth, I am a excellent photographer and I can offer my

services to the Sasekile for a reduced rate!

Last, I am humble! This comes from my religious beliefs about God and all He has given me. I do not take credit for all my talents – these are from Above although I work hard to make these even better (with God's help).

So that's me, Jerome le Roux!

I can't wait to enhance the Sasekile's brand with my talents and passion!

Kind Regards,
Jerome le Roux

I was laughing out loud by the time I reached the end of this – astounded that he'd been granted an interview let alone a place on the training course. The only other page on the CV contained his education (some sort of game-guiding qualification from a training college in Johannesburg) and a list of 'skills acquired from the University of Life – some might call these things hobbies but I do nothing without full passion!' The most 'impressive' included:

- *An ability to communicate with black people!*

- *A love of females (not in a perverted way!)*

- *Scuba diving (38 dives!)*

- *Fishing (fly or bait!)*

- *River boat skippers (almost complete!)*

- *4x4 driving (yeah!)*

- *Crossfit (where's your Box!)*

- *Rugby!*

- *A great ability to hold a lot of alcohol which is very useful when entertaining guests!*

There was not much to ascertain from the other CVs – just mugshots, lists of education and previous employment. There seemed to be one missing so I returned to my inbox, and found another email from PJ.

I clicked on the attachment labelled 'Jasper Henderson'. What opened on my screen was a badly taken photograph of a handwritten document. Over the course of the next few weeks, it would become clear that Jasper Henderson, aged 39, was not someone anyone with a modicum of sense would have employed to dig holes, let alone guide high-paying international travellers around the hallowed turf of the Sasekile Private Game Reserve. Dennis Hogan, illustrious and increasingly demented owner of Sasekile, was apparently a person without a modicum of sense.

As I was considering the CVs, a phone began to ring. This was odd. There was, as far as I knew, no phone in the BC – there was barely electricity. Investigation of the storeroom revealed a phone next to the Internet router – Craig had assembled this without being asked, and it clearly worked.

'Bat Cave University, dean of the faculty speaking,' I said into the receiver.

'Um, no, that's not right,' said the other end.

'What?'

'Eh, I'm not Dean,' said the voice ponderously.

'And who *are* you?'

Silence for a few seconds.

'I'm Jasper.'

'I see. Hello, Jasper.' I paused, expecting some explanation for the phone call – perhaps he needed directions or to confirm how many toiletries he'd need for the duration of his training. The silence stretched.

'Hello?' Jasper again.

'Oh God. Jasper, what do you want – why are you phoning me?'

'Who am I talking to?' This was clearly not a man in a rush.

'You are talking to Angus MacNaughton – who the hell do you think you are talking to? I assume you asked to speak to me?'

'Yes.'

Nothing further, just the sound of traffic in the background. I very nearly put the phone down.

'Let's start again,' I sighed. 'Hello, this is Angus MacNaughton speaking. Who is this and how may I be of assistance?'

'Hello, this is Jasper.'

Another pause.

'And how are you, Jasper?'

'Fine.'

'Good – I'm also fine, in case you were worried. Now, can we please move this along? What is it that you want?'

'Oh, ja, I'm, like, in a jam, bru ... a bit confused. Like ... I don't really know how to get there.'

'What do you mean? Are you lost?'

'No ... I, like, hitched to Ohrigstad, but I can't find a ride from here ... Can you send someone to get me?'

'What?' I was now completely focused on the phone call. 'Jasper, you are required to get yourself to work. There is no way that I am sending someone to fetch you – it's a two-hour drive from here.'

'Jissus ... no need to get so tense, bru. I just need some help, man.'

'Jasper, everyone else is managing – and you will too. If you are not here by the end of the day to start your training tomorrow morning at 05h00, then you can consider the offer of said training rescinded.'

'Ja, but, bru –'

'Thank you and goodbye.' I replaced the receiver, satisfied that I had solved the problem of training Jasper.

Ten minutes later, PJ arrived at a run, sweating.

'Angus, what the hell is going on? I've just had an irate call from Dennis saying that you've tried to fire Jasper before he's even begun and I'd better sort it out ...'

During the lengthy and angry discussion that followed, I tried to impress upon PJ the need to instil discipline from the outset, while he tried to impress on me the need to placate Sasekile's owners and not be completely inflexible with the people responsible for paying my salary.

Cormack, as the most junior member of the ranging team, was duly dispatched to fetch Jasper Henderson from Ohrigstad.

11

The rest of the trainees arrived over the course of the afternoon. PJ had decided that their first night should be in the lodge – to give them a taste for the place before being plunged into the joys of the Bat Cave. (Some might interpret that as rather sick.) They were told to meet me in the Main Camp boma at 18h30, before the guests arrived back from their drive.

At precisely 18h20 I walked through the back entrance of the boma and into the bar – I wanted to have a quick look at my charges before meeting them to guess who was who. On one side of the boma was a small flowerbed surrounded by a low wall, on which sat seven people – two women and five men. I guessed that the missing trainee was Jasper.

Phanuel looked up and I mimed for him to be quiet. He nodded and continued polishing the glasses. Incredible and a few other butlers were putting finishing touches to the tables, and Clifford-the-pyromaniac was in the process of pouring paraffin onto the wood in the central brazier.

There was an awkward nervousness about the group of trainees. This was good – the less they knew of what was coming, the more quick-ly their real personalities would be revealed.

Two of them – a woman in her early twenties, dark hair swept back into an untidy ponytail, and a redhead man of roughly the same age – clearly had no qualms about ordering a drink on their first night. She had a beer in her hand and the redhead was sipping from a full glass of Scotch. The woman was wearing loose-fitting khaki trousers and a shapeless fleece – Katie Howley, I guessed. I knew from her CV that the other woman was of Hungarian descent, so I pinned the big-boned and muscled woman with dense blonde hair as Franci Varga. The other drinker was expensively decked in pristine bush couture and sat with the easy arrogance that comes with having mounds of cash. Toby Steinbank or Gary Wells.

Next to Katie was a well-built man, older than the others, also in khakis and a holey jersey. He was leaning forward, elbows on knees, contemplating something in the middle distance. This was Solomon Mphanza – easy to deduce from his complexion. On the other side of Katie sat a tall, dark-haired man with an easy smile. He looked to be in his mid- to late-thirties – old for a ranger, and a few years older than me. Gary or Toby. I guessed that this was a man tired of the corporate world and in need of a change, or even a fellow who'd had change forced upon him by a divorce or tragedy.

At that moment, Clifford ignited his fire – shocking unless you were used to the mighty flash of heat and flame. Clifford almost incinerated himself every evening but would take no advice on the matter.

Six trainees sat back in shock. One adopted some sort of fighting stance – Jerome le Roux, with a plunging neckline and clad in pants so tight I mistook them for tights. He'd also eschewed the use of a jersey, presumably to show off his biceps.

The only person who didn't flinch at the conflagration was a dozy, dejected-looking fellow of medium build with curly dark hair. I deduced that he had seen Clifford light fires before – so he must be Donald Schultz, erstwhile trainee for seven months.

As I left the bar and walked into the boma, Jerome le Roux returned to his seat next to, predictably, the blonde I assumed was Franci. She shifted away from him.

'Good evening, everyone,' I said formally. 'I'm Angus MacNaughton – your trainer. Welcome to Sasekile'

The trainees stood and we shook hands. They were suitably impressed that I'd guessed their names – it turned out that Toby was the wealthy redhead and Gary the tall, dark, older chap. I simply do not have the personality to give rousing pep talks, so that was about it for their warm welcome.

'I see we're missing Jasper Henderson,' I continued. 'Who is rooming with him tonight?'

'I am,' said Donald. 'I think he was asleep on the pool lounger when I left.'

Jasper Henderson chose to make his entrance just then. He was about six feet and two inches and decked in a pair of old grey tracksuit pants, slip-slops and a jersey that looked as if it had passed through a combine harvester. His long, greasy dreadlocks were tied in an untidy ponytail and his face was covered in a wispy beard. He had a lean build but for a little potbelly.

'Hello, Jasper,' I said.

'Howzit, bru ...' He looked about him in wonder. 'Howzit, okes,' he said to the group.

'You aren't going to make a habit of being late, are you?' I said without smiling.

'Bru, jissus, it was a rough trip here.' He ran a hand through his dreadlocks.

'Have a seat, everyone,' I said. 'This won't take long.'

The trainees sat down on the little wall again. Katie drained her beer and put the glass down between her legs. On seeing this, Jasper stood up.

'I'm just gonna get a bezza, bru.'

At this point I thought it prudent to assert myself. (Actually, I just snapped.)

'Sit down!' I shouted. Jasper froze. 'Now!'

'Jissus, chill, bru.' Jasper looked at his colleagues and sat down muttering.

'Now,' I said, calm again, sixteen wide eyes regarding me. 'Tomorrow you will start your training. We have three months to get you ready for an assessment drive. That's not a lot of time, so you're going to need to keep your heads down and work hard. It's not boot camp and you are, apparently, all adults, so I'm not going to micromanage your time. If you don't meet your targets then, well, the ranks of the unemployed will no doubt welcome you into their chilly embrace. That said, I'm at your disposal any time. Any questions so far?'

'Where will we be living?' asked Jerome, his exposed skin covered in gooseflesh.

'Do you own a jersey, Jerome?' I asked.

'Ja, but I'm not cold,' he said, shivering slightly.

'Were your arms recently plucked free of feathers?'

'Huh?'

'Never mind. You will be living in tents for the duration of the training and operating out of a magnificent schloss known as the Bat Cave. I, too, will be living there but unlike you, I will be luxuriating indoors.'

They all stared at me. Franci chuckled slightly.

'What's a slosh?' asked Jasper.

'As I say, this is not boot camp or high school. You are not expected to maintain the discipline of celibate, manslaying gladiators – there are no rules against drinking or sex, etcetera. There *are* a few rules that cannot be broken, however. Firstly, during your training, you need to be shaved, dressed and ready by 05h30 every day, unless I say otherwise. That begins tomorrow. Secondly, if I catch you walking without a torch at night, I will make sure the bearhug of unemployment comes swiftly. Thirdly, you will treat everyone here with respect – there are people from just about every background you can imagine, and you will need to learn about the cultural sensitivities at play. Lastly, safety is paramount. You'll be spending time in a wild place where very few of you have much experience, you'll be learning to use high-calibre hunting rifles and, at the end of this, you'll be responsible for the lives of your guests and the poor chap allocated to you as a tracker.'

I let the silence hang for a little while. The effect was somewhat ruined by O'Reilly arriving in the boma with a wheel of Gorgonzola.

'Fekkin hell,' he yelled. 'Mathias, Oi told you ta clean dis fekking candelabrum!'

'As I said, all backgrounds.'

Franci, Katie and Solomon giggled and I waited for O'Reilly to depart.

'So, with regards to safety, you are to follow my instructions to the letter and without question until you qualify. Understood?'

There were muttered yeses and head nods from all but Jasper, who seemed to be examining his dreadlocks.

'Jasper, do I have your concurrence in this matter?'

He looked up. 'Bru?'

'While doing your lice study, did you hear what I said about safety?'

'Ja, bru, no troubles.'

'Excellent. Well, I'll leave you all to have your dinner here and see you tomorrow, 05h30 at the Bat Cave – Donald knows where it is, so he'll bring you over.'

By 05h25 the next morning I was sitting on a folding director's chair outside the BC, sipping coffee in the frigid air. It was still pitch black with no hint of the dawn. On the trestle tables in front of me was the comprehensive training file.

I had visited Bradley in the tip that used to be the rangers' room around 14h00 the previous day. He'd been sitting at his desk, tapping away at his keyboard with one finger, cigarette in hand while Mishak – the world's most useless tracker or, more positively, the world's most enthusiastic hood ornament – was haranguing him, no doubt about extra leave or an increase or more food ... Mishak one of the main reasons I'd been unable to maintain any enjoyment when I'd sat on Bradley's (admittedly much cleaner) seat.

Mishak's face had turned sour as he'd seen me.

'Why are you here?' he snapped mid-flow.

'Mishak, I've returned to bewitch you,' I replied evenly.

Bradley swung round to look at me. 'Oh, well, um, goodness ...'

'Mishak, go away. I need to talk to Brad.'

'You can't talk to me – you are not my boss!' Mishak's fat cheeks wobbled. 'I am going nowhere!'

I ignored him.

'Brad, I was wondering if the training manual has been updated and where I might find the digital copy?'

The look on Brad's face indicated that he had no idea what I was talking about. Before he could respond, a voice came from the back of the room, where a grime-coloured chair with shredded upholstery seemed to be rotting into the floor. On it slouched Mark, one leg over the chair's arm, perusing his phone.

'Sasekile rangers don't use that training plan any more – it's old school,' he said. 'We needed something more dynamic.'

Resentment mingled with the dusty atmosphere.

'A more dynamic training plan would be great,' I said. 'Where would I find a copy?'

'There's no copy – it's more like an institutional culture built over years. It's IP.'

'I see,' I replied. 'You mean you just make it up as you go along?'

Mark stood and pointed at me.

'Things have changed since you left here, MacNaughton – we have a way of doing stuff. We have a group of mentors who decide when a trainee is ready. The process can't be rushed.'

'Oh, spare me.' I'd lost patience. 'This nicotine-infused tip is an excellent indication of how things are being done around here.'

'Now, just wait ... a second there ...' said Bradley, but I was already out the door.

An hour later, I'd printed out my old training programme and put it in the eight files Bertie had helped me lift from Hilda's office while she'd been at lunch (or post-lunch snack or pre-tea – it was difficult to tell).

At 05h30 on the dot, I heard the approach of footsteps and saw the flickering of a torch on the path between the kitchen and the BC. As expected, seven people were soon gawping at the façade, such as it was, of the BC.

There was no piece of me that expected Jasper to be with the crew, shaved and ready.

'Morning, all. Donald, was there any movement from your flatmate this morning?'

Donald shook his head and sighed. 'I oath, I tried to wake him but he just groaned at me. Those dreadlocks ... I'm not sharing a tent with that guy.'

I showed the seven present their training files and told them to help themselves to coffee.

A few minutes later I barged into Main Camp room 3.

The bed was occupied by a dishevelled creature – butt naked. His clothes and buggered-up backpack lay on the floor next to him. He was lying on his back, mouth open and snoring loudly. The acrid odour that slapped me in the face was that of stale human mixed with marijuana and rotting onions. The latter I deduced quickly came from the arrangement on his head, which must have contained a number of invertebrates hitherto unclassified.

I cupped my hands to my mouth and yelled at the top of my lungs: 'JASPER!'

He sat bolt upright. 'It wasn't me, I didn't take it!'

'Good morning, Jasper,' I said.

'What ... where ...?' He looked around frantically, trying to place himself.

'Sasekile Private Game Reserve. You are a trainee ranger and you are late for your first day.'

While thoroughly irritated, I found Jasper fascinating – it was like discovering a proto-human. I watched as the adrenalin ebbed in his body and he slowly (*very* slowly) became aware of his surroundings. Eventually, he inhaled sharply and rubbed his face with both hands. His next action was so incredible, I could but watch in awe.

Instead of covering his nakedness, leaping up and apologising for being an indolent waste of oxygen, he leant over to the bedside table, where a half-smoked joint rested next to a box of matches. He popped the joint into his mouth, eventually found an unused match in the box, struck it, held it to the tip of the joint and inhaled loudly. A cloud of smoke filled the room and he sighed in satisfaction before turning slightly and leaning against the headboard.

'Phew – gave me a fright there, bru.' His voice sounded like a recording on a stretched tape – deep, slow, irregular. 'You shouldn't wake a dude up like that,' he admonished.

I was speechless. He took a second puff, clearly interpreting my silence for contrition.

'So, bru ... What's up?'

I swallowed, thankful that his nakedness was preventing a physical attack.

'Jasper, do you think choofing a reefer in your birthday suit is a good way to start your first day of employment?'

He stared blankly at the first wisps of dawn through the glass sliding door, and then leant forward to stub out the last two millimetres of his joint on the matchbox.

'Just waking up, bru – had a rough one yesterday.'

'Jasper, I don't want us to get off on the wrong footing here, do you?'

'No, bru, 'course not. It's all chilled.'

'No, Jasper, it is *not* chilled. Indeed, I'm heating up rather quickly. So, let me tell you what is going to happen if you wish to remain on this game reserve for longer than the next 60 minutes. You are going to wash that stink off your body, shave your face and present yourself at the Bat Cave. While you may be under the impression that you enjoy some protection from Dennis, let me assure you that when his wife cottons on to the fact that her bat-shit crazy husband has employed a dreadlocked pothead that smells like a compost heap, dung will fly – and not in *my* direction. The choice is yours.'

I turned to leave and then stopped as I reached the door.

'And another thing. Those parasite-riddled rolls of stale gunk growing out of your head are coming off today. They may have suited whatever Wild Coast drinking house-cum-brothel you oozed from, but when Mrs Schwartz of the Upper East Side arrives here for her safari, she does not expect to be attacked by an evil-smelling kraken emanating from her guide's bonce. Savvy?'

Forty minutes later, dawn was brightening the chilly winter morning at the BC. The trainees and I were going through the extensive training file when a young security guard called Sergeant (name, not rank) delivered

Jasper with the words: 'This one is lost.'

'In many more ways than one,' I muttered.

The creature looked about the BC with the fascination of one experiencing sight for the first time. He'd managed to dress in a pair of torn khaki shorts and moth-devoured jersey from the previous evening. His feet boasted slops, which on closer inspection I could see had been gaffer-taped together. It was his face that drew our attention most: in his mouth was a collection of discoloured ivory in various states of disrepair. He'd attempted to shave, but clearly with a very blunt razor. Amongst the tufts of sparse hair, about 20 small pieces of tissue were stuck to little nicks and scratches. I shuddered at the thought of what Nicolette Hogan would say about this biological marvel.

An intervention was sorely needed, so I asked trainee-veteran Donald to take the others on a tour of the lodge and familiarise them with the somewhat confusing layout of camps, kitchen, laundry, bomas, workshop and maintenance store.

'Jasper, sit down please.'

He mooched over to a chair and slumped down into it – not before leering at Franci's retreating figure.

'Let's start again, shall we? Why don't you tell me a bit about yourself?'

I made him a cup of coffee and an hour later I had two pieces of ammunition. Nicolette was one, and the other was the fact that Jasper was up to his eyeballs in debt – two children and their (different) mothers were hounding him for maintenance. If this gig didn't work out, he had nowhere to go.

Through the rambling yarn, I gathered that Jasper had met Dennis at a backpackers near Coffee Bay. (I assume Dennis had chosen such a hostelry as part of his late-life earthiness.) There, Jasper had managed to sell Dennis a substantial quantity of top-quality marijuana and appoint himself surf instructor. Having thus ingratiated himself to our rapidly maddening owner, and after three months of teaching the septuagenarian to surf, Jasper prevailed upon him for financial assistance. Unfortunately for him, Dennis was infamously parsimonious with anyone other than himself: 'Don't give a man a fish! Taych him to fish!' he was fond of saying.

So instead of a large cash payout, Dennis offered Jasper a job at Sasekile – an offer I have no doubt he would have refused outright if he'd had even a vague hope of an alternative income.

I coaxed all this from Jasper while pretending to be deeply impressed, sympathetic and concerned, but the long tail of woe did nothing to endear the hopeless creature to me. He appeared to have a chronic inability to take even the slightest responsibility for himself.

'Thanks, I've heard all I need to,' I said when he'd finished. I stood up. 'So let me tell you how this is going to work. If you want to stay employed – and, frankly, it is difficult to see what part of your personality is suited to this job – then you are going to do the following. First, you're going to have a haircut – that bird's nest might be groovy for a dodgy Wild Coast backpackers, but it ain't gonna fly here. Second, your face will be shaved every morning with a sharp razor – ask someone for help if you don't know how. Lastly, if I so much as smell a hint of that Coffee Bay skunk on you or around the BC, you will be departing immediately.'

'Bru, why you so hectic? It's all chilled – I just need to settle a bit.'

'No, *bru*. Find the staff shop, get a razor and learn how to use it. And one other thing: please brush your teeth so that they are less the colour of custard and more that of milk.'

Jasper stared mournfully at the dawn.

When the rest of the group returned from their tour, I pointed out the tents, poles and bush-cutting equipment and told them to set everything up and then split themselves into rooming pairs. I was at pains to point out that anyone found to be fouling our communal bathroom and not fixing their mess would be consigned to using the bush and a spade.

'If you need anything – and by that I mean things that might be missing from the tent set-up, not sushi or Egyptian cotton – let me know.'

'Well, I'm not sleeping with Jasper,' repeated Donald. 'One night was enough.'

Sorting out their tents was an interesting task to observe because the group would, I knew, arrange themselves into a natural hierarchy.

Predictably, Jerome attempted to take control, dressed as he was in another pair of tights/jodhpurs.

'Okay, okes, let's grab those pangas and slashers and clear the place where the tents are gonna go.' He picked up a panga.

Natural leadership is very rare – most people, myself included, need to have it bestowed on them or earn it. As stated in his CV, Jerome du Toit thought he was a leader on account of his size, strength and personality. He was wrong, though, because his instruction was universally ignored. Franci's eyes rolled heavenward, Katie stared, Donald coughed, Jasper looked like he might cry, and Gary and Toby sniffed.

Solomon stepped forward. He walked to a patch of ground next to the BC and surveyed it.

'How big the tents are?' he asked me.

'Three metres by three metres.'

Solomon paced out the space between the biggest trees. He checked the position of the sun, did some more pacing and then retrieved a spade from the pile of tools. With this he scraped out a three-by-three-metre square between a large red bushwillow and the jackalberry that shaded most of what would become known as the Smuts Hall of Student Residence. Jerome stared, panga in hand, as Donald stepped forward and picked up another spade.

'Maybe the second one here?' He looked at Solomon hopefully, indicating the area between the jackalberry and a clump of blue sweetberry.

'We'll need to chop that bush, but it can fit. Maybe another one in there, but we must chop the buffalo thorn.' Solomon pointed his spade at a space shaded by a large, leafless tree.

Franci picked up a panga and made for the spot. Jerome stood in the middle of the group as they filtered around him beginning to clear the tent areas, then he headed for the place Franci had chosen beneath the buffalo thorn. He clearly thought it best to do physical labour sans shirt – at the time that he revealed his naked torso to the Lowveld, I put the temperature at around fourteen degrees. His physique was not particularly 'cut', as gym people like to say. There was a goodly covering of adipose tissue around his vast muscles that spoke of a previous enthusiasm for anabolic vitamin S. A tattoo of a lion ran up the right arm, its bared teeth threatening to bite his head off. On the back of his neck were some Chinese symbols.

'Jerome, do you speak Mandarin?' I asked, picking up a panga – I figured I'd better earn some credibility.

'Huh?' He stood to face me from beneath the buffalo thorn and a scraggly branch's vicious thorns caught the flesh around his clavicle. 'Aaaah!'

If you've ever been caught by a buffalo thorn, you would know that the only course of action is to stand dead still and plead for help or risk being enmeshed for life. Jerome, despite having explained his extensive experience of the wilderness in his CV, was obviously unfamiliar with the murderous thorns of *Ziziphus mucronata*. In less than ten seconds, another five branches had attached themselves to the squirming flesh on his back. His cool-cat demeanour vanished as he gave a high-pitched, plaintive moan.

'Can someone help me?'

Franci looked up from where she was scraping the ground. 'Oh my God. What the hell are you doing, Jerome? It's freezing fucking degrees out here – where are your clothes?'

'I'm stuck, bud,' Jerome said sadly. 'Can someone help?'

Katie and Donald eventually walked over to unpick the hooked thorns from Jerome's flesh.

'Dude, you're bleeding,' said Donald. 'Next time, wear a shirt.'

'Other than Donald,' I asked the group, 'does anyone know what tree has claimed the dignity of Jerome le Roux?'

They all looked at the tree. Gary walked over to examine it, touching the thorns and causing those remaining in Jerome to bite deeper.

'Aaah!' he yelped. 'Don't pull the branches!'

'Oh, quit your whining,' said Franci.

'UmLahlankosi,' Solomon said from where he was leaning on his spade. 'The buffalo thorn.'

'So it is,' I replied. 'Can you tell us why it is called umLahlankosi?'

And so, as Jerome was released and redressed, and while the rest of the crew continued their labours, Solomon explained that the branches of the tree would have been placed on the grave of a dead Zulu chief. Donald chipped in with some info about using the fruit to make beer. All in all, a good learning experience – biologically for eight and physically for one.

It took the trainees about three hours to sort out the camp, with gentle prodding from Solomon and very little help from Jasper, whose hands blistered after 20 minutes. At some stage during the morning he lit a cigarette, which I chopped out of his mouth with my panga – in hindsight a reckless action, but it had the desired effect.

'Jissus, bru! What are you even doing? You could have chopped my face off!'

'Jasper, I will not tolerate choofing – it is the foulest habit and you choofers do not understand how vile it is for those of us who don't partake. You've murdered your own sense of smell, but that doesn't mean your foulness won't affect the rest of us.'

I noticed Katie and Donald glancing at each other. They too would have to find somewhere else to have their ciggies.

Donald, having decided that one night with Jasper was more than enough for the rest of his life, simply put his sleeping kit into the tent Solomon had set up. The older man didn't object. The two girls, naturally enough, took a tent together; Gary and Toby another. The one beneath the buffalo thorn was thus occupied by Jasper and Jerome. The latter was the sort of person who likes to be associated with persons of influence, and anyone who met Jasper would immediately appreciate that he was not a person of influence – except in the procurement of *Cannabis sativa* in the hills of the Wild Coast.

I thought it would do them both good to be stuck together.

By 09h30, we had created quite an appealing little camp. The tents and the BC made five sides of a drunk pentagon. Solomon even constructed a little fire pit in the middle. By then, we were peckish and made our way to the Avuxeni Eatery for some breakfast.

Afterwards, I took the trainees up to the staff village to show them around, though my main purpose was in fact to visit Zebulon, the self-appointed village barber. Normally he could be found cleaning and fuel-ling the hundreds of lanterns that lit the pathways and bomas of Sasekile when the sun set, but by 10h00 I knew he'd be back in the village, sitting in the sun on an old cable spindle, waiting for customers.

First, though, we met Mynah at the staff shop. She explained how the account system worked should the trainees wish to purchase canned fish, soap, toothpaste, cheap biscuits (made of palm oil, sugar and saw-dust), oil, maize meal, shoe polish, toffees, chips, scrubbing brushes or beer. Then we made our way to the centre of the village to Salon Zeb-ulon. I am not making that name up – he had a six-by-three-foot sign cut from a rusty piece of corrugated iron, painted in bright-red letters.

Jasper, being the doziest human being in the Lowveld, did not realise what was about to happen. Franci and Solomon did, however, and began to chuckle.

'Avuxeni, Zebulon,' I greeted the barber. 'You are well?'

'Ah, yes, good, very fine!' he said, eyeing Jasper's dreadlocks.

'These are the new trainees,' I replied, indicating my charges and in-troducing them. 'This, chaps, is Zebulon and for the slower among you, he is the village barber.'

Realisation very slowly seeped into the cannabis-addled neurology belonging to Jasper Henderson.

'Um,' he said.

'Yes, Jasper. You will be Salon Zebulon's first customer this morning.' This galvanised the fellow.

'You can't do that!' he moaned. 'You know how long it took me to grow these, bru?'

'I do not give a flying piece of faeces,' I replied. 'They are an affront to civilisation. They go or you go. Your choice.'

'Bru, that's not cool, man. Dennis said I was cool.'

'Dennis's wife will take them off at your throat if she sees them. Sit down.'

From our earlier conversation we both knew he was in a hopeless situation. He sat down on the white plastic chair (painted with words 'SZ customers only') outside Zebulon's home and cowered.

The clippers roared to life. I wondered what sort of reaction this might provoke in the rest of the trainees so I watched them carefully as the dreadlocks fell to the dust. Initially, they just stared. Jerome, Gary and Toby looked around disinterested. Franci laughed openly. Donald's expression didn't change at all. Solomon looked from me to Zebulon to Jasper, his right eyebrow cocked. Katie wore a face of concern.

A few minutes later there was a pile of hairy snakes lying on the floor around the white chair.

'He must take this away.' Zebulon, disgusted, indicated the hair on the ground. 'My other customers will not come.'

When it was over, Jasper sat unmoving. His scalp was something to behold – it had apparently not had the benefit of shampoo or any cosmetic for some decades, and was covered in red spots, blackheads and blotchy patches.

Katie spoke first. 'Come on, dude, it's not that bad. You just need some shampoo – I'll lend you some.'

Donald was next. 'Ja, you look much better – this place has a way of doing things, and that hair wasn't going to work with these rich guests. Also, this is healthier.'

'Come on, Jasper,' I said. 'Pick up your head-worms and let's go.'

12

The next morning, training proper started. The first week would contain very little in the way of natural history and guiding technique, and much more by way of physical tasks. The objective was to explain nothing about what was expected – a form of torture perhaps, but very effective at unearthing personalities. The idea wasn't to 'break the trainees down' so much as to remove the comforts that allowed them to mask their true characters.

The first of these was a lengthy walk of some 35 kilometres.

At 05h30, we gathered at the trestle tables for coffee and rusks – well, most of us. Jerome insisted that he only drank herbal tea. I suggested he might need a rusk for the day's activities because I couldn't say when he'd eat again.

'I'm good thanks, bud – I'm on a detox.'

I knew he would be in some distress by day's end, but figured he'd learn soon enough.

'All I am going to tell you about this week is that it's going to be a physical strain – that's it. When you've finished your coffee, please take one of these sacks and fill it with sand. It must be full. We leave here in 20 minutes.'

Jacob had delivered the sandbags the previous afternoon and placed a small trowel next to them. The trainees set to their work immediately. Well, most of them did. Jasper, who looked like he'd just woken from a 20-year slumber – which was probably not entirely inaccurate – stood to one side and scratched his recently shaven head. He'd spent a good deal of time in the shower after his traumatic haircut and had severely tested Katie's sympathy by using all of her shampoo. That said, he looked relatively human, if you could ignore his appalling dentistry.

It was clear to some that they were not going to be able to load all eight bags with the tiny trowel in the allotted time. Once again, Solomon came to the rescue. Without saying anything, he found a sharpened stick and began to loosen the earth around the base of a combretum tree. Eventually everyone else got in on the act. Jerome, relishing the opportunity to display his strength, pounded the earth with a sharpened log. The effect was destroyed somewhat when his stick snapped and he fell into the dirt. Everyone laughed – even Jasper looked slightly less suicidal.

'Right,' I said when they were done, 'we're going for a walk. Each of you pick up a bag and let's go.' I turned on my heel.

'What must we bring?' asked Gary.

'Whatever you need,' I replied. 'Come!'

And so, as the sun rose, we started off on what would turn out to be a rather long stroll. Now, it does not require great feats of physical fitness to be a guide at a high-end game lodge. In fact, being a guide at Sasekile required almost no physical aptitude whatsoever – it's not like rangers had to carry their guests to safety across great distances, hounded by man-eaters. If there was a problem in the field, help was never more than a radio-call away, and the rangers didn't do any physical labour unless they were serving on the conservation team as punishment (as Hugh and I had had to do many years previously).

The reason for the long walk was to test what the trainees were like under mental strain. They had no idea how long we would be walking for, or the consequences of not finishing – a situation that nicely exposed people's characters without the painful process of actual conversation. It's easy to lie in a conversation. It's not easy to lie 25 kilometres into a walk carrying a 10-kilogram sandbag when you have blisters all over your feet, you're thirsty and your blood sugar is through the floor. That's when it's very difficult to maintain a façade.

I was leading the walk with one of the young trackers – an enthusiastic and hawk-eyed youth called Slumber. I wanted an extra set of eyes to make sure nothing leapt from a bush and mauled us. The previous day, I'd explained to Elvis that I needed someone to accompany us. His eyes had widened in fright until I'd added that I didn't expect him to lug his 120-kilogram bulk around the reserve.

Slumber arrived at 06h15, just as dawn began to break.

Everyone was rather jovial but for Jasper, of course, who looked like the weight of his sandbag might crack whichever part of his malnourished skeleton he prevailed upon to bear its weight. Jerome had gone to great lengths to look magnificent for the outing. He'd donned a new pair of khaki tights, some brand-new veldskoen with green soles and a green T-shirt with his favoured plunging neckline. No jersey did he require on the nine-degree winter's morning. On his head he wore a wide-brimmed, leather safari hat.

'Jerome,' said Franci as we left the BC.

'Yes?' he replied, delighted at being addressed by the blonde.

'Are you cycling today?'

'What's that?'

'I was wondering why you're wearing cycling pants?'

'They not cycling pants,' he snapped. 'They Lacoste action pants.'

'Unfortunately, we can see your action bits,' Donald said flatly.

We walked out of the Main Camp entrance, down through a little tributary of the Tsessebe River and up onto a road heading east, parallel with the Tsessebe bank. It was wonderful to be in the bush again and for the next little while we strode along in a satisfied silence. It felt as if years' worth of dirt and rust were being chipped off me. My senses began to resharpen, ears picking out sounds I knew but couldn't quite place – a bird call, a movement in the grass. My nose revelled the most, however, because even at its best, Cape Town smells nothing like the bush. My olfactory system greedily picked out the wild smells of old buffalo dung, dry grass, desiccated bushwillow leaves, dust and even the faintest hint of popcorn from a leopard or genet marking its territory.

A red-billed hornbill pair, objecting to the cold, sat atop a dead knob-thorn as the first rays touched the tip of the tree. They bowed to the sun in their inimitable way, opening their wings and ko-ko-ko-koking at each other. A fish eagle called down on the northern bank of the river and suddenly I was aware of the muted winter-dawn chorus – more like chamber music than the summer symphony. Crested francolins squarked, a crested barbet trilled and ring-necked doves provided the constant chorus.

I inhaled as my body began to connect with the wild once more. Muscles loosened and the gorgeous sensation of being out on foot on a lowveld morning infused me. Naturally enough, the feeling didn't last long.

We'd been going east for about 20 minutes when Jasper's plaintive voice shattered the atmosphere. His voice was fairly high-pitched and nasal, but years of chain smoking had also made it gravelly such that Jasper Henderson sounded like a miniature chainsaw on its last legs.

'Annngus,' came the voice from the back of the line.

I stopped and turned around. The group came to a halt.

'What is it, Jasper?'

'Bru, I gotta take a dump. Can we go back or get picked up or something?' For the second time in two days, Jasper had stunned me. But just briefly.

'Jasper, we cannot and will not go back. I told you to be ready for a day out. If you need to void your bowels, you can have five minutes and the roll of white gold I carry in my bag.'

'What, like, take a dump in the bush?'

'If you'd prefer to do it in your backpack, that's up to you,' I replied.

He looked horrified. Solomon chuckled and so did Franci. Jerome shifted the contents of his crotch.

'I'll just hold it for now.'

Thus began a very, very long day for Jasper Henderson.

I spun round and we continued – me in front, Slumber just behind. He spoke almost no English so everything he saw he pointed to with explanations in rapid-fire Shangane. I had to ask him to repeat himself slowly because my ears were no longer accustomed to the language's whistling sounds. He was very sharp though, and I felt confident that he'd see anything I missed.

In each clearing I'd announce a brief jog and then begin running, which did wonders to warm me up but did little for the humour of those in the group who had neglected to maintain a rigorous exercise regime. By the time we'd completed about six kilometres, some were looking a bit worse for wear. This was good – the sooner they tired, the sooner their personalities would emerge and I'd be able to see who went inside themselves, who needed encouragement and who was able, despite the strain, to give encouragement. I called a brief halt and told everyone they could relieve themselves and drink some water if they wished.

'This sucks,' said Toby to Jerome as he dumped his bag on the road. 'I've never seen a ranger do this. And my family's been coming to these lodges for years.'

'Ja, it's pretty kak,' agreed Gary. 'Didn't know I was signing up for this.'

Solomon and Franci had barely broken a sweat. Katie and Donald were red in the face and dropped their sandbags immediately. Jerome apparently lived by the mantra 'No cardio, just lifting'. His breath was laboured, all the more because he was trying very hard to pretend that he wasn't tired. Jasper looked like he was going to die. Little veins had appeared all over his cheeks and drops of sweat dripped from beneath his very oddly shaped beanie. His eyes wore a terrified, vacant stare and his hands were shaking.

'All okay?' I asked.

'How long are we doing this for?' asked Katie.

'As long as it takes,' I replied, taking a sip of water.

'How long is that?' moaned Jasper. There was no subterfuge here – Jasper was a lazy wastrel.

'Could be another five minutes, could be all day.'

'For fuck sake's,' muttered Toby.

After five minutes, I picked up my bag. 'Right, let's go!'

In other surroundings, Jasper would have simply have given up. Unfortunately for him, he was now six kilometres into the greater Kruger. He had no bush experience and was therefore not only desperately in need of the job, but also utterly terrified. He groaned as the sandbag slowly made its way onto his right shoulder.

About 20 minutes later, Slumber clicked his fingers and pointed. I held up my hand for the group to halt.

'Can we rest here?' said Jasper loudly.

'Shut up,' I hissed, pointing to a thicket about 30 metres in front of us. 'Be very, very quiet.'

Under my left foot were the steaming fresh tracks of a white rhino bull. My eyes followed them to the bush Slumber had indicated and, through the yellowing foliage of a variable bushwillow, the tip of a horn became visible. We were badly exposed so I quickly scanned the area, spotting an elephant-destroyed marula tree about 20 metres to the right.

When rhino get a fright, they often just run willy-nilly. Their eyesight is so poor that they really can't tell where they're going, so you might or might not find yourself in the path of the lumbering beast – even if he really has no desire to skewer you. I pulled the ash bag from my belt and shook it. What little breeze there was wasn't in our favour. We couldn't just stand there, exposed.

The rhino bull snorted, a sure sign that he'd picked up a scent.

Jasper whimpered. I turned to the group.

'Move quietly and quickly behind that dead tree,' I instructed. 'Slumber, go to the back and lead them.'

Perhaps I should have been clearer about what to do with the sandbags. Solomon, Donald, Toby, Gary and Katie placed their bags on the road and retreated.

'What about our sandbags?' Jasper asked loudly, oblivious to the atmospheric tension.

This convinced the rhino bull that his suspicions were well-founded. He burst out from behind his thicket onto the road, his massive head swaying from side to side, snorting as he tried to figure out where we were.

'Fuuuuck!' yelled Jerome.

His sandbag hit the ground and he ran for the cover of the marula, overtaking the others, who were about halfway there. The bull turned to face us and took two steps forward, head held high. He paused for long enough for me to shout: 'Behind the tree *now!*'

Then the rhino came at a gallop. We were lined up like a set of ten-pins facing a 2.5-tonne bowling ball.

A rhino moves with incredible speed. Some humans can move with great speed too – Jerome was behind that marula tree before the rhino had come ten metres. Jasper Henderson was frozen solid in fear and years of cannabis funk. He just stared. With the rifle in one hand, I grabbed Jasper by the collar and hauled with all the strength I could muster. Luckily, he was built like an emaciated toothpick.

The bull, distracted by the movement, veered towards Jasper and me as we struggled behind the others.

'Dive!' I shouted.

We flung ourselves over the thick, fallen marula trunk and rolled. The sound of the bull smashing into the log reverberated through the winter bush.

'Jissus, br–'

I clamped a hand over Jasper's mouth. 'Don't say a fucking thing!' I hissed.

We were lying in a patch of forbs and dry grass. The log wasn't particularly wide and if the rhino really wanted to have at us, it wouldn't take a great deal of effort.

'Roll!' I snarled at Jasper. 'Towards the others.'

I shoved him and he began to roll, the adrenalin finally doing its job and dulling his pain receptors. The others were behind a mass of fallen timber. Solomon came round, grabbed Jasper by the arm and dragged him back to where they were all cowering. I crawled after him as fast as possible with the rifle still in my hands as the rhino clambered over the first log and began to horn the backpack I'd jettisoned.

We were relatively safe huddled behind the timber fortress, the rhino distracted by his destruction of my pack. The brand-new bag was obliterated in seconds and a role of loo paper flew into the air, unravelling as it went. The bright-white streamer caught the morning sun, completely freaking the rhino out. He squealed at the white snake, swatted at it a few times with his horn and then ran like hell.

Calm returned. Towards the river, a white-browed robin-chat began to sing and some babblers cackled at each other from a scraggly raisin bush. A breeze caressed the long red grass. Slumber was the first human to make a sound. He started laughing at the sight of Jasper who, in his efforts to find cover, had scrambled through a patch of thorny forbs, grazing his legs and tearing his already threadbare jersey. As the adrenalin slowly ebbed, the part of his brain that told the rest of him about pain kicked in.

'Ow, fuck, jissus, bru, fuck,' he moaned, gingerly pulling the multi-pointed thorns from his lower legs and hands.

Katie and Donald, who were closest to him, helped remove the spikes and somehow managed to muster some sympathy.

'Bru, I have to go back. I'm injured, I can't carry on. I feel like I'm gonna die.'

'Jasper, if you really are going to die, could I ask you to use your remaining strength to fashion a shallow grave?' He didn't smile. 'I strongly submit, however, that death is further away than you think.' I turned to the rest of the group. 'Now, what can we learn from this experience?'

No one said anything. Jerome checked his clothes for signs of damage – there was a tear over his right bicep, which he enlarged slightly and then flexed, making sure the skin (with the tattoo of a dragon) could be seen through the hole. Katie was wide-eyed as she dusted herself off.

'Get a bit of fright there, babes?' asked Toby with a laugh.

Franci's face was implacable and Solomon picked a bit of grass and began to chew it thoughtfully.

'We need to take this seriously or someone could die,' Donald offered in his mild monotone. He shrugged mournfully.

'And how do you think we could best do that?' I asked.

Donald glanced at Katie and then looked at the ground, apparently embarrassed.

'We could start,' I said, 'by not making a noise when there's a potentially dangerous animal in front of us. Jasper, if I say stand still, you do that and you shut up. Savvy? That rhino came at us because you failed to follow instructions.'

'Bru, please, I need to go back to the camp,' he whined.

'I'll radio for someone to come and fetch you,' I said. His face lit up. 'And you can pack your stuff and be out of camp by the time the rest of us get back.'

Jasper's visage went green. 'Come on, bru.'

'Oh, for fuck sake's,' snapped Franci. 'Stop whining like a toddler.'

Of course they didn't know there was someone on standby in case there was a genuine issue. I knew they wouldn't all make it – blisters, fitness, lack of food and mostly the mental torture of not knowing how far they had to go would contribute to their eventually running out of steam. They also didn't know that this wouldn't mean automatic exclusion from the training.

'Let's go,' said Solomon. 'I can carry your sandbag for a while, Jasper.'

'He can't do that!' snapped Toby. 'That's not fair!'

'Is he allowed to do that?' asked Katie.

I shrugged. 'Eight sandbags, eight people. One of you can carry him too if you like.'

And so we set off again, the morning pleasantly warm and everyone hyperaware. A few minutes later, the road met the Tsessebe riverbank as it turned south. The precipitous bank was about ten metres above the bed and we enjoyed a gorgeous view of an elephant herd feeding in the reeds. None of the elephants saw us. Jasper seemed to have revived slightly with Solomon carrying his sandbag – one slung over each shoulder.

'Stunning,' Franci whispered.

We sat in the shade of a leadwood as the elephants browsed below and, possibly for the first time, the crew began to feel some sense of wonder at where they found themselves. All had their insecurities, foibles, fears and stories, but the wilderness is a great leveller. I'm not one who goes in for 'energy, auras and spirits' but something about sitting with those elephants changed the atmosphere. I'd obviously had many similar experiences, but it was fascinating to see the wild work its magic on this disparate group. Even Jasper watched the herd with something approaching appreciation. He sat with his back up against the tree and gawped, the hint of a smile on his thin lips. Jerome was almost more impressed by the scene in front of him than he was with himself. But Gary seemed rather bored, and spent the time with his shoes off, removing three-awn seeds from his socks.

I thought it best to let the moment linger so that everyone could gain maximum benefit from the elephant sighting – especially after our near-death experience.

Ten minutes later, the herd melted into the bush on the opposite bank and I bade everyone stand. As we moved off, Jasper did not offer to take his sandbag back; Solomon shouldered it uncomplaining.

By 11h00, the physical strain of the morning was beginning to tell, even on the fit. But for Solomon, they had all eaten almost nothing on waking. He, as I subsequently found out, was a person who understood true hunger, and had stuffed at least a dozen rusks into his pockets before we left. These he chewed on periodically. Jasper had been late out of bed and hadn't even had a cup of coffee.

Up on a crest I called a brief halt so that I could take an apple from my bag and have a sip of water.

'Are we going to eat anything?' asked Toby.

'Did you bring anything?' I asked.

'No – you didn't tell us to,' he snapped.

'I didn't tell Solomon to bring anything either,' I replied, indicating the large Zulu man munching contentedly on one of O'Reilly's home-made rusks.

'Bud, I don't eat carbs,' said Jerome, to which a derisive snort emanated from Franci's nose.

'You have a pretty good covering of flesh for someone who doesn't eat carbs,' said Katie staring straight at him. Franci chuckled again and Jerome went red.

'But seriously,' said Toby, his face pinched with anger, 'this is bullshit. We're not Navy SEALs in training. We're just rangers.'

Donald leant against a marula tree watching. He said nothing and looked sad.

'Right, let's get going,' I said, and they staggered to their feet.

Solomon walked over to Jasper and held out his sandbag.

'It's your turn now,' he said and dropped the bag on Jasper's right shoulder. The spindly surfer nearly buckled.

'I can't carry on,' he said.

'Well, there is a hyena den not far from here,' I said. 'I'm sure they'll be along presently, and your misery will come to a swift – well, swiftish – end.'

'Can you lose the sarcasm?' snapped Toby. 'You're the trainer. Do your training job.'

I let that hang for a while before replying.

'Toby, that's precisely what I'm doing.' I began to walk.

Five minutes later, Slumber put a hand on my shoulder.

'Angus, that one like a stick is not coming. He is sitting and crying,' he said in Shangane, concerned.

I turned and there on the road was Jasper, head in his hands, sitting in the dirt.

We had our first quitter.

I pulled the radio from my belt. 'Bradley, come in.' I waited a few seconds. 'Bradley, do you copy?' Still nothing. This was annoying because he'd promised to be on the radio in case of an emergency. 'Does anyone with an intact cerebrum copy this message?'

'Go ahead for Rhirandzu, reception,' said Rhirandzu.

'Good day, Rhirandzu. Please could you send someone to find Bradley, kick his backside and then tell him to call me on the radio.'

'Copy, will do it,' she replied.

A moment later, Bradley's breathless voice came over the airwaves.

'Angus, um, yes, um, go ahead for me ... It's Bradley.'

'Good morning, Bradley,' I said. 'I need you to affect a rescue operation, please, 100 metres east of the junction Nuntlwa Road and Ingwe Alley.'

'Oh, yes, gosh – is someone hurt? Shall I alert the medical-rescue doctor-people?'

'No, nothing of that nature. Jasper has just given up.'

'Oh, good, yes, okay – someone will be there in ten minutes.'

I struggled to feel any sympathy for the wreckage of a human crying in the dirt against the tree trunk. Katie and Donald, however, were crouched down next to him. Katie put her hand on Jasper's shoulder and was telling him that everything would be okay. Donald gave him some water. Solomon took a rusk from his pocket and Jasper took it without any apparent gratitude. Franci looked disgusted and Jerome sat down on a rock saying nothing. He picked a few burrs from his socks, face red with exertion.

'Jasper,' I said eventually, 'quit your snivelling. Someone is coming to get you.'

The look Katie gave me would have frozen the balls off a buffalo. Jasper wiped his nose with the back of his hand, leaving a line of snot across his arm hairs.

A few minutes later a vehicle arrived – Bradley was driving it himself – and Jasper climbed into the front seat without greeting his rescuer.

'Oh, well, I see you must be quite tired,' said Bradley. 'Does anybody else want to come home?'

I was astounded. He seemed to think we were out for a voluntary stroll and that anyone who'd had enough could simply head back for lunch and a massage.

Jerome looked at the vehicle and then at Franci.

'Not me,' he said.

'I'm done with this shit,' said Toby. He threw his bag into the car and climbed in.

No one else moved. I shook my head at Bradley, who waved cheerfully and drove off. Jasper, unsurprisingly, had left his sandbag on the road. Donald noticed first.

'What do we do with that?' he asked.

'Well, it can't stay there,' I replied, 'so someone had better pick it up. You'll have to all share the load, I guess. Let's get going.' I turned on my heel and began to walk.

'Christ,' muttered Gary.

The sky was that deep winter-blue I've only seen in the Lowveld, and there wasn't a single cloud. High above, a small flock of vultures wheeled and then sped off to something edible or perhaps just a better thermal. An orange-breasted bush shrike gave its whistling po-po-po-po-poo-pooo. Then a covey of crested francolins burst from the cover of a fallen red bushwillow, squawking in wild alarm.

'Ahh, fuck,' shouted Franci.

I swung round in time to see her recover, but not before the rest of the group had begun to laugh.

'I don't think francolins eat people,' Katie said mildly, and we continued on.

We pushed hard for the next hour and I had decided I wouldn't stop again unless prevailed upon to do so. My legs were also starting to take strain – it had been some time since I'd propelled myself this sort of distance on foot. It's an amazing thing, however, when you know how far you have to go – you can set little goals and keep moving. When, like the trainees, you have no idea, it's perfect torture.

At around 12h30, as we crossed a sodic area in the full sun, Slumber clicked at me and I turned to see that Jerome, limping badly, was lagging 20 metres behind. His face was a twisted grimace of pain.

'Jerome,' I said, 'catch up quickly. We can't spread out.'

'I – I ...' he gasped.

'He's got blisters in them new designer shoes,' muttered Donald, who'd become quieter and quieter as the walk continued. Here was someone who coped with stress by turning inward.

I called a halt.

'Jerome, do you need to be picked up?' I asked.

'I ... well ... It's just ... I've got a blister,' he said, stumbling to catch up. He fell to the ground and took off his brand-new shoe. A blister at least an inch in diameter had spread around his Achilles and then burst. A mixture of blood, sweat and blister fluid congealed on the worse-than-useless secret socks Jerome thought made his legs look so good.

Franci gagged and reeled away. Solomon said, 'Oh my Jesus!' and backed off.

'Can you carry on?' I asked.

'Dude, I can try but, jeez, this is really sore.' The pain had wiped away any bravado.

'I didn't ask if you can try,' I said. 'Can you carry on?'

Silence ensued, punctuated only by the clicking of a flock of white-crowned helmet shrikes foraging in a knobthorn nearby. 'Jerome, can you carry on or must I call someone to fetch you?'

'Well, how far do we still have to go?'

'As far as it takes.'

'I'm not tired, it's just my shoes are too small.' He looked hopefully at the group.

'Sure, pal,' said Franci, 'and your pants are even smaller.'

'Am I kicked off the course if I don't make it?' Jerome looked terrified.

'If you hadn't realised yet,' said Franci, 'I think not knowing is the point.'

There was more silence.

'Bradley, come in,' I said into the radio.

This time there was no delay. The doleful look on Jerome's face as he drove off with the head ranger would have made the casual observer think his family had just been kidnapped by a Mexican cartel.

'On we go!' I turned, and we continued.

About 5 kilometres later – a good 25 kilometres into the walk – Katie's voice stopped the group.

'Angus?'

I turned. She stopped, dropped her sandbag on the ground, untied her oversized fleece from her waist, dropped it in the dirt and sat down. Her face was bright red, forehead dripping with sweat.

'I can't carry on. I'm fucked. I need to be fetched.' She wasn't being dramatic.

A few minutes later we were down to three.

We had about ten kilometres to go when we lost one more. Donald twisted his ankle when he stood in a harvester-termite hole about three kilometres from the end.

'Aaargh!' he yelled, dropping to the ground faster than his sandbag. 'Fuck, my ankle,' he wheezed, gasping in pain.

Donald was no more, and Bradley made his fourth foray into the field for the day – apparently unable to prevail upon anyone in his team to help.

Half an hour later, we jogged into a clearing where a vehicle, once again with Bradley in the driver's seat, was waiting to take us back to camp. It was 15h00.

Franci, Solomon and Gary dumped their sandbags and sat down on the Land Rover running board. They were spent. I went round the other side, dropped my bag into the vehicle, put the rifle on the rack and sat down on the opposite running board. Out of the gaze of my charges, I allowed my hitherto placid visage to express the exhaustion I felt. I gasped under my breath as I took off my new shoes and socks, and looked at the raw, bloodied patches around my heels and ankle. One sock made an audible tearing sound as I pulled it from my right foot, a flap of skin deciding it would rather stay with the sock than with my big toe.

I, too, was done.

We returned to camp a few minutes later. Bradley parked outside the rangers' room, where, under a blue sweetberry bush, Mark sat on an upturned crate sucking on a cigarette. He snorted derisively as Franci and Solomon walked past to deposit the sandbags just outside the door.

'Only three of you made it?' he asked.

'Eh, yes,' said Franci, unsure if he was impressed or not.

'Gonna be tough to find another three trainees at such short notice,' he replied. 'Hogan Camp opens in twelve weeks.'

'Are the others going to be fired?' Solomon asked, alarmed.

'They would be if I was in charge,' Mark replied, taking a long drag and then stubbing out his cigarette into a small paint can overflowing with butts.

'Mark,' I hobbled over to replace the rifle in the safe, 'do you think your guests enjoy the smell of Styvie Blues when you greet them on the deck?'

Jason emerged from the rangers' room carrying two rifles.

'Bud,' he said to me, 'it's a long time since you guided anyone. The job isn't the same as it was – it's much more sophisticated.' He handed a rifle, with no safety checks, to Mark and the two of them stalked off to meet their guests.

The three of us made our way back to the BC.

There was silence when we arrived. I walked straight in to put the kettle on – all I wanted was a cup of coffee and a rusk. Unsurprisingly, Jasper was fast asleep in his tent. Jerome was sitting at the trestle table with a mug in front of him, his face a picture of despair. Donald had his foot up on the other table where Katie, freshly showered, was expertly wrapping a bandage around his damaged ankle.

'You know what you're doing there, do you?' I asked as I came outside.

She glared at me. 'Yes, if you'd read my CV, you'd know I have an advanced first-aid qualification.'

'Now, now,' I replied evenly, 'no need for hostility. No one's died – yet. How's it feeling, Donald?'

'It's bloody sore,' he said quietly, 'but I don't think anything's broken.'

I returned inside and made a brief call to the kitchen. I'd prepared O'Reilly for our return and he'd promised to sort some grub for us. As I was plunging the coffee, Hayley and Sam arrived with two trays of sandwiches.

This was the first time the trainee chefs had clapped eyes on the trainees, but I'm not sure Sam noticed anyone other than Franci Varga. She was sitting at the table unpacking things from her bag. A lock of hair had fallen over her right cheek, lit gold by the late afternoon. Her face lifted, cheeks still flushed from the day's exertions. As her blue eyes passed over Sam's round face, I could almost see his adrenalin surge. Her full lips parted slightly as she smiled (most likely at the sandwiches), and pushed the hair behind her ear. Sam's face resembled a ripe pomegranate.

Jerome rallied remarkably on sighting Hayley.

'Howzit, I'm Jerome,' he began. 'Let me take that from you.' He smiled greasily and carried the laden tray the final 1.5 metres to the table.

'Well done, Jerome,' I said. 'Your chivalry is a credit to our gender.'

'I like to be a gentleman,' he replied, pleased with his contribution.

Hayley surveyed the camp and its occupants. 'You all look kind of pooped.'

'Not too bad, hey,' said Jerome, a bit too quickly.

'I'm fucked,' said Franci.

Sam, who was trying to steel glances at her, gasped at the invective.

'Could someone wake that cretin Jasper?' I said. 'We need to talk about the walk and the consequences thereof. Thank you for the grub, chaps, and please pass on my thanks to O'Reilly.'

Hayley smiled warmly. 'No problem at all. Come on, Sam.'

The male chef glowed as they departed.

Solomon, possibly impatient to get some food into his belly, walked over to Jerome and Jasper's tent. A moment later, having provoked an alarmed squeal not unlike a duiker being savaged by a leopard, he emerged with a bleary-eyed Jasper in tow.

'Lose the self-pity, Jasper – you look like a soldier who's barely survived the Somme. In fact, you walked fifteen kilometres in paradise. Maybe give some consideration to sucking it up, as they say.'

When everyone was seated around the table and munching O'Reilly's delicious creations, I began.

'Only three of you completed the walk.'

This made everyone except Franci, Solomon and Gary put down their sandwiches. Katie exchanged a nervous glance with Jerome, and Donald sighed heavily.

'Ja, but, bud, I got a blister. I would defos have –'

'Shut up, Jerome.' I snapped. 'And don't ever call me "bud" again.' I took a sip of my coffee. 'The purpose of the walk was not to assess your fitness – although clearly many of you are taking your youth for granted. It was to see how you react under physical strain – how hard you were prepared to push yourselves.'

'Before you start,' said Gary, 'I need to tell you this isn't for me – no offence or anything, but I've made a mistake coming here. It's just not gonna work out – like, I'm done living in tents and stuff. I thought it would be fine, but I can see I'm past this stuff. I'm just not gonna enjoy this.'

There was a shocked silence, broken– naturally enough – by Jasper.

'Bru,' he said to Franci, 'can you pass me one of those chicken zarms?'

She absently pushed the tray towards him.

'No offence taken, Gary,' I replied. 'Thanks for your honesty. You can leave tomorrow morning.'

'My girlfriend's in Hoedspruit,' he said. 'I think I'll leave now if that's cool.' And within ten minutes, Gary had departed Sasekile forever.

'Anyone else like to leave now?' I looked around the table.

Toby spoke up next. 'I don't see the point of this. We're supposed to be rangers. We not in the army. Today was bullshit and I don't appreciate being spoken to like ... like a common soldier in basics or something. I'm not doing that stuff again.'

This was a fellow used to getting what he wanted – prefect at his Johannesburg private school, recently qualified chartered accountant, father an influential banker.

'Well, Toby,' I replied, 'you won't have to do it again.'

'Good,' he said.

'You will not have to do *anything* at Sasekile again. Indeed, you will be precluded from doing anything at Sasekile again. You may get up from the table, go to your tent and pack your bags. You may leave now or tomorrow morning, I care not.'

He stared at me. 'Is this another sarcastic joke?' There was a touch of uncertainty in his voice.

'Nope, no sarcasm. This is not the place for you. Pack up and leave.'

A puffback shrike called from just behind the BC.

Toby took a bite of his sandwich. An awkward silence grew as I observed him. The others started squirming in their chairs. It was like watching a child ignoring an instruction, just sitting hoping the adult will forget.

'You seem to be having some difficulty understanding. Let me be clearer.' I sipped my coffee. 'You're an arrogant, entitled dickhead and you are therefore not welcome on this training course.'

A few gasps from round the table.

'Who the fuck do you think you are?' Toby exploded from his seat and smashed his hands onto the rickety table, which collapsed under the assault. Sandwiches and mugs hit the dust, scalding coffee and tea covered laps and faces. Everybody leapt, yowling as boiling beverage hit them and the precious food hit the ground.

I too exploded from my seat. 'I'm the fucking trainer, you asshole! Now pack up and piss off!'

At this point, Toby launched himself across the ruined furniture at me – apparently believing that attacking me would help his cause.

I've thrown the odd haymaker in my time (mostly at Hugh), but to describe myself as a competent fighter would be ridiculous. I raised my fists in preparation but there was no need. Toby tripped on the fallen trestle, cracking his knee as he came down. He yelled and rolled onto his back.

'Probably time to go, Toby,' said Donald, who'd miraculously managed to maintain hold of his mug and its contents.

Franci agreed. 'Ja, don't think this is gonna work out for you.'

The fight extinguished by his fall, Toby stood, paused, and then mooched off to his tent. He left while the rest of us did our best to fix the table.

Day two and we were already down to six.

13

For the rest of the first week, the trainees completed various team-orientated tasks: first-aid scenarios, building bridges with poles, crossing gullies with ropes (fake crocodiles snapping at their toes), that sort of stuff. I told them next to nothing about the tasks and they were only allowed to be on task or at the BC, where all meals – small ones – were delivered. There was never quite enough food, and the tasks were sufficiently physical to keep them all at the verge of hangry outbursts. That might be considered cruel by some, but I'm no psychologist – any other method of deciphering the trainees' strengths and weaknesses and discerning when they were lying was simply beyond the scope of my emotional intelligence (not to mention my patience).

With some modification, this was the way I'd found training to be most effective during my ten months in charge of the ranging team. I'd started off just handing new rangers a training file and beginning the training straight away, but it had soon become apparent that I needed a different approach. Then I'd read a book on training SAS operatives and decided that physical tasks were a far easier way to unmask how people coped under pressure and, more importantly, if they took out their frustrations on others.

This had all become necessary after the arrival of two disastrous trainees shortly after I'd started as head ranger. Roger Ballamy and Nicholas Ras's CVs had indicated intelligent young graduates with a good knowledge of the wild and a desire to make a difference to conservation and ecotourism. They were friends from school and university – and possibly two of the most reprehensible, malingering ingrates I have ever had the displeasure of meeting.

I'd handed them the training file and told them we'd go into the field once a day for practical game-drive training. The rest of the time, they'd be left alone to study.

'As long as you keep up with the schedule, you can allocate your time as required,' I'd told them at our first meeting, during which they'd stared at me with almost disconcerting awe.

Of course, someone with greater social skills would have worked out that these two paragons of the South Africa private-education system were about as sincere as an ANC promise. The lodge was particularly busy and I was driving flat out during the first two weeks of Roger and Nicholas's Sasekile stay. There'd been precious little time to check up on them and I assumed, given their glowing references and awestruck attitudes on arrival, that they'd just get on with it.

Well, within a fortnight, Roger had stolen a crate of beer from the staff shop and received a broken nose from Jacob. His schnoz had taken a punch at 06h00 one morning when Jacob arrived at the workshop to discover the conservation-team vehicle missing. It was found parked outside the Bat Cave, an unconscious Roger on a mattress in the back with a newly impregnated trainee chef naked in his arms. They were both covered in mosquito bites, and she enjoyed a bout of malaria shortly before leaving the lodge a few weeks later.

On day ten of Nicholas's stay I was eating dinner with my guests when the trainee strode into the Kingfisher Camp boma carrying a quart of Castle Lager, dressed in a pair of baggies and slops with no shirt. He had the hairless body of Adonis, and had stumbled over to where Allegra was standing at the bar.

'Hey, babes, how about I come to your place for a massage a bit later – you know you'd like your hands on this body.'

Allegra carefully put down the glass of Sauvignon blanc she was holding.

'You do know I live with your boss, right?'

'Ja, so? He look like this without a shirt on?'

Nicholas didn't notice her right knee until it collected him on his undercarriage. He almost dropped to the floor, but Allegra quietly guided him from the boma to collapse on the dust outside.

Roger and Nicholas left shortly thereafter and I had modified my training approach to accommodate my emotional shortcomings.

We spent the final day of week one with the conservation team under the able (if somewhat brutal) leadership of Jacob 'Spear of the Lowveld' Mkhonto. Jacob also had absolutely no sympathy for shirkers. Before the final day, we'd agreed that he would push the trainees really hard from dawn until dark – even more than he pushed his normal team of battle-hardened men and women.

We met at the dark and freezing workshop at 05h30. Jacob and his crew were already there and we piled into the back of a stuffed old Land Rover, huddling for warmth. Even Jerome had donned something warm – a designer puffer jacket. Jacob insisted that someone else drive, so I assigned Donald to this task.

There were eleven of us in the load bin amongst the spades, picks, pangas and saws. It wasn't comfortable, but I ended up squashed between Franci and Katie, which wasn't entirely unpleasant. Opposite me sat Nhlanhla – he who had lost his left eye on a twig when Hugh and I were working our punishment with the conservation crew all those years ago.

Jerome, still buzzing from the effects of Solomon's tar-strength coffee, was all bonhomie as we rattled out into the frigid dawn. I had wondered what he'd meant in his CV when he mentioned the skill of 'communicating with black people' – I was about to find out as he soon struck up a conversation with the conservation crew using some appalling Fanakalo.

I must digress briefly to describe this language.

Fanakalo is a pidgin combining Nguni languages (predominantly Zulu), English and Afrikaans. It was used on the mines and allowed white bosses, too indolent to learn the languages of their workers, to communicate with them. Over the years, various rangers and guests had arrived at Sasekile and used Fanakalo to communicate with the black staff, which I always found cringeworthy.

One delightful woman from Hillcrest near Durban, on hearing me speak my bad Shangane with Elvis, confided, 'I can also speak Zulu,' as we drove on from the leopard tracks we'd been discussing. 'So important in the new South Africa,' she finished – and I wondered how long South Africa would be 'new' to her.

'That's great,' I'd replied.

At the drinks stop an hour or so later, she'd decided to address Elvis in her 'Zulu'.

'Elvis,' she began as he poured her a gin and tonic, 'uphi lo khaya ka wena?' [Where this home of you?]

Elvis stopped pouring and looked around. He handed the drink to the woman and, with a slight sigh, replied, 'Boxa Huku Village.'

'Ai, mina yazi lo village. Mina shlala lapha Hillcrest,' she explained without being prompted. [No, me know this village. Me live here Hillcrest.]

Elvis nodded and took an Appletiser from the cooler box.

'Wena khona lo mantawna?' she asked. [You have this childs?]

'Three,' he'd replied.

'Ah, kashle. Zonke lo muntus ka lo South Africa yena khona too much mantwana. Wena and lo mafazi ka wena clever kakhulu!' [Ah, goodly. All this peoples of this South Africa they be too much childs.]

She'd given me a satisfied wink. Elvis had forced a smile.

In the back of the vehicle, as we rattled out into the dawn that cold Friday morning, Jerome thought he'd attempt something similar. The five members of the conservation crew – three women and two men, who looked as if they'd been forged of barbed wire – regarded their helpers for the day. Jerome lifted his head.

'Sakabona, mafazis and magents!' he said cheerfully.

The team just stared at him.

'Mina Jerome le Roux. Mina thanda sebenza with wenas! Kunjani?' [Me Jerome le Roux. Me love work with yous! How are you?]

Dorris muttered something in Shangane and the three women began to titter.

Jerome was oblivious. 'Yena khona makhulu makhaza laphaside, ne?' [There be big cold here side, huh?]

More blank stares.

He turned to me. 'I thought all South African blacks spoke Zulu. Why don't these people?'

Solomon overheard this and replied, 'They do speak Zulu. It is you who don't speak Zulu.'

Jerome was scandalised. 'I learnt that from my oupa – the Lord rest his soul. That's how he used to speak to the workers on our farm!'

Solomon looked away and sighed.

I said, 'Your oupa, then, with whatever respect is due his dearly departed soul, did not speak Zulu either. He spoke Fanakalo – which is an affront to the act of speaking. If you don't want to come across as a dinosaur, you might like to extirpate it from your lexicon.'

Jerome's face went red and he fixated on the bottom of the rusted vehicle as it bumped along.

'So, what language do they speak?' asked Katie.

'Why not ask them?' I suggested.

'Oh, um, okay.' Katie looked across the vehicle and Dorris caught her eye. 'What language do you speak at home?'

Dorris smiled. 'Ahe,' she replied, clearly not understanding a word.

Solomon rolled his eyes. 'They speak Xitsonga or Shangane,' he said to Katie. 'I'm surprised you came here not knowing this.'

'Oh, yes, I suppose I should have found out.' Katie was abashed.

'I bet you ain't the only one,' I said as the white trainees suddenly found themselves fascinated by whatever tools were closest to them.

As the sun came up, Donald stopped the vehicle on the side of a clearing, and we clambered out, our condensing breath catching the sun. We rubbed our hands together and moved around to warm up – all except Jasper, whose long face spoke of the world on his skinny shoulders. He was wearing every piece of clothing he possessed, and being a surfer, his wardrobe was a collection of T-shirts, shorts and God knows how many sarongs. The latter items, at least four, he had wrapped around his waist, chest, shoulders and head such that he looked like a colourful Bedouin tramp fallen on hard times. It was his balaclava that really caught my attention, however – it was like a hood, but with one hole in the middle of it, big enough for his nose and one eye.

'Jasper,' I said as Jacob instructed his team, 'where on earth did you find that balaclava?'

'At ... a market ... in Coffee Bay,' he replied slowly.

'Where? At a stall for drunk toe-knitters?'

Jasper shrugged, and turned his body to warm the other side. As he did so, he adjusted the sarong on his head and the back of the balaclava was revealed to have another small hole in the back.

'Jasper, I think you may have purchased a tea cosy,' I said.

He swung round and touched the back of his head then his face.

'Oooh,' he said, realisation dawning. 'That's why it's got two holes!'

Nhlanhla, who was also wearing a balaclava of sorts, but one that exposed both eyes, clicked his teeth. He walked over to Jasper, whipped the tea cosy off his head and placed it on his own.

'Much better!' he exclaimed. With his one glass eye, the tea cosy was a perfect fit. He handed Jasper the grubby brown one he'd just taken off.

Jasper pulled it over his head and might have actually smiled.

Jacob's team was in the process of clearing a section of mopane woodland. A natural pan, dry in the winter, was fringed with some beautiful cathedral mopane, but the tall trees had made babies that were obscuring a view of the water which, in summer, was a favourite spot for wallowing rhino, elephant, buffalo and the odd overheated hyena.

Jacob gathered us together and explained in Shangane that we needed to remove a section of smaller trees (about head height), the most difficult part being digging out the stumps. Mopane wood is incredibly hard – more than 1 300 kilograms per cubic metre. This means that cutting it is bloody difficult, especially for hands not used to manual labour. We could see where the conservation crew had been working over the last few days and, after I had more or less translated Jacob's words, we set to work.

My prediction that Jasper would be the first to buckle came true about 20 minutes later. The very gentle and slow chopping sound on my right stopped. Jasper was standing looking in horror at his hands. Franci, hacking powerfully next to him, looked up.

'Christ, your hands are soft as soap!'

'I'm a surfer not a woodcutter,' he moaned, staring at his ruined palms.

I kept chopping, my eye on the unfolding scene. Katie walked over and took a look. Why she felt such sympathy for the useless laggard, I cannot say.

'Jasper, let's wrap your hands in cloth. That will help.' He'd discarded one of his tatty sarongs when we'd begun chopping. 'Let's tear this one in two and then we can cover your hands.'

'But that's my sarong ...' he wailed.

'Oh, for fuck sake's,' said Franci. She dropped her panga, grabbed the torn piece of cloth and ripped it in two. 'There, now please quit your fucking whining.'

Katie wrapped the morose twig-with-a-paunch's hands and he picked up his panga to continue tickling the mopane tree.

We shed layers as the sun warmed our backs and the work heated us from within. Mixed with the dawn chorus was the sound of a game-drive vehicle in the distance. A flock of Burchell's starlings squabbled in the trees above us and a bearded woodpecker tapped out its territorial call on a dead leadwood in the valley just to the north. Everyone lost themselves in their task and chatter amongst the trainees ebbed to nothing. The ladies on the conservation team, however, kept up a constant refrain in Shangane so rapid I caught one in every 20 words.

I noticed that the ladies set to the task with less gusto than the trainees (except for Jasper, who was only able to smoke pot with gusto). They used a slow, steady but ceaseless rhythm, chopping and hacking without pause for hours. Not only that, but their chopping was much more efficient than ours. Where I would take 25 chops to remove a branch, they'd take four or five.

I found myself working next to Solomon, who had the same efficiency with his panga as the ladies. He observed each branch, then expertly sliced it with a few well-aimed chops.

'You've done this before,' I said.

'Yes, much times,' he admitted.

'Tell me where you grew up,' I said. And so, as the chopping continued, Solomon shared his story.

'I am from a village called Nkangala near Eshowe. You know Eshowe?'

'I spent a night there once.'

'It's on the western side. A small village, very poor, not much going on.'

'There must be a pretty good school there.'

'It is okay, but my father was a priest, educated at a mission school. From the day I could read, he was making me sit with books. Books.' Chop. 'Books.' Chop. 'Books.' A thick branch came off the tree. Solomon tossed it onto the neat pile he'd made. 'When I left home to try to find work, I was sixteen and I never wanted to see a book again!'

'So your father was a good man,' I commented.

'Good man? No – my father wasn't a good man. He was a snake.' Solomon spat on the ground. 'I hated him. He beat us all – my mother and my four sisters. But by the time we left home, we could all speak English.' Solomon shrugged. 'At least he gave us that.'

'What happened to him?' I asked.

Solomon stood up, stretched and snorted. 'He died of a "long illness".' He made the inverted commas with his fingers and shook his head. 'I think I have brothers and sisters all over KwaZulu.'

'And your mother?'

'She is still at Nkangala. I have built her a small house with two of my sisters who can't find work.'

'How old is she?'

'About 75, we think – she doesn't know for sure.' Solomon moved on to the next tree while I flailed at mine.

'And what made you want to become a ranger?'

At this Solomon's face lit up. 'There is a forest near Nkangala called Entumeni.' He stopped his work to tell me this part. 'My father sent me to Eshowe one Saturday to buy something – I can't remember what. I was fourteen. I had always gone past this forest on my way to and from Eshowe, but never inside. I remember I was angry that day – just growing up and beginning to think for myself. I was on the family's old bicycle and for some reason I turned onto the road that led to the forest and I just kept on pedalling – I was so lost in my anger. After some minutes, I stopped. My legs were aching and I was panting.'

Solomon paused and looked into the trees behind the pan.

'I remember just looking around then. There were just trees, the sound of me breathing and birds. So many birds. In a few minutes, my anger was gone – my whole body was smiling.'

He carried on chopping.

'That's when I knew I was going to work in nature – I didn't know what jobs there were, but I knew I just had to work in nature.'

'That's a brilliant story,' I said, standing up to stretch and check who was shirking. Jerome (shirtless, of course) was operating next to Franci (of course). He was laying into a small mopane with disturbing violence and the hapless sapling wasn't putting up much of a fight. Every time he raised his arm, the lion on his shoulder threatened to sink its teeth into his neck.

I was about to ask Solomon about his bush education when Jerome, with a wild slash, missed the branch he was aiming at. The blade whistled past the twig and cracked into his shin. His desire to impress Franci evaporated. He dropped the panga and set to a wailing so dreadful, I expected a clan of hyenas to arrive and investigate what was being murdered. He fell to the dust clutching his shin. Everyone ceased their chopping and ran over.

'What's wrong?' asked Katie.

'My leg!' he yelled.

'Did a snake bite you?' Jasper cast about for a serpent.

'Aaaaargh!' Jerome moaned.

'He chopped himself with his panga,' said Donald, shaking his head.

'Jerome, let me see.' I tried to pry away his hands.

'No, it hurts. It hurts!' he wailed.

'Jerome, move your bloody hand now!'

'It's so fucken sore!'

Jacob clicked his teeth and knelt in the dust. He took both of Jerome's substantial wrists in his own powerful hands and pulled.

'Aaaargh!' Jerome yelled again, trying to wrench free.

Franci stepped in and grabbed one of his hands. 'Hold still, you big baby.' The sound of Franci's voice caused the part of Jerome's brain occupied by his ego (in other words, most of it) to override the part responsible for registering pain. He finally went still, and I was able to observe the injury.

It's fortunate that the shin is not home to more blood vessels because if it was, Jerome would probably have bled out before I'd had time to drum up the sympathy to help him. He had caught the tibia with an angled blow that tore his jodhpurs and sliced into the little bit of flesh that covered the bone. This had come away from the leg and dangled with the piece of cloth. The white tibia shone in the mid-morning light. There was still a substantial amount of blood.

'Oh, Jesus!' said Franci.

'Is it bad?' said Jasper, disturbingly excited. He pushed past the others to have a look. 'Oh!' he exclaimed before turning and vomiting into the dust.

'Yoh!' said Dorris, covering her mouth and walking off. Cindy and Minah did the same. Abednigo said, 'Aieee!' then covered his eyes and went to sit down.

'Fetch first aid,' said Jacob to Nhlanhla.

'Jerome, just try to lie still. Donald, get his jacket and put it under his head,' Katie said – de facto paramedic.

As is the case, I suspect, with first-aid kits in most game lodges, the small green bag that Nhlanhla brought to Katie was not exactly in a state to deal with severe human trauma. A tube of antihistamine had burst and covered everything in the little bag. This had occurred in the distant past, so it had crusted dry and smelt iffy. Over the years, members of the conservation crew had used bits and pieces – plasters, aspirins, safety pins, bandages for minor injuries and ailments. The only thing of any use was a bottle of disinfectant and a crepe bandage. Katie grabbed the bottle of disinfectant and handed it me, nodding at the wound.

'This is going to hurt,' I said to Jerome.

His eyes widened in his pale face. I poured a cap full into the wound. Jerome yelled, then went suddenly silent.

'He's out,' said Katie.

She wound the bandage around the leg of the unconscious trainee, tore the end in half and tied it in place. The best she could do for a field dressing.

'He'll need a doctor,' I said. 'Someone needs to take him to Hoed-spruit.'

Donald sighed. 'I'll do it – I need some stuff there anyway.'

Eventually, Jerome, his face the colour of troll, came round. Jacob and Donald dragged him to his feet and he groggily climbed into the car. It rattled off presently and peace returned to the Lowveld.

'Back to work!' said Jacob and the chopping resumed.

The one thing that Jacob did allow was a 60-minute lunch break. He called a halt at exactly 12h30, whereupon we all found ourselves a little spot of shade and settled into our meagre food package, which consisted of a sandwich each, some water and a few rusks – not exactly fuel for labour. The conservation crew brought tubs full of maize porridge and a stew they'd cooked the night before. It looked substantially more appetising than the peanut-butter-and-jam affairs the trainees (and I, in solidarity) consumed.

Being out in the Lowveld in the middle of a perfect winter's day is wonderful (in summer, it's volcanic). We settled into the shade of a massive mopane tree – one of the only trees with leaves left on it – and relaxed. The ladies of the crew kept up their good-natured chatter as they shared their porridge and stew. Solomon sat next to Jacob and addressed him quietly in Zulu, apologising first for his inability to speak Shangane and using the respectful 'Baba' to address him rather than his name.

'You Zulus,' said Jacob in Zulu, 'you think the rest of us must learn your language but you never learn ours.'

Solomon nodded slowly. He'd made sure to be sitting lower than Jacob, which I knew was a sign of respect for the older man. My attention drifted to Franci and Katie, who were both eating silently, looking into the woodland. Jasper had fashioned one of his many diseased sarongs into a pillow and was curled up fast asleep in the foetal position, crumbs and dried peanut butter littering mouth and chin.

I put my back against the tree and sighed with satisfaction. The temperature was perfect, and I too began to doze off.

'There's an elephant!' hissed Katie.

I came to with a start. A young elephant bull was making his way towards the pan, perhaps hoping for a bit of late-season mud. He hadn't noticed us yet, clustered as we were around a huge tree on the side opposite to his approach. The trainees looked at me, their faces expressing fear and excitement – all except Jasper, that is, who did not stir. Jacob began to stand – his approach to this sort of thing was to make as much noise as possible and put the animal to flight. I clicked my tongue and he looked at me. I motioned for him to sit. He looked at the elephant and then me, shrugged and resumed his place on the ground.

I looked at all the trainees and mouthed, 'Just sit still and be silent.' I put my finger over my lips. They took their cue from me and sat back down.

The elephant kept coming, the scraping of mopane branches against his thick skin the only sound of his approach. A Burchell's starling called lazily above the pan and fluttered off. A breeze blew gently from him to us so there was no chance of his smelling the human observers. Even so, his trunk moved from side to side, picking up scents well beyond those of the human olfactory system. When he was about 10 metres from the end of the pan (about 25 metres from us), Franci shuffled slightly, preparing to stand if necessary. I motioned for her to be still.

Right at the edge of the pan, the bull froze. His trunk snuffled on the ground where one of us had walked sometime during the day. His ears flapped gently, trying to hear if anything was amiss. It was at this rather sensitive point that Jasper had some sort of daymare.

He sat bolt upright next to Franci and shouted: 'Yes, it was me but

I didn't mean to!' Then he saw the elephant and his state of alarm ratcheted up with astonishing speed. 'E-e-e-elephant!' he yelled. 'There's a fucking elephant!' He stood up and ran for the car, which had disappeared with Jerome and Donald. He dived behind a sandpaper bush so small it wouldn't have hidden a gerbil.

The elephant's hitherto placid disposition changed instantly. He threw his head up, ears splayed, and trumpeted. The conservation team, with the exception of Jacob, departed with a haste that defied biokinetics – eddies of rising dust the only indication of their departure.

This caused some panic in the trainees.

Franci, Katie and Solomon stood up, caught in two minds – they went a few metres, then stopped, then took a few more steps, stranding themselves in no man's land while the conservation crew was already most of the way to Zimbabwe. I'd never tell this to anyone I was responsible for, but if you're going to break the golden rule and run, make sure you run fast and far.

The elephant decided that our bunch of idiots was more than he could stomach. He turned tail and scarpered into the woodland, the sound of breaking branches slowly receding.

A minute later, I was haranguing four bashful trainees while Jacob was doing the same to his crew. One positive of the dressing down was a small seed of solidarity between Jasper and the others.

After the elephant, we saw no further signs of animal life. The afternoon progressed with us digging out the stumps, a mighty task involving picks, shovels, skin, sweat and one dislocated finger.

We were working away, the pleasant afternoon slowly passing overhead, when Katie, operating a spade, became frustrated with a mopane root that wouldn't break. She lost her temper and began hacking at it with her shovel. The root held fast, and in frustration she slammed the flat of the spade against the stump. The tool bounced, Katie let go and its shaft smacked into Franci's hand, which was clasped around her pick.

Franci dropped her tool immediately, grabbed her left hand with her right and yelled.

'Fuck, fuck, fuck, ow, fuck!'

'Oh, shit, I'm so sorry!' said Katie, her hands over her mouth. 'Is it bad?'

'I don't know if it's fucking bad – I can't look!' Franci gritted her teeth.

I heard Nhlanhla bemoaning the dreadful language to Abednigo.

'Franci, look at me,' I said.

'Christ, it's fucking sore,' she wheezed.

'Look at me!' I snapped.

She looked at me, her face pale.

'Let me see.'

She slowly removed her right hand from her left and it became immediately apparent that her language was entirely justified. The second joint on her middle finger was bent 45 degrees to the side, resting over her ring finger.

'Oh,' I said without thinking, 'that does look serious.'

'Yoh, yoh, yoh!' said Nhlanhla, hand to mouth.

'Bloody fuck,' said Abednigo, forgetting that he didn't swear.

There was a thump like a sack of rice being dropped on the ground. We turned to see Jasper once again in the dust. No one paid him the slightest mind.

Franci starting going as green as the remaining mopane leaves. I led her over to a small rock and she sat down.

'It's dislocated,' I said.

'You'll have to put it back!' Katie said, studying the offending hand.

'I can't put it back!' I snapped. 'You're the one with advanced first-aid training!'

'Yes, but I'll pass out. I can't do it!' She backed off, head shaking from side to side. 'You do it, I'll tell you how.'

'Oh God, fine – I'll do it,' I replied. 'Franci, this will probably hurt, um, quite a lot.'

'No shit!' the patient wheezed.

Gagging slightly, I took her injured hand gently in mine.

From three metres behind me, Katie spoke: 'You need to pull it out to separate the joint and then put it back in place – it should just slip back in if the ligaments are still intact. You'll have to pull quite hard – if you

139

don't use enough strength, it'll just hurt like hell.'

'Right,' I replied. 'On the count of three. One ... t–' On two, I pulled the finger out, attempted to line it up and let go. Franci screamed. Her right foot came up from the ground and she kicked me full in the chest with her size eight. I sprawled into the dust.

The conservation crew began to guffaw. This set off Solomon and Katie (Jasper was sitting with his head in his hands). I turned to look at Franci who was examining her hand – all fingers in place.

'I think you did it!' she said.

'My pleasure.' I wiped the dirt from my face.

Katie strapped the errant finger to its neighbour for support and the work continued – Franci insisting she was fine to carry on.

After the final day with the conservation team, we walked onto the BC veranda at around 18h00, dirty, sore and, in my case, satisfied with a job well done. Donald and Jerome had returned from Hoedspruit a bit earlier so there were only five of us to share the shower. I gathered everyone at the trestle tables for a quick bathroom chat – Jasper arrived with his towel and 'washbag', which consisted of a Checkers packet containing a toothbrush, paste and some wet soap.

'Jasper,' I said, 'from this moment on, you will shower *after* everyone else.'

'Why, bru? I worked just as hard as them!'

'That is debatable, but you will be last because you take too long – there is but one geyser and no one showering after you has ever had hot water.' Everyone nodded in exhausted appreciation. 'And as for the rest, I am implementing a strict two-minute rule in the bathroom unless you are having a dump – then you can take as long as you like.'

'How do I wash my hair in two minutes?' asked Franci.

'I would suggest you shave it off or find a time of day when no one else needs the bathroom.' I sincerely hoped that she wouldn't choose the former. 'Far more important than the showering is the fact that we have a phantom shitter in our midst,' I continued. 'Someone in this group doesn't see the need to clean the bowl after an explosive movement.

This is not acceptable. Make sure that the loo is pristine – it is not fair to expect anyone to go in there and see the productions of your alimentary canal.'

'What's a ailminty canal?' asked Jerome.

'Alimentary,' I repeated. '*Alimentary* canal. Anyone care to enlighten Jerome?'

'Your digestive tract,' said Katie.

'Correct – the pipe between your mouth and your sphincter, Jerome. If the phantom shitter continues, I will investigate and when I discover their identity, that person will be given a shovel with which to dig a personal latrine. All clear?'

There were mutters of agreement.

'Bru ... are we going to eat properly tonight?' asked Jasper.

'That's the next discussion,' I replied. 'Today's exercise was the final day of what I call "physical week". Tomorrow we start your actual ranger training and your integration into the lodge, as per the timetable in your files. From tonight, we eat at the Avuxeni Eatery with the rest of the staff.'

'That sounds great!' said Jerome, who was sporting some heavy bandaging on his right leg – beneath which, he had proudly announced, were eight stitches.

'There is also what is known as a "Twin Palms" tonight,' I continued. 'These are, in my opinion, detestable gatherings where the staff drink themselves into a stupor before attempting various acts of depravity on each other. You are to receive your welcome drinks at this evening's affair. I remind you that you are to be up and ready at 05h30 tomorrow morning.'

'That also sounds great!' said Jerome. 'Lekker to meet some new people and make friends! You must have been to a few, Donny?' Jerome seemed to be under the impression that his trip to town with Donald had made them best mates.

Donald looked at Jerome. 'Please don't call me that. No, I've actually never been to one,' he admitted. 'Trainees must not drink or have relations with other staff members until they are qualified. No parties!' He did a fair take of Mark's gravelly accent.

'Hang on,' I said. 'You mean that in your seven months at Sasekile you haven't had a drink or even seen the inside of the Twin Palms?'

'Nope, not a drop – but I *have* seen the Twin Palms. I've been the one who's cleaned up the morning after.'

'Well, tonight will be an ... um ... experience for you as well then.'

I retired to my room and was pleased to hear some animated chatter outside suggesting general relief that 'physical' was finished and, more importantly, that the trainees were forging the beginnings of a team. I'd already prepared myself for the fact that some were going to be worse for wear the following morning.

14

There weren't many others at the Avuxeni Eatery when we arrived – it was relatively late, and the camps were all about to serve dinner. Claire, the massage therapist, was sitting with a book in one hand, a plate of rabbit food in front of her. She glanced up as we arrived, nodded a half-hearted greeting and continued with her meal. Francois and Hilda were just getting up to leave.

'Fok,' said Hilda. 'Angus MacNaughton, making a whole uvver lot like him. Fok.'

Francois just glared at me, animal fat glistening in his beard.

'Good evening, Hilda,' I said. 'These fellows will be over to sort out their details with you in the morning. Please extend them every courtesy.'

'Fok,' she replied, and waddled off.

'Who was that?' said Katie.

'That was the head of finance,' replied Donald. 'She pays us so it's quite a good idea to be nice to her.'

He looked at me.

'This is more a case of do as I say, not as I do,' I said.

Craig was also there, a mound of unadulterated pasta on his plate. He was shovelling this into his mouth with a teaspoon, and with his other hand viciously tapping on a micro-computer, perhaps playing a game. At least ten strands of spaghetti hung from his mouth, and he did not so much as blink when we arrived.

'Good evening, Craig,' I ventured.

'Mmmmm!' he said, giving me a thumbs-up with the hand he was using to fill his mouth.

The trainees, ravenous, went into the eatery and began filling their plates with piles of bolognese.

Jerome, predictably, took his plate over to where Claire was sitting.

'Howzit,' he said to her.

She glanced up.

'Jerome le Roux.' He held out a hand.

Claire just looked at him.

'One of the new rangers,' he continued, confidence ebbing.

'*Trainee* rangers, you mean?' She cocked an eye at him.

'Well, ja, but nearly a ranger.'

'Yes,' she replied, returning to her book.

'What you reading?' he tucked into his bolognese.

'A *Passage to India*,' she replied without looking up.

'Any good?' Jerome shovelled another mouthful home.

'Hmm.' Claire turned her body slightly away from him.

'Is it about India?'

'No, it's about Kazakhstan,' I said, sitting down on the opposite side of the table.

Katie spat out a piece of carrot but Claire didn't twitch. She placed the last neat forkful of lettuce into her mouth, closed the book and left without a word.

'I think she likes you,' said Franci, smiling across the table.

'You reckon?' said Jerome.

'No, you arse,' said Franci, 'she left because of you!'

'Don't worry,' said Donald, 'she doesn't like anyone.'

'Bud, we'll see about that at the party!' said Jerome.

'Oh, that we shall,' I said.

Before I could subject myself to the perceived joys of the Twin Palms, I had two things to do. This was PJ's final night at Sasekile: on the morrow, he would depart for Kenya to set up the Hogans' new camp in the Masai Mara. He and his wife, Amy, were spending their final night in a Rhino

Camp suite, their belongings already en route to the Mara. I wandered down to the camp, torch in hand. All was quiet but for faint sounds from the camp kitchen. Brave crickets sang from the bush, somehow managing to maintain their physiology despite the cold. The familiar smell of the potato bush made me smile – the scent always reminded me of my first year in the wild.

I knocked on PJ's door.

'Come in,' said Amy.

They were sitting on a sofa, each with a glass of wine in hand.

'Angus,' said PJ warmly, 'have a glass of Shiraz.'

'Thanks,' I replied.

As we sipped our wine, we chatted about memories and the future. The Woodstocks were very excited about the new chapter in their lives. We laughed about my disciplinary hearings in the early days and my near-death-by-impalement on Mitchell-the-elephant's remaining tusk. PJ and I were never particularly close, but I had come to enjoy his forthright manner and competence. I left a few minutes later after a warm hug from Amy, a firm handshake from PJ and an open invitation to visit the Mara any time.

From there, I went to PJ's old house – now Hugh and Simone's. Their Land Rover Discovery was parked outside, light spilling from the passenger door and boot, where the unpacking process had not yet been completed. My, my, how my brother had come up in the world since the days of our shared Toyota Tazz. Simone emerged from the front door.

'Angus!' she said, enfolding me. 'It just feels so right that you're back here. Help me take that cooler box, will you?'

My brother was arranging wine bottles in a substantial rack that covered most of one wall in the kitchen-dining area.

'Hello, String Bean,' I said, lifting the cooler box onto the granite countertop.

'Ah, Angus!' He placed an expensive-looking bottle and turned round. 'Welcome to our not-so-humble home!'

I looked around. 'Yes, certainly, as fast as you have ascended, I have done the opposite.'

'Choices, choices ...' He shook his head. 'How about a glass of this gorgeous Chardonnay?'

He took a bottle out of a box. We sat on some garden chairs surrounded by unopened boxes and chatted about the honeymoon they had just enjoyed in the Seychelles. The newest MacNaughton couple's stay at North Island had cost them about the same as a stay at Ouma Koenie se B&B in Kempton Park – such was the reciprocal deal he'd managed to organise.

'And how are you feeling about your new work responsibilities?' I enquired, draining my glass.

'All under control – I have lots of ideas and I reckon a fresh perspective will be good for Sasekile. I have huge plans for this place – starting with overseeing the new build.' String Bean's eyes had a faraway look, no doubt as he imagined future glories.

We then had a good laugh remembering his wedding, but I didn't stay long – the happy couple was keen to unpack and settle in.

Now, in order to understand the goings on at a Twin Palms party, you need to understand the general stage of life of the frontline staff at a place like Sasekile. They are, by and large, in their mid-twenties and maximally infused with sex hormones. The new trainees' arrival coincided with a period of general staff turnover – in other words, there were a lot of staff members who hadn't paired off yet. So it was that there was a slavering desire to interact with the trainees – 'new meat' – at the great unveiling. When I walked into the Twin Palms, the sexual tension was palpable to at least four of my senses.

You also need to understand that the Twin Palms was an insufferably stuffy chamber with no windows. After an hour of dancing on a mid-summer's evening, the place was clogged with every human odour imaginable. By this stage, remaining revellers were so blinded by moonshine or the desire to copulate that they didn't notice.

I arrived at the BC to fetch my charges at 20h50. Tradition dictated that I, as their command master chief, lead them into the room at the designated time, whereupon the obligatory welcome drink would be administered by the head ranger after a word of welcome from the general manager – my brother, on debut, this evening.

Five of the trainees were sitting around the trestle tables – all, with the exception of Solomon, fizzing with nervous energy. Solomon was sitting with his feet up, leaning precariously on his chair, reading a field guide on snakes

Jerome emerged from the BC, where he had been beautifying himself. He was dressed for a night at a swanky Joburg club – well, I think that's what someone going to a swanky Joburg club would wear. His Viking undercut was perfectly in place, and he wore a navy-blue shirt made of shiny material that looked like it shouldn't be near an open flame. His bottom half boasted the obligatory spray-on pants, this time black, and on his feet he'd donned a pair of pointy black brogues. The ensemble was completed by a leather (plastic?) jacket and a gold neck chain. Even in the open air, the power of his aftershave hit me like a sledgehammer.

'So, we going now?' he asked in a twitter of excitement, hands fiddling, touching his ears, eyes darting around like pinballs.

Everyone turned to look at him. There was a stunned silence as we took in the visage and our noses fought to find sufficient oxygen molecules amongst those of the aggressive aftershave.

Franci, dressed in a pair of jeans and a warm top, hair tied in a neat ponytail, coughed. 'Sweet fuck, Jerome, what is that smell?'

'What smell? My cologne? It's DKNY, obvs.'

'I think she's asking why you applied so much of it,' Donald said without smiling.

'Jerome, I fear I may have given you the wrong impression of the Twin Palms. It is not the Ministry of Sound – it is a den of hedonistic vice that smells like Satan's bowels. And it is not unusual to find its occupants completely without clothes,' I said. 'Let's go.'

At 21h00, we walked into the Twin Palms. The place was heaving with lascivious humanity, the music pounding and booze flowing. I sighed heavily.

As we arrived, the music ceased and my brother took to the stage (well, he stood on the three stacked crates that sufficed), carrying a tankard of some foul brew.

I took a position behind the crowd next to O'Reilly, who was chatting with Mayan. She laughed at something he said, her smile flashing like the diamond at the top of her right ear. Then she nodded in my direction, the smile falling from her face. O'Reilly slapped me on the back.

'Dis is your very favourite ting in the world!' he said.

'Laaaadieeees and gentlemen!' yelled String Bean. All eyes turned expectantly. 'You all know that this is an important night.'

'Drink for the GM, drink for the GM.' September Mathebula, Main Camp manager and one-time mentor to the new GM, took up the chant. It was quickly joined by the rest of the room. A second later, Hugh put the full tankard to his lips and drank.

'One, two, three, four, five –' they all counted. On six, the tankard went onto his head as dribbles of vile punch and bits of fruit dripped off his chin. The crowd roared and String Bean smiled benignly like a king to his subjects.

'Ladies and gentlemen, thank you very much! It's great to be back. There are going to be some changes around here but that's not a discussion for now. Now, we are here to welcome the newbies and celebrate the future.' Another roar followed and then the chant of: 'Newbies, newbies, newbies!'

'That's your cue!' I shouted at my six slightly alarmed recruits. 'Go up to the stage!'

The crowd parted as the trainees made their way to the front. They couldn't all stand on the stage so they shuffled to either side and faced the rest of the baying mass. Bradley also came forward, shook Hugh's hand, and replaced him on the stage – or he would have had he not tripped on the lip of the top crate, kicked it off and then fallen over the precarious construction with a sickening thud. There was a collective gasp and then laughter from many in his ranging team – none of whom moved to help him. I looked over at his wife, Kelly-Anne, and noticed her roll her eyes and take a long draw from her glass.

Bradley righted himself while Donald and Solomon reconstituted the stage. 'Um, so, howzit, everyone. Um, so, ja, a big welcome to the new guys –'

There was an awkward pause because the inflection of his sentence had indicated that he would go on. He didn't. There were a few giggles and some people gave perfunctory claps.

'So, um, ja, welcome, guys – oh, um, and girls. Great to have you here in the, um, family here at, eh, Sasekile ...'

Another dreadful pause as the two trainee chefs arrived. The Irishman started to giggle.

'Did we miss anything?' asked Hayley, out of breath.

'Are you joking?' I asked.

'Oh, fek. He's a good goi, dis fella, but he ain't mooch of a pooblic speaker.'

'Not quite Obama,' I agreed.

Hayley chuckled and Bradley at last continued.

'So, can, um, someone bring the drinks up for them?' He looked plaintively into the crowd.

Mark, Jason, Brandon and Jabu brought forward six tankards of God-knows-what. When each of the trainees had their concoctions, Jason basically shoved his boss off and climbed up on 'stage'.

'Right, okes, as you know, you training to join the best ranging team in Africa. That's a big call but it's true. It's an honour to be here and you gonna have to earn it. You need to show you part of the team – and this is the first way to show you wanna be one of us.'

The rest of the rangers roared.

'Have we turned into a frat house?' I asked O'Reilly.

'Dat goi is sooch a tit,' he replied.

Jerome watched Jason, nodding at everything he said, quivering in anticipation at the chance to prove himself one of the boys.

'Shoot a tiger, shoot a cat ...' began Jason.

The rest of the room took up the chant: 'Chunder, chunder on your back. Chunder, chunder, cotch and spew. Cotch on me, I cotch on you.'

No matter how many times I heard it, the poetry in this drinking chant eluded me entirely.

'Singing one, two, three ...'

Tankards were raised to trainees' lips. By the time they got to four, Katie's tankard was on her head with Jasper's following almost immediately. Jerome, seeing his two colleagues finish before him, tipped his and spilt most of the concoction down the front of his shiny blue shirt. Bits of fruit dangled in his designer beard. Franci and Donald finished on ten. At this point, Solomon took his glass from his lips and poured the remainder into Katie's glass, glaring at Jason and defying him to suggest he do otherwise. Katie was about to toss Solomon's leftovers down her gullet when Jasper grabbed her tankard and emptied it into his own throat.

A great cheer rose up and the music began to pound. Jerome lifted his hands to the sky as if he'd just won the Olympic 100 metres. Sweat dripped from his brow – his leather jacket, general anxiety and the airless room threatening to overheat him. The trainees disappeared into the back-slapping crowd from which, I surmised, the wise would shortly emerge and the unwise not until much later. Above the mass of people, the white Afro of Craig was visible like a giant pom-pom floating in an angry sea.

'Thank God that's done,' I said.

'You not big on drinking games?' asked Hayley sipping from a glass of punch.

'Not this sort.'

'Why not?' she asked.

'Because I find the idea of ascribing legendary status to people with a poor gag reflex and a genetic predisposition to processing booze effectively utterly ridiculous.'

'Angus can't hold his liquor,' chimed in O'Reilly.

'That's also true,' I admitted.

'Ag, shampies,' said Hayley. She stood for a while, observing the heaving mass in front of us. 'I've never really thought about it – guess I just assumed it was for fun.' She smiled. 'Well, enjoy your evening.' She emptied her glass and headed into the throng.

Jason swaggered towards her and they began to dance.

Hugh strode up to me and slapped me on the back. 'Well, did you miss this? I did – nothing like a Twin Palms with the full team!'

'I agree, there is literally nothing like a Twin Palms.' I paused to check my watch. 'In the same way that there is nothing like being impaled on a spike.'

But Hugh was so excited that he either didn't hear me or pretended not to.

'Looks like that big fellow is having a good time. Good God, which one is he?' SB pointed at Jerome.

'That would be Jerome le Roux.' Jerome was in the middle of the dance floor. He'd removed his jacket but the synthetic material from which his shirt had been moulded was soaked in sweat. In one hand he held a tankard, its contents sloshing over the top, and in the other he held Candice, recently returned from leave, around the waist. He was gyrating his pelvis at hers and, given Candice's lack of, shall we say, discernment, it was easy to see where the evening was going to end for them both.

Free booze was something Jasper was going to take full advantage of no matter its providence. He sat on the rickety bar, leaning against the wall, drinking from his plastic tankard and then refilling it from the steel bath of punch. He only moved from his position to satisfy his other addiction – nicotine. There was no smoking allowed in the Twin Palms.

The rest of the trainees seemed to be having a relatively good time and as The Killers' 'All These Things That I've Done' began to pound out of the speakers, Hugh flung himself into the crowd.

I turned to leave.

'You are not a dancer?' Mayan peered at me.

'In here, I am not a dancer, no,' I replied as I headed for the door.

The cold night air and silence were a sweet, blessed release. I wandered slowly back to the BC, the sound of the party receding, replaced with the subtle sounds of the chilly winter's night. A hippo called from the river and a lonely fiery-necked nightjar called in the woodlands as it searched for the few insects still moving in the midwinter.

The walk to the BC took me around the main staff village on an unlit path. Halfway back, my torch gave up – it wasn't a quality piece of camping gear. In fact, it came from a garage shop, because until then, I'd never shared the other rangers' fascination with powerful, expensive torches. I shook the cheap plastic implement, but it was quite dead.

There was no moon, and a thick blanket of cloud covered the sky. I held up my hand in front of my face and could not see it. I had two choices – walk back to the Twin Palms along the path that I knew was free of animals or continue to the BC. Facing the Twin Palms wasn't an option.

I stepped cautiously forward, my nose and ears on high alert. As my eyes adjusted, I began to make out the outlines of a few trees. My greatest fear was coming across a buffalo, as Julia had four and a bit years back – the memory of which still sometimes woke me in a cold sweat.

So when the hippopotamus appeared next to me, I was somewhat surprised and slow to react.

The enraged or terrified creature – I didn't stop to find out – let out a bellow loud enough to wake a week-old corpse and began to run. I knew it was a hippo only because the bush about 20 metres to my left sounded as if it was being mauled by a hurricane-force wind. I turned and looked in gobsmacked surprise as the hippo came steaming towards me. At the last second, I ran. I had no idea where – I just moved as fast as my legs would carry me. Three seconds later I collided with a spindly bush, tripped, grabbed at it, caught the trunk and the momentum swung me round. My back collected the trunk of a large marula and I fell, winded, at the base of the tree.

In the end, my sudden disappearance behind the marula tree must have confused the irate creature as it made for the river. The sound of vegetation being eviscerated receded into the distance as my breath came slowly back. I cursed, disorientated, my back aching. It hurt to breathe. I staggered to my feet and tried to think where the path was. After a minute or two I found it, and limped the last 40 metres to the BC, every sound making me jump, expecting to be ironed at any moment.

At 05h00 the following morning, I switched on the kettle and went to the bathroom, where I examined the damage to my person. There was a nasty blue bruise the size of a hand covering the left rear of my rib cage. I forced myself into a bracing cold shower, and then set about making some very strong coffee. I wasn't feeling tiptop and my observations of the trainees the previous evening indicated that I would not be the worst off.

Slowly the trainees began to emerge from their tents – Solomon and Donald first. Donald was subdued as a rule, but the apathy with which Solomon set to the coffee indicated some physiological distress. The girls came next. Franci was neat and tidy as always, if a little red-eyed. Katie, however, resembled the victim of a mauling from a rabid horde of hyenas. Her hair was still in the previous evening's ponytail, such that the elastic looked like it had been stuck to her head with Velcro. There was a dry red-wine stain around her lips. Her baggy shirt was untucked, her boot laces and belt undone.

'Rough night, Katie?'

'Phew,' she exhaled. 'Rough morning.' She made to pour some coffee.

'No, no,' I said. 'You look like a sick zombie – this is not the face that you will ever present to your guests, and nor will you present it to us. Go and sort yourself out, then coffee.'

'Ag,' she muttered and turned back to her tent.

At 05h20, there was a scuffling of bushes behind the BC and a flickering of torchlight. We turned to look as Jerome, still in last night's garb, swaggered onto the scene, grinning.

'Howzit!' he said, rubbing his hands together. 'Everyone have a good night?'

'We didn't get the clap, if that's what you're asking,' muttered Donald.

'What's that, bud?' asked Jerome.

'It obviously wasn't as good as yours,' said Franci.

'Well, that would be hard! Mine was epic and ...' Jerome tittered '... hard, if you know what I mean.'

'I'm going to be sick,' said Franci.

'I suspect Jerome's undercarriage will also be sick soon,' I added. 'I hope you wore double protection – you are not the first to have been lured into Candice's boudoir.'

Jerome's grin increased. 'I've never heard it called that!'

'Oh God,' said Franci.

'Jerome, you have precisely five minutes to get ready. We can talk about the potential infection to your nethers later.' Jerome strutted off towards his tent. 'And tell your tent mate he has the same amount of time.'

Jasper didn't actually look too bad – although Solomon had to wake him with a cold glass of water to the face.

15

That morning saw the beginning of our game-drive training, something I had not received in any great detail from my 'mentor' Anton – he with the muscles of Superman and the brain of a dung beetle, mercifully no longer anywhere near Sasekile.

We headed out as the sun pinkened the eastern sky. I loved being out of camp before any guest had stirred. Solomon was in the driver's seat, I was on the rear bench alone and the others were spread between us. They each had a map of the reserve, and I'd told them to navigate us onto the airstrip.

'Okay, bud' – Jerome, head covered in some sort of designer beanie that he'd carefully placed Boyzone-style with his fringe sticking out, was still on a high after his evening with Candice – 'take a left, then first left again.' He turned his map around, trying to orientate himself.

Solomon turned right out of camp.

'I said left!' squeaked Jerome. 'You not even using a map!'

'Planes land every day.' Solomon pointed to the southwest. 'The airstrip must be there.'

Jerome was silenced, and in five minutes we were on the apron of the strip.

'Now we listen,' I said.

Solomon cut the engine to take in the slowly building winter oratorio. First a grey-headed sparrow chirruped on a fallen knobthorn just off the apron, then a crested francolin squarked from the drainage line south of the strip. This set off a few others. The Cape turtle dove chorus rose with the brightening day. Finally, a lion roared, his calls reverberating through the Tsessebe River valley.

A lion calling is a great test of how connected people feel to nature. Most people don't need to be hushed when a lion roars; they do it instinctively, overwhelmed by the power of the sound and its primal resonance.

'Hey! That's a lion vocalising!' burst Jerome. 'My oupa and me, we used to –'

'Quiet, Jerome!' I snapped.

The rest of the roars we enjoyed in silence, right until the last grunt. Jerome made to speak again but I held up my hand as we let the sound ebb.

'Oh, wow,' Franci said eventually.

'Epic,' said Katie.

'Jissus, bru,' said Jasper. 'Is he angry?'

'My oupa –'

'Jerome, shut up about your oupa. If you had guests, this would be a golden opportunity – they want to find the lion, not talk about your oupa. When that lion is fast asleep under a bush in bad light, and you've exhausted your knowledge of lion biology, then, and *only* then, may you consider telling stories about your oupa. Right now there's a lion to be found!'

The group looked at me, expectant.

'Donald, where do you think he is?' I asked the man who'd been 'training' for seven months.

'Just north of the river, on Black Mane Clearings.'

'I would agree. Katie, you navigate us to Black Mane Clearings quick as you can.'

Donald pointed at a spot on the map and a few seconds later we were bumping through the dawn towards the Tsessebe. Katie, with a little help from Donald, took us down to the river and in the middle of the causeway I told Solomon to stop and turn off the engine.

The Tsessebe was a winter trickle but life on the river was waking – a hamerkop called from upstream, a red-faced cisticola flitted onto a reed next to the car and whistled 'Psss, pss, pss ps ps ...' and a Goliath heron stepped through a curtain of reeds to examine another pool for breakfast. Then the lion roared again, much closer this time.

'There!' Franci pointed to the northeast.

'That's Black Mane Clearings,' said Donald.

'Let's go!' said Katie. 'Over the causeway and take the next left!'

Excitement fizzed through the vehicle.

'My oupa said –' began Jerome.

'Shut up, Jerome,' said Franci and Katie in unison.

A minute later we moved through a copse of combretum trees onto Black Mane Clearings. I spotted the cat almost immediately but I was used to looking for leonine shapes in the half-light. Bar Jasper, everyone searched frantically, desperate to be the first to find him.

'Huh, check it out, there he is,' Jasper said quietly, having done nothing more than glance around him.

No one heard him. I suppose he could have pointed, but his body was too wrapped up in sarongs to extricate a hand.

'There! He's there!' shouted Jerome. 'I found him!' He pointed frantically.

Solomon stopped the vehicle – we were 50 metres or so from the great cat.

'Jerome,' I whispered, 'there is no need to shout at us – if we were guests, you'd want to enhance the sense of wilderness we were feeling. This is all about creating an atmosphere of wonder. Blethering at high volume into the dawn is going to do the opposite.'

Jerome's eyes glazed over. 'Let's get closer!'

'Just wait a sec – there's no need to park on top of the animal. Solomon, switch off the car and let's all be quiet for a minute.' I spoke softly yet urgently, as I might to guests seeing a lion for the first time.

The engine died as the sun finally peeped up over the horizon. The lion sat up and looked around him – he'd obviously heard something out of our pathetic human earshot. A single ray caught him on the right side of his face, his eye shone and he began to roar once again. Puffs of condensed breath caught the sunlight with each roar.

All the trainees bar Jerome were mesmerised. Sitting in the first row of the game viewer, Jerome was fiddling with a bag at his feet.

'Jerome, what are you doing?' hissed Katie, who was sitting next to him. 'Can't you sit still?'

'I'm getting my camera!'

Soon a large DSLR with a 600-millimetre lens emerged from under his feet. The lion was in the final stages of his roar when Jerome aimed and depressed the shutter, eliciting the photographic equivalent of rapid fire.

For Franci, who was hungover and hangry, this was too much.

'Fuck sakes, Jerome, is that really necessary? I mean, *shit*' – she pointed at the cat – 'the fucking lion is dead still? Why the fuck do you need to take seven thousand pictures like that?'

'You don't know photography,' Jerome replied, defiant. 'And don't swear at me like that.' He aimed the camera again and fired off a few more shots.

The radio crackled to life. The game drives were heading out – many of them to find our lion. I instructed Solomon to drive slowly to about 20 metres from the cat and switch off. Then we would begin the most painful lesson of being a guide – operating the game-drive radio while trying to impart wilderness wonder to clueless guests.

When I'd left Sasekile previously, the game-drive radio procedures were excellent. I'd love to take credit for this, but all I did was make sure the procedures Carrie (my predecessor) put in place were adhered to on pain of death. There is little more irritating than morons on the radio.

One of the main rules was that you spoke English on the game-drive channel. This was so that everyone would understand, but more than that, it was so that the god-awful game-drive Fanakalo that befouled the radio waves of other lodges did not do the same at hallowed Sasekile.

I'd visited a number of other lodges over the years and heard some gems. On one occasion, PJ had organised that Allegra and I spend a weekend at a supposedly swanky establishment on a reserve close to Sasekile – he was always sending staff on 'rewards', which actually meant he wanted to check out the competition. Our ranger there was everything I hoped the new trainees would never become. He'd arrived at tea with bulging muscles and acne, despite his being at least 25, which indicated a fondness for intravenous testosterone. His shirt was undone to just above the diaphragm, the vast pectoral muscles (free of fluff) on display. These were dotted with an outbreak of pimples from his post-wax ingrown hairs.

This creature's first action on game drive was to call into the radio: 'Afternoon, buggers. My malungus wanna see some skankaahn, so I'll be making my way to the three madoda skankies from this morning.'

The reason for speaking in this manner was apparently to prevent guests from understanding what was going on – it allowed the brave ranger to 'surprise his guests', claim credit for 'finding an animal' and also talk about his guests without their knowledge. 'Skankaahn', or 'skankie' for short, is a bastardisation of the word 'Xikankanka', meaning cheetah in Xitsonga – something one of the unfortunate couples on our drive had asked to see.

'Copy that,' said another ranger. 'I'm gonna head to the gonnies [lions] first, then join you at the skankies.'

Then the real pearler: 'I got a skankie on my mova. Proper skankie,' said our guide into his radio.

A mova is a car. A skankie or skankaahn is also a way to refer to an attractive lady guest.

'Ja, saw that one earlier,' came the reply. 'Nice one, bru!'

It was clear they were referring to Allegra – the other two women on our vehicle were over-strudelled Germans in their seventh decade.

'Travis,' I addressed our guide from the back seat as we drove out of camp.

'Ja?' He turned, smiling cheerfully.

'If you refer to my girlfriend by any name other than the one given by her parents, I shall come to the front of the vehicle and clock you one in the teeth.' The smile on his face vanished. 'I realise that I do not possess the musculature that you do, but I'll take the risk.'

'Ja, I'm not sure what you ... um ... I was just –'

'Shut up, Travis.'

So at Sasekile we had always spoken English on the radio – an approach that allowed the guests to understand what was happening on the drive, and made them feel a part of the tracking process rather than a bunch of halfwits (which many were, of course).

In my absence, however, radio procedures had changed.

'Howzit, mobile stations, can I get a route and sightings update …? Great skop last night, buggers.'

'Sweet lord, who is that?' I asked Donald.

'Sean – he's 23. Newest guide,' replied Donald, eyes fixed on the lion.

'Morning, only me out so far. I'm heading south towards Hyena Pans.' Jeff, trying to maintain standards.

'Copy that, heading up north to find the khalering pussycat!' Sean replied.

'Morning, buggers and buggesses. Copied the routes, gonna follow S-bone up north for the gonnie. Feeling rough AF.' Jason this time.

'Lekka, chinas. Copied the routes, gonna go River Road north, also for the khalering gonnie.'

I looked at Donald again.

'Johnno. Been here two years.'

'Morning, fellas. I'll be heading up north as well; can I get a standby for that cat if you okes get him?' I recognised Mark's voice.

Another three vehicles called themselves up to the north before I could instruct Solomon to call in the lion they were all looking for. They had 15 000 hectares to explore, but the low-hanging fruit of a soon-to-be comatose lion was what they wanted.

I gave Solomon some brief instructions on how to call in the sighting, explaining to them all that if I ever heard anything other than English on the game-drive radio, they'd be on short rations for a week. Solomon went over it in his head once and then depressed the mouthpiece.

'Stations, this is Solomon, trainee ranger. We have located this male lion, static on Black Mane Clearings.'

I gave him a thumbs-up. Pandemonium erupted on the radio.

'Who is that?' Jason, aggressive.

'Trainees on Black Mane Clearings.' Johnno.

'What you got there?' Mark, deeply confused.

'Trainees can't be in a sighting!' Jason, incensed.

'They must be on standby!' Mark.

I climbed over the seats to the front row and took the radio from Solomon.

'Stations, we'll move out as soon as the first drive arrives here,' I said firmly.

'Ja, but now my malungus are gonna see you found the gonnie.' Sean, whining.

The lion rose during this discussion and began to walk north, most likely to seek cover.

I lost patience. 'Copy that,' I said into the radio. Then I instructed Solomon to take us out of the sighting, the sound of vehicles converging from all angles changing the glorious wilderness atmosphere into something that resembled rush hour in New York City. It gave me some satisfaction to see the lion disappear into a bushwillow thicket.

An hour later, I told Solomon to turn off the game-drive radio. It had been a ceaseless barrage of desperate rangers trying, and failing, to track the lion.

At 11h00, we were sitting around the tables at the BC, the trainees with their heads down writing notes about lion biology. I was explaining infanticide in mammals to Katie when Jason and Mark, with Brad a few steps behind, stormed up the path, steaming from their ears.

'Good morning,' I said breezily.

'Well, yes, um. Hello, Ang–' began Brad.

'What the *actual* fuck?' yelled Mark. 'What do you trainees think you playing at?'

I looked around the table. The trainees looked up. Jerome shrunk back, trying to distance himself from his colleagues.

'What are you talking about?' I asked.

'You okes caused a complete shit-show this morning. We *all* had malungus that needed to see that gonnie!'

Solomon, taking a sip of water, snorted.

'Something funny?' If Jason thought to intimidate Solomon, ten years his senior, he'd made a mistake.

'Your Zulu is funny,' said Solomon, deadpan.

Jason pointed a finger, but under Solomon's unwavering gaze, the finger shifted to indicate everyone at the table.

'You okes better learn your place. You not here for a jol! If you wanna be part of this team, you gonna have to work for it and show some respect to the seniors,' said Jason.

'Not gonna happen with this oke in charge.' Mark looked at me and then Brad. 'We should be training these okes, not some outsider.'

'He's, um, not, ah ... really an, um, outsider.' Brad, making a piss-poor attempt at leadership.

'Guys,' I said, 'Donald here has been so-called "training" under you and the so-called "seniors" for the last seven months. I'm willing to bet a lobotomised macaque could be trained to take a safari in seven months.'

'Now, um, let's just try and stay calm,' said Brad.

Jason ignored him. Frothing and gesticulating, he shouted, 'You don't get it, buddy. Your day is long gone. Things have changed – we the best ranging team in Africa. Anyone wanting to join has to prove they worth it. This is not for just anyone!' He looked dismissively around the group and then glared at me.

I'd had enough. 'This team, with respect to you, Brad, is a joke. You behave like a bunch of Jeep jockeys feeling threatened about the little fiefdom you've created, so now you've come here to piss on my patch.'

Mark and Jason took a step forward.

'Don't you fucken talk to us like that!' Mark pointed a menacing finger at me, at which point I thought it advisable to stand up in case I needed to beat a hasty retreat. They were both bigger than me and I am no fighter. Naturally enough, it took a woman to calm the situation.

'God, this is pathetic.' Franci stood up. 'Can you all just put your dicks away. Maybe you need to go sort this out in private, but this is embarrassing.'

'Yes, I think, that's um, probably, best. Let's have a chat ... some other time,' said Bradley.

The 'senior rangers' departed and I walked into the BC to cool off.

There was muttering outside.

'Lobotomised macaque,' I heard Katie say. 'I think we have our first nickname. Donald, henceforth, you will be known as ...' She paused for effect. 'The Macaque.'

'Thank you,' said Donald. 'It's an honour.'

For the next week, we headed into the bush each morning and afternoon learning how to conduct sightings from the vehicle, use the radio and drive the Land Rover. The latter does not take great feats of strength, but it does require some learning and experience to drive off-road or negotiate steep gullies.

One morning we went to an old quarry, which was useful for lessons on how to drive a four-by-four without destroying the bush or killing guests. We parked in the shade of a marula tree, and I went about explaining the very boring but very important mechanics of the Land Rover drivetrain. Franci took notes, Jasper stared at the tree, Solomon nodded gravely, Donald looked surprised, and Jerome and Katie looked bored.

'Donald, why do you look so perplexed?' I asked. 'Presumably you know all this already.'

'No, I've never heard any of this. I've never had a lesson on this car.'

'I see. And you two?' I pointed at Katie and Jerome. 'Are you bored because this is all deeply familiar to you?'

'Well, um, sorry, but yes,' said Katie. 'My dad and I have stripped and rebuilt four Land Rovers.'

'Good to know,' I said, surprised. 'Did I get anything wrong?'

'Um, no – I mean, your understanding of the central diff is a little dodge, but it won't make any difference to the driving.'

This new knowledge came as something of a relief. I had no idea what went on under the hood.

'Katie, perhaps you'd like to take us through the engine?' I suggested, and her face lit up.

For the next 30 minutes, Katie explained the workings of the ancient V8 we, as the training team, had been allocated. Jerome continued to look as if he was an astrophysicist being forced to learn basic arithmetic.

'Jerome,' I said, 'your CV suggested you were an excellent exponent of four-by-four driving. So perhaps you'd like to have the first go?'

'Ja, my oupa taught me when I was still a laaitie.'

I pointed out the tracks that led out and back into the quarry in three progressively difficult runs, although nothing too alarming. Before I could finish, he'd leapt into the driver's seat.

'No problem, bud!' The engine roared and he was off. The Landie raced up the first hill, wheels spinning, turned at the top and raced down again with Jerome pumping the accelerator.

'You need to lock the diff and put it in low range!' I shouted as he raced past, turned and sped towards the second hill. 'And slow down!'

'I got this, bud!' he shouted back and sped towards the second hill – substantially steeper than the first and covered in loose stones.

The aged Land Rover ran out of puff halfway up the hill and, instead of stopping and putting the car in low range, he just revved mightily and rode the clutch until he'd crawled over the lip. An acrid smell filled the air.

'He's stuffing up the clutch,' observed Katie.

Having turned at the top of the hill, Jerome came haring down again, waving his right fist in triumph as he made for the third slope. He was too far away and the engine was objecting too loudly for my shouts to reach him. The third slope was very steep and strewn with rocks. The first section cut left out of the quarry, the track angling down the slope. The last section wasn't in the quarry but part of a massive disused termite mound with a brown ivory tree growing out of it. This time, Jerome engaged the low range (but did not stop to do so). There was a grinding noise and then a loud clunk as the old gearbox finally acquiesced. He slammed it into second gear, pounded the accelerator and aimed for the hill.

'Oh no,' said Katie.

I covered my eyes briefly.

Halfway up, the front right tyre hit a huge rock. The steering wheel flung itself out of Jerome's hands and the vehicle lurched to the left –

down the slope. Jerome's foot froze on the accelerator as he grappled with the steering wheel. The engine roared and then the back right hit the same rock. Jerome lost control and the Land Rover began to roll.

'Sweet fuck,' said Franci.

'Yoh,' said Solomon.

'Jissus, bru,' said Jasper, registering genuine alarm.

The Land Rover tipped onto its two left wheels and began to roll down the slope.

'Fuuuuuuuuuck!' Jerome shouted in terror.

The car fell onto its side and would have rolled all the way back into the quarry, almost certainly crushing Jerome to a pulp, but for the tree on the old termite mound. The bonnet smashed into the trunk, and then the Land Rover twisted and slid on its left side to the base of the quarry.

We all ran.

When the dust settled, Jerome was still sitting, 90 degrees from horizontal, in the driver's seat, gripping the steering wheel and staring straight ahead. His face had changed from its usual olive complexion to that of startled milk.

'You moron, Jerome!' yelled Katie. 'Look what you've done to our vehicle.'

'Phew,' whistled Jasper, looking over the wreckage. 'Gnarly, bru.'

'It's going to be difficult for the rest of us to practise now,' observed Donald.

We eventually extricated the shaken Jerome and sat him in some shade.

'Something wrong with that car,' he mumbled. 'My oupa ...' He put his head in his hands.

I called Jacob on the radio, and about an hour later he arrived with Nhlanhla and the tractor. They attached a towrope to the underside of the stricken Land Rover and pulled. It crashed down onto its four wheels and bounced once. Then the back right tyre exploded. We spent another 40 minutes learning how to use the high-lift jack with Jerome, still in shock, sitting under a tree looking sorry for himself.

On our return to the BC, I was unsurprised to be summoned to the office of the Lord High Commander of the Universe.

'Angus,' SB began without pleasantries, 'Mechanic Douglas arrived here ten minutes ago hyperventilating and pointing at the workshop. I could get no sense out of him and had to go back there myself. Having seen the training vehicle, I am surprised he didn't have a stroke!'

'My lord, it is highly unusual for a 25 year old to have a stroke.'

His face went red. 'Angus, do you think we have the budget for this? And don't call me that!'

'I am unaware of the financial constraints on the vehicle budget,' I replied, picking up a decorative clock on SB's desk.

He stood and snatched it from my hand. 'Angus, what the hell happened?'

'Ah, I was waiting for the purpose of this visit!' I sat down to explain, and promised to try and keep Jerome in check.

'This never happened when the other guys did the training,' my brother muttered, head back, fingers pinching the bridge of his nose.

'String Bean, I shall endeavour to make sure this doesn't happen again. I am sincerely sorry about it – as I told Douglas when we returned.' When nothing further came from the general manager, I tipped my hat, bowed deeply and said, 'I shall now humbly withdraw, my lord.'

'Don't bloody call me that!'

For the next week we continued with game-drive training (in a savagely dented vehicle). It was very pleasant looking for animals and spending time in their company without the hassle of guests and their bottomless desires. After the first radio disaster, I decided that if we found an animal, we would spend as much time with it as we liked before calling it in for 'the best ranging team in Africa'. Unsurprisingly, 'the best ranging team in Africa' didn't call us in to any sightings – but for those found by Jabu, Brandon or the ever-loyal Jeff.

16

One morning, when our decrepit Land Rover was due for a service – although I failed to understand what a month, let alone half a day, could do for the rattling, belching piece of engineering – we went for a walk around the Sasekile lodge.

Myriad walkways ran between the camps, the rooms and the back-of-house areas, around which, over the years, hundreds if not thousands of trees had been planted. The proximity to the river and a relentless watering regime meant that the camp gardens were always green (unlike wild vegetation in late winter, which can look pretty rough before the first rains). The greenery was great for the guests and, as evidenced by my near-death experience with Mitchell-the-elephant (who had nearly flattened me in the rain one fateful night five years previously), extremely attractive to herbivores when the bush offered nothing but sticks and dried pods to eat.

The gardens were also brilliant for learning indigenous trees.

Just as dawn broke, we left the Bat Cave armed with a few tree books. The camp was just waking and muted sounds emanated from the main kitchen as the chefs began their breakfast preparations. The security guards were walking around the camp waking guests – one of them, Willy, taking a slightly perverse pleasure and banging loudly on each door and shouting, 'Wakey-wakey, guesty-guesty!' before chuckling and moving on to the next room.

Our plan was to start at the camp furthest to the east, Tamboti Camp, and walk the path west all the way to Rhino Camp, learning the trees as we went. We strolled through the rear of the Tamboti boma as the guests were making their way onto the deck for coffee. Down in the river, an irate hamerkop squawked about some perceived injustice while grey-headed sparrows chirruped at each other from various here-tofore-unidentified trees. Way in the distance, a fish eagle called.

We began on the path leading past the Tamboti Camp rooms to-wards Main Camp. I stopped at a snuff-box tree and prevailed upon the trainees to name it. This was going to be a boring task because the train-ees had to learn how to use the key in their tree books – a laborious pro-cess initially. I split them into three teams with rewards (one tenth of a beer or cider) for the team who identified the tree first, and punishment (ten push-ups) for the others. Jerome was delighted when I paired him with Franci. Katie went with Jasper, with Donald and Solomon making up the final team.

They set to the task of identifying the snuff-box tree while I looked for a bearded robin scrabbling around the base of a plumbago bush.

The first individual to come across us was Sliver, the security guard. The average camp security guard has no interest in security at all – the work consists of escorting incredibly rich people to and from their rooms in the dark, and then making them coffee in the mornings. It's supposed to include patrolling the camp at night for marauding crea-tures (both animal and human) but, as the lowest-paid employment at the lodge, sleeping by the fire is much more enthusiastically embraced.

That morning I was to discover an exception to the rule. Sliver was about 23 years old, and possibly the most serious person I have ever come across. After the guests have been woken and their coffee made, tired guards normally drift back up to the staff village to have a shower and return to their slumber. Sliver emerged from the Tamboti Camp main area at a quick march. When he saw us mustered around a tree in the gathering light, he halted, stamped his foot, turned 90 degrees, stamped his foot again and marched up the path towards us. He halted in front of me, stamped his right foot again and then saluted.

I returned his salute, fighting not to laugh.

'Good morning!' Sliver shouted at me.

'Hello,' I said.

'I am Sliver, security,' he announced, staring over the top of my head to a point in the distance.

'I am Angus, superhero,' I replied more quietly.

'What are you doing in my camp? I am in charge of safety here!' Sliver bellowed and stamped his foot again.

I came to attention and stamped my foot too.

'We are here to learn about trees!' I shouted back at him. 'We do not intend to pillage any of the rooms or violate any of your guests!'

There was a pause as Sliver considered this.

'Good, please proceed!' he yelled, before turning on his heel and marching back to camp.

'*Oncoba spinosa*,' said Jasper, breaking the amused and stunned silence.

I wheeled around.

'What did you say?'

Jasper looked up from Katie's tree book. 'This tree, it's a snuff-box tree. *Oncoba spinosa*, bru.'

The others stared with faces as incredulous as mine.

'Who told you that?' I asked.

Jasper shrugged. 'It's in the book, bru.'

'Is he right?' his teammate, Katie, asked.

'Against all expectations, yes,' I said.

Katie started to dance around the tree, ecstatic.

'That's one-tenth of a beer for us and ten push-ups for you, one-tenth beer for us and ten push-ups for you ...'

'Well, you heard her,' I said. 'Ten push-ups for the rest of you.'

'Just ten?' asked Jerome, whose face was soon the colour of beetroot.

'You can do as many as you want, Jerome,' I replied.

They all dropped down, did their push-ups and we moved on to the next tree.

Over the course of the next hour, Jasper Henderson and Katie Howley were the only ones to not take off their jerseys. They did not do even one push-up while the rest completed almost a hundred. I believe, on that day, we found Jasper's one true talent (other than being a marijuana-soaked laggard). He caught on to the tree key with confounding speed and, even more remarkably, remembered everything. By the end of two hours, he was walking in front of the group pointing out all the species we'd already identified, and searching for new ones. The others (except Katie, who made zero contribution to her team's efforts) spent the time doing push-ups or taking frantic notes from Jasper of all people.

Just after 08h00, we came to the building site of the brand-new Hogan Camp, situated between Main and Kingfisher. There were great piles of building material and, while I am no authority on engineering, I couldn't see how on earth the six-bed camp would be up and running by the time the Condé Nast people came to see it at the end of the year.

This, apparently, was an opinion shared by Nicolette Hogan.

We came upon a blue sweetberry bush just next to a pile of bricks and I set the trainees to it, instructing Jasper to keep his answer to himself this time. While they were busy, I observed the builders mooching around, chatting, haphazardly moving a few bits and pieces. Then, marching down the entrance to the new camp came Nicolette Hogan. She was moving with purpose, trailed by her personal assistant, a pale, thin young woman named Mary. Mary was carrying a clipboard and a pen in her hands, and the top pocket of her pristine white shirt contained another three writing instruments.

Nicolette was not someone given to shouting, but was one of those people whose anger can be felt at a hundred paces. When displeased, her mouth turned down at the sides and her voice became a deathly hiss. The object of her ire would feel a burning in their soul that manifested in a sense of impending doom. She was the sort of person who makes even the innocent feel like they are about to be found out for murder.

Nicolette nodded briefly at our group, thankfully engrossed with the tree and their books, as she flew past. Then she stopped and turned slowly.

My heart arrived in my throat. The group ceased their tree investigation as she regarded us, jaw working from side to side.

'Angus,' she said quietly.

I wanted to vomit.

'Morning, Nicolette,' I said with fake jocularity.

'Who is *that?*'

Everyone looked at Jasper, who was looking at his tree book. I clipped him over the head.

'Hey, bru?' he complained and then looked into the face of doom.

There was no chance I was taking responsibility for him.

'This is Jasper Henderson,' I replied. 'Um, he is the fellow Dennis found on the Wild Coast.'

'Why is he dressed like he lives in a desert?' Her jaw was working furiously.

Jasper was, as usual, covered in his sarongs for warmth.

'He doesn't have anything else to wear, I'm afraid,' I replied.

Nicolette inhaled and then exhaled deeply. 'Angus, do you think it appropriate that our guests see this ... creature?'

'Well, I, um ...'

'Yes or no.'

'No.'

'Then, why have you allowed it to happen?'

'Eh, I –'

'I'm not interested. If I see him looking like that again, both you and he will leave within the hour. Do I make myself clear?'

Mary made a note on her clipboard, looking at Jasper with an inscrutable expression.

'Abundantly,' I replied, feeling the size of an amoeba.

Nicolette wheeled and strode off towards the building site.

As we completed our identification of the blue sweetberry bush, once again deciphered by Jasper (who hadn't bothered to follow the conversation with Nicolette), there was a sudden flurry of activity and shouting at the construction site. A builder ran past, pushing a wheelbarrow.

In theory, trainee rangers were supposed to clothe themselves. If they qualified, then Sasekile would issue them with a uniform. I had connections, though, so I went to see Hugh after breakfast. He was at his desk, tapping furiously on a new laptop. He'd taken to wearing a pair of glasses that made him look much older than his 28 years. I observed as he picked up the phone and pushed three buttons.

'Candice,' he began, 'find out when the new boma chairs are arriving.'

There was a pause as she, no doubt, gave some excuse as to why this was going to be a problem.

'I don't care!' SB shouted. 'This is a priority and when I say something needs to get done now, then it needs to get done *now!*' He slammed down the phone.

I walked in and sat on the chair in front of his desk.

'Good day, my lord.'

He didn't look up.

'I told you not to call me that. What do you want?'

'Yes, good, I'm fine, thank you – and you?'

'Oh God. Yes, I'm fine – busy, as you can probably see,' he sighed, still tapping away.

'I'll get to the point then. I need a uniform for Jasper. He looks like a tramp, and Nicolette saw him today. He will not be able to afford any clothing until his first pay cheque – which, as I am sure you are aware, is little more than slave wage for a trainee ranger.'

Hugh sighed, pushed his glasses onto his forehead and squeezed the bridge of his nose.

'This is not something I need to be dealing with, Angus. Go and see Kelly-Anne. She's the new ops manager. She looks after small-picture stuff like this.' He pushed his glasses back onto his nose.

'You mean the unfriendly one who runs Main Camp with September?'

'She's not unfriendly, she's efficient – now, please, I'm really snowed under here.' He picked up the phone again and began bellowing something to an underling.

'Thank you, my lord.' I bowed deeply four or five times as I exited his office.

Next I made my way to where Kelly-Anne, Candice and Hilda shared a space. Mark was leaving as I approached the door – he barged out and didn't greet me.

'Morning, Mark,' I said to his back. 'Good chat, thanks!'

Kelly-Anne, like the Gruppenführer next door, was tapping away on her computer. Her desk was disturbingly neat, as was her dark hair, which was pulled into a severe ponytail that seemed to take the skin on her forehead to stretching point. Her mouth was pinched in concentration, and a pair of fashionable (I think) glasses rested on her straight nose. She was dressed entirely in black.

'Morning, all,' I said breezily.

'Fok,' said Hilda, looking up and shaking her head.

Candice, talking quietly into the phone, spun on her chair, showing me her back.

'Morning,' said Kelly-Anne, unsmiling, so I walked over to her desk.

'How are you?' I asked.

'Fine thanks and you?' This was said without a hint of interest.

'Good.' I thought it best to just get on with it. 'I need some old uniform for one of the trainees – Nicolette's orders.' This wasn't exactly true, but I seriously doubted Kelly-Anne would check.

She sighed heavily.

'Can you come back tomorrow or the next day?' she asked.

There was a mound of uniforms in the open steel cupboard off to one side.

'Have you *met* Nicolette?' I asked.

Kelly-Anne stared at me. She would have been good-looking but for the disdainful look on her face.

I pointed. 'Just reach into that cupboard and hand me two shirts, two pairs of shorts and that old jacket.'

'You know you can't just come in here and demand things?' she said. 'We have a system here that falls apart if people just come in and take stuff.'

It was my turn to sigh.

'Kelly-Anne, I am not asking you to build a rocket ship in your spare time. I need some clothes for an employee – this is part of your job.'

'Don't you tell me what my job is!' she snipped as I walked to the cupboard and pulled out what I wanted.

This galvanised her. She shot from her chair, which went skidding across the floor.

'You can't just take stuff!' she shrilled, grabbing me by the shoulder.

I feinted left and then swung right, my booty cradled at my midriff. This loosened her grip and I made for the door.

'Victory!' I shouted, and I could have sworn that Hilda cracked a smile.

Back at the BC, the trainees were sitting around the trestles with their tree books. Jasper was standing away from the group, examining a seedling growing where the ground was wet next to the bathroom wall.

I handed him the khaki uniform. 'Jasper, please go and put this on. And don't take it off unless you're getting into bed or taking a shower. Savvy?'

'Cool,' he said, putting the clothes down on the ground. 'So what's this tree, bru?'

'Looks like a tree wisteria,' I replied. 'Jasper, I'm not kidding – go and take off your glad rags and put this stuff on *now*. Nicolette Hogan is not to be trifled with.'

Jasper lazily picked a wilting leaf from the seedling, took his kit and headed for the tent – and not a moment too soon because something utterly unprecedented in the illustrious history of Sasekile was about to occur. The sound of approaching footsteps arrested our attention and Solomon, rocking on his chair again, got such a fright that he tipped over backwards.

Down the path strode Nicolette Hogan, trailed by Mary. She'd never visited the place during my previous stint at Sasekile.

They arrived in front of the veranda just as Jasper emerged from his tent. Typically oblivious, he was wearing only a pair of khaki shorts. These he had failed to fasten, such that his fraying cotton briefs protruded from the top, not entirely covering the thick hair of his nether regions. He had a new shirt slung over his shoulder, head still buried in the tree book. He rubbed his little pot belly with the hand not holding the book.

A small squeak emanated from the mousie form of Mary and she scribbled something on her clipboard.

'*Bolusanthus speciosus*,' he said, looking up and registering very slight alarm at the sight of Nicolette and Mary. 'Um, howzit.'

Nicolette stared at him.

'Um, I'll just, I think, put my shirt on.'

'What a very good idea.' Nicolette's voice could have frozen the sun.

But instead of returning to his tent, Jasper decided it was a good idea for him to dress in full view of everyone else. He put the book on the ground, whipped the shirt over his head, tucked it in and fastened the button on his shorts. Then he rearranged his package, grunted, wiped his nose with the back of his hand and retrieved his book from the dust.

Nicolette observed with a mixture of fascination and disgust. She then turned her attention to the BC and examined our little university. It was neat and tidy – Franci had been on post-breakfast clean-up detail, and she'd done an excellent job. I was standing in the doorway of the BC with a mug in my hand. When Katie looked at me, I pointed at my mug and indicated Nicolette with a frantic head nod.

Katie's brow furrowed and then she understood.

'Um, may we offer you some coffee or tea?'

Nicolette turned back from her examination of the tents.

'No, I think not. Mary, do you want coffee?'

Mary shook her head vigorously. 'No, thank you very much,' she squeaked and wrote something down.

'You can all sit down now,' Nicolette said.

The trainees took their seats. Jasper just sat on the ground.

'I came through here to see what was happening at this, um, facility.' She paused and no one breathed. 'It looks adequate, although I want those creepers removed from the window.' She pointed at a fragment of *Jasminum* that had managed to make its way up the wall in the last few weeks. 'Details, details, you must all learn to see details.' Mary made a note. 'Angus, walk with me.'

Nicolette spun on her heel.

'Angus,' she said as we strode down the path. 'At the end of the year, Condé Nast is coming – you know about that. They have decided, however, that instead of sending two evaluators, they are going to give Sasekile the honour of hosting their end-of-year congress. We were their second choice – actually, their third – but I am determined they will regret this. At the end of the congress, they will announce the winner of the Pink Flute and this year the ceremony will be broadcast live from Sasekile – from the Hogan Camp deck.'

She stopped and spun to face me just before the path opened onto the little clearing in front of the kitchen. Mary moved around her with a smoothness that indicated lots of practice.

'I expect everyone at this lodge to ensure that we are awarded the Pink Flute – and I mean everyone, from Jacob in the conservation team to Hugh and all the way down to that apparition you are training. Understand?'

'I understand the sentiment but I'm afraid I have no idea what the Pink Flute is,' I said.

Nicolette scowled and exhaled loudly. 'The Pink Flute is a yearly award handed out by Condé Nast to the best hotel or lodge in the world.'

'Why a flute?'

'It's not a flute one might play a tune on,' she was getting exasperated. 'It's a ceremonial champagne flute.'

'Oh, right, I see.'

'Good. Now make sure your charges understand its importance.'

17

For the next three weeks we continued with game-drive training, going out morning and evening – approaching sightings, operating the radio and simulating guest situations.

Jerome would only arrive at the BC around 05h25 to dress himself. He was having an affair with Candice, the thought of which made me gag. Whether he just preferred her sleeping quarters, I'm not sure, but I didn't ask. In all honesty, given the choice between sharing a cramped tent with Jasper or sleeping in Candice's well-used bordello, even I would have considered the latter.

I had a visit one morning from Craig while the trainees were doing another tree patrol. The IT manager arrived at the BC while I was redesigning the written tests the trainees would have to complete during the next month or so. I first saw his head, the vast, puffy white Afro moving through the trees like a lost cumulus cloud. He wandered up to the veranda and lifted his finger as if about to announce something. I waited for him to speak but nothing came.

'Hello, Craig,' I said eventually.

'Hmmmm,' he replied, looking at the Wi-Fi router attached to the roof.

'How are you?'

'Yes.' He nodded and then sat down.

'Can I offer you some tea or coffee?' I ventured.

'Hmmm, yes.' He nodded, still apparently appraising the BC.

'Which one?' I asked.

'I'm, yes, coffee ... No, tea ... Yes, coffee.'

I went inside to fill the plunger and emerged presently with two mugs, the plunger, a sugar bowl and the rusks. I poured him a cup.

'Milk?'

He shook his head and slowly pulled the mug and sugar bowl towards him. He then proceeded to ladle seven teaspoons of refined white sugar into his mug. He mixed it, took a sip and then added another two. He picked up the mug and settled back in his chair, making no attempt to explain himself.

'Craig, is there something specific you came to see me about, or is this just a social visit?'

He put down his cup on the table and I could see him trying to figure out how to say what he needed to. He held up two fingers.

'Two things you need to say?'

He nodded.

I foresaw a lengthy game of charades. 'I'm afraid I don't have all morning, so you will need to tell me.'

The colour drained from his face.

'Too much night noise,' he said quietly.

'Too much night noise?' I repeated.

'Hmmm,' he nodded.

I thought about this as a red-billed hornbill landed on the veranda and began to pick up rusk crumbs, utterly unafraid. Then realisation dawned.

'You live next door to Candice?'

'Hmmm.' Craig nodded vigorously.

'And Jerome's nightly activities are causing a lack of sleep?'

More nodding.

'Is it him or her?'

'I think him,' said Craig.

'Ah, well, I'll have a word with him, no problem.' I was trying hard not to laugh. 'And the second thing?'

'I want to learn some bush,' he said.

'You want to come out on training drives?'

More enthusiastic nodding.

'Okay, that's fine. I don't suppose you'll make much noise or distract the trainees too much.'

Craig stood immediately and disappeared without another word.

The trainees returned presently, tree-guru Jasper at the front, new uniform far too big for his odd shape. The others carried four or five samples each and wore expressions ranging from frustration to determination.

'How many new ones?' I asked.

'Seven million,' said Donald, flopping down.

Jerome came up the path last. He looked exhausted and Craig had just explained why.

'Jerome,' I said, 'before you sit down, a word inside.'

He sighed and followed me into the BC storeroom.

'I've had some complaints.' I got straight to the point.

'From who, about what?' He was alarmed.

'Never mind from *whom*,' I replied. 'And about – well – about the noises coming from your person during your nightly coitus with Candice.'

'Huh?'

'About the grunting and groaning you're making while having sex with Candice.'

'Oh, that's not me,' he immediately shot back.

'Are you saying someone *else* is having sex with her or that *she's* making the noise?'

'I'm the only one!' he snapped.

'I seriously doubt that, but I don't really want to discuss it. Just make sure you both take your carnal pleasures in relative silence from now on.' I walked out.

Craig came out with us every afternoon from then on. This was useful because the trainees had a 'guest' to direct their new knowledge towards. The IT manager, however, said almost nothing and asked even less. He was particularly silent when Katie or Franci addressed him. His eyes, however, turned out to be spectacular.

'Hmmm!' he'd shout-hum, pointing.

Whoever was driving would stop the car and we'd all peer into the bush trying to discern what Craig was looking at. Often it was a small bird – a crombec or an eremomela foraging in the leaves. Or sometimes he discerned a leopard's pelage in the deep shade of a tree that the rest of us had missed.

In the fifth week, the walk training began. This consisted of us approaching large mammals on foot so that the trainees could learn how animals would react to them. The ultimate goal being to prepare them for their greatest challenge – the unarmed walks. I convinced Brad to lend me Slumber the tracker for two weeks (he who'd done the long walk with us). This was for his excellent tracking skills and also for the extra safety of having someone around who knew what he was doing.

In the mornings we headed out on foot from camp just as it grew light. It never ceased to amaze me how quickly the winter turned to summer in the Lowveld. The first week of August was frigid but on the day we headed out from camp, a warm breeze was blowing in from the northwest. For once, Jerome wasn't covered with goose flesh and the rest of us shed our layers almost as soon as the sun shone on us.

On our last morning before the unarmed walks began, we cut through the block due south of the camp. The dry grass crunched underfoot, sending little puffs of dust up with each step. The subtle potpourri smell of winter woodland had been replaced with the subtle honey scent of the first knobthorn blossoms and a hint of smoke from fires outside the reserve in the communal rangelands. The sky was hazy and there was a heat to the dawn that heralded the dry copper, bronze, gold and grey months.

We settled onto a game path with Slumber and me up front, the trainees in single file behind us. No one spoke – the group was becoming attuned to the bush and no longer needed to be told to keep things down. Well, most of them anyway. Jasper still lacked bush sense and his passing interest in plants had turned into an obsession.

'Hey, check this!' he semi-shouted.

The group froze, expecting to see an elephant cow charging from behind a thicket. Instead, Jasper sat down on the ground and stared at what looked like a fibrous sausage sticking out of the hard soil. He was completely oblivious to anything else.

'Jasper, keep your voice down – we cannot hear anything murderous if you keep yelling at us,' I said.

'But what *is* this?' he asked.

'It's called a baboon's tail,' I replied. '*Xerophyta retinervis.*' I really wanted to get on, but Jasper was so fascinated by the bizarre plant that I figured we'd better spend a bit of time with it. 'It produces leaves and pretty mauve flowers as soon as the soil is wet, no matter what the season.'

We continued our walk as the sun began to warm our backs. Then we found a lioness track crossing east over the game path. Slumber went forward a few metres and then came back.

'It is a pride,' he said. 'About four, maybe more. They are hunting.'

A ripple of excitement touched the group.

'Are we going to track them?' Jerome lifted his eyes from where he'd been examining Franci's well-muscled calf.

'How fresh do you think these tracks are?' I asked the group.

Donald squatted on his haunches to examine them.

'Late last night,' he said. 'The wind was blowing at sunset, and these haven't been disturbed by wind.' He took a step forward. 'A dove walked on this one, so it was well before first light.'

I looked at Slumber, who nodded.

'What can we tell about their behaviour?' I asked. I was met with blank stares, then Donald's face lit up, as much as this was possible.

'They were hunting. Lions like to use paths and often walk in a straight line – these lionesses are spread apart.'

'Indeed,' I replied. 'Let's go and find them.'

The game drives were just starting to move out of camp, but I decided not to call in the tracks. The vultures on the ranging team would just speed around and ruin our chances of finding the pride on foot.

We headed east on the tracks – tough going because the ground was hard and dry, and the cats weren't walking in a straight line. Ten minutes later we picked up the very obvious tracks of a large buffalo herd heading south, the lion pugmarks on top of the buffalo hooves. One of the lions had stepped neatly into the middle of a wet buffalo pattie and the trainees examined the footprint in the dung.

'So cool!' said Katie.

'What's happening here?' I whispered.

'Lions picked up the buff way back. Now they're tracking them.' Donald pointed at a cat track amongst the buffalo. 'They've turned south.'

'Were the buffalos running?' asked Katie.

'No,' said Slumber.

'Maybe the lions were not yet close enough?' Katie asked.

Slumber nodded.

Everyone was whispering now. I gave a thumbs-up and we continued, losing the lion tracks many times but our guess that they were following the buffalo was vindicated each time we picked up a lioness print amongst the herd.

We continued for half an hour in silence, Slumber in front, me just behind him. I asked Solomon to walk at the back because if we did bump into the lions, I reckoned he would stand firm and catch Jasper if (when) he tried to flee.

Then something changed. The tracks of the buffalo suddenly spread out in all directions, and each footprint became less distinct, almost twisted. The ground was noticeably more churned up. Slumber looked at me and raised his eyebrows. I turned to the group, all of whom had noticed the change.

'Now they run,' said Solomon.

The lion tracks, however, disappeared. The pride had obviously given chase, but in the ensuing panic the buffalo and lions had stampeded in all directions. Situations like that require patience – and define a good tracker. I was no great tracker – I was too impatient. Slumber, I realised that day, would become a master of his craft.

'Walk circle,' he said. 'Find more lion nkondzo.' He was already doing this. Katie wisely joined him. Jerome stood around looking at the sun reflecting off his bicep while Jasper examined a scraggly shrub that a fleeing buffalo had eviscerated.

'Here,' said Donald. There was almost excitement in his voice. 'Two of them, I think, went this way.' He pointed towards a shallow drainage line fringed with thick bush. The excited 'trackers' forgot themselves entirely and headed off in a broad front.

'Hey!' I hissed and they stopped. 'What do you think is going to happen if you lot blunder into a wounded bull?' Suddenly, the impenetrable thicket of spike-thorn and guarri looked a bit more intimidating. 'Get behind the rifle and absolutely no talking as we go through the thicket – this is the perfect spot for an old bull to be lurking.'

We slowly edged forward on the lionesses' tracks. I thought it unlikely that the cats were close – we would have heard them if they were squabbling over a carcass. Belying his name, Slumber was hyper-alert, each footstep carefully placed so as to minimise noise. His eyes darted from side to side, peering into the thick bush.

A firefinch alarmed from the thicket. We stopped to listen. And then moved gingerly on.

Then all hell broke loose.

A covey of four crested francolins exploded from the dry grass at the base of a spike-thorn bush. They screeched, panicked wings flapping against the vegetation. If you are not used to this, the sound is so ear-splitting and sudden that you'd be forgiven for thinking Armageddon had arrived. The trainees, all bar Donald, leapt back a few paces and simultaneously swore.

'Fucking hell!' Jasper.

'Oh my God!' Katie.

'Christ!' Franci.

'Eish, jirre, fok!' Solomon.

I'm not sure what Jerome said but his reaction was something to behold. He hit the deck like he'd just been sniped from behind and covered his head. The ensuing silence was broken by Slumber, who doubled over, hands slapping his knees until he looked like he might join Jerome in the dust. Donald almost cracked a smile.

'Jerome,' I addressed the prostrate figure as he began to roll over, 'can you talk me through your plan there?'

He stood. 'Getting a good angle on the threat,' he replied, brushing dirt from his jodhpurs.

'Sure, pal,' said Franci.

'I was!' he almost shouted. 'Um ... gets you out of the threat's view field. Ja, you don't wanna be in a buffalo's view field.'

'I have never heard the term "view field" before,' said Franci.

'Ja, well, I read it in a book.' Jerome looked triumphant.

'Throw that book away,' I said, knowing he was talking absolute cods. 'Next time stand up straight and look at me – I'll tell you what to do.'

Slumber had recovered and we proceeded with caution, easing through the thicket and into a shallow, dry riverbed, sand crunching under our feet. Neither buffalo nor lion had lingered in the sand; instead, they'd continued up the opposite bank into another thicket. The cat tracks were almost impossible to follow but the panicked herd had left a swathe of destroyed vegetation and churned soil in their wake.

A southern boubou called from downstream, searching for its partner. The thicket gave way to more open woodland and we happened on a game path that headed to a nearby pan.

It was there that we found evidence of violence for the first time. Slumber stopped at a little patch of wet soil, holding up his hand for us to halt. He knelt, and touched the patch, rubbing his fingers together.

'Blood,' he whispered.

There was a collective intake of excited breath behind me. Some tracks headed down the game path and others bombshelled into the surrounding woodland.

'I need not remind you of the need for complete silence now – especially you, Jasper,' I whispered. 'Either there is a wounded animal not too far away, or there is a dead one surrounded by some protective cats having an early breakfast.' I looked at Slumber.

'We check the path,' he said. 'You want to call on the radio?'

'No,' I said, 'we find and then we call it in.'

Slumber nodded.

The pan was pumped during the winter so it was a favourite for thirsty animals as the hot and dry part of the year took hold. We walked two abreast up front – me with the rifle, Slumber with his brilliant eyes. The winter landscape gave little cover on the path and the vegetation thickened slightly as we approached. Then Slumber stopped and pointed. All I saw was the sharp point of a buffalo horn just above the water level, the view largely obscured by kooboo-berry bush.

I brought the group closer so that they could see through the gap in the bushes. I also put my hand over my lips, impressing the need for silence. We'd have a better view from behind the fallen apple-leaf tree to the left so I signed to the group that we would move there to take a closer look. We retreated ten metres or so, crept left and then reapproached the pan from behind a screen of bush until we were tucked up behind the apple-leaf.

The buffalo bull was lying half in and half out of the water, his back to us. The source of the blood on the path was immediately apparent: there were three horrendous gashes across his back, the blood beginning to congeal in the fur around them, an enthusiastic swarm of flies feasting on the wound. The buffalo sighed loudly and we collectively held our breath.

'That' – I turned to whisper – 'is not an animal you want to trifle with.'

'Where the lions?' asked Jerome, looking around.

'Not here, or that bull would be in the process of becoming lion scat,' I replied.

'We go back to the path.' Slumber turned to go.

Back at the original blood patch, we waited while Slumber walked an arc then beckoned us to follow. He'd found the lion tracks, which we followed ... and followed ... and followed.

Two hours later, we were still hacking around in the woodland. We'd crossed four roads, heard the game drives moving hither and yon, possibly also looking for the lions, although I hadn't turned on the radio to find out. The sun was making its presence felt, and, in some cases, so was hunger.

I called a brief halt at a fallen marula. Solomon bent to tie his shoelaces and then removed a rusk from his backpack. Franci looked at it hungrily. He smiled, reached into his bag and took out another one. Jerome reached into his designer khaki shoulder-pack and pulled out a protein bar, the provenance of which I could not work out – perhaps Candice had ordered him a stash from town. Katie and Donald hadn't brought anything except water, which they sipped. Jasper hadn't even brought that and begged from Katie, who gave him some.

'Jasper, why didn't you bring water?' I asked.

'Bru, I dunno. I didn't think I'd need it.' He shrugged. 'Slumber didn't bring any either.'

'Slumber is young, fit and strong, but mostly he is not begging from anyone else …'

'Bru, can we go back for breakfast now?' Jasper continued, pulling an ancient digital-watch head from his pocket. 'It's nearly nine o'clock.'

'We are going to find these lions,' I replied. 'Then we'll go home for breakfast.'

We moved on, concentration waning as the heat intensified. Footfalls grew heavier and less careful. For an inexperienced tracker, it was almost impossible to fathom what Slumber was following. The birds of the midmorning lull began to call – chinspot batis, orange-breasted bush shrike, white-browed scrub robin. A bateleur soaring far to the north let out its baboon-like 'quark'.

I too was finding it hard to focus, my mind drifting. The night with Kerry … That made me think of Anna, then Arthur, Anna's surrogate father. The old man's beautiful letters to me had suddenly stopped the previous year. Eventually I received a missive from his girlfriend, Mavis, stating that the old boy had had a massive stroke and died quickly. It was dreadfully sad – my last connection to Anna severed – but he hadn't suffered, and had died at home with his beloved Mavis.

My reverie was disturbed by an unpleasant smell as we came into a clearing in the woodland. The previous season's long grass suddenly began to wave like a golden pond in a vicious wind.

I could utter one word – 'Stand!' – as a blur of lion fur whirled around us.

In the long grass we couldn't see how many there were or where they were running. The incredible volume of their angry growling added to the terrifying confusion.

'Stand still!' I shouted again, my head whirring to locate the irate cats.

Then I saw the bloodied rib of a carcass. A half-eaten buffalo cow lay in the deep shade to the side of the clearing. We'd blundered into the middle of the sleeping cats, full of meat and warming in the sun. The flailing grass resolved into four lionesses and two sub-adult males. While the latter scarpered into the woodland behind the carcass, their sisters, mothers and aunts took deep umbrage at our presence. Slumber and I, at the front of the group, had snarling lions on both sides. I hoped everyone behind me would stand their ground.

'Hey!' we both shouted. 'Voetsek!' (This word has a universal meaning that even animals seem to understand.)

'Shoot a warning!' yelled Jerome.

I hadn't even raised the rifle – in the confusion of grass and lions, it would have been impossible to know where to shoot.

'Just stand still!' I yelled again. Shouting at the trainees hopefully had the double effect of stilling them and getting the lions to back off (their English not being up to much).

Slumber and I instinctively stood back to back, which negated the need for my turning side to side. The less movement the better at that point.

'Shoot!' Jerome shouted again.

I stole a look and saw all eyes on me and not on the lions. Solomon stood at the back of the group, his hands on Jerome's shoulders just in front of him. Franci, Katie and Jasper just stared wide-eyed and pale-faced while Donald looked on, registering but mild concern.

We stood rooted while the cats – arranged like a flower, with our group as the stem – growled and hissed. They took turns rushing forward, slamming their front paws into the ground before retreating a few steps. We couldn't move back because at the slightest movement one or more of the cats would advance in a whir of slashing paws and tails.

Eventually, the incensed growling became a low, blood-icing rumble.

'Take one step back,' I instructed.

There was a shuffling behind me. All eyes fixed on the growling death, no one was watching where they were going. It was at that point that Jasper tripped over his own feet and dropped into the grass.

'Aaargh!'

The cats took exception and the oldest lioness – one eye milky from an old injury – advanced two steps, her growl becoming a deafening grate.

'Aaargh!' yelled Jasper again, scrabbling and slipping, trying to stand.

'STAND STILL!' I shouted.

We all froze, but for the panicked Jasper. To be fair, it must have been enormously scary being eye level with the feline faces of doom. The other three lionesses also came on, perhaps anticipating that Jasper would perform a flanking manoeuvre and bite them in the bum or drag off their buffalo.

The scrabbling behind me continued and the growls escalated.

I lifted the rifle to my shoulder, pulled the bolt back and drove a round into the chamber.

'Fire, for fuck sake's!' shouted Jerome.

The scrabbling on the ground finally ceased – Solomon had grabbed Jasper by the collar and hauled him to his feet.

Another stalemate ensued.

'Everyone grab the belt of the person in front and take one more step back,' I said, 'and no one fucking fall over, for God's sake!'

We took one more step. The lions stood.

'And again,' I ordered.

We retreated once more, and the growling dissipated slightly.

'Again!'

And so we retreated painfully slowly out of the clearing. When we were a good 30 metres from the cats, they turned and walked back to their carcass.

'Turn around and walk – do not run – straight towards that marula tree on the crest,' I instructed.

In the shade of the tree, I unchambered the round, made the rifle safe and leant it against the trunk. It was then that I allowed myself to breathe. My head swam and I had to sit, my legs shaking. Everyone else joined me on the floor around the trunk. For a moment the only sound was that of human beings breathing heavily and a cardinal woodpecker prying away bits of bark above our heads.

'That was interesting,' said Donald, finally. This set everyone off.

'Jissus, bru, I thought we were toast.' Jasper.

'Christ, how close was that?!' Katie.

'The Lord saved us.' Jerome.

'Fuck me.' Franci. 'I seriously doubt God had anything to do with it.'

'Yoh,' said Solomon. 'I'm still shaking.'

'Eish, it was good!' said Slumber, laughing. This broke the tension somewhat and an excited gaggle of conversation broke out as everyone relived the experience. It is amazing how close proximity to death fosters solidarity.

'Why didn't you shoot at them?' Jerome asked when the sound dimmed. There was a hint of accusation in his voice.

'Which one should I have shot, Jerome?'

'I dunno, a warning or something would have made them back off.'

'I see. And what if a warning shot had precipitated an attack?'

'Then you load and shoot again!'

'Have you any idea how long it takes a lioness to cover five metres, Jerome? Let me tell you. Less than half a second. If you fire a warning shot and they decide to fuck you up – all of them – then only Superman would be fast enough to reload, aim and kill one, never mind the other three.'

The woodpecker finished his foraging and flew off.

'Well, in my humble opinion, you should have shot,' said Jerome.

'Fuck-all humble about your opinion,' said Franci.

An awkward silence ensued. I really didn't give a shit what Jerome thought.

Back at camp, however, he found fertile ground for his concerns.

That afternoon, the trainees were in their books outside the BC and I was sitting on my bed reading a book on human origins.

My study was interrupted by the phone, so I rose to answer it. But Jasper reached it first.

'Howzit,' he said, into the receiver. There was loud remonstrating on the other end. Jasper held the receiver away from ear and scowled. 'I think this is for you, bru,' he said as the torrent continued from the other end.

I put my ear to the phone.

'... and if you ever answer a Sasekile phone like that again, I'll have you up on a disciplinary!'

'Hello, String Bean,' I said.

'What? Where is Jasper? Why haven't you taught them how to answer the phone properly? What if I was a guest?'

'My lord, under what circumstances is a guest going to phone the Bat Cave?'

'That's not the point,' he shouted. 'Anyway, I need you up at the office right now. I can't believe you've started your shit again.'

'What are you talking about?'

'Just get up here in five minutes.' The phone went dead.

I considered ignoring him, but was actually quite intrigued about what could have got him in such a frothy.

On the veranda, Franci and Solomon were poring over a book together, Katie was drawing a picture of a lion skull and Jasper, against instruction, was back in the tree book. Jerome was absent.

'Jasper, I told you to focus on predators today – you can barely tell a lion from a cheetah. Put the tree book away or I'll confiscate it.'

'Come on, bru, I dig trees lank.'

'Predators, then trees.' And I departed.

Jerome's absence from the BC was explained the moment I walked into the general manager's office. String Bean had organised himself a little conference space that he called 'the round table'. He obviously had little clue as to why the original round table had been round, however. At the table were Brad, Jason, Mark, String Bean and, somewhat to my surprise, Jerome. There was one other seat at the table.

'Sit down, please,' said the Lord High Commander of the Universe.

My jaw clenched as I sat. Jerome was looking at a spot in front of him.

'I really do not have time for this, Angus,' String Bean continued.

'Time for what exactly, my lord?'

'Don't call me that!' he snapped. 'For conflict resolution! I'm under tremendous pressure.'

'Well, perhaps you'd like to tell me the reason for this little gathering instead of playing your small violin,' I suggested.

SB glared at me. Jerome looked up briefly.

'We are here because there is concern that you are taking unnecessary risks in the field and undermining the culture of the ranging team,' said SB.

'Oh God,' I sighed, 'here we go.'

'This is serious!' snapped Mark. 'You can't just come in here and try change things – you not even a ranger any more! How can you be teaching this team?'

'You're quite riled up about this,' I commented. This got him going.

'Fuck you, man! You think this is a joke?'

'That's enough!' yelled String Bean. 'Angus, these guys have got legitimate concerns. Jerome says you all nearly died this morning – that you blundered into the Mapogo Pride and nearly got everyone killed.'

'And you didn't even try to call in the lions on the radio!' shouted Mark. 'We were looking for them the whole morning!'

'Now our malungus who left this morning haven't even seen lions!' Jason leapt to his feet. 'You think that's good for our reputation?'

'Jerome also says you told them never to use Shangane on the radio – only English. I mean, where do you even come from?' Mark again.

Jerome was furiously biting his nails. The silence hung as I looked out the window, suddenly exhausted after six nonstop weeks. A yellow-billed hornbill alighted on a small red ivory and peered into the glass. The peace was broken by the bird attacking his reflection. *Crack* – the beak hit the glass and everyone jumped.

'What the fu-?' String Bean. I spluttered a laugh.

'This really isn't funny, Angus.'

'Except it is,' I began. 'Judas, I mean Jerome, sorry, is qualified to buy too-small clothing and nothing else. Yet here we sit considering my actions based on his assessment. That is funny – it's also ridiculous.'

'I know a lot about the bush!' said Jerome. 'My oupa –'

'Yes, yes, yes, your oupa taught you blah blah fishcakes – fuck, if I hear that again, I swear I'll –'

'Angus!' snapped String Bean. 'You'll behave with respect at the round table!'

But I was too far gone.

'Your "Shangane" on the radio is nothing more than archaic Fanakalo – lazy at best, deeply racist at worst.'

It's amazing how an accusation like this focuses people's attention.

'We're not racist!' said Mark. 'Every lodge uses game-drive Shangane – that's how we keep each other informed and surprise our guests!'

'No, it's how you talk smack to each other and hide things from your guests because you're too incompetent to give them decent information.'

'Angus!' String Bean.

'No, my lord, this ranging team exists in the Dark Ages.'

'Stop calling me my lord!'

'Sorry, your grace.'

I thought he may have a conniption. His mouth puckered into the cat's sphincter and his ears turned bright red.

'You see what this fucking dude is like?' Jason was back on his feet. 'I say we get rid of him and let the real team train the new okes.'

'It'll take you lot till the next ice age to train six new guides,' I said.

'Now ... um ... Angus,' stammered Brad for the first time.

'That's it, everyone out!' bellowed Hugh. 'Now! All of you!'

I raised an eyebrow and rose to leave.

'Not you, Angus!'

I settled myself back down as the rest stormed out. We sat awkwardly for a while as the hornbill continued its suicidal attacks on the window.

Then String Bean spoke very quietly. 'Why must you always do this?

Why can't you just get along with people?'

'String Bean, you and PJ hired me to do a job. That's what I'm doing. You did not hire me to make friends. My crew have learnt more in six weeks than that lot of half-arsed dimwits managed to impart on Donald in seven months.'

String Bean's forehead fell to the table and he began to bang it gently. This combined with surprisingly good timing with the hornbill's efforts on the window.

Bump bump bump CRACK, bump bump bump CRACK.

'The building is a disaster,' he said at last. 'They are so far behind that I cannot see how they'll ever be done by the time the Condé Nast people come. Nicolette holds me responsible.'

I shrugged. 'Well, that is the mantle of leadership.'

'What the hell would you know about that?' he snapped, sitting up.

'I did run the ranging team for almost a year,' I offered.

'Hmph. We all know how that turned out.'

'Quite,' I replied, feeling my face flush.

The silence hung for a while, the hornbill defeated by his reflection, Hugh's forehead resting on the table.

'Those guys in the ranging team are good okes,' he said at last. 'They're a strong unit.'

'Some of them are, but your head ranger is weaker than a sponge and your so-called mentorship team are a bunch of rah-rah men's men.'

'So what? Does that make them bad – why do you have such an issue with men's men? They're my mates, man, and you're ruining that.'

'String Bean, these are crises you are going to have to deal with. You are the general manager now. The buck stops with you. I've got no time for this nonsense. Fire me if you like and get someone else to do your training. But if you think those "mates" of yours are capable of it, you're off your head.'

I walked out of the office and across the walkway to the rangers' room. Those rangers driving had departed already. Brad was the only person there, smoke rising from a cigarette in his mouth. He was typing into his computer with one finger.

'Brad.'

He looked up. 'Oh ... um ... yes, eh, hello, Angus,' he said, as if we hadn't seen each other the whole day.

'I've come to tell you that Slumber is an excellent tracker and that whatever you believe or don't about today's walk – and frankly it is only you who should have come to ask me about it if you were concerned; that is your job after all – Slumber behaved with great skill and calm.'

I walked out before he could respond.

Next I went across to the section of staff housing where Candice and Craig lived in a block of four double units surrounding a grassy court-yard. Craig was sitting on an old cane chair outside his house. The smell of marijuana filled the small space. The IT manager's head was envel-oped in a cloud of smoke as I came round the corner. He spluttered once and coughed.

'Hello, Craig. Where is Candice's room?'

'Hmmm.' He pointed his massive bat at the door next to him.

I walked in without knocking. Candice was lying on the bed, tapping something into her smartphone. Jerome was emerging from the bath-room, shirtless, doing up his pants.

'What the fuck, you can't walk in here!' shouted Candice.

'Shut up, Candice. Jerome, you'd best join me outside immediately.'

Outside, Craig had disappeared. Jerome emerged a few seconds later, not bothering to dress himself. He attempted a look of confident insolence. Candice came to the door behind him, which Jerome appar-ently misinterpreted as support instead of the morbid curiosity it was.

'I –' he began.

I cut him off.

'You just listen and don't say a damn word. Next time you have a problem with the way I do something, have the balls to come to talk to me about it. If you go snitching behind my back again to your new friends, I'll make damn sure you find yourself cutting onions with O'Reil-ly for a month.' I pointed a finger at him. 'You're a fucking spineless sal-amander, Jerome.'

I didn't wait for a response.

18

Rage stewed as I walked back towards the BC, taking the long route through the staff village. The sun was setting, and a northwesterly breeze warmed the coming dusk. The lowveld spring was on its way, although there wouldn't be proper rain for the next few months. I was walking past my old house (well, a room with a bathroom), muttering to myself, when I heard my name called.

'Hello, Angus.'

I turned to see Hayley, sitting on a director's chair. She was leaning against the wall, a glass of white wine in one hand, a book in the other. Her hair was wet and tied up loosely. She wore an oversized T-shirt and baggy track pants.

'Good evening, Hayley,' I said, looking into the knobthorn outside the room. The tree still bore scars from Mitchell's attentions – a few scraggly twigs now grew from the stump of the branch he'd removed. Remembering the old elephant made me smile. I wondered where he was.

'Why are you smiling?'

'Just memories – I used to live here,' I replied.

'Oh.'

'Bertie used to live next door.'

'Sam's there now.' On cue, the door swung open and the perfectly rounded shape of Sam Willemse emerged in a pristine chef's uniform.

'Hello, Samuel,' I said.

'Oh!' he startled. 'You. Yes, H-h-hello.' His brown cheeks were flushed from exercise or a hot shower – the latter most likely, given the cosmetic whiff that followed him. 'It's actually S-S-Samson, not Samuel.'

'My apologies,' I said.

'N-no problem.' Sam closed the door behind him. 'Y-y-you on t-t-to-night?' he asked Hayley.

'Nope. Good luck down there.'

Sam departed with a cheerful wave. The silence hung again.

'You want a glass of wine?' Hayley offered.

'I should get back to the Bat Cave,' I replied, turning to leave.

A group of fork-tailed drongos began to fight over something in the knobthorn, their darting black forms silhouetted against a sky tinged with fuchsia.

'What are those? They always make a noise around this time of day.'

'Those are fork-tailed drongos,' I said. 'How long have you been here?'

'Seven months, but we don't have a great deal of time to learn the birds.' She was slightly defensive.

'Clearly,' I responded. The drongos continued their jamboree. 'See the slightly paler one? That's a youngster. Looks like it's got something in its beak that the bigger ones want.'

'Oh,' she said, taking a sip of her wine. 'Sure you won't have a glass?'

'Oh, alright,' I replied.

She wandered inside and emerged a few seconds later with an old plastic desk chair and a glass. She placed the chair next to hers under the window and poured some wine from the bottle stashed under her chair.

'Cheers,' she said.

We clinked glasses and I took a long sip. It was just what I needed after the day and the nonstop six weeks. We sat in silence as the drongos continued their game in the branches.

When standing, Hayley was about five feet and three inches, her strawberry-blonde hair almost always tied in a loose bun, strands drift-ing down the nape of her neck. She lifted the glass to her lips again and I made note of the fact that her hands and nails were fastidiously clean. She had a round mouth with full lips that didn't have much of a dent in the top. They parted to reveal straight white teeth, although the bottom ones seemed slightly less aligned than top. I couldn't tell much about her figure beneath the shapeless outfit she wore.

'How's the training going?' she asked eventually.

'Not bad,' I said. 'Some are better than others, but they're relatively on track.'

'Even the weird surfer dude? He's not much like the other rangers here.'

'No, he's not.' I shrugged. 'Astoundingly, he's become something of a plant expert – no doubt he's hoping to find the next big floral narcotic.' She giggled.

A few minutes later, as the drongos finally flew off she said, 'And the big dude? The one that's schtoomping Candice.'

'Schtoomping?' I asked.

'Yes, schtoomping,' she said. 'It means having sex in young-speak.'

'Ah. He's doing fine,' I lied, taking another sip.

A fiery-necked nightjar called from the veggie garden near Jacob's place.

'Well, he doesn't think he's doing fine,' she added.

I looked over at her as the light from the window caught the golden liquid in her glass. I didn't know how to respond – not knowing Hayley from a bar of soap, I had no idea if she had allegiances, or where they lay. I drained my glass, thinking it best to leave. As fast as my glass emptied, the bottle came up from under Hayley's chair.

'You look like you need to relax a bit,' she said. 'Quite uptight, aren't you?'

'Probably,' I replied.

A scops owl began to call quietly in a tree behind Hayley's room. People were drifting down to the camps – butlers, barmen, chefs, scullery staff – for the evening shifts. The game drives were set to return in the next 30 minutes or so.

'Anyway,' she continued, 'I think you should know that Jerome spends quite a lot of time drinking with Mark and Jason. I pass Jason's place on the way back from the kitchen at night and they're often out there – Brad, Mark, Jason, Candice, Kelly-Anne, Jerome and sometimes a few others – sitting around a fire. I've heard your name mentioned more than once ... They invite me over for a drink if they see me. That Jason likes the ladies.'

'Why are you telling me this?' I asked.

The scops owl continued its rather mournful prrp as darkness began to gather.

She took a long sip of her drink and shrugged. 'I dunno, you just seem genuine. I also dig this place and your bro, although – jeez, no offence – he can be a bit arrogant sometimes.'

Fair comment, I thought. Silence returned, the breeze ruffling the last brave leaves hanging in the knobthorn and carrying down the subtle honey scent of its flowers – always the first tree to flower just before spring. The wine was working and I began to relax.

'Those fellows are not my best,' I said eventually.

She shrugged again. 'They're not great, but I cut them some slack. Jason's had a bit of a rough time.'

'Oh please,' I said. 'He's a private-school-educated trust-fund kid – how hard could his life be? Have you looked around you?'

'Don't get testy,' she soothed. 'He's the youngest of four brothers – and the others are all successful businessmen. Apparently, his parents see him as the family failure.'

'How the hell do you know that?'

'We had a thing at the beginning of the year.'

I rolled my eyes. 'What happened to your, um, thing?'

'Nothing much. He wanted commitment, I don't do commitment – I just like to fool around for now.' She looked at me and winked.

'I see.' I took another sip. 'Anyway, what is it you think I should know about them?'

'Just that those guys don't dig you. They reckon you shouldn't be here – they call you the Short-Shit.'

'That is imaginative!'

Hayley laughed and adjusted her wet hair. She drained her glass, picked up the bottle and held it up. 'We can't leave this to waste.'

I held out my glass and she emptied it between us.

We sat in silence as a pleasant buzz began to infuse me. I was momentarily mesmerised by the sounds of the evening village, the smell of the wood fires ... and the glow of the light that lined Hayley's neck and head. She tossed back the glass, examined it and then she looked at me from the corner of her eye.

'You got a girlfriend?'

I looked at her. 'No.'

Her eyes didn't waver. She took a deep breath. I found myself staring at the captivating space between her chin and naval, where her shirt, despite its bagginess, stretched.

'You? Boyfriend ... or girlfriend.'

'I told you, I like to fool around,' she replied. 'I like a fluid situation.'

She placed her glass down on the floor and stood. She put her hands on her hips and stretched again. Our drink was over, so I stood too, heart racing slightly. Hayley walked in through her door and leant over to place the wine glasses on a low stool. Her shirt lifted slightly to reveal a floral tattoo on the base of her back. She stood, removed her hairband and shook her hair free, curls cascading down her back.

'Are you coming in?' she asked, turning to face me.

I considered her standing there for a few seconds, took two steps forward and closed the door.

About three hours later I arrived at the BC attempting leopard stealth, a task made difficult by the darkness, the booze and a pain in my lower back – an injury from the evening's, um, vigorous activities. (I'd fallen off Hayley's bed – my old bed – onto the concrete floor.) There was no one on the veranda, so I figured I was safe.

As I stepped inside, the bathroom door opened and there stood Katie in her pyjamas, holding her wash bag. I don't think I managed a particularly effective nonchalance.

'Where've you been?' she asked. 'You didn't come back all afternoon.'

'Well, I ... um ... I'm glad you all missed me,' I said.

'Why you so flustered?' She frowned.

'Oh, just lots on my mind with the upcoming unarmed walks – and you startled me.'

Katie looked at me, deadpan.

'Go to bed,' I said and walked into my room.

19

I woke feeling rather good – in a 'I came right last night' kind of way. Hayley was refreshingly uncomplicated. While a repeat performance would no doubt be enjoyable, I had no desire for anything more serious than that.

I wandered onto the veranda to find three of the trainees packed for a day out and the other three with their books in front of them – except for Jerome, who was examining his meaty forearm. Solomon, Donald and Franci were about to begin the biggest challenge of their training to date.

In my first few months in the wild, the unarmed walks had proved a profound experience. I'd seen lions, elephants and buffalo, and learnt how human beings fit into the wilderness. As the head ranger, the few people I'd trained had completed their walks without incident, although I'd been in a state of abject fear that they'd not return – horrific images of dismembered trainees haunting my thoughts.

Now, all six would have to get through the walks – three at a time, all on different routes. I wasn't particularly afraid of how these three would get on. Donald had experience, was unflappable (or depressed?) and would barely register an emotion when faced with death by the horns of a buffalo. Solomon was so imbued with a love of nature that I reckoned he'd figure his place in the wild quickly. As far as Franci was concerned, I was more worried for the safety of the animals she'd encounter than hers.

Jerome seemed to be in two minds about the whole affair. He was put out by the fact that he wasn't being sent out first but, as I'd heard on the post-coital pillow the evening before, most of the current crop had not done the unarmed walks. Hayley described how Jason and Mark had pontificated around their fire one evening that the walks were an accident waiting to happen and should be banned immediately. Thus far, SB had not seen fit to step in and tell me they were right.

Equipped with a map (GPS drawn as opposed to the cartoon I'd been given), a first-aid kit (brand new) and a fully charged radio each, the three of them set off just after dawn with instructions to radio in when they reached three waypoints.

I took the other three trainees out into the field for some intensive game-drive training.

Jerome was becoming more of a pain in the arse by the second. His general attitude around the BC and on training drives was monosyllabic and when asked to use the radio, he was torn between doing what I'd told him and using the idiotic Fanakalo the rest of the guides (except Jeff) used. That morning, about ten minutes out of camp, Katie spotted a male leopard in a tree just off the road. He'd just murdered an impala ewe and hung her in a leafless marula.

Jerome was driving. He positioned the car and took out his camera.

'Jerome,' I said, 'call in the sighting before you start blazing away with that thing.'

Wordlessly, he picked up the radio and then thought about what he was going to say. 'Stations,' he began, 'I have located a madoda ingwe with a mala bamba in a marula shlashla on River Road South.'

Apart from the Fanakalo, the implication was that he had tracked and found the leopard.

'What did you locate, bru?' This was Jasper, sitting in the back seat peering at the feeding leopard through an ancient pair of binoculars I'd managed to find in a storeroom. 'This dude was just chilling here when we came along.'

Jerome shrugged. Katie sighed and looked at me. I sat there grinding my teeth as the radio went wild with excitement.

'Where's that madoda?' Jason.

'River Road South,' replied Jerome.

'What's he doing?' Sean this time.

Jerome looked quickly at me and then at the cat. 'He's phuzaring the bamba.'

This was too much.

'Get out of the driver's seat now,' I instructed. 'Get into the back.'

'This is *my* sighting!' he objected.

'Not any more. You can't speak on the radio so get in the back now. Katie, you take over.' I was spitting mad.

Jerome packed his vast camera into its bag and climbed out of the driver's seat. Katie swapped into the front as the incessant radio babble continued.

'Okes, where's that ingwe? My malungus need ingwe shteam.' This was the only current lady ranger, Jackie.

Katie looked at me and I nodded.

'The animal is on South River Road, static in a marula tree' – she thought for a second – 'a hundred metres west of the junction with Jake's Road.' The change of voice created mayhem among the collective idiocy.

'Is there *another* ingwe on South River Road?' Mark.

'Negative, one ... leopard,' said Katie.

'Where's Jerome's ingwe?' Jason, now irritated.

'It's the same animal. I have taken over the sighting,' said Katie, turning red.

Jasper was chortling away in the back seat.

'Okes get so wound up here,' he observed.

For the first time, I looked at Jasper with something approaching respect. He'd understood a basic tenet of being a ranger in the bush (one that I frequently forgot): to infuse guests with a sense of wonder for the wild rather than racing around trying to show them the bloody Big Five.

Eventually, Jackie arrived with her guests. She looked palpably relieved when she saw the leopard still in his tree, nonchalantly plucking the hairs from the deceased antelope's belly.

'Let's get out of here,' I said, and we departed.

We were sitting at breakfast a bit later when the radio crackled to life for the 10h00 check-in. Franci, Solomon and Donald were fine and proceeding without incident. Then Bradley came in over the airwaves.

'Um, Angus, come back in, please.'

'Go,' I said.

'Um, could you and the, eh, new rangers well the, um' – there was some shouting in the background – 'that is to say the *trainees* ... come to the, eh, rangers' meeting at ten thirty, please.'

This was a new one, and I could guess the reason.

'Copy,' I replied.

We walked into the rangers' room at exactly 10h30. All the rangers and trackers were there, lounging about. The so-called mentors sat together on the sofas – Mark, Jason and Johnno. Jabu and Sipho sat next to them, looking bored, while the younger guys stood or leant on the furniture. Jeff was seated on a wooden stool, reading an *Africa Geographic* magazine, his lips moving slowly as his less-than-speedy brain tried to absorb the information. Last in the door was Jackie. Jeff noticed immediately, stood and offered her his stool. The others didn't move. She declined and leant against the rifle safe, pulling out a phone from her breast pocket.

Brad was at his desk, ubiquitous cigarette hanging from his mouth. Eventually, he turned his seat.

'Oh.' He seemed surprised that the room was full. 'Well, um, hi, everyone ... eh, thanks for, um, coming.' Ash fell from his cigarette to the ground, but he didn't appear to notice. 'Basically, just, uh, usual, um ... stuff this week.' He went through a few things related to guest requests, upcoming leave and general rules at a pace so slow I found it difficult not to tear out my hair. It was the same old waffle from every rangers' meeting since the dawn of safari.

I looked around the room at bored faces, no one paying particular attention except Jeff, of course, who was diligently taking notes.

'... then, um, we need to, eh, chat about the, um ... radio procedures.'

Radio procedures have also been spoken of at every rangers' meeting in ecotourism history.

'Jason is, eh, going to remind us of, um ... the, eh, procedures.'

'Okes, we've been through this stuff before,' began Jason, 'so get it right. Especially you trainees.' He mouthed off for a while about the need for accuracy and listening to the radio at all times. 'We've discussed using Shangane on the radio a hundred times,' he continued. 'We agreed to do it, so do it – again, especially the trainees and you, Jeff.'

It was interesting watching Jabu and Sipho's reaction to this. Highly experienced veterans, they had never been elevated to leadership positions. Jabu had been asked to lead the team at various times but had steadfastly refused, while Sipho had done some training but always asked to return to driving guests because he detested admin. Sifiso, the only other black man on the team and one of the youngest, was on leave.

The two veterans stared forward, looking pained – they were both men who abhorred conflict as a rule. I said nothing.

The meeting was then opened to the floor and after people had aired various grievances about nothing useful whatsoever, the meeting broke up.

I headed out into the fresh air and wandered to the office section to say hello to Bertie. He wasn't at his desk. Craig was in his section, a giant packet of disgusting orange chips open next to his keyboard. He must have recently run his hand through his head because there was a streak of fine orange powder over the top of his white Afro.

'Hello, Craig,' I said.

'Hmmm,' he replied.

'Where is Bertie?'

He took a chip from the bag and used it to point at the wall between their office and the one where SB operated.

I left and walked towards the general manager's office. Through the window, I could see SB standing at the round table opposite a man I didn't recognise. Bertie sat looking from one to the other like a tennis spectator, but I couldn't hear what was going on.

There was a door between the GM's office and the admin office where Kelly-Anne, Hilda and Candice worked. As I entered the office, I could hear muffled shouting from the other side. Candice, as ever, was on the phone and turned her back to me. Hilda looked up and grunted – by far the warmest interaction we'd ever had. Kelly-Anne scowled.

'Whadoyouwant?' She'd not forgiven me for stealing Jasper's uniform.

'Fine thanks and you?' I replied.

Hilda grunted again – if I wasn't mistaken, it was a grunt of mirth. Without looking up, she reached into a massive jar of chocolate-chip cookies and began to masticate.

'Seriously,' said Kelly-Anne, 'what do you want?'

'I want silence ... nothing more.' I walked to the interleading door and pushed my ear to it.

'... but how did you not know the foundations were going to subside on that soil?' said an exasperated SB. 'I mean, that's your job!'

'No, that is the job of a geo-technical engineer who didn't do his job,' said a deep voice with a strong South African accent. 'I cannot be blamed for his bad work.'

'But you hired the geo-geo-whatsit engineer!' SB, displeased.

'What are you doing?' Kelly-Anne shouted from her desk. 'You can't eavesdrop on management meetings!'

I waved a hand at her for silence.

'... as I said, we need to bring in another contractor – I know a guy who can fix this. It's no help blaming people ...'

'Get away from the door!' Kelly-Anne shouting.

'Shhh!' I hissed, pushing my ear closer.

'Don't you shhh me – I am the operations manager here!'

'Not *blame* anyone?!' SB exploded. 'This is human error. What are you talking about not blame anyone!'

'Please, don't get emotional. It cannot help the situation,' the deep voice said smoothly.

'Emotional? *Emotional!*' SB yelled. (I didn't need to bother pressing my ear to the door now.) 'You get out of here and get that so-called other contractor and have this issue fixed by tomorrow, do you understand me!'

'Please, I will get him in, but I cannot guarantee a timeframe. This is a complex problem – I'll see what I can do.' A few seconds later the main door opened and the big man's footsteps receded.

'I mean it!' said Kelly-Anne, coming towards me.

I turned as she lunged towards me like an angry leopardess, stopping with her face inches from mine.

'Who the *fuck* do you think you are coming in here like this, hey? You do as you are fucking told in this office!'

I gazed into her dark, cold, unmoving eyes. Her skin was perfectly smooth, but for a frown line on the bridge of her nose. She smelt vaguely of roses – a scent too old for her.

I leant very slightly forward and planted a kiss on her lips.

The reaction this precipitated was magnificent. She reeled back, tripped on the carpet edge, spun and then clattered onto Hilda's desk, sending the cookie jar crashing to the ground. Hilda lost any sense of decorum.

'What the fok, Kelly-Anne! Vat's my fokken cookies! Fokken hell!'

I figured it best not to hang around and departed for the relative sanctuary of the BC.

Just after 16h00 the three walkers returned, tired but otherwise in one piece. We had a lengthy debrief about the day's animal encounters, which had mercifully been without trauma. Solomon had seen a few buffalo as he walked along River Road, but they hadn't seen him. Donald had had to skirt around an elephant herd; he admitted that he hadn't given them a wide enough birth and a cow had seen him.

'She put her ears out and lifted her head,' he said blandly, 'so I just quickly moved away into some thicker bush and made it back to the road about 100 metres ahead of them. Should have given them more space to start with.' He remained utterly unflustered.

Franci hadn't seen any big animals but her sojourn to the central sections of the reserve had netted some plains' game: 'My highlight was sitting at Nkombe Pan watching a village weaver build his nest while I had my lunch. Could have sat there all day – it's brilliant how they manage to weave the grass together without fingers or thumbs.' She then showed us a beautiful drawing she'd made of the bird hanging on the frame of the nest. She pinned her drawing to the BC door.

To my great relief, the three first trainees finished their nine days of unarmed walks without incident. Only Franci saw a cat – she happened upon a pride of lions late one morning. The cats bombshelled out of the grass and disappeared into the woodland.

20

On the morning Jerome, Jasper and Katie headed out on their walks, I gave Franci, Solomon and Donald the day off – eight weeks into training, they were exhausted. They decided to go into town for some basic supplies – toiletries and so on.

'Please can you get me some KFC?' begged Katie just before she departed at dawn.

I nearly gagged. 'What the hell do you want that for?'

'Just need some takeaways,' she replied.

It never ceases to amaze me the things that people miss when away from what passes for civilisation.

As for me, I went in search of Bertie because I needed some help. The joys of spring had brought about an enthusiastic effort by the bat colony to augment their numbers, and their noise and copious defecation was causing more trouble than usual. I was waking every morning to the smell and feel of guano dropping onto my face where one of the foul chiroptera had drilled a hole through the asbestos – if I didn't die of a bat-borne disease, it would be asbestosis for sure.

As I went past the GM's office, Bertie and Francois – the two men able to help me – were walking in, so I followed.

'Morning, Bertie, Francois, my lord,' I said.

'Morn–' SB looked up from the round table. 'Stop calling me that! What do you want?'

'Trouble with my ceiling residents – I really think it's time you had the ceiling replaced.'

'I cannot possibly assign any resources to the Bat Cave. Have you any idea how badly this new building is going?'

'No, I have no idea how badly the new building is going – none whatsoever. I'm guessing not very well?'

'There's no way it's going to be even half ready by the time the Condé Nast people are supposed to take up residence there.'

'I take it this is a bad thing?'

'Do you think we'll win 'best hotel in the world' when the inspectors unpack their belongings onto a subsiding concrete shelf surrounded by unpainted walls, with a couple of sleeping bags tossed onto the compacted dirt floor for comfort?'

'That would certainly be a surprising victory,' I offered.

String Bean turned his attention to Francois.

'Francois, what the hell is going on down there – you're our maintenance manager, you must have *some* idea of building.'

The enormous man's beard moved about as the massive jaws stretched.

'To me, yes, well, that is a problem there by the sand,' he announced.

'What the hell does that mean?' asked SB.

Francois looked down at the table and, in the manner of South African men of all cultures, found himself unable to utter the words 'I don't know'.

'Bertie, I need you and Francois to find out what is going on down there. I am starting to think that I cannot trust Billy.'

'Who is Billy?' I asked.

'He's the bloody builder – came with a helluva CV, but I'm concerned he isn't all he's cracked up to be. Every day there's some new problem that isn't his fault. I mean, he's building a six-bed camp, not the bloody Burj al Arab.'

'What does Nicolette say?' I asked.

String Bean turned white and Francois shuddered.

'She doesn't know – she's been in the Mara for the last three weeks with PJ, and I haven't told her. I need to handle this myself.'

I looked at Bertie, who shrugged his shoulders.

'That is an extremely risky strategy,' I suggested. Hugh continued to stare at a small spot on the table in front of him. 'If it doesn't work out and you haven't told her ... When is she getting back to Sasekile?'

'Tomorrow.'

'My lord, that is not goo-'

'Yes! Fuck. I know!' He slammed his hand onto the table. 'This is not helping, and to make things worse, I had to have two of his bricklayers thrown off the property yesterday. They got drunk in the village and then one of them got amorous with Incredible.'

'With *Incredible*?' I was dumbfounded.

Bertie began to giggle and very quickly became hysterical. Hugh was not amused.

'It's not bloody funny! He walked into Incredible's room and tried to climb into his bed. Yesterday morning a delegation arrived from the village to demand the builder's removal. It took them an hour to finish haranguing me about the fact that this man couldn't possibly be a Shangane because, in the words of Mishak, "there are no gay Shanganes in the world".'

Bertie was howling, tears rolling down his cheeks.

'I don't give a damn about the sexual orientation of our staff or the builders. I care that the bloody camp is finished, and I cannot see how that's going to happen – and if it doesn't, that will be the end of my time here.'

'So just to be clear, you aren't going to send anyone to fix my roof?'

'No!' He slammed his fists down on the table again.

I got up to leave, but Hugh wasn't finished.

'Oh, bloody hell, Angus – I forgot to tell you, you're going to have to drive some guests this afternoon.'

I froze. 'That's not part of the deal,' I said evenly.

'Angus, between these four walls, there is a problem – Jackie thinks she's pregnant and needs to go to a doctor today. Jason assumed he was the father until Jackie informed him that Sipho could also be the father – if there is a father of anything.'

'A liberal man like Jason must have loved that,' I commented.

'Exactly – he confronted Sipho last night outside the boma. Fists flew. O'Reilly copped one while trying to separate them and had to be carted off to his bedroom. Anyway – I've suspended them both for a week, which means we're short of guides and full of guests. You are the only option ...'

I opened my mouth to object. String Bean held up his hand.

'Please, don't give me shit about this. Things are difficult enough as it is – it's just for a week.' He looked close to tears.

I sighed heavily. 'Which camp?'

'Kingfisher.'

'Oh God – you mean I must suffer guests *and* Melitha?'

He looked up at me in a deeply pained manner.

'Right, my lord, Kingfisher it is.' I turned to leave.

'Stop fucking calling me that!' he shouted as I departed.

I strolled across to the rangers' room to find out from Brad which tracker I'd be teamed with. He was out so I consulted the day's driving roster on the rangers' board. Sipho's name had been crossed out and replaced with a question mark – I assumed this was now me. But Sipho, being a superb tracker himself, had been assigned the weakest tracker in the group: the cretinous Mishak.

That afternoon, at 15h00, I presented myself at Kingfisher Camp, where Jeff, the other ranger driving out of Kingfisher, and his lover, Melitha, were excitedly chatting at the tea table. They both turned as I walked down the stairs into the main area.

'Oh, Anguth,' said Melitha, 'welcome home to Kingfisher Camp!'

'Yes, good, brilliant,' said Jeff, sloshing tea onto his saucer, where a half-eaten biscuit was forced to set sail.

'Howzit,' said Sean, the third Kingfisher ranger for the day. He was a tall blond fellow of around 24 who had apparently been a professional cricket player at one stage of his life. He was sitting on an ottoman next to the tea table, slurping from a cup.

'Quite,' I said.

'You mutht be tho exthited to be guiding again!' said Melitha, having clearly learnt nothing about my personality in all the time we'd known each other.

'Um, yes, can't wait,' I said, helping myself to a cup of coffee and choc-chip biscuit.

'Where you gonna drive this afternoon?' asked Jeff, before sucking the soggy biscuit off his saucer.

'As far from everyone else as I possibly can,' I replied.

'Oh.' Jeff nodded as if I'd just revealed a great profundity.

I leant against the deck railing, close to the ottoman where Sean was slouched. As I was about to sip my coffee, the most terrific smell assailed my nostrils.

'Good grief,' I said, 'what the hell is that god-awful stink?'

'I can't smell anything,' said Sean, taking a pack of Marlboros from his top-left breast pocket.

'There was a time,' I said, 'when guides carried notebooks in their top pockets.'

Sean lit up. I looked at Jeff, who was pointing not-so-subtly at Sean's feet, and then at Sean, who was wearing a pair of stylish Chelsea boots and, apparently, no socks. Presumably, the assembled company was too polite to inform him of the malodorous atmosphere his feet were creating.

'Sean,' I said.

He exhaled a long line of smoke and looked at me. 'Huh?'

'You have clearly killed your sense of smell with those things – so it is beholden on me to tell you that your feet smell like a mixture of Stilton with rotting carcass.'

'What are you talking about?' he snapped and then tossed his cigarette butt over the edge of the deck as we heard the chatter of approaching guests.

My lot consisted of a group of four recently retired Americans who lived between Florida and Wyoming, and a couple from Johannesburg.

From his physique, it was apparent that the South African man was someone who owned an exorbitantly priced mountain bike, which he would tell us about within the first ten minutes of acquaintance. He was

around 50 years old and stood at six feet and two inches with miraculously thick dark hair. His wife, who introduced herself as Daisy, was
made up to the nines, clothed in expensive shades of khaki, dripping
with jewels. Her hair was platinum blonde and the porcelain texture
and immobility of her face suggested a substantial portion of the family
wealth was being diverted to a plastic surgeon. This made her age difficult to discern, but I guessed she was mid-forties.

The Americans were early retirees – in other words, people who'd
amassed an obscene amount of money and retired in their mid-fifties.
Something I was not, in any way, on my way to achieving.

Once they'd had their tea, I gathered them together for a bit of an
orientation and to find out what they expected to see in the great wilderness of Sasekile. Hylton Robinson, the South African, was last to join
us. We waited as he finished a loud conversation with Melitha.

'So, has the gym got a bike?' he asked as she refilled his iced coffee.
'I'm training for the Epic – coming up in a few weeks.' He was referring
to the Cape Epic cycle race, but of course assumed that everyone in the
world would know what 'the Epic' was.

And there it was, the cycling hobby had been announced.

'Well, yeth, Hylton, the thame bike you uthed the latht three timeth
you were here.' Melitha was confused by his question.

'Ah cool, lekka, gonna need to do some training while I'm here.' He
took a banana from the fruit bowl and made his way over to where the
rest of us were waiting for him. 'Howzit, everyone. I'm Hylton Robinson
with a Y.' He pronounced the Y as 'waah' and then went round the group,
shaking hands firmly and looking everyone in the eye (or 'aah', as he'd
have said).

A little later, we were out on drive, enjoying the slow cooling of the
afternoon – spring can be beastly hot. With the rains still a good few
weeks off, the bush was grey and brown so we headed for the river,
where I hoped there'd be elephants feeding in the reeds and coming
down for their afternoon drink.

'Oh, we're great birders,' announced Daisy when I asked what everyone wanted to see. She brandished a pair of 10x42 Swarovskis.

'Great', in this sense, could mean one of a few things. The Robinsons were: a) excellent birders; b) enthusiastic birders; c) thought they were excellent birders.

We drove onto the Tsessebe River bank, where I stopped the Land Rover to listen for a minute. If there were elephants about, we'd be able to hear them feeding, rumbling and moving through the riverine vegetation. Just next to us there was a gorgeous little oasis in the dry heat of the day: a little pool surrounded by reeds, too small for the hippos to befoul with their dung. The surface was littered with lily pads, and one of the lilies had flowered soft purple. Off to one side, a malachite kingfisher perched on a reed, the stalk gently swaying in the breeze. The bird somehow managed to keep his head perfectly still as his body swayed with the reed.

I was about to point out the colourful little piscivore when Hylton-with-a-waah spoke up.

'Ah, cool, pygmy kingfisher,' he announced with the confidence that comes from having people kowtow to you on a daily basis.

So the Robinsons fell into category c.

As I was about to correct him, Ashleigh Shultz of Key West spoke up: 'Where? I can't see it!'

I turned to see her flailing around with her binoculars like she was searching for an approaching Messerschmitt. Again, before I could answer:

'Just above that lily pad with the flower,' Hylton advised.

'What's a lily pad?' asked Paul Shultz.

'It's like a water-leaf-thing,' Daisy replied.

'It's a malachite kingfisher.' I finally got a word in edgeways. 'See the mauve flower in the pool, a foot up and a foot to the left you'll see a small, colourful bird pitched on a reed. It's got a bright-orange beak and a blue head.'

'Oh, I see it, I see it!' exclaimed Devereaux Benedict, also of Key West and, if his outfit and equipment were anything to go by, a substantial contributor to the local economy. As with many safari goers, he was the quintessential example of a man with all the gear and absolutely no idea.

He'd purchased himself two professional-grade camera bodies and an array of lenses.

'Gonna take me some pitchures!' he'd announced as he'd hauled himself and his massive camera bag into the back seat. There was a great shuffling as Devereaux began to affix a brand-new lens to one of his bodies.

'It's a pygmy,' said Daisy, training her Swarovskis on the bird.

'Where's a pygmy?!' Annette Benedict this time, looking alarmed. 'Are they dangerous?'

In the time-honoured tradition of guests hailing from the United States, Mrs Benedict heard nothing unless she was directly addressed – and even then there was a 50 per cent chance the answer to her query wouldn't penetrate and she'd ask precisely the same question a few minutes later. In this case, she had no idea we were talking about a bird and began to scan the undergrowth for a band of very small humans.

'You don't git pygmies here, do ya?' Paul Shultz. 'They's extinct.'

'I can't see the bird!' Devereaux was pointing his camera in the general direction of the world's most patient kingfisher (malachite). Unfortunately, he had affixed a 14–24 millimetre lens onto the front of it and the bird was a good 30 metres away.

I was getting testy. 'There are no pygmies!'

'Don't pygmies eat people?' Annette, red-faced in the heat, alarmed and confused.

'No, that's Brazil,' said Paul.

'It's a kingfisher!' said Hylton.

'D'ya get Brazils here?' Annette was now consumed with the threat of cannibals.

'A *pygmy* kingfisher!' said Daisy, irritated that no one was listening to her or Hylton-with-a-waah.

'I still can't see the damn bird!' Devereaux was using a fisheye now.

'No, you get Africans here!' said Paul.

'Oh, okay. Do *they* eat people?' Annette was sweating.

I put my head onto the steering wheel and exhaled loudly, remembering why I had given up guiding. The mindless drivel escalated in volume until I could take it no longer. I stamped on the floorboard, turned around and stood on the driver's seat.

'Ladies and gentlemen!' The bird mercifully took flight. 'Your attention please!'

Debates about cannibals, cameras and kingfishers came to an end and twelve eyes focused on me.

'Firstly, there are no man-eating humans out here of any stature or ethnic origin. Secondly,' I took up my bird book and paged to the kingfishers, 'that was a malachite kingfisher we were looking at – easily confused with a pygmy, but that bird had no purple about the ears and it was fishing. Pygmy kingfishers are normally found away from water and they do not eat fish.' I sat back down and started the engine. 'Let us move along and see what else we can find.'

'Still think it was a pygmy,' muttered Hylton.

A while later, I spotted a leopard splayed out on the rocks in the middle of the river, shaded by a small matumi tree. As a courtesy, I first told Mishak in Shangane.

'Leopard!' he shouted, pointing triumphantly at the reclining cat and grinning at the guests.

'Brilliant spotting – they have such good eyes!' said Daisy.

'Oh my gaad!' said Ashleigh. 'Is it dangerous?'

'No, leopards are chilled here,' advised Hylton. He was looking with his Swarovskis but obviously hadn't seen the cat yet.

'Devereaux,' I said, 'I am no expert, but I'd suggest you take out the longest piece of glass you have in that bag of yours – this will have the effect of bringing the subject of your photograph close enough for you to see it.'

'Hmmm,' he grunted, scuffling about until a lens the size of a Howitzer emerged. 'Like this?' he asked. He looked at the top of the lens. 'This one says 600 millimetres and F4. Ya think that'll work?'

'I suspect it will work very nicely,' I replied.

'It's so goddam heavy!' he complained as the mighty thing smacked onto the seat frame. He aimed it in the direction of the leopard. 'I still can't see shit!' Devereaux was becoming frustrated.

'Again, I am no expert,' I offered, 'but I think you'll find it easier to capture images without the lens cap affixed to the lens.'

He scowled at me. There was some more expensive-sounding banging as the lens was withdrawn to a point where Devereaux could reach the front. He removed the cap.

'Oh my!' he exclaimed as, finally, an image of African fauna appeared in his viewfinder. 'A jagwaar!'

'Oh God,' I muttered.

The afternoon progressed relatively pleasantly from there – the comatose state of the leopard meant that everyone had time to bicker, ask their questions, ignore the answers, re-ask their questions, take appalling photographs and, in the case of the Robinsons, mouth off about their Sasekile knowledge while hinting that Nicolette Hogan was their very best friend in the world. Pretty standard stuff for South African guests.

I called in the sighting on the radio and Jeff joined us briefly but left after a few minutes – he was driving a family with three ill-disciplined, sugar-saturated under-twelves. Sean, no doubt wildly concerned that his guests wouldn't see what their camp mates were seeing, hared in a few minutes after that.

He approached with the speed of a rally driver, bringing his Land Rover to a halt in a cloud of dust. There was a loud clang as a guest's bag full of accoutrements slid off the seat and onto the floor. Oblivious, Sean rose on his seat to sit on the dashboard. He pulled a massive knife from the scabbard on his belt and pointed the blade at the sleeping cat.

'There, in the shade there, is a leopard,' he announced at the volume of a nineteenth-century newspaper peddler. 'She's resting in the shade because it's hot.'

Such insight.

Sean wasn't wearing a hat, despite the heat – I can only assume it was to preserve his perfectly kept hairstyle. It looked something like Keith Urban's – straightened with highlights in the manner of an expensive 'shaggy surfer'. He carefully adjusted it with a glance at the side mirror of the Land Rover. Then he addressed his tracker, a tiny, irritable man by the name of Zub Zub (an onomatopoeic moniker he'd gained from his habit of blowing bubbles into his beer when drunk).

'Yini lo ingwee, mfo?' Sean asked quietly. [What this leopard, brother?]

Zub Zub sighed audibly. 'Shadow, five-five spot pattern,' he said, clearly not feeling as brotherly as the preening ranger.

'This leopard is called Shadow,' Sean announced to his guests. 'She's eight years old, has had four cubs and is a great hunter. Her father is the Sharp Rock tomcat and her mother is called Sasha.'

He yelled all this in the time it took his guests to find their binoculars and train them on the cat. There was no attempt to build any kind of atmosphere of wonder.

'I've seen her on foot a few times. She can be a bit aggro!' he chuckled, eyeing the attractive young woman in the back seat.

After ten minutes, Sean departed in another cloud of dust, at least two of his guests still observing the cat with their binoculars. The noise of his departure made the leopard briefly lift her head, and Devereaux fired his camera like a machine gunner.

After an hour or so, with the sun setting behind her, the leopard stood, stretched and came out of the shade. She sauntered down the rock, the red-faced cisticolas in the reeds nearby setting up an alarmed chorus. She strolled to the water's edge and began to drink. I moved the vehicle slightly so that Devereaux could bring his Howitzer to bear, the leopard gorgeously backlit by the departing sun. It was a magical scene that I thought would be best enjoyed with a background of evening birdsong and the gentle lapping of water from the river.

'Leopards don't akshilly have to drink,' announced Daisy.

'Ja,' agreed Hylton. 'We seen them in the desert at Tswalu and they don't need water.'

Guests usually pick up on the guide's energy so I whispered, 'Everyone, just listen to the birds calling, and the sound of the leopard drinking – that's a white-browed robin-chat over there.' I pointed towards a tangle of greenery on the bank from which the bird was piping an evening concert.

'Ah can't see the jagwaar no more!' said Devereaux, still fighting with his camera.

It was getting dark and I seriously doubted he had any idea how to adjust his settings for this.

'Haven't you got a spotlight?' asked Hylton.

'I do,' I replied, becoming testy, 'but we've had such a great sighting that I don't think we need to light her up like she's about to face a fast bowler at the Wanderers. She's a nocturnal animal, after all – she likes the dark.'

'Mark used a spotlight last time we were here,' said Daisy.

'Mark also smokes 20 a day. That doesn't make it a good idea,' I retorted.

The leopardess stood, stretched and then melted off across the river. (Devereaux failed to take a photo.)

'Goddammit! I didn't git her yawnin!' said the photographer.

Once back at camp, I rushed to the BC to make sure the walkers had returned safely, which they had. Jasper had seen a buffalo in the riverbed.

'Bru, I was bricking it for a while, hey – I hid behind a *Euclea natalensis* for about an hour, just breathing. After that I was still bricking for most of the day but I made it okay. Feel like I really need a drink.'

'That's fine,' I said. 'You'll find comfort or you won't – that's what you're there to discover. That's why this is the greatest test of your training.'

Jerome scoffed. 'I saw an elie – but he was far off. Hoping for some more action tomorrow.'

'Jerome, I remind you that the purpose of your walks is not to seek out "action", as you put it – it is to avoid any kind of encounter with potentially dangerous animals. Is that clear?'

Jerome shrugged. The closer he came to the end of his training, the more he was aligning himself with the senior rangers. In other words, the less credence he gave to anything I said.

The Hoedspruit travellers had also returned. They were thoroughly drunk, sitting around a fire in the middle of their tent camp, chatting away. I didn't mind hugely, given that they appeared to have become inebriated once home. Jerome thought it thoroughly unfair.

'Why these guys allowed to have a bender while we out there risking our lives?' he moaned as I threw my game-drive bag onto my bed.

He was standing at the bathroom door and I pushed past him so that I could go to wash my face.

'Because, Jerome, they've finished their walks.' I looked at myself in the blotchy mirror. A rather haggard visage returned my gaze – not very surprising after eight weeks of nonstop training.

'Ja, but I didn't choose to be in the second group – I should have been in the first.'

'Why is that?'

'Because I've got more experience than them – I've been going to the bush since I could walk.'

'Jerome, do you think I influenced the random hat draw we had?' I pushed past him again – he was oblivious to my personal space.

'Well, it sucks.'

'I don't give a shit. Stop whining and get on with it. You can have a drink in nine days' time.'

The very last thing in the universe I felt like was dinner with the Robinsons, Shultzes and Benedicts. Worse, Melitha had, as they were climbing off the Land Rover, suggested I bring down my guitar and play them a song or two post dinner. I very nearly threw myself off the deck into the lethal horns of a buffalo grazing nearby.

I began to drink heavily as soon as I arrived at the camp, the task made easier by a new butler called Hanyani who, inexplicably, had been sent to work under Melitha's tutelage. He was a teetotaller (actually, a Fanta Orange-totaller) and had no concept of what constituted an acceptable measure of Scotch.

'Good evening. Welcome to Kingfisher Camp,' he intoned seriously as I walked onto the deck with my guitar.

'Hanyani, you do know that I work here?' I scowled at him. 'There is no need to welcome me to the deck – it's like welcoming a slave to the salt mines.'

He was an enormous young man, with a gentle face and nervous eyes that regarded me blankly.

'How about a drink?' I suggested.

'Yes!' he said. 'What you like to drink?'

'A Scotch please.' This flummoxed him. 'Whisky,' I clarified.

He departed for the bar and I went to the scullery to put down my guitar. Hayley was in the kitchen with Rufina and they were chatting away as various bits of the gourmet meal sent up delicious fragrances.

I hadn't seen much of Hayley since our, ahem, encounter in her room ten nights past. She'd been on leave and, frankly, I hadn't had the time.

'Evening, chefs,' I said.

They both looked up and smiled. 'Riperile,' said Rufina.

'Hello, trainer,' said Hayley. She'd not seemed in the least affected by our interaction. I'd been slightly afraid that she might expect some sort of relationship or, worse, talk about what had happened. Neither of these things occurred and she went back to her cooking and chatting.

Back out on deck, the guests were standing in small groups talking about the afternoon's drive. Sean was sitting on the arm of a sofa, drinking a light beer from a bottle. He was being addressed by a middle-aged German man. Sean was paying no heed; instead he was eyeing the olive legs emerging from the extremely short skirt of the man's teenaged daughter.

Hanyani arrived with my Scotch – a full glass of neat spirit with four blocks of ice. That would ease me into the evening nicely. I thanked him, took a great gulp and wandered over to the Americans, who were crowded around Devereaux and his camera – he still had the massive lens attached to it.

'Here – now if I just push this here button, we should be able to see that jagwaar drinkin.' Nothing appeared on the screen. 'This goddam thing!' he snapped. He had a pair of reading glasses perched on the end of his nose, sweat glistening on his brow, his turkeyesque jowls wobbling with frustration.

I took another gulp and waded in.

'Devereaux, if I might ...' I took the camera without waiting for an answer, looked at the back, pushed a button and a blurry, overexposed photo appeared on the screen. It could have been the leopard, but it was difficult to say. I scrolled through the collection of what could only be described as abstract images. Eventually I found one of the leopard that was in relative focus. Alas, it was only half the animal, it's front half somewhere left of the frame. I sighed and handed the machine back to its owner.

My Scotch was finished.

At dinner, I didn't have to say much as Hylton-with-a-waah held forth about various subjects in which he considered himself an expert. Daisy discussed her jewellery with Annette, who seemed keen to buy some 'real African daahmnds'. There was no actual conversation amongst the men. It was amazing to behold. Hylton would finish a story and then Devereaux or Paul would tell one, utterly unrelated.

Hanyani kept my glass full throughout the meal.

By the time pudding came around, the room was reeling somewhat. Melitha then took it upon herself to announce a 'conthert with Anguth, the Jimmy Hendrikth of Thathekile!' As she bade everyone gather on the comfortable seats, I went to the scullery to fetch my guitar.

I performed five songs, at the conclusion of which there was some polite applause. I could not tell you if I played them well or not, such was the level of my inebriation. Melitha asked for an encore but by then I was too pleased to be done. I bowed deeply, said good night and tottered out through the kitchen swing door.

As I took my guitar case off the counter in the scullery, Hayley came in from outside, removing her apron – service was done for the night.

'I didn't take you for a public performer,' she said.

'I'm not,' I slurred. 'This is Melitha's doing.'

'You had a bit to drink tonight?'

'A substantial volume.' I turned around, my guitar in hand.

'I left my torch behind. Walk me home?'

'Where's Rufina?' I asked.

'She took the golf cart back to the main kitchen.'

'I am sure I will manage to escort you,' I said.

A second later, we were standing in the dark, me fumbling for my torch. Each night, the security guards lined the pathways to the guest rooms with paraffin lanterns – a massively impractical lighting technique that looked great but was entirely ineffective for seeing murderous creatures coming out of the dark. Eventually I found my torch's on switch and was momentarily blinded as the beam shone straight into my eyes. We then proceeded, me in front and Hayley behind. The sky had clouded over, and a strong wind was up, creating an eerie atmosphere.

The security team had not seen fit to light the path that diverged from the guest one. We could have continued to the village on the golf-cart track but there was a shorter path that led past the BC. This we took instead. Even in my inebriated state I was very careful – the wind and dark made for high risk on the short section between the golf-cart track and the BC. Halfway along, a rustle in the bushes arrested our movement. Hayley, in the manner of one who has never nearly been ironed by a tusked or horned animal bent on homicide, was not paying attention. She walked into my back.

'Ow!' she said, her thigh collecting with my guitar.

'Shhh!' I hissed, scanning ahead with my torch. It was difficult to pinpoint the source of the rustle with the wind whistling in the leafless branches around us. But then there was more rustling, louder this time.

'What is it?' She was alarmed now. 'A leopard or lion?'

'No, it's something small.'

At that moment, a genet emerged onto the path in front of us. It looked up into the glare of the torchlight, completely unconcerned, an unfortunate and very dead gerbil hanging from its mouth. The genet regarded us briefly and then continued on its way.

'That's cool!' whispered Hayley.

'Forward march,' I said, and we continued down the pathway.

We were just passing the BC when there was a mighty crack of wood followed by loud trumpeting. The exact direction of breaking branches and trumpeting was difficult to discern against the gusty wind.

'That's bigger than a genet,' I said.

The noise became deafening and we instinctively moved to the cover of the BC's veranda.

'Are they angry?' Hayley whispered.

'No, they're singing Verdi's *Requiem*,' I replied. 'Yes, they're upset – I suspect there's a bull trying to have sex with one or more of the cows and they're not particularly keen. Or maybe there are two musth bulls in the herd having a fight over a cow in oestrus.'

A choking eddy of thick dust spiralled in under the veranda as the sound of elephants came closer. The roof began to creak – I had some doubt about its ability to withstand the gale.

In the end, it didn't have to. As a peel of thunder cracked overhead, a massive elephant bull's backside emerged from the darkness in reverse. I assume he was being pushed by another one, but I never found out. Instead, I dropped my guitar, swung out my right arm and pushed Hayley back towards the BC door.

'Inside quickly!'

She stumbled and then righted as the elephant's derriere clattered into the spindly veranda pillar. It provided zero resistance and collapsed, bringing down the other one. We just managed to fall inside the door before the entire edifice came down on the trestle tables, and my guitar.

'Fuck,' said Hayley, breathing heavily as we looked out.

There wasn't much to see. The veranda roof and beams had completely blocked the doorway. The elephants continued their battle, but thankfully the noise of the rending corrugated iron drove them away from the tents.

Given the excitement, the eerie wind and thunder and the half-bottle of Scotch I'd consumed, it is unsurprising that Hayley and I became enthusiastically entwined.

21

I woke at 05h50 with a pounding headache. My consciousness slowly rebooted as I came to the realisation that there was another person in my tiny, lopsided bed. On lifting the covers, I was greeted by Hayley's back tattoo, but my consideration of what species of plant it was meant to depict was disturbed by a loud banging from outside.

'Angus!' It was Katie. 'Angus, are you in there?'

The memory of the veranda destruction came back to me as I tried to sit up, pinned as I was between the wall and the sleeping chef.

'Angus!' she called again.

I rubbed my eyes.

'Yes,' I said. 'All good, you go on your walk – I'll sort all this out after game drive.'

'Okay, cool, thanks – see you later.'

'Be careful out there!' I shouted. 'Of elephants especially!'

'Morning,' Hayley stirred and mumbled.

'Good day,' I replied, squeezing my way up and out of the bed.

There were clothes everywhere. The room wheeled momentarily and waves of nausea forced me to sit back down on the end of the bed. I checked the time – just ten minutes until the guests arrived on the Kingfisher deck. After a quick cold shower and hunt for my clothes, I climbed out of the window, leaving Hayley fast asleep, the sheet rather invitingly draped about her. I shook my head – no time to be thinking what I was thinking.

The morning drive was a trial.

The sun beat enthusiastically down on us as soon as it had broken the horizon – one of those days when there is almost no colour in the sky. There wasn't a hint of moisture in the air, the previous night's cloud and wind a distant memory.

By 08h00 it was white-hot, the only breeze provided by the moving Land Rover. We found a pride of lions devouring a zebra they'd killed just before dawn, but the selfish cats had dragged it into the only shade, so we had to park out in the open to watch them.

The guests wilted under the solar assault.

'Oh my Gaad,' said Annette, her face resembling a plump plum. She seemed to be melting into the vehicle – slowly sliding off the seat. 'It's so hot – I need AC.'

'Goddam!' said Devereaux, still fighting with his camera, sweat pouring down his face as he took photo after photo of the lions fast asleep in full shade. 'Why don't they look up?'

'They're not as interested in us as we are in them,' I suggested, trying to swallow my nausea.

'Lions sleep for 16 to 20 hours of the day,' announced Hylton-with-a-waah.

He was wearing a leather safari hat and beneath this an item of clothing the function of which I still cannot fathom. There was a fashion among well-to-do male safari-goers of wearing a tasselled scarf around the neck, regardless of the temperature. Hylton was wearing what I called the 'Red Arafat' – like a colourful version of old Yasser's headdress. Next to him, his wife's face seemed to be melting off her skull.

We were home by 09h00.

I returned to the BC to find Franci, Solomon and Donald making a valiant attempt at cleaning up the elephants' mess. Somewhat miraculously, it appeared that although the case was badly scuffed and pitted, my guitar had survived the ordeal. The trainees had borrowed some tools from the conservation team and set to work detaching the mangled corrugated iron from the broken wooden struts. All three were hungover, but hard at it.

I therefore had no option but to muck in, thankful that the BC was in relative shade.

By 13h00, we had the mess cleared, the trestles up and a temporary shade cloth strung between the trees so that the university could be functional again. An hour later, I was marking written exams at the newly shaded trestles. The trees around us were just starting to get their new leaves so our little camp was bathed in a pale green hue. I looked up to find Donald peering into the trees, pen in between his lips.

'What is wrong, Donald? Has one of my avian exam questions flummoxed you?'

He looked down at me. 'No. I am contemplating the unarmed walks and whether or not someone is going to die one day.'

'You are worried about Katie?' I suggested.

There was a very slight flush to his face that said all I needed to know.

'I am concerned about all my colleagues – present and future.' He returned his attention to the bird exam he was writing.

'Sure, pal,' said Franci with a snort.

A flock of white-crested helmet shrikes flew up into branches above our heads. We watched them settle, and then returned to our tasks.

The temperature was blisteringly hot when I made my way onto the Kingfisher deck at 15h30.

Everything seemed to be wilting, the air completely still. The sulking lilies on the lounge's mantlepiece were aggrieved at having to live in a vase so far from their temperate origins and the leaves of the jackalberry mimicked Hanyani's hang-dog expression as he sweated over the tea table. A red-billed hornbill sat in the tree, staring at the deck, his wings drooping, beak wide open as his gular flap fluttered in a desperate attempt to stay cool.

Melitha and Jeff were just standing looking shell-shocked.

As I sipped a tall glass of iced coffee, looking out over the heat-zonked wilderness, I noticed a thin plume of smoke rising far over the northern horizon. It appeared to be a long way from Sasekile's northern boundary, but just to be safe I borrowed Melitha's radio and called Jacob. If there was to be fire danger, Jacob was the man to handle it.

There was no answer from the 'Spear of the Lowveld', and I remembered that he was on leave. Instead, Nhlanhla came on the radio – he whose name means 'lucky', but whose life had been anything but. He had only one eye from a nasty incident with a thorn bush six years previously, and sported only eight toes, having lost two while digging a grave for a deceased uncle after six quarts of commiserating home-brew.

'Go for Conservation Team,' he said into the radio.

I explained the evidence of combustion. He thanked me and said he'd go and have a look immediately, but that one of our northern neighbours had already reported a fire well north of their boundary. In other words, there didn't seem to be any immediate danger to Sasekile, especially with the air so still.

The guests appeared in various states of heat-induced stupefaction not long after, and we headed out on drive, the moving air something of a relief. My plan was to head to the river again and find some deep shade where we could sit and try not to expire. Instead of taking the previous afternoon's route, we crossed north over the river at a wide, sandy causeway where the late dry season had reduced the river to a trickle. West of the crossing, on the northern bank, was an ancient sycamore fig which I knew would give shade and, with luck, a view of animals coming down to drink, and perhaps a troop of baboons trying to stay cool. The tree was perched atop a steep cliff, three metres above the riverbed. The rocks near the opposite bank made pools that held water year round.

As we crested the northern bank, I cast my eye to the smoke plume on the horizon, but I couldn't see it over the vegetation and took this as a good sign.

Once under the fig tree, my plan began to play out perfectly. Dazed by the temperature, two buffalo bulls had occupied some muddy wallows on the opposite bank. A baboon troop lazily foraged in the shade below the bank, no doubt hoping we'd bugger off so that they could occupy the fig tree when dusk began to fall. We could hear elephants up and down the bank, but none was in view. Above us, in the branches, the liquid calls from a black-headed oriole combined with a small flock of green pigeons to make a beautiful soundtrack.

'I can't git a pichure of that there buffalo,' said Devereaux, clunking his 600-millimetre lens on the back of the seat frame. It was already starting to show signs of wear. This, of course, did not stop him depressing the shutter. He'd worked out how to use the rapid-fire setting and every time he aimed the camera, there was an accompanying burst of loud clicks. God knows how many shots he'd taken over the 24 hours I'd suffered him.

After ten minutes, the baboon troop reached a pool. The young ones amused themselves jumping into the water and out again in the manner of humans the same age. Baboons are not animals who mate with any sense of decorum or obvious courtship. It was hilarious watching two young males trying their luck with various females in the troop. It is beyond biology's understanding how a baboon male can find the swollen pink rear end, encrusted with the day's bowel movements, of a lady baboon attractive – but then, so is the attraction some humans feel for each other.

'Angus, what are they doin?' asked Annette as one of males stood on the heels of a female drinking from the pool and began to thrust vigorously.

'I believe they are making love,' I replied.

'Oh!' Annette covered her mouth in shock.

'Animals don't "make love",' Hylton corrected. 'They mate – they don't do it for pleasure.'

The male baboon let out a groan of ecstasy as he completed the task Hylton believed he wasn't enjoying.

'He looks like he's havin a pretty good time to me!' said Paul, giggling like a teenager.

'Paul, that's disgustin,' said Ashleigh, turning red and averting her eyes.

'Sheat, I missed it,' said the photographer.

'Oooh, here come the elephants!' said Annette, pointing in the opposite direction.

'Ja, it's a herd led by the matriarch,' said Hylton, desperately needing to give some input.

'Oh, thank Gaad for that breeze that's come up.' Annette was fanning herself and I saw that she wasn't wrong: a northwest wind was ruffling the fig leaves above.

In amongst the smell of baboon dung and dry grass was the unmistakable hint of smoke.

Then everyone turned their attention to the ten or so elephants that suddenly emerged from the riverine forest on the southern bank, making their way straight towards a small pool occupied by another buffalo bull. Charging down the bank, they were clearly in some distress, the cows herding the youngsters in front and the whole group making deafening trumpets and screams. The reason for their speed came soon after – two gargantuan bulls in musth, one in reverse, being pushed by the other. Almost certainly the same two who had obliterated the BC veranda.

Choking dust rose from around the charging pachyderms. All were heading for the pool where the buffalo, hitherto fast asleep, looked up, groggy from heat and slumber.

He couldn't see the elephants behind the reeds but his tiny buffalo brain slowly registered that his hitherto peaceful afternoon was about to change. The elephants, making for the water, burst through the reeds onto the sandy riverbed and turned for the pool. One of the cows, still in a state of defensive fury and mad with thirst, saw the buffalo and decided to take out her frustrations on him. She charged.

The alarmed bovid grunted and tried to stand, but the mud he was lying in made him sluggish. The elephant, mercifully for the buffalo, only had one short tusk on the left, otherwise she'd have impaled him. Instead, she caught him on the right flank with the top of her head and sent him flying into the rocks on the southern bank. He set to a deafening bellow, trying to right himself, hooves slipping and scraping against the rocks. The elephant came through the pool, still bent on murder. As the buffalo regained his footing, she hit him again, sending him rolling over the rocks and onto a game path behind.

Devereaux's lens sounded like an artillery barrage.

'Hotdamn, I'm gonna git me some good ones here!' he yelled.

There followed a brief moment of calm. Then the buffalo righted himself and ran off into the woodland. The elephant cow calmed down and the herd began to drink, the calves tossing water and mud about.

The developing peace was shattered by the radio. Sean had driven onto the northern boundary and seen the column of smoke. Instead of calmly calling the conservation team or reception, he just bellowed, 'Fire, fire, fayaah!' into his radio. He made no mention of where or size.

This, inevitably, created mayhem.

'Take this to channel 2, dude – only animal sightings on the game-drive channel,' said Mark.

Strictly speaking, this was correct – the idea being to keep the game-drive channel free for game-drive-related talk. Of course, once everyone on the game-drive channel heard there was a fire, they all (me included) switched to channel 2 to find out what was happening, leaving the game-drive channel with no one on it.

'Where's the fire?' Mark.

'Who's on fire?' Jeff.

'Where's the fire going, okes?' Jason.

'Jirre, fires are dangerous. My pax are scared now – must we evacuate the lodge?' Sifiso.

'Could everyone not clog the radio! We need to find out what's going on!' SB came over the airwaves sounding about as calm as a clan of enraged hyenas. With the new building slipping into the river, Nicolette none the wiser and the prospect of Sasekile going up in flames as she arrived, I could only imagine his psychological state.

As per normal in these sorts of places, Sasekile had hundreds of theoretical emergency procedures that should kick in during an emergency, but no one takes the training seriously and no one ever practises them, with the result that as soon as there is an actual problem, everyone runs about like a bunch of headless francolins. There was a loud beeping noise from the radio and no one could say or hear a thing as everyone tried to speak at once.

I turned down my radio and followed the developments while the guests enjoyed the elephants, blissfully unaware. And this is how it should have remained for them – except that Mishak also liked to carry a radio. And he thought it best to tell the guests they were in imminent danger.

'Sasekile is burning!' he shouted from the front of the vehicle.

'What's that?' asked Ashleigh in alarm.

'Nothing to worry about,' I said. 'Small fire on the northern boundary, perfectly routine for this time of the year.'

'Fires are dangerous!' said Mishak loudly.

'Are we in danger?' Annette this time. 'The fires in California kill hun'reds of people –'

'An African veld fire is a terrifying thing,' Hylton said loudly, in case anyone should think the African variety of a wildfire less virile than the American version.

'Oh my God,' said Daisy, her immobile face defying her concern. 'There was a fire on my brother-in-law's farm and it killed all the sheep.'

'I don't wanna be cooked like a sheep!' said Ashleigh.

I knelt on the driver's seat and turned to face the group.

'Please would everyone remain calm. There is no danger. There is a small fire in the north of the reserve – nothing the conversation team can't handle.' As I said this, a gust of hot wind blew across the vehicle, sending a dust devil into the river.

The elephants took fright and headed to the southern bank, leaving an eerie silence.

I looked up to the sky, which had turned hazy. Another sustained gust of hot northwest wind hit us. I wasn't overly alarmed – the conservation team was competent, although their talismanic leader, Jacob 'Spear of the Lowveld', was away. Still, this was hardly the first fire that illustrious Sasekile had dealt with.

Finally, the radio noise cleared and the general manager exploded onto the airwaves.

'For Christ's sake, could someone tell me what is going on!' he yelled.

This outburst was heard by my guests since I had, on account of the radio silence up to that point, turned my radio up.

'Oh my!' said Annette. 'He takes the Lord's name in vain!'

'Is not good!' This was Nhlanhla, de facto head firefighter. 'This fire is too big and the wind is too strong coming from northwest. Send help!'

'Everyone is driving!' shouted String Bean.

'Shit, okes.' Jason came on air. 'We better get up there to help!'

I took the gap to get onto the radio.

'String Bean, phone the three trainees in camp – they can help.' I had no idea if he heard me or not because Candice, genius of reception, had just received a call from Buffalo Plains informing us of a fire on our northern boundary.

'Hugh, Hugh, Hugh, Hugh,' she shrieked into the radio. 'Buffalo Plains says there is a fire – a *fire*!' She then forgot to release the microphone button, so we were all treated to her shouting to the rest of the office: 'Girls, there's a fire! Last time the lodge nearly burnt down – so hectic!'

'Fuck!' This was Kelly-Anne.

'Fok!' Hilda.

Then she must have let go of the microphone because String Bean came back on: 'For Christ's sakes, will you all *please* stop clogging the fucking airwaves!'

'He takes the Lord's name in vain *again*!' gasped Annette.

'Candice, I do not need to hear this from Buffalo Plains – I know there's a fucking fire because a fucking massive wall of smoke is blotting out the fucking sun!' String Bean was not handling the situation with what might be described as calm and measured leadership.

For the sake of the guests, I should have turned down the radio but I was becoming quite concerned. In theory, Brad – as head ranger – should have taken control. But Brad, inoffensive as he appeared, had the leadership skills of legless millipede. By the time he'd waffled his ponderous thoughts into the radio, we'd all be cinders. Nhlanhla, bless his holey nylon socks, had simply not been trained to take charge of a high-adrenalin situation like this.

The radio finally cleared again.

'String Bean,' I yelled into it, 'get Bertie to the fire front to control it, and tell him to take the three remaining trainees with him. Do it now!'

There was a pause.

'Copy,' said String Bean.

Bertie had worked in the conservation team for the better part of six years and although he'd been in charge of community development for a year, he was – despite a generally quiet disposition – the best qualified to handle a firefight in the absence of Jacob. He was no doubt resting after a hard day in the communities, oblivious to the fact that his house was about to burn down around him.

In the meantime, I thought I'd better go and have a look. This wasn't the ideal guest experience but Hylton-with-a-waah was excited about the prospect.

'We better go check it out, hey?' he suggested.

'What?' asked Ashleigh.

'The fire – we need to help!'

The thought of the Benedicts, the Shultzes and Daisy – in various states of decrepitude and corpulence – wielding fire-beaters as the raging inferno devoured a year's worth of exuberant grass growth was ridiculous, but I didn't argue. I put the car in gear and drove north, straight into what had developed into a gale-force northwester.

What had started out as a gentle plume of smoke was now a vast, grey, billowing wall about two kilometres wide. I prayed that Jacob had done the firebreaks surrounding the lodge well because it was going to be very, very hard to stop this one if the wind and heat continued.

I drove to the top of a small hillock that afforded a view of the northern horizon. Mishak complained loudly that we needed to get the guests back to the lodge, but this was purely so that *he* could get back – Mishak had never shown the slightest concern for another human in all the time I'd known him. I parked, jumped out of the car and shimmied to the top of a leafless marula tree.

It appeared that Mishak's assertion that 'Sasekile is burning' was, if anything, an understatement.

I'd never seen a fire like it. There was no way this wall of flame could be beaten out. The only option would be a backburn – an extremely delicate operation requiring a lot of manpower and calm coordination.

The most difficult part of lighting a backburn is stopping it jumping back over the fire break in a strong wind. Every tiny ember on the fire line has to be beaten dead so that it doesn't blow over the line and ignite the grass on the windward side, causing a second fire front and trapping the firefighters.

Nhlanhla had appeared to come to the same conclusion, but hopelessly underestimated the manpower, cool head and coordination required. From my perch on the marula limb, I could see him about 200 metres north of me, armed with just four helpers. Suddenly they fanned out along a line and I realised what they were going to attempt. My radio was back in the car.

'Mishak!' I shouted down. 'Throw me the radio quickly!'

The useless man looked up ponderously and then tossed the thing in my general direction. It smacked into a branch, split apart and fell to the ground.

'It break,' said Mishak.

I looked up in time to see flames leaping up at the feet of the four fighters. On the driving wind, I heard a shout and one of them pointed behind him. The group was suddenly obscured by flames exploding out of the grass on both sides of them. There was more shouting and the roar of a Land Rover as the group made their escape.

I needed to move my Land Rover (and guests) from harm's way, and hastily clambered down the tree

'This is not what I paid for!' said Ashleigh as I fell the last few feet, twisting my ankle.

'Ow, fu–' I stopped myself and hobbled over to the car. 'My apologies. I know this is not a traditional safari, but this fire is now out of hand. Rest assured I will not put you in any danger, but we do need to cut your game drive short.'

'Damn fire's comin'!' Devereaux in the back seat was alarmed and, worse, he was right. The ill-considered backburn – now the new fire front – was approaching with alarming speed.

And finally Bertie came over the airwaves.

'Everyone must stay off the radio,' he instructed. 'I am in charge of this fire. You only speak if there is emergency. We are going to start a backburn from Watika Clearings to the north. Everybody who is not driving a guest must come there now.'

This was just what was required. I slammed the car in gear and drove along the fire front to the first junction, and then turned south for Watika Clearings. There, Bertie was standing on the bonnet of the conservation-team Land Rover, radio in one hand, stick in the other, shouting instructions at his team. Franci, Solomon, Donald and all able-bodied members of the lodge staff were with them and began to fan out according to Bertie's instructions.

'Let's go!' Hylton leapt out of our car.

Naturally enough, no one else moved – including his wife.

Bertie came rushing over. 'We need everybody!' he said breathlessly, and I agreed.

Before I could say anything, Hylton had grabbed a fire-beater from a pile and rushed to join the line. I didn't stop him – he seemed able-bodied enough.

'String Bean,' I called into the radio.

'Go ahead,' he said. 'What the hell's going on there? I'm driving up to the airstrip now. Nicolette's plane is about to land.'

I imagined Sasekile's illustrious owner flying through a tsunami of smoke to her lodge.

'I'm going to get my guests back to camp. Most of the drives are cycling through a leopard sighting south of the river. I'm the only one in the north. I'd strongly suggest sending the rangers and trackers to help with the backburn. This is going to be a big fight.'

'No, that'll be really bad for guest feedback,' he said.

'Not nearly as bad as guests sleeping on the smouldering ruins of what used to be their five-star lodge!' I shouted into the mouthpiece. 'I'm taking my guests back – we need everyone on this thing!'

I slammed my car into gear and started for camp.

'What about Hylton?' wailed Daisy.

'Hylton will have to take his chances,' I said, fuelled by a sudden resolve to get the other guests out of the way.

But there was something bugging me as I hurried for the lodge. I couldn't quite put my finger on it until the vehicle radio crackled back to life.

'Angus, do you copy?' The voice was quavering.

My heart hit my toes.

'Katie, go to channel 3,' I instructed and flipped the radio channel.

'Angus, I'm just north of Watika Clearings and, um, I think I'm surrounded by fire.'

I stood on the brakes. She should have been back at camp or close to it – nowhere near where the fire was now raging on three fronts.

'Why are you so far behind?'

'I fell asleep under a tree, and I-I had a sore foot ...' She sounded on the verge of tears.

'What's going on? Why d'ya stop the car?' said Annette.

'Give me a second,' I snapped and then spoke into the radio again. 'Katie, where exactly are you?'

'I'm not actually sure – I'm a bit lost, but I'm on a road between the fires. I'm heading east but it looks like the fires are closing behind me and in front of me.

As a general rule, African grass fires are not as terrifying as Californian or Australian tree fires. That said, a high fuel load from good rains combined with ambient heat and a driving berg wind can make them extremely scary. There was only one road she could have been on – Vulture's Nest was a long track running parallel with the northern boundary. Without evacuation, she'd be incinerated.

'I'm coming,' I said. 'I want you to jog east – I'll be coming from that side. Stay on the road. And stay calm.'

'Copy that. Please hurry,' Katie said.

'We have to go and save someone,' I shouted at the guests as I executed a three-point turn at high speed. The howling wind kicked up dust and cinders into our faces. There was a lot of coughing and spluttering. Mishak took the opportunity to climb off his perch and hop onto the ground.

'This is not good!' he lowed at me. 'We must go back to lodge.'

'Stay here then and take your chances,' I said to him, throwing the car into gear and driving off. He'd have to walk back to the lodge on his own – or run if the backburn failed.

I drove as fast as I could. In order to try and intercept Katie, we needed to go east around the fire front, turn north and then west onto Vulture's Nest Road.

'Hold on!' I shouted, gunning the engine, dimly aware of Devereaux shouting, 'Where ya goin?' as his 600-millimetre clanged into the seat frame at the back.

'My hat!' screeched Ashleigh as I swung the wheel, and accelerated.

At the Sasekile eastern boundary, I nearly collided with a vehicle full of people from Buffalo Plains coming to help fight the fire.

'Down this road!' I pointed back the way we'd come.

Then we turned north and sped down the hill. Unfortunately for all concerned, the road crossed a dry riverbed with steep banks and two huge berms on either side for road drainage.

'You can't go down there at speed!' shouted Devereaux.

But I barely heard him. I plunged over the edge, hoping that if I didn't touch the brakes, we wouldn't flip over frontwards. Very briefly, all four tyres left the ground. Cars are not designed to fly, and just those few inches of altitude caused catastrophe in the back of the vehicle. As the tyres hit the ground, the Land Rover bounced. Everyone's backsides (mine included) left their seats. Knees and elbows cracked into seat frames and guests began to scream.

Devereaux's 600-milimetre, body attached, flew off his lap, caught him in the jaw and then fell out of the bouncing Land Rover. On the riverbed I accelerated for the opposite bank, wheels churning sand, engine screaming.

We narrowly avoided a herd of terrified elephants charging away from the fire along the riverbed and then hit the lip of the bank with a crunch. The vehicle bounced up, causing more limbs to smack into the various parts of the Land Rover.

'My bag!' Ashleigh yelped as her belongings tipped out of the vehicle.

We sped up over the relatively smooth section of the road and then the front wheels left the ground as we came up and over the berm. More wailing from the back.

'Sorry!' I yelled, as my foot kicked onto the accelerator. To the left I could see the fires: the original one streaming down the slope, enthused by the gale and the massive fuel load; the backburn creeping up into the wind. The sound of the engine, screaming guests and northwesterly in my ears was deafening.

Then the radio crackled.

'Angus, please come quick,' Katie's breathless voice filled with panic. She was running. 'The one on the slope is almost at the road, I have to off-road!'

This would make finding her extremely difficult and dangerous.

'Copy,' I said. 'I'm coming. Try to stay close to the road!'

Finally, we reached the turn to Vulture's Nest Road. The last of Devereaux's camera bags were expelled as we executed a four-wheel drift around the corner. He'd long since given up hope of saving his stuff.

The road sloped up towards the fire front and then turned parallel with it at the top of the crest. As we reached the bend, so did the fire. I had no choice but to turn off-road, hoping like hell that we'd spot Katie in the rapidly diminishing space between the two infernos.

I needed to look around me so I stopped the car, stood up on the driver's seat and peered into the smoke. The guests were coughing behind me, covering their mouths with their clothing.

I couldn't see Katie.

I turned to look behind us. The fire roared and crackled, and I had the distinct impression that the wilderness was profoundly pissed off.

'Angus!' I just heard the radio above the inferno. 'I'm on the termite mound under the big tree with the red flowers to your left.'

There she was, perched on a low termite mound beneath a boer-bean tree about 50 metres away. I dropped into the seat and gunned the engine through the block, mowing over a few small trees. As the Land Rover drew level with the mound, Katie leapt into the passenger seat, her clothes wet with sweat, face covered in black grime. I turned the car, aiming to drive through the block to where the eastern boundary met the drainage line. To my horror, I saw that this avenue was closed by the fire and a ridge of rocks over which we couldn't drive. I turned down the slope for the drainage line.

'It's too steep, you can't cross there!' shouted Katie.

I said nothing, my mind working furiously as the fire chased us towards the almost sheer bank of the narrow drainage line. We pulled up at the edge. There was no way down in the vehicle, and the fire was raging towards us on three sides. Further downstream the flames had jumped, on their way to meet the backburn.

'We're all gonna die!' moaned Paul.

Katie looked at me.

'Everyone out of the car immediately!' I shouted. They all just stared. 'Get out now or you will die!'

This galvanised them, and a few seconds later they'd all tumbled out. Ashleigh – someone who had exercised only the muscles of her jaw for at least three decades – fell to the ground and screeched: 'My leg! My leg!'

'Get into the riverbed!' I shouted. 'Hurry up!' I took Ashleigh under one arm. 'Katie, help me here!'

She took Ashleigh's other arm, the fire now so close I could feel the heat through my shirt.

'Get up!' I screamed at her. 'Now!'

Katie and I yanked and we semi-dragged her to the edge of the drainage line. The others had made it to the bottom of a steep game path, still surrounded by dry vegetation that would ignite at the slightest provocation. Paul was limping badly and Daisy's white top had torn to reveal a lacy khaki bra.

'I can't go down th–'

I had no choice but to pull Ashleigh backwards so that she sat down with a thud, then I moved to the front and pulled her legs, dragging her onto the gravelly path that led into the riverbed. Gravity did the rest.

In the riverbed, I saw our salvation to the right – a small muddy pan under a rocky overhang.

'Get into the mud,' I pointed, grabbing the arms of the now semiconscious Ashleigh and dragging her towards the pan.

With not a second to spare, we all squelched into the mud and pushed ourselves up against the rocky drainage-line wall as the flames took to the dry vegetation on the banks and overhead. We felt a tremendous heat and then there was mighty roar as the Land Rover's diesel tank exploded.

'Oh, sweet Lord!' wailed Devereaux.

Cowering in the stinking mud we pressed ourselves against the rocky overhang. I was holding one of Katie's hands and one of Ashleigh's, and we all squeezed instinctively as the tank exploded.

In five minutes, it was over.

The flames had sped off to meet the backburn. Slowly, silently everyone began to climb out of the mud. Ashleigh was pale as a ghost and in need a stiff drink and possibly a medical evacuation.

We all flopped onto the sand, looking up towards what had once been the Land Rover – aluminium, it turns out, burns rather well and our vehicle was now the only thing still flaming, surrounded by the embers of the bushfire.

'Shit dammit to hell,' said Paul, head in his hands.

Over the sound of the receding flames came the distinctive whup-whup-whup of a helicopter. I looked up into the smoke, and saw a flash of yellow. And then, just as I thought the day couldn't get any worse, a torrent of water crashed over us as the firefighting chopper lost its load (inaccurately, it must be said) onto our heads. Thankfully we didn't take the full brunt, but it was sufficient to thoroughly soak us in the evil-smelling water retrieved from a dam where hippos had been enthusiastically defecating for 35 years.

'Oh, for the love of God!' Annette finally lost patience with her Lord.

There we sat, traumatised, clothes torn, faces covered with soot, coughing up smoke, wet and smelling of hippo dung. And we had no way home.

22

Katie and I made the guests as comfortable as possible in the sand, and then I departed to find help. From a tree on the southern side of the drainage line, I could see that between the backburn and the chopper, the fire had ceased to be a danger to Sasekile or its inhabitants. There was a road a few hundred metres south of the drainage line we were sitting in and I crunched over the blackened ground, dodging bits of glowing elephant dung. The sun was setting so there were only about 30 minutes left of light.

On the road, thankfully, I met a vehicle full of firefighters on their way home, all full of joyous bonhomie post the trauma of the fight. I smiled as a memory surfaced of the fire fight during my first year in the wild. Anna and I had sat on the back seat on the way home, legs touching, irresistibly attracted to one another.

Now the group stared at my grubby, soaking, smelly visage.

'What happened to you?' asked Claire, her white massage-therapist's uniform now black.

September started to laugh, and this set off the rest of them – Mayan, Kelly-Anne, Melitha, Craig, Solomon and Franci. The only person not laughing was Mishak, who, like me, had been covered in hippo sewage.

'You leave me!' he lowed. 'You leave me – I will make a grievance complaint against you!'

'Join the queue, Mishak,' I said.

Five minutes later, another vehicle arrived into which the occupants were decanted so that I could take the first vehicle to retrieve my guests.

Fifty minutes after that we arrived back at the lodge. I had radioed ahead and there was a paramedic on hand to help Ashleigh, who was still in-communicado. Also in the car park to meet us, full of excited chat for his contribution, was Hylton-with-a-waah. As far as he was concerned, this was his best-ever safari experience.

The other guests silently climbed from the vehicle and walked back to their rooms, Ashleigh supported by a paramedic and Hanyani the butler. Paul – her husband – left them in the car park in his haste to get to the bar.

I returned to the BC to make sure the other two walkers had made it back safely. With all trainees present and accounted for, I went to shower, shave and take stock.

Some time later, I made my way back to Kingfisher Camp. I knew there was going to be shit, but was unsure as to exactly how much of it would be flying in my direction.

Quite a lot, as it turned out.

Hugh was on the deck. To say he looked harassed would be akin to describing a three-week-old corpse as looking unwell. His hair was all over the place, his shirt untucked (I'd never seen this before) and there were black bags under his eyes. A group of five angry people were yelling at him, all talking over each other in their efforts to denounce me as the most dangerous human being on God's earth.

I slunk behind the bar to observe.

'We were told to watch out for mosquitos and hippos!' shouted Devereaux. 'We didn't expect to have to defend ourselves from our driver!'

'... complete maniac ...'

'... barbecued to death while that crazy fool ...'

'... literally into the fires of hell!'

'... didn't pay for this ...'

'... goddamn near killed us!'

'If I could just –' String Bean tried to interject.

'How in the hell can he be working at a place like *this*?' This came from Paul, who was sitting with his foot up on an ottoman, sprained ankle bandaged, a livid bruise starting to form over his left eye.'

'I understand –' String Bean again failed to get a word in.

'He's insane, I tell ya! He pulled Ashleigh into that ravine like she was a sack of garbage!'

'I'll be picken gravel outta my ass for years!' said Ashleigh, having been fortified with a massive bourbon.

Out of the corner of my eye, I saw butlers Luzile and Phanuel, hitherto enjoying the sport, evacuate at tremendous speed. I looked round, and went cold.

Nicolette Hogan.

She strode through the Kingfisher Camp entrance unsmiling.

Hanyani and I shrunk behind the bar.

'Please, if you would just let me –' String Bean was becoming testy.

'We better not see that asshole again,' concluded Devereaux. 'You'll be hearin from my lawyers! All my cameras are destroyed – most of em are still out there in the jungle!'

'I am sure –' SB was cut off again.

'And another thing,' said Paul, 'what in the hell were you doin dropping six tonnes of hippo shit on us?'

In almost six years, I had never heard String Bean so much whisper anything impolite to a guest, no matter how awful they were. Now, with quite the worst timing in the world, he snapped.

'Will you all just *shuddup!*' he shouted. 'For God's sake, I know you've had a tough afternoon but so have we all, so sit down, put a cold towel around your heads and calm down to a mild panic – no one died this afternoon, and for that you should all be fucking grateful!'

It was then that String Bean felt it.

He slowly turned his head, the colour draining from his face as he beheld Nicolette glaring at him with one eye cocked. It may as well have been a cocked .45 Magnum.

'Leave the deck immediately,' she addressed him quietly.

'Eish.' Hanyani peeped from behind the bar, where he was pretending to be engrossed in glass cleaning.

String Bean didn't utter another word. He turned on his heel and walked out. Nicolette stood there for a moment, and no one spoke. Then her head turned quietly towards the bar. Catching my eye, she gave a barely perceptible shake.

'Yes, ma'am,' I said, and scuttled out from behind the bar and left via the entrance.

The last thing I heard was Hylton who, against any expectation, became my ally: 'We did save Sasekile and that girl though.'

'And you just ran into the flames!' began Daisy. 'I thought that was the end!'

'Babe, sometimes you gotta make sacrifices for the greater good.'

Outside, the wind had dropped but the smell of smoke hung in the air. At the Bat Cave, all was silent as the trainees (except Jerome) sat around reading or looking at maps for the next days' walks. Someone had found some flex with coloured bulbs in it – from some long-distant '80s New Year's party, probably – and strung them up around the veranda. It gave the place a surprisingly inviting atmosphere.

'What's happening at Kingfisher?' asked Katie.

'Oh, the usual – drinks, dinner, threats of litigation,' I replied.

Jasper was in his hammock examining a forb of some description. He looked up with mild concern.

'You in the shit?'

'Swimming in it.'

'Sorry, bru. Sounds hectic.'

'Couldn't have been helped – but I am not sure the powers that be will see it that way.' I walked inside and sat on my bed. A few seconds later, Katie came in.

'You saved me,' she said, standing awkwardly at the door.

'I should have just told you to run to the drainage line and wait there,' I said.

'I've never been so scared in my life.'

Before we could continue, the phone rang and I was about to answer it when Franci, cheery as you like, came out of the bathroom and picked it up.

'Bat Cave University,' she said into the receiver.

Then all colour drained from her face.

'Yes, of course, I'm sorry,' Franci began. 'Yes, of course ... no problem at all. My apologies once again.' She replaced the receiver and turned to me. 'That was –'

'I know,' I said.

'She says you mus–'

'I know that too.'

In the office, Nicolette was sitting at the round table, though somehow she made it look like it had a head. Arranged around her were Kelly-Anne, Mary (to take minutes), Mishak, Abednigo (the union shop steward), Brad and Hugh. The latter was staring at his hands in his lap. God, it irritated me how sorry he could feel for himself.

'Sit down,' Nicolette instructed and I complied immediately. 'I am going to give you a chance to present your case for how you behaved this afternoon. If I do not find there to be completely exceptional circumstances for' – she held up her right fist, releasing her fingers one by one as she reeled off the list – 'why all of your guests are injured, one was fighting the fire, there's a burnt Land Rover in the middle of the fire path and Sasekile is about to face a claim for camera equipment to the value of almost a million rand, then you will leave this property before midnight. Do I make myself clear?'

Kelly-Anne smirked as she fixated on a pen on the table in front of her.

'Yes, ma'am,' I said. 'It is perfectly clear.'

I then set about explaining the events of the afternoon. I managed to control my emotions – placing enormous emphasis on my fear for Katie's safety while trying to keep my guests safe. I confessed things had got slightly out of control by the time I was dragging Ashleigh down the gravel bank on her arse (but I didn't use the word 'arse').

All the while, Mishak made little grunts, desperate to have his say – utterly unconcerned for any part of the story that didn't involve him. I made a point of not mentioning him at all.

'You'd describe pulling a semiconscious guest down a gravel path and depositing her in the mud just before your Land Rover exploded as "slightly out of control"?' Nicolette looked at me, face unmoving.

I did my best to look apologetic. 'I'm not sure what else I could have done once we were surrounded by the fire.'

'What you should have done,' Nicolette took a deep breath, 'what you *should* have done was radio someone else to fetch her and then taken your guests back to the lodge.' She raised her fist slightly off the table and then knocked it down again – this was her version of a temper tantrum.

She wasn't necessarily wrong, but she also hadn't been in the teeth of the inferno. I remained silent – not about to admit to being completely in the wrong. I, unlike my brother, was not about to grovel – if she wanted to get rid of me, then so be it.

'Would anyone else like to say anything?' She looked around the table.

Mishak needed no encouragement. 'Yes! This guy left me!' He pointed at his barrel chest. 'He just left me in the bush. I could have been murdered by a lion or an elephant or a black mamba! I demand compensation!' He brought his meaty hand down like a gavel.

My experience of union representatives up to that point had not been positive. Abednigo, however, was clearly a man who'd been harassed by Mishak as often as I had, and his heart was clearly not in it when he mumbled, 'Yes, compensation,' before returning to the magazine he'd been reading when I came in.

No one else said anything so Nicolette took the floor again.

'I feel that bringing you back here was a poor idea. You're a menace to tourism and I am frankly concerned about those six trainees after your so-called training. Wherever you go, disaster follows.'

Mary typed away furiously on her laptop.

'Look,' I said, 'I am actually quite sorry about this. It's possible I overreacted this afternoon, but in the moment I think I did the right thing.'

'I don't want to hear any more from you. Brad finished with his guests this morning and is going to have to take yours for the rest of their stay – those that will not be visiting the Nelspruit Mediclinic tomorrow. We are still short, so you are going to have to take the guests he was going to drive out of ... um,' she looked at Kelly-Anne.

'Rhino Camp,' said the operations manager.

Nicolette paled. 'In case you've forgotten, Angus, that is our most exclusive camp – if I had any other options, you'd be leaving, never to set foot in this place again.'

'So, just to be clear, I shouldn't go back to have dinner with the current lot?' I thought this might lighten the mood.

Brad finally opened his mouth. 'Um, no, eh, Angus ... that would not be, um ... appropriate, eh, at all ...'

'He thinks he's being funny,' Hugh explained quietly.

'I fail to see any humour at all, Angus,' said Nicolette. 'Now get out while I deal with your brother.'

'If I could just ask, who is managing Rhino?' I asked.

'Mayan,' replied Nicolette. 'She'll take no nonsense from you, so maybe it's not all bad.'

I began to feel a little sorry for Hugh as I wandered back to the BC. After almost six years, he was still in love with Sasekile, body and soul. I hoped he wouldn't be fired. I also hoped he'd find himself a spine and not blub in front of Nicolette.

Half an hour later I was lying on my bed staring at the ceiling when SB walked into my room. His face was longer than a zebra's.

'Not good news then,' I said sitting up. I could see that he wanted to rage at me; indeed this was why he was at the BC and not at home with the fair Simone. But he was out of puff.

'No,' he said. 'She said I was obviously way out of my depth and incapable of handling the lodge. She cited the building, the handling of the fire, my shouting at the guests and "a sense of increasing entropy" in the lodge.'

'Ah.'

'I don't even know what "entropy" means.'

'Chaos, basically,' I explained.

'She said I had underestimated the task and treated it with ... how did she put it? Oh, "gobsmacking arrogance". She was incensed that I hadn't told her about the building.' He rubbed his face and exhaled loud-ly. 'I just don't fucking get it – I work harder than anyone else here for fuck sake's. Surely she can see that?'

'String Bean, Nicolette is successful because she is ruthless in her expectation of results. If you cock up, she doesn't give two hoots how hard you tried.' I felt bad for him despite his apparent inability to see how this had come to pass. 'What are you going to do?'

'She gave me two options: leave Sasekile or accept demotion to Tamboti Camp manager.'

'Ouch.'

'I don't know. Simone and I are going on leave tomorrow so I guess we'll just have to see. I need to tell her in a week.'

'Who's taking over?'

This made him swallow hard, tears brimming.

'Kelly-Anne. Nicolette is going to bounce between here and Kenya until the end of the year, but basically Kelly-Anne's in charge.'

'That is not going to be fun,' I noted.

He wanted to be angry with me, but for once his troubles weren't of my making. My brother mooched out.

23

Mayan Kholi, aged 28, hailed from Mumbai. Her parents owned a chain of hotels and lodges in the wildlife areas of India and her purpose for being at Sasekile was not the salary. Indeed, Mayan's family was so fabulously wealthy that she'd been dropped off on the airstrip by the private jet on which she'd flown out from India. Nicolette Hogan had struck up a relationship with Mayan's parents some years previously at an international luxury-tourism conference. Their daughter was at Sasekile to learn about African safaris in the hopes that she might be able to apply some of the lessons to the Indian variety.

I'd met her in passing but other than greeting across the table at the Avuxeni Eatery, I'd barely said two words to her. My information on her background came from snippets eavesdropped from various conversations and from Jeff, who was constantly imparting bits of random information – normally I came across him in the little staff gym.

Mayan's bearing was regal and aloof, and her best friend seemed to be Claire, the massage therapist. She had, as far as I could tell, the personality of razor wire.

The morning after the fire, I headed down to Rhino Camp to meet my new guests. They'd arrived late the previous evening and not yet been on a drive. Normally the camp manager would not be on deck at 05h30. Not so this morning. I presume Ms Kholi was there because she'd heard who was coming to drive her guests and wished to impress upon that person that she wasn't about to have her guests suffer the same fate as his previous lot.

I strolled onto the deck at 05h10, hoping for a quiet cup of coffee before the guests arrived. I still got pangs when I walked into Rhino Camp – the sofa was the same one on which Anna and I had shared a bottle of Luddite Shiraz on the night we first kissed. I bit my lip and made for the kitchen. In Rhino, the guests get their coffee served to them in their rooms so the ranger (just one in this case) has to help himself in the kitchen.

I poured some fresh grounds into a plunger and added some water from the HydroBoil. As I was waiting for the coffee to steep, the door to the deck swung open and in strode Mayan Kholi.

She was exquisitely turned out in a white Sasekile uniform top and tight-fitting khaki slacks. Her long black hair was tied up in an elaborate bun that defied physics, and her full lips were finely coated in dark lipstick. Diamond studs rested in each earlobe; the right ear was pierced and adorned with at least four other bits of metal. Her nose also contained a diamond stud. Our eyes met as the smell of jasmine floated to my nostrils. I began to feel a bit awkward, but she was apparently entirely at ease.

'Um, good morning,' I said, turning to the plunger and beginning to depress it.

'Good morning,' she said at last, without the hint of a smile.

'Would you like some coffee?' I offered.

'No, thank you,' she said. 'I would like to talk to you about my expectations for my guests' stay.'

'Right,' I said, pouring the coffee into a cup and taking a rusk from a jar.

She spun and walked out of the kitchen to the deck. As I came out behind her, she turned her brown eyes on me.

'I do not wish for us to get off on the wrong footing,' she began, 'but I do not expect my guests to be treated as some sort of irritation or hindrance to your enjoyment of this reserve.'

I dipped my rusk and took a bite. 'That sounds fair,' I replied.

'Your reputation as a volatile and unpredictable ranger precedes you and it is generally agreed among the camp managers that no one wants you driving out of their camps. Apart from Melissa. Obviously.'

'You have an interesting method of not getting off on the wrong foot,' I suggested.

'Further, I do not appreciate sarcasm, especially when it comes to the people paying to keep this lodge running, both in terms of the conservation of the reserve and the salaries of the people who work here.'

'Right,' I nodded.

Mayan then explained that the guests were four elderly French people who spoke little English. One woman was very frail and needed to be treated with great care. Apparently they were a family who owned a large wine operation in the Loire Valley. On cue, I heard a loud clicking sound and some French chatter. I put down my cup.

'I will introduce you,' Mayan said, leading me out into the car park.

There stood four of the most ancient Gallic ruins you could ever hope to see. One of them was using a walker, which explained the clicking. Mayan greeted them in what sounded like perfect French, and then indicated me. The four fossils smiled and nodded. The camp manager then looked at me and turned up the corners of her mouth in a smile that went nowhere near her eyes.

'Bonjour,' I said.

'Ah! Vous parlez Français!' exclaimed the one leaning heavily on his walker.

'Non, non, non!' I shook my head. '"Bonjour" is all I can say.'

They looked a saddened by this, but shrugged.

'Do not worry. We speak some Anglaise,' said an old man with a handlebar moustaches.

Using a mounting block and a lot of patience, we managed to seat the guests and set off. Mishak had refused to drive with me so Elvis and I were joyfully reunited. He chuckled away on his seat, the guests nattering to each other in French.

It was a cool, overcast morning, and the French relics seemed satisfied with simply taking in the scenery. I pointed out bits and pieces of ecology that they may or may not have understood.

Thirty minutes into the drive, I turned a corner off the river road, and trotting across a clearing in our direction came a pack of twelve wild dogs. A sighting of these animals is always fun, especially when the dogs are on the hunt. The pack had yet to find a target, but it wouldn't be long before they flushed a duiker or spooked a herd of impala – then there would be great entertainment.

'Those are wild dogs!' I said excitedly to the guests as I stopped the car. 'Very rare animals.'

All four began looking in entirely different directions – one behind us, 180 degrees from the dogs, one with her binoculars trained on the sky and the man with the walker was staring at something of interest in the bottom of the vehicle.

'There!' I pointed at the dogs. 'Look ... um ... regardez les ... um ... chiens!' I remembered the noun finally.

'Les chiens?' Jean, the man with the handlebar moustache, followed the line of my pointing finger.

'Well, more wolf than chien,' I explained.

'Où sont les chiens?' asked Marie, her binoculars flailing wildly in the vague direction of the fast-disappearing pack of hounds.

I started the engine again.

'Why you have, eh, dogs, 'ere?' asked Jean as I fought the urge to speed off-road after the pack.

'They are wild dogs – painted wolves,' I tried to explain as I turned a corner, hoping the pack would cross the road in front of us.

There was some animated French in the back and then the inevitable tap on the shoulder (which I hate profoundly).

'Why you are showing us ze dog?' asked Jean, 'We 'ave ze dogs en France.'

'Yes, I understand,' I attempted, 'but these are not normal dogs. They are wild dogs – very special. The second most endangered carnivore in Africa!'

At this point the hounds emerged onto the road in front of us – at roughly the same time as a small herd of impala appeared from the other side. I kicked the brakes (thankfully we were going slowly). The dogs immediately gave chase, the impala panicked, and one, a youngster about to reach his first birthday, dithered for slightly too long. He leapt into the air and turned but it was too late. The alpha male grabbed the loose skin on the inside of the impala's back leg and dragged him down to the road with a dull thud.

The rest of the pack were on the stricken antelope in a flash. We could do naught but watch the gory scene unfold in front of us as three hounds tore open the belly, viscera exploding in all directions. Four went for the front legs and began to pull while the rest grabbed whatever exposed bits they could. The impala made one bleat before he was entirely dismembered. There was blood, organs, limbs, intestines and bone all over the road between excitedly twittering dogs.

The scene was gruesome in the extreme – even Elvis looked away.

The noise died down as the pack retreated with their individual bits of impala. In fact, the ensuing silence became concerning. I turned to see the faces of the prehistoric French now the colour of driven snow, their mouths hanging open. All eight hands were affixed to the seat frames, knuckles white. Given my present status as the Sasekile's least-loved turd, it was tricky to see how I might convince anyone that I wasn't to blame for the brutality the ancients had just witnessed.

'Merde,' said Jean.

'Oh, mon Dieu!' exclaimed Marie, a polka-dot handkerchief over her mouth.

'Putain,' muttered Phillipe, eyes wide with horror.

Clarisse just stared, slack-jawed, and said nothing.

'I, um, am very sorry if that was difficult to see,' I said. No one paid me the slightest attention. 'Should we perhaps see if we can find something less, um, gory to look at?'

I started the engine, reversed slowly, turned and drove away as two other game-drive vehicles arrived.

'Bru, you can't leave a madush sighting before anyone else has got here!' This came from Mark with a group of six white-knuckled Americans on the back of his vehicle.

I kept driving.

Ten minutes later, I stopped on the banks of the river. A tranquil scene, it was a high point that overlooked some rocks and reeds below. Still the guests had said nothing.

'Give them drink,' Elvis said.

'Coffee?' I asked.

'No – brandy.'

'We only have Amarula for the coffee,' I hissed.

'Use that one,' he instructed.

Without asking, I walked to the back of the car, took out the little tin of Amarula miniatures, returned to my seat and handed them to guests. They each took one wordlessly, twisted off the tops and finished them in one gulp. We just sat there for a while, watching a green-backed heron standing perfectly still, fishing on the edge of a little pool. Above, a pied kingfisher hovered and occasionally plunged into the water.

The effect of the booze and the relative peace seemed to ease the tension on the back of the vehicle. Eventually, Jean tapped me on the shoulder and pointed a finger at me.

'No more, 'ow you say, sang ...' He looked confused.

'No singing?' I asked.

'Non, non, non, no more, eh, red, eh, sang ... *blood!*' He shouted as the translation came to him. 'We come to relax, eh, not, eh, for 'orrible death.'

'Oui!' agreed the others in unison.

Later that morning, I was marking tests at the trestles while the three trainees wrote yet more of them. The previous season's fallen leaves still littered the ground so it was impossible to approach the BC without being heard. So it was that we all heard the approach of light footsteps. We looked up to see the unfamiliar and slight figure of Mayan Kholi walking up the path from the kitchen.

For the first time in our brief acquaintance, it appeared that she seemed unsure of herself. The BC had that effect on people. The trainees leapt to their feet – it was a standing order that any member of the hospitality staff who arrived should be greeted warmly and offered refreshment. (I told them not to bother with the rangers, which was probably not great for their integration into the team.)

'Good morning, Mayan,' said Solomon. 'Welcome to the Bat Cave University. Can I offer you some tea, coffee or orange squash?' He grinned at her.

'Oh, good morning – um, well, no – no, thank you. I won't have anything.'

The trainees sat down and looked at her expectantly, as did I.

Her big brown eyes grew even larger as they took in the ruin of the BC and the neat little camp next to it. The silence grew slightly awkward.

'Can we help you with something?' I asked, eventually.

'No, I just came to say that the guests were traumatised by this morning's kill.'

I didn't fancy being admonished in front of the trainees, so I said, 'Shall we go and talk about this somewhere private?'

'No, that won't be necessary. They do not blame you but have insisted that they see no more wild dogs or blood on safari. Please make sure that this is the case.'

'I'll do my best,' I replied.

'Thank you.' Mayan cast a final glance around the BC and departed.

'She's a toughie,' said Franci.

'Indeed.' I looked along the path down which the faint scent of jasmine was disappearing.

'Interesting,' said Donald.

We all looked at him but he said nothing further, his eyes focused on the amphibians and reptiles test.

'What, pray, is interesting, Donald?' I asked.

He looked up to see our eyes all locked on him.

'Oh, that she came all the way here to tell you that. There is a phone, after all.'

'Given that you have known her for the longest, what can we deduce from this?'

Donald looked thoughtfully into the trees above his head.

'I would say she's really scared of the potential damage you could do to the reputation of her camp and to her guests.'

'So, not that she has a crush on me?'

Franci snorted and Donald frowned.

'That is very unlikely.'

The afternoon's game drive went off without a hitch – Elvis and I showed our guests some rhino, general game and an elephant bull at a great distance across the river. There was no blood but for the greenish hae-molymph leaking from a centipede that we watched a brown-hooded kingfisher beating to death. They appeared unaffected by the arthro-pod's demise.

I was excused from sitting for dinner with the guests because they spoke so little English and Mayan felt it would be awkward for them to try and include me in conversation – I was strangely put out by this because I'd found myself warming to the genuinely interested antiques.

My early return to the BC for walk debriefs turned a pleasant af-ternoon into an unpleasant evening. The walkers were waiting for me, showered and clean but for Jerome, who always showered at Candice's house and he hadn't left yet. He was lounging on one of the chairs at the trestle tables chewing a matchstick and examining the tattoo on his right bicep – some sort of Celtic symbol. Katie was writing in her note-book, Donald sitting next to her pretending to study his insect book. Jasper had strung a hammock between a rickety pole holding up the veranda roof and a combretum tree. In this he lay, a head torch casting light onto a very well-thumbed tree book. Franci and Solomon were in deep discussion about translating light years into kilometres, the former drawing on a page, the latter trying to catch up on a physics education the government hadn't seen fit to provide him with.

'Evening, all,' I said. 'Let's have a quick chat about the walks.' I pulled up a chair and sat down.

Jasper eased himself out of his hammock and mooched over. Jerome didn't sit up.

'Jerome, what did you see today?' I asked, trying not to be irritated by him.

'Just some elies.' He shrugged.

'How many elephants, where were they, how did they react? You know the drill,' I said.

Jerome sighed heavily. 'Couple of cows by Old Pump Road and a bull on Clarence Clearings.'

'Did they see you?'

'Not the first ones. The bull was coming down the road towards me, but he was chilled.'

'Jerome, I am going to try to not become enraged by your shitty attitude and give you another chance to explain your interaction with the elephant bull.'

At this, Jerome sat up and glared at me. 'How can you even be training us? You wouldn't even have a job here if there wasn't a staff shortage – none of the camp managers want you in their camp, the okes in the rangers' team reckon you gonna get someone killed. So why should we take shit from you when you can't even do the job you training us to be doing?'

There was a shocked silence, from me as much as from anyone else – largely because the question was a valid one. I looked out into the bush and considered the query. It would have to be answered without flippancy – not for the putrid Jerome's benefit, but for the others.

Nevertheless, I'd worked very hard over the previous ten weeks and was actually quite proud of how my charges were coming along. I thought they would all actually become pretty good rangers.

I sighed and looked around the group; all eyes were glued on me.

'I guess that's a valid question,' I said to Jerome.

'Fuck it is!' he replied, hitting the table.

'I guess the answer is that I have an experience and understanding of what it takes to do this job that I have clearly struggled to demonstrate in practice. But, as a group, it would be well within your rights to go to Nicolette or Brad and suggest that you no longer wish to be trained by me, because you don't believe I'm up to it. I don't suppose either of them would disagree with you.'

The silence hung for a while.

'I vote we do that,' said Jerome. 'Mark and the boys will train us for the rest, and those okes are sharp. They reckon these walks are mad – someone's gonna get ironed.'

But Jerome had failed to read the room.

'You're forgetting something,' said Donald.

'What's that, bud?'

'I learnt more in one week with this group than I did in seven months with those senior rangers.'

Another silence ensued.

'Bru,' Jasper addressed Jerome, 'I like to be chilled AF but, jirre, you can be a doos, hey.' He picked up his tree book.

'Anyone else like to say anything?' I asked.

Heads moved from side to side.

'Fuck sakes, okes.' Jerome looked at the ground.

'Right, back to the walks,' I said. 'Jerome, tell me about your elephant encounter – make it detailed and lose the attitude.'

24

The rest of the unarmed walks proceeded without incident, as did my driving duties. The French ruins left after three days and then I had a honeymoon couple, also out of Rhino Camp. They spent far more time in their room than they did on game drive – but of course they saw no need to tell me of their intentions to stay in bed of a morning, so each day I presented myself at Rhino Camp at 05h15 to enjoy an eye-opening coffee before returning to the BC to mark tests.

Terrified that I was going to do something awful to her guests, Mayan arrived each dawn as I was pouring my coffee. This is not camp-manager behaviour – normally they stagger to the 07h00 meeting, the idea of being spruced up and ready by 05h15 a complete anathema.

Mayan was all light and joy in front of the guests and to the other camp staff but for me she reserved a defiant disdain. On the fourth morning, on cue as I was pouring my coffee, the swing doors to the kitchen opened and she wafted in.

'Good morning, Mayan,' I said, taking a fortifying sip. I was feeling chipper – this was my final day of driving, and the trainees were about to finish their unarmed walks.

'Good morning,' she replied, inspecting me like an officer might a moronic private.

'Anything specific this morning, or just checking that I don't cock up again?' I took a rusk from the jar, placed it on a saucer and smiled at her.

The glare did not waiver. Her hair was in a French plait, the tail hanging over her right shoulder, wound with gold thread.

'You must get out of bed at a beastly hour to achieve that hair by 05h00.' I walked past her onto the deck. There I placed my cup and saucer on the railing overlooking the river, and dipped my rusk.

In the sausage tree above my head, a black-headed oriole made his liquid call – no doubt overcome by the desire to mate for ''twas the season' for it.

I heard the kitchen door swing as Mayan walked out with a cup of her own.

'You do take nutrients per mouth!' I said. 'I thought you lived on prana.'

'Because I'm Indian?' The hostility was undiminished.

'No, because I've never seen you ingest anything – well, except for a lettuce leaf.'

She moved to a sofa, sitting on the edge and balancing the cup of tea on her knees.

'I don't like to eat in front of the guests,' she offered.

'Ah,' I said. 'And what's making you break your rule to share a morning hot drink with me?'

'I am not sharing anything with you.'

'You are, unwittingly perhaps, sharing the dawn with me. This marks a new phase in our relationship.'

'We do not have a relationship,' she said evenly.

'Of course we do – in the same way that a recalcitrant child has a relationship with a fractious teacher.' I turned my attention back to the tree.

'Are you unable to be conciliatory?' she asked after taking a sip of tea.

'Mostly, yes,' I admitted, 'especially when I'm being observed like a bacterium under a microscope.'

The oriole flew off with a frightened squark as a little raptor alighted in the sausage tree. I peered into the branches, trying to find a clear view of it.

'It's a little sparrow-hawk,' said Mayan.

'Oh, yes?'

'Yes,' she replied. 'Yellow cere, yellow feet, yellow around the eye.

Small raptor.'

'You saw all that as it flew in?' I was impressed.

'No, I am looking at it right now.' From her perch on the edge of the sofa she was looking into the branches, but then the little bird took off, causing a flock of crested francolins to trumpet their disapproval as they scurried for cover below.

'You are shocked that I know anything about birds,' Mayan said.

'Well, the camp managers hereabouts – especially these days – are not exactly topping the lists of world-class ornithologists.'

'Do you know how many bird species there are in India?'

'No, I don't,'

'There are more than 1 300 birds in India and approximately 80 of those are endemic – my family operates properties in most of the good wildlife areas, so I have learnt about birds.'

'Right,' I said, draining my coffee. 'Well, looks like the honeymoon couple will not be making their last opportunity for a morning game drive.'

'No, it would seem not.' She stood and smoothed her trousers. 'And I am very relieved that you have caused no further trouble in my camp.' She made for the kitchen.

'You know,' I snapped, 'I am not in the habit of accepting being spoken to like a piece of lion scat. I took it after the incident at Kingfisher Camp, but I won't take it any more! So I'd appreciate a little less outright disdain when you address me.'

She stopped and turned, her jaw clenched. 'It is precisely this sort of childish outburst that will preclude that from happening.'

I stomped off the deck and out of the camp.

I had a few more tests to mark and then that tedious task would be complete. Most of the tests were pretty well handled, each trainee showing where their strengths and weaknesses lay. In Jerome's case, the latter was his ability to write a comprehensible form of English.

Katie, it turned out, was extremely dyslexic. This was not something she had chosen to disclose at the commencement of her training, with the result that when I read the words 'lyins liv in prids with 2 – 5 relatid femals + the cups', I thought she was taking the piss. The evening of her first walk, I had called her into the BC. This was always a little awkward as the only private space in the BC was my room or the storeroom (Jeff's old room), and the dimensions of these spaces were such that standing in them with another person was uncomfortably intimate.

In the storeroom I made sure to stand near the window so that she could stand near the door – I guessed this would feel less threatening. She closed the door and looked at her feet, standing between the door frame and a row of ancient metal shelves that held our bits and pieces.

'I guess you've seen,' she said, despondent.

'I have, yes.'

'What now?' she asked.

'Well, I want to know what the problem is, its extent and why you chose not to say anything when you were hired.'

'I'm dyslexic and it's really bad – well, that's what I'm told. I obviously can't tell the difference.' She shrugged. 'I didn't tell anyone because I thought I'd finally found something where it wouldn't be a problem.' Her left hand was on the shelf, fiddling with a sock that had lost its partner.

'How on earth did you finish school?' I asked.

'That's not very sensitive,' she said.

'Sorry, I suppose it's not.' It was my turn to look at my shoes.

'They have ways of assessing people like me,' she shrugged. 'I did mostly oral exams and I had a voice-operated computer.'

'Ah.'

'Does this mean I can't be a ranger?' She looked up, her hair even messier than normal, eyes turning glassy. She blew a piece of fringe out of her eyes.

'Not unless you plan on writing to your guests,' I said. 'It just would have been good to know, that's all. Do you struggle to read?'

'Yes,' she admitted, 'but I don't struggle to listen and absorb information.'

'Well, your Big Five test answers were pretty good, despite my needing an Enigma machine to decode them.'

'Huh?'

'Never mind – how did you study?'

Her face flushed slightly and she looked down at the ground.

'I had some help,' she said.

Things began to click into place.

'Has Donald been helping you?'

She went bright red.

'Ah, good – I see.'

Solomon, punished with a school staffed by loyal cadres of the government revolution, also had a tough time writing in English. His knowledge, however, was superb so once I'd learnt to decipher his dreadful handwriting, it quickly became clear that his brain was filled with fascinating nuggets that would delight his future guests.

Franci and Donald delivered excellent results, as expected, although the former's grasp and appreciation of weapons was slightly disturbing.

Jasper, being born of a disposition that made him unable to complete tasks he didn't feel like doing, delivered brilliantly on all things plants, passably on invertebrates and horribly on birds and mammals.

'Jasper,' I said after reading his bird test, 'you are going to have to do this again. It is, frankly, crap.' I was once again in the storeroom having a one-on-one. 'Have you not actually read anything about birds? Do you even know what a bird is?'

'Bru, I just don't dig birds – they don't sit still ... It's hard, bru.'

'Jasper, do you think that because you do not feel like learning about birds, we can simply accept that you don't need to learn about them? Shall we offer you as Sasekile's first plant-only guide? Do you know how many guests ask to see *plants* on their game drives?'

He looked towards a corner of the room where a gecko was about to ambush a moth attracted to the bare bulb in the ceiling. He seemed to be genuinely considering the question.

'The answer is zero, Jasper – absolutely no one comes out here and says, "Ooh, we'd like to have a plant-specialist guide and only see flora. Fauna is so last-decade safari."'

'Bru, studying is hard ... I mean, I finished school like 20 years ago.'

'Bullshit, you've amassed a massive amount of plant knowledge – now get off your arse and do the other stuff. You will rewrite the mammals, Big Five and bird tests in three days' time – you had better do them properly.'

In general, I was feeling utterly exhausted. I'd been going for three months straight and needed some time off. The final chapter before the assessment drives would be shooting training, and the amazingly complicated, admin-intensive and often utterly nonsensical array of firearms laws meant that Sasekile had been farming out rifle training to specialists for the last few years. Albert 'Groot Skoot' van Schalkwyk was arriving the following day to spend a week with my charges.

That suited me down to the ground.

25

I had leave, but no idea how to actually *leave* Sasekile. I'd sooner have walked than experience the shuttle bus from Hoedspruit again but, mercifully, rescue came from my previous landlord. Boris had sent me an email a week previously.

> *From: Boris van der Veen*
> *To: Boy Lodger*
> *Subject: Soiree*
>
> *Dear Boy,*
> *Hope you're well, blah blah fishcakes, etc.*
>   *We're having a shindig at the house next Saturday and need some entertainment. Clarice wanted some foul Cape Town jazz band to come and sully our home for an exorbitant cost, but I said we'd get you instead. Attached is your e-ticket to Cape Town from Hoedspruit.*
>
> *See you in a week.*
> *Boris*
> *P.S. Don't forget your guitar. You can use Harry's DJ.*

Notwithstanding the incredible presumption, this did solve my problem. I prevailed upon Bertie to take me to Hoedspruit but he explained that Craig was already doing a town trip and dropping another staff member at the airport.

On the day in question, I packed my bag, polished my guitar and went to where the Land Rover Discovery was waiting. Craig sat in the driver's seat staring fixedly ahead, a bag of NikNaks in his lap. Next to him sat the other passenger.

Mayan.

At least it will only be 90 minutes of awkwardness then.

As I put my stuff in the boot, Kelly-Anne emerged from the office.

'Angus,' she snapped, 'have you handed over the week's training to Brad like I told you to?'

'Good morning,' I replied.

'Have you?'

'How are you?' I smiled.

'You're on thin ice here, Angus!'

As I climbed into the back seat, I considered how amazing it was that one so finely constructed could contrive to be so unattractive.

'Your Eminence, I have complied with all reasonable instructions.'

'Don't call me that!' she snapped as I closed the door.

I opened the shade-tinted window. 'I feel your irritation is simply a façade. You're going to miss me. Please don't worry, Your Worship – we shall meet again in just one short week.' Before she could respond I pushed the window button to raise the dark glass. 'Drive, Craig, quickly.'

He needed no encouragement. The wheels spun and the car sped out of the lodge.

'Oh, sweet Muruga,' said Mayan, gripping the arm rest.

Craig achieved the normally 90-minute trip over rough roads in just 60 minutes. By the time Mayan and I fell out of the vehicle at the tiny Hoedspruit airport, the driving combined with the odour of NikNaks had made us nauseous.

We wandered silently to the check-in counter. I assumed Mayan was flying to Johannesburg – normally only tourists took the Hoedspruit–Cape Town flight.

'Hello, yes, you are going where?' said the woman on check-in duty between chewing on her bubblegum.

'Cape Town,' said Mayan.

'You, sir?' said the woman blowing a bubble.

'Cape Town,' I replied.

She tapped on her computer, pulled out two boarding passes and handed them to us.

'We are not travelling together!' said Mayan in alarm.

The woman shrugged.

'You are now.' She looked past us. 'Next please!'

I'd been allocated the window seat, Mayan the middle. As we waited for the passengers to board, I read my book, pressing against the bulkhead. Mayan sat in the aisle seat, leaving a seat between us in the hope that the plane would not be full. But alas, just before the doors closed, a middle-aged woman bustled down the aisle carrying a mountain of small bags, a huge wooden giraffe and some sort of multicoloured poncho. She was sweating profusely, dressed in long flowing rags completely inappropriate for the heat of the Lowveld. On her head sprouted a collection of dreadlocks not dissimilar to those we had detached from Jasper.

I couldn't help but smile – this is, after all, how the universe gets its kicks. I watched her coming from the corner of my eye, knowing beyond doubt that she was headed for our row.

'Excuse me, I'm so sorry to be a bother but ... I think you're in my seat.' The woman addressed Mayan in a midwestern American accent.

Mayan smiled graciously. 'My apologies,' she said. She undid her buckle and slid gracefully into place next to me, staring straight ahead.

The new passenger then attempted to fit her mounds of curios, handbags and superfluous clothing into the overhead lockers, which were, naturally, already full.

'Oh dear, oh golly,' she said as she began to stuff bits and pieces into the seat pocket, under the seat, under Mayan's seat and around her person. Such was my mirth that when the giraffe-head lanced Mayan's chest, collecting her on the collarbone, tears began to leak from my eyes.

'Excuse me,' said Mayan firmly. 'Would you mind keeping your giraffe to yourself?'

'What? Oh golly, yes, oh, I'm sorry.' She promptly withdrew the animal, only to swing it into the aisle as a flight attendant came past. There was a loud crack as the giraffe's neck broke at the shoulder, combined with a grunt from the attendant who'd received its horns in the solar plexus.

'Oh golly!' said the woman. 'My giraffe! Oh golly, are you hurt?'

We took off not too long after that, Mayan staring fixedly ahead, trying not to touch either of the passengers next to her. Naturally, the chaotic woman had to go to the loo three times during the course of the flight.

When she left the first time, I commented, 'So, who would you rather be sitting next to? Me or hapless Harriet?'

Mayan turned her head slowly to me, the diamond in her nose glinting as it caught the sunlight coming through the window. 'An impossibly unpleasant choice,' she said, closing her eyes.

I returned to my book.

A few hours later, I was back in the Bishopscourt (actually Newlands) garden cottage, Hansel and Gretel slobbering at my feet, the southeaster threatening to rip the mountain from its moorings and fling it into the Atlantic. I was due in the 'drawing room at 19h00'. (Who has a drawing room in the twenty-first century?)

The evening was fun, if a little raucous. I began with some gentle predinner instrumentals, my Scotch being continually topped up by Boris. After pudding, I began to sing. Two hours later, everyone was roaring drunk, my audience dancing around in their finery, champagne and brandy sloshing onto the priceless Persian carpets. I was standing on the dining-room table, hammering my guitar and bellowing like Dave Grohl in a packed stadium.

I fell into bed in the wee hours and passed out despite the loud banging on my locked door from one of the Van der Veens' more amorous guests. The last thing I heard was, 'Oh, Angus, this body may be old but there is life in it yet!'

I left the Cape as my hangover subsided two days later – Boris had booked me a business-class ticket back to Johannesburg for the remainder of my week off. Before I left, I'd told him stories of my time in the bush over Sunday brunch, which had consisted largely of kippers and cognac. He'd laughed uproariously and then, naturally, probed for information on any sexual exploits. Thankfully, Clarice had been reading a magazine on interior design, sipping from a dainty coffee cup.

'Oh, Boris, for God's sake ...'

He'd winked at me but didn't press the subject.

On the way to the airport the next morning, the Rolls purring gently along the N2 highway, he'd decided to share some musings on me.

'Boy, you've probably heard this before, but Christ almighty, you do make things hard for yourself. It's all very well being weird as fuck at my age. You, however, live closer to the poverty line than most street people and yet you don't seem to appreciate that in order to make a living you have to be a genius like that Musk fellow, a rock star or heir to vast fortune. Failing that, one may have to depend on being generally pleasant to other people. You're a clever chap but you're no business genius, you're an acceptable rock star of a drunken Bishopscourt night but I don't see you tearing it up at the Albert Hall, and you're unlikely to inherit much.'

'Boris, I strongly suspect that you're about to give me some advice.'

'Advice? Are you fucking mad? I'm an alcoholic millionaire who inherited a massive fortune and made it very slightly larger. No, I'm just trying to understand your methods. I assume you want to make some tom at some stage? You're not the average Cape Town wastrel, after all.'

'Well, yes, I guess I would like to make some tom – honestly, I just haven't foggiest how to.'

'Yes, I can't really see how you will – still, you are an entertaining sort.'

Boris, against all laws, pulled the Rolls into the VIP section at the airport, told the irate guard to 'piss off back to the gutter' and then bade me a fond farewell.

'Till the next time then, boy – and good luck. Stay in touch!'

I spent most of the remaining five days of my leave either asleep or sitting on a bench beneath the oak tree in my parents' garden, reading a mindless novel, Trubshaw (now getting long in the tooth) snoring like a warthog at my feet.

The same could not be said for String Bean. He and Simone – what with their being married – were staying in the guest room, and Simone spent her days rushing around seeing as many of her friends as possible. For most of his leave, her husband remained in his pyjamas and moped around with a bowl of cornflakes, watching daytime TV.

Our mother, rather typically, felt profoundly sorry for her youngest.

'Oh, Hugh,' she said as he lay staring at Australian *MasterChef*, 'what can I get you? Some coffee? I promise this pain will pass.'

'You can get me a job,' he moaned.

'Oh, darling, you have a job – it's just not the one you want right now, that's all.'

In answer to which he grunted and waited for his coffee.

He made the incredible error of being on the sofa in his pyjamas at 17h30 when our father returned from a week-long work trip. I was just coming in from the garden where I'd been doing my exercises while Trubshaw did his best to bite whatever part of my body was in contact with the ground.

'Are you sick?' Our father appraised his youngest, married son.

'Hi,' said Hugh, not looking up.

Our father's jaw clenched. 'You sit up, or better still stand when I come into the room!' he shouted.

SB sat up abruptly.

'I'm having a tough time, Dad,' he said, wiping cornflakes from his chin.

'You're a married man! What the hell do you think you're doing lying around in my house like a slovenly teenager. I won't have it! If you are not showered and shaved in fifteen minutes, you can find somewhere else to stay! Your wife is welcome to remain.'

Hugh, wisely, didn't argue.

We had a braai that Friday night. Julia and The Legend came round, and we sat outside in the fragrant spring air, my mother's highveld garden a colourful, scented wonderland. Sadly there wasn't much meat to eat – Trubshaw had removed five lamb chops and a length of boerewors when our father's back was turned. The sight of him chasing the dog into the flowerbed and around the pool, armed with his tongs and shouting blue murder, made even Hugh crack a small smile.

Over mounds of salad, we all discussed Hugh and Simone's future. He was shaved and clean but still hang-dog. For the most part I sat silently as they all agreed that the courageous thing to do would be to accept his demotion with dignity and return to do the best possible job he could. The fact that Simone was starting an exciting new role in community development made it very unfair on her had they decided to forge a life elsewhere.

'What do *you* think, Angus?' my father asked as I tucked into a bowl of ice cream.

I shrugged. 'String Bean has no desire to hear what I think.'

'No, I don't need to hear from the man who nearly incinerated his guests,' agreed SB.

'Oh, come on, Angus,' said Simone.

I put down my spoon. 'Well,' I said. 'I think String Bean grossly underestimated the task he was given and failed to admit it. He spent more time trying to please his friends at the lodge than actually showing leadership in an admittedly complex situation: his head ranger was a pleasant imbecile and his operations manager was as trustworthy as a schizophrenic mamba. So he had little support. But his greatest failing was a chronic inability to admit to his own cockups and that, essentially, is why he finds himself in his current position.'

String Bean made to speak but I held up my hand.

'I say none of this under the misapprehension that I could have done a better job. These are simply my observations.'

String Bean leapt up from his seat and stormed off. Simone glared at me and rose to follow her husband.

'Oh, Angus!' said our mother. 'That's very harsh!'

I picked up my spoon.

'Could you have done that without the sarcasm?' asked Julia.

'No,' I replied. 'I'm sick of his moping.'

The clinking of cutlery mixed with Trubshaw's snoring coming from beneath the table.

26

I felt rejuvenated after my leave and managed to hitch a ride back to the lodge with Claire the massage therapist in her beastly little Renault Cleo. She was the perfect travelling companion; I've spent time with furniture possessed of greater conversational skills. After greeting me without smiling, she declared she had an audiobook that we'd be listening to. As it turned out, she'd chosen a heroic fantasy novel, surprising since I'd half expected a treatise on naturopathic medicine or the benefits of essential oils on human psychology. The only awkward moment came during a profoundly raunchy sex scene. I looked across to Claire as her cheeks flamed, her hands gripping the steering wheel, but her expression didn't waver.

On arrival, I made sure to bypass the office, prevailing upon Claire to drop me near the kitchen, which allowed me to avoid management. My return to the Bat Cave was pleasant. The woodland all around had flushed green (not in the week I'd been away; I just hadn't really paid it much attention). There was frantic activity in the boughs as the birds went about the business of breeding – many must have had chicks stashed away in concealed nests and tree holes.

I smiled at the thought.

Along with the spring, there was a subtle change in confidence and energy among the trainees. Everyone except Jasper and Jerome were settled in reading at the tables. The ex-surfer was in his hammock examining a herb, the other was simply absent.

'Hello, all,' I said.

'Good day,' said Donald mildly, which for him was the equivalent of being hugged.

Franci, Katie and Jasper did come and hug me. Solomon shook my hand and smiled.

'Welcome back, 'mfundisi,' he said warmly.

'Where's Jerome?' I asked.

'Dunno,' said Franci, 'but he hasn't been around here since you left.'

'And how was rifle training?'

'Fuck, bru,' said Jasper. 'Jissis, I thought I'd broken my shoulder, bru. Don't dig those things. It was hectic.'

'Did you all get through the assessment?'

'We did,' said Donald, 'but one of us was – and this is according to Albert "Groot Skoot" van Schalkwyk – 'the best damn rifleman in the whole of South Africa.'

'Really?' I asked. 'And who was that?'

'Franci,' said Solomon. 'She didn't need any training. Actually, she taught Groot Skoot many things.' The admiration in his voice was palpable.

Franci just shrugged. 'I know guns.'

'Well, we've reached the last phase of your training now,' I said. 'The assessment drives.' The assessment drive was supposed to mimic a real guest drive and put some pressure on the candidates. 'Each of you will take a drive with me, the GM – which I suppose now means Kelly-Anne – and a few others. Might I prevail upon one of you to go and fetch Jerome from Candice's boudoir? We need to do a hat draw.'

Ten minutes later, Jerome sauntered in and when they were all sitting around the table, I placed their names in an old peak cap of mine.

I pulled out a name. 'Jerome, you'll be first.'

'Yes!' he said, pumping his fist. 'Soon I'll be on the road with guests and their tips.'

'You have to pass first,' I reminded him. Then I drew out the rest. Last would be Donald, which seemed very unfair so Katie, drawn second, offered to swap.

'No, no,' he intoned. 'I'll do as the universe has decreed.'

'Tomorrow afternoon, Jerome,' I said.

He stood and stretched. 'No worries, bud. I got this.'

The following afternoon we gathered on the Main Camp deck. I was early, so I poured myself a coffee and purloined a slice of lemon-drizzle cake with Hayley's help.

'How was your leave?' she asked, moving things around on the buffet table.

'Relaxing, thanks,' I replied. 'Much needed. Anything important happen while I was gone?'

She blew a curl out of her eyes. 'Well, Queen Kelly-Anne has wasted no time letting everyone know who's boss. She's fired two chefs and one of the maintenance guys, and the union is up in arms.'

'Fun times,' I said.

'Between you and me, I don't think the result of Jerome's drive is in dispute.'

'I see.' The cake was delicious. 'And why do you say that?'

'I might be wrong, but it sounds like Mark, Jason, Brad and Kelly-Anne have decided he's ready.'

'Well, that wouldn't surprise me,' I said finishing the confectionery. A slightly awkward silence followed. 'Um, we're all good, are we?' I asked.

'Pfff, Angus,' she said, smiling, 'I told you I don't take that stuff seriously. Please don't go asking me out or anything.'

'Good to know,' I said as Jerome swaggered onto the deck. 'And thanks for the info.'

The ranger candidate looked about like he owned the place. He'd already been given a new Sasekile uniform – which used to be a reward for those ready to drive guests. His Viking undercut was neatly and immovably gelled in place, and he had eschewed the use of a hat despite the blistering October sun.

He made no attempt to engage me and instead oozed over to Hayley.

'Howzit, Hayls, can I get a slice of that cake and coffee?' he said as though addressing a waiter.

At that moment the Main Camp manager arrived. I had never seen the universally affable September Mathebula run before, and I'd certain-ly never seen him confront anyone.

With his face two inches from Jerome's, he said, 'Who you think you are talking to?'

'Chill, bud,' said Jerome.

'You wait till the guests are finished – you're not even a ranger yet!'

Jerome shrugged. 'Give me four hours.'

His 'guests' arrived presently: Kelly-Anne; her downtrodden hus-band, Brad; Jason; Mark and O'Reilly. But for O'Reilly, I had no allies. I began to suspect – nay, I was sure – that young Jerome had known pre-cisely who would be on his assessment drive, despite the fact that this was only supposed to be revealed at tea. I also had an inkling that he'd already been told about the outcome. I realised suddenly that I wasn't going to have any say in the trainees' fates.

'We'll skip the introductions. I'm sure you can do those,' Kelly-Anne addressed Jerome as they all settled in with tea and cake.

'You've seen him do an introduction?' I asked, leaning on a pillar be-cause all the seats were taken, one by the candidate himself.

She didn't bother to acknowledge me. Brad turned red and then fixed his gaze on the milky tea in his cup.

'We'd like a few big cat sightings and a few birds,' said Kelly-Anne. 'That will be sufficient – no one wants to spend their lives on game drive. Let's be back before the real guests return.'

This was unprecedented – the drive was supposed to be a challeng-ing rite of passage. Eventually, after the 'guests' had chatted and con-sumed two cups of tea each, Kelly-Anne decided we should go on drive.

I sat in the back seat with O'Reilly and so began two of the most painful hours of my life. Jerome, predictably, ignored just about every piece of training I'd ever given him. He loaded the rounds into his rifle in full view of the 'guests', drove the bolt home loudly and dumped the weapon into the rack. He then stood up on the running board, tattooed bicep threatening to tear the tiny shirt he'd sprayed on.

'I'd like to introduce my best friend,' said Jerome, adopting a solemn expression like he was about to deliver a eulogy. He pointed at the tracker's seat, where Slumber was staring disinterestedly from the front of the Land Rover. 'This is Slumber. He's not only my tracker but also my best friend.' He paused and looked pensive. I looked around; everyone was nodding. 'He's a Shangaahn and is a great tracker of animals.' Jerome continued. 'Together, we'll find you the best.'

He was about to begin the safety briefing when Kelly-Anne said, 'If I have to hear that speech again, I'll kill myself or someone else.'

Moving swiftly on, his opening gambit on the radio was spectacular: 'Howzit, stations. Ranger Jerome out. Give us a sightings' update, please. My pax wanna see gonnies or ingwees.' Jason was sitting in front of me and he turned to give me a sarcastic thumbs-up.

'Good luck, my bud,' came Sean's voice. 'There's a madoda ingwee phezulu a shidulu [men leopard up termite mound] on Wildebeest Clearings. I'm in charge. Pull in, bud.'

It was a struggle for my eyes not to roll.

We pulled out of camp onto the dam wall. Two fish eagles sat in plain view, eyeing the water. They suddenly began calling at each other, throwing their heads back in their duet.

Jerome's contribution to this was, 'Cool song, hey!' before turning around, dropping a gear and haring forward. The acceleration made my cheeks billow.

'Jerome,' I shouted from the back, 'where are we going at such a lick?'

He swung around and glared at me.

'It's a surprise!'

'Woohooo,' said Jason. 'Famba, shteam.' [Go, steam.]

I could hear some talking on the radio but so loud was the movement of air over my ears that I couldn't follow what was happening. The warp speed at which we were driving made me think that the animal we sought must be running somewhere in a hurry. After fifteen minutes, during which O'Reilly and I came dangerously close to developing piles from all the bouncing, we pulled off-road into Wildebeest Clearings. There were two other vehicles at the far end of the clearings, guests pointing cameras at something in between them.

Jerome said nothing as we approached. I spotted the leopard walking between the cars, but Jerome just kept speeding towards it. Eventually he too saw the cat sauntering out into the clearing.

'There!' he shouted. The leopard started and ran a few steps before continuing its slow stroll across the clearings. Jerome then slammed on the brakes and O'Reilly's elbow smacked into the seat frame in front of him.

'Fek!' he yelled.

Jerome swung around and said, without irony: 'Please try and keep noise levels to a minimum.'

The only reason I could fathom for the rapidity of our approach was that Jerome had been terrified to miss the leopard as he had no idea what else to show his 'guests'.

'This is a male leopard,' he began, whipping out his camera before anyone had even raised their binoculars. 'We call this guy Bruiser because he is so big!' Click, click went the shutter. 'He's dominant over three females, Shadow, Annie and Pretty.' Click, click. 'Leopards like to hunt small to medium-sized antelope.' Click, click. 'They live alone.' Click, click. 'Unless they're getting up to hanky-panky! Ha ha!' Click click. 'Leopards are ambush predators.' Click, click.

'Bud, look!' Jason was pointing to the edge of the clearing where an oblivious duiker was foraging along the fringes. 'Check, Bruiser's seen it too!'

'Like, I said,' began Jerome, click, click, 'leopards like to eat small to medium-sized antelope. That duiker is a small antelope and weighs around fifteen kilograms. They mostly browse on herbs and tree leaves but sometimes eat guineafowl chicks.'

The leopard had certainly clocked the antelope. Staying low to the ground, the cat snuck around the back of our vehicle, using it for cover.

Jerome grabbed the radio.

'Okes, this ingwee has spotted a munti. Looks like he wants to bamba it shteam!'

The other two vehicles arrived presently, keeping their distance in the hopes the leopard would kill. This would have been a pretty good test for Jerome – a tricky situation for a new ranger to handle.

'Bud, just stay where you are,' instructed Jason, negating the need for Jerome to make any decisions of his own. 'Don't wanna disturb the situation.'

Between us and the edge of the clearing was a termite mound. After five minutes of waiting patiently (during which time Jerome must have taken 300 photos and delivered the same number of facts utterly unrelated to the scene in front of us), the duiker moved to forage behind the mound. The leopard took his gap, quickly crossing the space and sinking into the grass, the white tip of his tail twitching from side to side.

A good guide, in a situation like this, might build some tension for the guests through whispers and not pointing out the bleeding obvious. At normal volume Jerome said, 'The duiker is behind the termite mound; the leopard is on our side. We need to keep quiet and not move.' He delivered this while staring through the viewfinder on his camera.

'Dis goi is a twat,' whispered O'Reilly to me. He was rubbing his elbow. 'Does he tink we're all fekking bloind?'

'Like I said, leopards are ambush predators so this big guy is gonna ambush the duiker if it comes round the si–'

The cat exploded from cover to the back of the mound. There was a strangled bleat and then silence ...

For exactly one nanosecond.

Three engines roared to life, gears ground. In the aggressive forward lurch, O'Reilly hit the back of his head on the seat frame.

'Oh, for fek sake's!' he shouted.

No one paid the slightest heed.

'Whoa!' shouted Jerome's 'best friend' Slumber. 'Go slowly – he is just there.'

'Gotta check the kill, bud,' Jerome ignored his advice. 'There he is!'

He hit the brakes once more and said nothing as he brought his camera to bare on the scene. Those of us in the back had our view obscured by a bush. The clicking of the shutter was all we could hear.

'Jerome,' I ventured, 'from the back seat we cannot see what is happening.'

He started the car, jumped forward a few feet and stopped. We were, at most, ten metres from the cat, as were the other two vehicles. He was surrounded on three sides by cars and backed up against a termite mound, jaws clamped around the duiker's throat.

The Tamboti male, or 'Bruiser' as the rangers had taken to calling him, was a tolerant fellow. He was about five years old and normally very relaxed around vehicles. Hemmed in like that, with a kill that would hopefully feed him for the next three days, he became a little testy. He looked up at our vehicle, pulled his lips over his teeth and snarled. Then he took three steps forward, tail swishing, so close that I couldn't even see him over the lip of the vehicle. O'Reilly slid over to my side.

'Shit,' said Jason. 'Back up, bud!'

Jerome started the vehicle and moved back a few metres.

'How cool was that!' he said to his 'guests' with a massive smile and a thumbs up.

'Awesome!' said Mark. 'Guests love this shit!'

I was gobsmacked at how far the ranging team at fabled Sasekile had fallen. We used to be at the cutting edge of guiding in the Lowveld, now we had joined the country's oblivious ranks of Jeep jockeys, harassing animals and chasing the Big Five.

'When did dis place become an attack-safari destination?' O'Reilly was clearly as nonplussed as I was.

'Jerome, why do you think that leopard charged us?' I asked our fearless ranger.

Jason and Mark rolled their eyes heavenward.

'Bud, leopards often get aggressive when they on a bamba. Check, he's relaxed now.' The cat was dragging his prize towards the edge of the clearing. Jerome made to start the vehicle.

'Hang on,' I said loudly, my face flushed with irritation. 'Do you think there is anything you could have done to negate his charging us?'

Jerome shrugged. 'No, not really. No harm done. Cat has his bamba and now he's chilled and gonna have a chow over there in the bush.' He pointed as the leopard disappeared into the safety and relative privacy of a spike-thorn thicket so dense it would have concealed an angry herd of elephants.

'Great, let's move,' said Kelly-Anne. 'Nice sighting. Time we had a drink.'

The leopard was our only sighting before a sundowner that went on for the best part of an hour. After this, everyone was roaring drunk except for Jerome, Slumber and me. On the way home, they joked amongst themselves, mostly about our ranger's affair with Candice.

When Slumber spotted a bush baby in a tree five minutes from camp, I hoped we might have a sighting with which to test our great candidate. The tracker shook his spotlight at the little primate. Jerome brought the Land Rover to a halt and peered into the darkness.

'What you got there, brother?' he asked Slumber.

'Bush baby.' Slumber flicked his light at the top of a small knobthorn tree 20 metres from the road. There was silence as Jerome tried to locate the animal.

'We got a bush baby, everyone. In that tree. From the right angle, you can see the eyes.' Without waiting to find out if anyone other than Slumber could see the creature, he launched into a list of facts: 'Ja, so bush babies. This one is a lesser bush baby, a small primate so it's related to monkeys. Eats tree gum and insects. Has huge eyes so that it can see well at night – it's a nocturnal animal. They can jump big distances between the trees. They make this loud tweeting alarm call when they see a predator. Live in small groups – maybe there's some others around here.'

Having thus exhausted his knowledge of the lesser bush baby, Jerome went quiet and stared vaguely towards the centre of the torchlight beam.

'Dat stchoopid fekker can't see shite,' muttered O'Reilly.

I had to agree – Jerome did not know where he was looking, and he made no attempt to explain the animal's whereabouts to anyone. In any event, it made no difference. Three of his guests were utterly unconcerned and barely took the time to look into the spotlight beam, so much were they enjoying Jason's story about how drunk he'd become after passing his assessment drive a few years previously.

Brad, who'd mumbled roughly two words during the course of the drive, decided to ask where the animal was as he peered at the tree with his binoculars.

'Um, well, so, Jerome, could you, eh, perhaps point out to me, um, where the bush baby is? I don't ... seem to be, eh, quite able to, um, see it.'

Before Jerome could answer, Brad's wife, de facto general manager, said, 'Oh God, Brad, you must have seen a thousand of these things. Let's move on!'

'Oh, well, yes ... I guess I have seen quite a few,' he agreed.

'Lily-liver,' muttered O'Reilly as we headed for camp.

The following morning, before breakfast, the people who'd been on the assessment drive met to discuss the outcome. I was in no doubt that Jerome wasn't ready to take game drives of an acceptable standard, but I was equally sure that becoming a member of the current Sasekile ranging team had very little to do with one's ability to entertain high-paying international travellers in the wilderness. To give credit where credit is due, Jerome had excelled himself in his ability to mimic and please his mentors.

Kelly-Anne opened the meeting.

'Hi, all. We don't have much time, so let's not drag this out. I'm happy that Jerome will be an excellent addition to the ranging team. He's made a good effort to fit in with the rest of the guys and adopt the culture of the existing team.' She looked my way during that last bit. 'I'm sure if the rest of the trainees demonstrate this, they will, like Jerome, pass with flying colours. Does everyone agree that Jerome is ready to become Sasekile's latest ranger?'

There was a chorus of yeses from around the office.

I spoke up. 'For what it's worth, and in this room it clearly ain't worth shit, I think Jerome has assimilated some good knowledge but his ability to deliver it in an appropriate manner is poor and his handling of that leopard sighting was embarrassing.'

Jason clicked his teeth, rolled his eyes and gave Kelly-Anne an 'I told you so' look.

'There was no need to push that poor cat to the point where it revved us. When did it become acceptable to do that? Not only Jerome, but the other two pillocks in the sighting too. How is it that three of them were within 20 metres of that poor animal, on a clearing? That just wasn't necessary.'

'Who you calling a pillock?' Mark stood up.

'Anyone who thinks harassing an animal is okay!' I shouted back.

Jason wafted his hand in my general direction. 'It was a one-off situation, oke. We've all let that happen from time to time and the guests love it. No harm done, let's move on.'

'Does the head ranger have nothing to say on the matter?' I began to shake with rage. 'I mean, Brad, what actually is your purpose on this earth other than to foul the air with your choofs? You said almost nothing on the drive, and now you're sitting there like a rotting blancmange with his tongue cut out. You're supposed to be leading this team, not watching it like a morbidly fascinated outsider!'

Naturally enough, Kelly-Anne interjected. 'Don't you dare speak like that to ...' She paused, realising that if she spoke for her husband, my point would be made. 'To anyone! You can drop the attitude or get out.'

I rubbed the bridge of my nose. 'I would very much like to hear from the head ranger on this matter.'

Brad had no option but to respond now, but he did so only once he'd looked at Kelly-Anne and she'd given him a subtle nod.

'I, eh, well, you know ... sometimes these things happen and, well, I think we can, um, probably all agree that a small ... incident – not that it was a bad incident – but, you know, one that is, um ...'

My desire to leap across the room and shake the idiot was almost overwhelming.

'The point,' I hammered in vain, 'is that on an assessment drive, the ranger should be delivering a near-perfect experience, like in a driving test. Passing Jerome now would be like handing someone a driver's licence after he'd created a pile-up. Yesterday's drive gave no indication of his capabilities, and I therefore fail to see how in the name of fucking sliced cucumber you think you can pass him!'

By then I was shouting again, which did absolutely nothing to remedy the situation and gave Kelly-Anne the excuse she needed to ignore me.

'Shouting is just not acceptable. Angus, get out.'

I took my hat off the dusty shelf that had once housed my prized skull collection and was now a shelf for lost property, and walked out.

Jerome was sitting on a bench in the little herb garden. His arms were stretched out along the back of the bench, his shirt undone so that the morning sun could bronze his expanding body. Waiting to be called into a meeting to find out if he had passed, he looked for all the world like he owned the place.

'Howzit, bud.' He looked up as I stalked passed. 'Guess my time taking orders from you is done.'

'So how did he do?' asked Katie, excitedly as I moped back to the BC.

Given that the others would soon have to face the dreaded assessment drive, I had to try and stay positive.

'He, um, ja, he did well,' I said, trying not to look like I'd been stabbed.

They all looked at me.

'And?' asked Donald. 'Did he pass?'

'Yes, he did pass,' I replied and quickly went into the BC.

Animated chatter broke out on the veranda as I closed the door and lay down on my bed. What the hell was the point? The place was clearly going down the drain. I decided that I'd work out my contract to the end of the year and then find something else to do with my life – though of course the possibility of being thrown out before then was high. Such was my despondence that I fired off two missives in the hopes of some usable advice – an email to my father and one to Boris. I figured two more disparate views of the world could not exist.

We saw Jerome once more that day when he came sauntering down the path into our little camp, singing tunelessly.

'Howzit, okes!'

Katie, ever conciliatory and generally unable to think poorly of anyone, leapt to her feet.

'Well done, Jerome! First one of our team to make it! I'm so proud!' She rushed over, put her arms around him and gave him a squeeze.

This inspired the rest to shake his hand. He then tried to hug Franci, which amounted to her standing like a stone statue while he briefly rubbed himself against her – extremely awkward to observe. Having made no effort to get up, Jasper frowned from his hammock.

'Nice, bru,' he muttered before returning to a field guide on mushrooms.

'Ja, it's lekker to be part of the *real* ranging team! So now I'm heading off on some leave – two weeks in Jozi for this ranger boy!'

Leaning on the door frame to the BC, I thought I should remind him of his final test: 'Jerome, any mention of when you are going to shoot your impala?'

'They said some time in the future – there's quite a few okes who haven't done it yet.' He turned back to the rest of the group. 'Anyway, just gotta get the last of my stuff. I got my own room now – gonna pimp it to the max!' With that he went into the tent that he and Jasper had briefly shared and emerged a minute later with a duffle bag.

'So long, trainees!' he chuckled before disappearing down the path.

Silence ensued.

Above our heads a flock of white-crested helmet shrikes foraged in the new green leaves of the red bushwillows and a yellow-fronted tinkerbird piped away in the distance – pip pip pip pip pip pip.

'I thought there was a staff-accommodation shortage,' said Donald.

'There is,' I replied. 'You'll recall, however, that you vacated your room when you moved to this university. I suspect that is the space that young Jerome is about to … pimp.'

Donald's shoulders sagged and even Katie looked pained.

'I'm sure they'll build more when we qualify,' she said.

'One can but hope,' I replied.

My father wrote back an hour later:

From: Dad
To: Angus
Subject: Recurring patterns – endlessly so

Dear Angus,
I find myself at something of a loss about your situation (not for the first time), especially as I only have one half of the story. I have little doubt Hugh would give me a different impression of what is happening there. With the information at my disposal and the knowledge I have of your general disposition, these are my thoughts.

Frankly, I would suggest you leave Sasekile as soon as your contract is up. I suspect if you remain you will only succeed in burning more bridges and, given your propensity for conflict, that will not make life any easier for Hugh, if he finally decides to return.

I am sure that you are not entirely to blame for the latest impasse, but it is difficult to see you managing to contrive a diplomatic solution. As for what you should do next, I would suggest something that doesn't involve working with other people.

This may come across harshly, but to paraphrase you at our last dinner when asked your opinion on your brother's situation, you asked for honesty.

Love
Dad

Boris's reply came that evening and was marginally more encouraging:

From: Boris van der Veen
To: Boy Lodger
Subject: Recurring fuck-ups

Dear Boy,

I would not presume to give you advice on your current bugger-up save to say the following – if being at Sasekile and the fate of your trainees is important to you, then you must hang around and fight. Hell's bell's, if there is one talent you have, it's fighting! What have you got to lose?

Good luck!
Boris
P.S. Found a girly yet? Send juicy details. Mrs Van der Veen took a dim view of my suggestion that we visit a gentlemen's club yesterday evening.

My immediate concern was not accommodation for the other trainees. It was for their chances in their assessment drives. I knew that none of them had done anything to ingratiate themselves to the senior rangers, but they also hadn't gone out of their way to cause trouble. I hoped whatever perceived faults they had would be blamed on me. In my opinion, they were five high-quality candidates. Even pothead Jasper. His second attempt at the non-floral written tests had been passable, his personal hygiene was much improved and although his teeth were still the colour of toffees, they were clean and he no longer smelt like a carcass.

Five days later, my fears, for the most part, had come true: only Katie had managed to pass a drive.

I had been excluded from the 'guest' list, and the others had been given only vague explanations as to their failure – Franci was 'trying too hard to be tough' and 'should allow her femininity to show', Solomon didn't treat his tracker with sufficient respect and Jasper's appearance wasn't up to scratch (fair comment). I felt worst for Donald: he 'just didn't fit in with the team culture'. Mark had suggested that he seek employment elsewhere.

Donald was one of the most philosophical people I ever met. He accepted life's knocks with fortitude and dignity, but this development nearly broke him.

'They said I could try again in a month's time,' he said sitting at the trestles, staring straight ahead. 'I haven't been home in ten months. I just don't think there's any point in continuing. Probably best for me to just head back to the city and find a job there.'

I poured a large measure of Scotch into my one whisky glass, and handed it to him.

'Sleep on it,' I advised.

'Oh, Don, I'm so sorry,' said Katie, tears welling, rubbing his back. Unsurprisingly, she had not been granted a room to live in, so her time in the tents was set to continue.

I looked around the table at the miserable crew.

'Let's all have a drink,' I said. 'Nothing that getting pissed won't cure for a couple of hours!'

I brought out the whisky bottle and another cheaper one, and we poured large measures into our coffee cups. Jasper roused himself from his hammock to join us at the table, and Solomon found another bottle of deeply foul moonshine.

We all proceeded to get sozzled. It was 12h00.

Two hours later I could barely see straight and retired to my bed. A few hours after that, I woke to the sound of thunder. There was a mighty crack and the heavens opened, ending the dry season. My mouth felt like it was full of sawdust as I staggered outside.

There is something magical about standing outside in the first storm of the season – and not only for humans. I'd been caught in the bush a few times during the first rains, and seen how the animals relished it. Impala frolicked in clearings, water spraying off their flicking tails and ears; warthogs dived into the first mud puddles, kudu eased out of the thickets to look at the sky and crop the wet, new leaves. Even the cats, normally so morose in the wet, appeared relieved as they were pelted by the first fat drops. I was probably projecting my own feelings ... but perhaps not.

As the first drops fell, I walked to the unsheltered spot in the middle of the tents, turned my head to the skies and opened my mouth.

The downpour's intensity grew and soon I was soaked, the rain washing away all the shit I'd been dealing with. I heard a movement next to me and looked down – Franci was emerging not from her tent, but from Solomon's.

'Oh, yes?' I said.

'Not what you think.' She pointed at her own tent. 'Don and Katie have whiled away the afternoon together. About fucking time, let's face it.'

Solomon came out next and then Jasper (from his own tent). We stood there together, showering in nature's blessing.

Suddenly, we heard shouting. We turned to see the bedraggled figure of Mayan Kholi charging towards the BC.

'Why don't you answer the phone?' she began.

'Hello, Mayan! Isn't this rain glorious!'

'But why didn't you answer?' Her French plait was dripping water over her left shoulder, black shirt clinging to what I realised was quite an arresting figure. She wiped her wet fringe from her forehead and glared at me.

This was the first time I'd seen Mayan lose composure.

'Mayan, the Bat Cave has a roof of corrugated iron – which, as you can deduce from the elevated volume of my voice, makes hearing anything softer than a Foo Fighters concert impossible.'

Mayan blew a droplet of water from the end of her nose.

'Can we be of assistance?' I asked. 'Or were you just phoning for a chat, in which case I'll put the kettle on and get you a towel?'

She flicked the plait back over her shoulder.

'My camp is flooding and I need some help ... please.'

A minute later we were running down to Rhino Camp in the deluge, Katie and Donald red about the face and grinning stupidly.

Mayan was not exaggerating. Water was literally pouring through the apex of the roof in the camp's main area. Gift, the butler, and Florence from housekeeping were running about with pots and buckets trying to catch the water. It was somewhat akin to trying to contain the Victoria Falls.

'Where is Francois and his team?' I yelled over peels of thunder.

'Who knows? I think there's some problem at the new building,' Mayan shouted back.

'We need plastic for the roof. Solly, you and Donald go to the sheds and get the biggest piece of builders' plastic you can find – and bring a ladder.'

The rest of us began to move sofas, tables, carpets, ottomans, vases and various costly bits of décor away from the flood.

As Franci, Jasper, Mayan and I wrestled a soused four-by-four-metre Persian rug towards the relative safety of the kitchen, Mayan's radio crackled to life. It was Sean announcing that his six guests wished to return to camp posthaste – they were no longer enjoying their game drive (what a surprise) and would appreciate some hot chocolate and red wine next to a fire in their rooms.

'Sweet Muruga, this is a disaster!' said Mayan, and she instructed Gift to make the hot chocolate.

We finally got the soggy, incredibly heavy roll of priceless carpet through the kitchen's swing doors and emerged onto the main deck as Solomon came down the steps, holding a ladder above his head. He failed to appreciate the wet floor and slid across the floor, the ladder swinging like a deranged helicopter blade. As Solomon overbalanced, the ladder took out an arrangement of five bottles of malt whisky displayed on the bar counter.

'Fuuuuuck,' he yelled, as all five shattered.

We couldn't help it – the residents of the Bat Cave began to laugh.

'This is not funny!' Mayan screamed.

'Mayan, fear not. We will sort this out.'

Soon Solomon was on the roof with Donald, covering the hole with the plastic. Katie continued with the smaller pieces of furniture while Franci and Jasper headed to Rhino Camp Room 1 to start lighting a fire in the hearth. Mayan and I went off to do the same in the other two rooms.

In Room 2, Mayan turned on the lights, turned down the bed and made things cosy, while I made a fire with the decorative firewood that lived in a basket next to the hearth. When I started tearing up a *Vanity Fair* magazine to ignite the pyre, I thought she may have a conniption.

'Do you have *any* idea what those things cost?' She slid over to me in her damp secret socks.

'None, whatsoever,' I replied, 'but unless you're able to conjure dragon's breath, this is the only way we're going to light a fire in this deluge. Are you?'

'Am I what?' Water dripped from her plait onto the magazine.

'Able to breathe like a dragon – I know you can speak like one.'

'Oh, shut up, Angus.' This was the first time she'd uttered my name.

While I lit the fire, she mopped the floor of our wet footprints. Although it smelt like burning plastic, I managed to get a reasonable blaze going and we departed to repeat the process in Room 3 – this time with a copy of *The Spectator*, which gave off a slightly nuttier aroma.

We were about to leave through Room 3's front door when we heard the approach of the guests – against the beating rain, the Floridian couple was yelling at each other.

'We can't go out there!' said Mayan. 'We look like drowned sewer rats!'

Haloed by the golden light of the crackling fire, Mayan failed to resemble a sewer rat. The golden thread in her plait shimmered as she anxiously wiped a piece of fringe from her eye.

'Well, it's raining, so being wet is part of the deal.' I tossed the matches into the little basket above the fireplace.

'No, we have to use the veranda door. Bring that towel with you and wipe your footprints as you come – but you'd better get our shoes from the front.'

I opened the door, grabbed the shoes, dropped the towel onto the ground and skated across the floor over our wet footprints. We slipped onto the deck and closed the door just as the Floridians entered from the front.

I tossed our shoes off the deck and jumped.

'Come on!' I said as Mayan baulked. 'If you think we looked ridiculous wet, wait till they catch you hanging off their deck!'

'It's too high!'

'Jump, I'll catch you!'

This inspired her to jump away from me, landing in a long patch of grass. 'Ow, damn!' She stumbled as her ankle struck a log hidden in the grass.

'I told you to jump into my arms.'

Panting heavily, Mayan hobbled over to where I was leaning against an ancient Natal mahogany tree. She slumped between two flutes of its trunk. The thick canopy of luxuriant green provided excellent shelter as we watched the storm rage. She removed the fashionable veldskoen from her left foot and began to rub her ankle.

'I do not need saving, especially by you ... But I think I have sprained it.'

'Yes, possibly. I could get you into a fireman's lift, but that would require your body being pressed against mine and I suspect you'd rather be torn to shreds by hyenas.'

'We are finally in agreement.' She lay her head on the trunk and there we remained in the eerie shadow for another ten minutes until the rain finally let up. When she stood, it was clear that her foot wasn't about to bear any weight.

'Come on,' I said. 'Let me help you, otherwise you're going to have to stay here. Put your arm around my shoulder.'

Reluctantly, Mayan put her left arm around my shoulders. My right arm went around her waist and slowly we made our way out from under the mahogany, around the side of Room 3 and onto the path leading to the main area. I couldn't help but notice the hint of jasmine and the firmness of her midriff. After three not entirely unpleasant minutes, we arrived at the main area and I deposited Mayan in a chair.

The roofing crew had done an adequate job – the leaks were stemmed and a few housekeepers had made it from the staff village to aid with the clean-up.

'Probably worth putting some ice on that,' I said to Mayan as the trainees (well four, plus Katie-the-ranger) returned to the deck. 'I believe our work here is done.'

Mayan looked up from her swelling ankle. 'Thank you. All of you.'

27

A few days after the great deluge, String Bean and Simone returned from leave. Kelly-Anne had taken about 25 seconds to have their clobber moved from the GM's quarters, and her own (and Brad's) installed. They found their worldly belongings stacked without ceremony in the Tamboti Camp manager's cottage – still about four levels more salubrious than the BC. It had an en-suite bedroom, a tiny sitting room and a little veranda (now packed with boxes).

I wandered over to say hello and found SB to be in slightly better spirits than when I'd left him in Johannesburg.

'We've decided to see how we feel at the end of the year,' he explained, wading through the boxes that contained the comforts of his previous home. 'Maybe I'll be able to win back Nicolette's favour and at least get a decent reference.'

Simone came in from the car. 'I believe the assessment drives didn't go so well.' She plugged a kettle into the wall and placed it on a table next to the cottage's moth-eaten sofa.

'Not well at all,' I confessed. 'I'm not sure how much that has to do with the skill of the candidates versus dislike of their trainer's methods. And with Kelly-Anne in charge, it's not like anyone is going to rush to their aid.'

String Bean shook his head. 'The ranging team has some good guys. They know what's cutting.'

'String Bean, that is precisely your problem – you have failed to see that although there are some good guys in the team, they have been dominated by a group of boet-boys more interested in humping guests and building their guns than they are in nature. Frankly, they are desecrating the memory of a once-proud guiding team.'

'This from a guy who left because he hit a guest in the face.'

I looked out of the window and sighed. 'Fair enough, but *you* employed me to train these new guys.'

'It was PJ's idea, not mine, and look how it's turned out – four trainees who don't understand the current team's culture. The lodge needs those guys on the road as soon as the new building is done! You don't seem to care about that.'

'Please don't fight, guys,' pleaded Simone.

I had no desire to continue the argument.

'Well, good luck back in the camp.' I rose from the veranda wall and wandered off.

I wasn't really sure what to do with the trainees now, as I waited for the gods of guiding to give an indication as to what they expected by the next assessment. Brad had been sent on leave (by his wife) so I had no choice but to approach the Source of All Evil herself.

I knocked briefly on her office door (actually, I didn't knock) and walked in. Kelly-Anne was hammering away at her computer.

'Candice, have you got hold of those flooring people yet?' She didn't look up.

'Not yet,' I said, falsetto with my best Brakpan twang. 'They was not in the office today ...'

Her head flicked up at such a speed that her glasses flew off her nose.

'What the fuck are you doing in here? Get the fuck out – you don't just barge in here!'

'Your Grace, I didn't really barge so much as open the door and walk in,' I replied. 'I'd like a short word, if possible.'

'You can make an appointment with Candice – that's how the new system works. And don't call me that!'

I decided to forge ahead rather than point out the stupidity of booking an appointment with Sasekile's GM – it was hardly like walking into the office of Anglo American's CEO.

'Your Grace, I have come to ask why it is that the four trainees failed their assessment drives. They were not provided with any written feedback, and I therefore do not understand what I need to remedy in the next few weeks.'

Her face was going red so I thought it best to continue before she exploded.

'No matter what you might think of me and my methods, it would be unfair to punish those four hardworking souls. If you have no intention of passing them, then please let me know so I can help them find other ranging jobs.'

Kelly-Anne rose from behind the desk and pointed a perfectly manicured finger at me.

'Don't you dare suggest that our assessments were biased – that we couldn't see their potential past the "training" you have given them. They need to toe the line culturally or they will not make it, simple as that. You need to stop undermining the leadership of this ranging team – the trainees have had this explained to them. Now get out.'

'Thank you, Your Grace.' I didn't wait for the invective that followed.

Back at the BC, Katie was bringing a bag out of her tent.

'Are you moving in with Donald? Bit soon, isn't it?' I asked.

'I'm moving into a staff room.'

'I thought they didn't have a room for you?'

'Jackie has just upped and left. Turns out she *is* pregnant. We think she's gone back to the family farm in the Eastern Cape. Jason and Sipho came to blows again yesterday – I think it's all too much for her to deal with.'

'How very soap operatic,' I replied.

'No leave for me – I have to start driving straight away. I pick up my first guests this afternoon. I'm really nervous – it all seems rather sudden.'

'That's a good thing,' I said, picking up two of her bags, and we started walking down the path towards the lodge. 'If you're a little nervous, you'll concentrate on all the things you have to do. That's way better than being overconfident. I think you're going to be just fine, and it will get easier after a week or two.'

We walked in silence for a bit.

'Would you have passed me on the assessment drive?' she asked.

This was tricky for me to answer. In honesty, she wasn't the strongest candidate in the group. I feared her lack of self-confidence would make her dither, especially in an emergency. But right now she was about to take a game drive with real guests and she needed as much confidence as possible.

'Katie,' I stopped and turned to face her. A grey-headed bush shrike gave its ghostly call and she looked up at me, hair in her eyes. 'I think you are one of the kindest people I have ever met, and I know you have all the knowledge you need to take a game drive. Would I have let you train a bit longer? Ideally, yes – just till you were able to get over those nerves. Do I think you can take a game drive now? Absolutely. I trust you, and I know you have the skills to be a good, safe ranger.'

I saw her eyes brim with tears.

'Thank you,' she sniffed. 'That means a lot to me – it means a lot to all of us, by the way.'

Katie's room was in a block of four en-suite rooms. Sadly for her, she was next to Jerome. I looked into his window and could but shake my head. He had certainly pimped out his room, and it was somewhere between South African boet and a Turkish brothel. His duvet was purple faux-satin, and next to it an orange lava lamp bubbled like a sad tribute to the eighties. On one wall hung a massive poster of a scarred male lion's face. Across it were the words, 'Take no prisoners, give no quarter – be a lion, my son, be a lion.'

On his bookshelf was a collection of field guides, a huge Bible and a large gathering of books the subjects of which covered things like corporate leadership, living in the now, winning friends and influencing people, and creating the 6 000 habits for success. It was all so kitsch and ridiculous that I had to laugh. Propping up the books on one side was a massive box of Durex Fetherlite condoms and a huge bottle of something described as 'intimate lubricant – strawberry'.

'You'd think he'd at least be discreet with that stuff.' Katie had come out of her room to see what I was doing.

'Would you, though?'

'No, I suppose not.'

I turned to face her. 'Who is tracking for you?'

'Johnson. I don't really know him.'

'He's a wonderful old man, and he'll look after you. Why don't you go to the village now and have a chat with him. Be respectful – you always are, but even more so. Then just follow his lead. Be the interpreter of his bush skill for your guests.'

She nodded. 'Just like you told us at the beginning.'

'Precisely.' She needed just a little more push. 'I trust you to do a good job out there, and I am relying on you to represent our little university with distinction, okay?'

'No pressure.' She smiled.

'Just the right amount,' I said.

She put her arms around me and squeezed. 'Thank you.'

'Go forth, young Padawan, and be brave.'

I took a circuitous route back from Katie and Jerome's block, needing to decide how on earth to approach the rest of the training. Frankly, I thought the other trainees would be better off going to another lodge, but at the same time it would reflect poorly on their CVs not to have made it at Sasekile. I decided to carry on with training drives and keep my head down in the hopes that attitudes would have softened towards the candidates during the next assessment cycle in two weeks' time.

The path took me past what might be termed Hugh's Great Catastrophe. While I was in no way qualified to judge the quality of any building, what I found at Hogan Camp looked to my untrained eye like an almighty cockup. The piles of sand, rubble, bricks and timber resembled a dodgy supply depot rather than a flag-ship safari camp. Worse, there didn't appear to be any kind of assembly going on.

I heard voices and walked to the end of the cracking concrete foundation to peer down through a pile of timber that, I assumed, was supposed to be supporting an unbuilt wall.

Below me, at a table on which a plan was stretched out, Kelly-Anne, Mayan and Francois stood.

They did not look pleased.

'I just can't see how vis can be done,' said Francois in his strangely high-pitched voice. 'Not in ve six weeks till vey come here.'

'I am not giving you an option, Francois,' said Kelly-Anne. 'I am not *asking* you, I am *telling* you that this must be done or you can go and find another job!'

'Vat's really not fair at all,' he moaned. 'I can like to do a good job here, but I am not a trained builder!' The enormous man looked like he might actually cry.

Kelly-Anne's radio crackled with Candice's voice: 'Kelly-Anne, the union shop stewards are ready for you in the office.' The GM whipped the radio from her belt like Billy the Kid and pointed the antennae at Francois.

'You have six weeks!' she snapped, and then into the radio: 'I'm on my way.'

Silence ensued, punctuated by the sound of perishing builders' plastic flapping in a gentle breeze. Under the leaves of a sausage tree shading what would, one hoped, become the Hogan Camp main deck, Mayan stood, hands on her hips, looking out over the Tsessebe River.

'I can't do it,' said Francois, 'and if I can lose vis job, ven I am broke and finished.'

Mayan turned to him. 'Francois, we have to make a plan here. We can't just give up.' She spoke quietly but firmly.

'Ahem.'

They both looked up sharply, squinting into the sun, in front of which I was standing. It occurred to me that with the sun streaming from behind, I cut a rather religious figure.

'Waddafok, who is dat?'

'It is, I, the Lord God,' I replied.

Mayan sighed. 'It is Angus MacNaughton.'

'Same thing,' I said, stepping out from the cage of timber and sitting on the edge of the crumbling foundation.

'Are you looking for something other than yet more trouble?' Mayan asked.

'No, just came to the new camp in the hopes of a Michelin-star meal and some fine malt whisky. Imagine my surprise.'

'Nee, fok!' Francois slammed down his fist on the trestle table, which promptly collapsed. 'Fo-o-o-k!' he yelled into the river.

'You can take that sarcasm somewhere else,' Mayan said. Her eyes blazed and one red-tipped finger came up to point. 'We have a genuine problem here – why don't you stop trying to make it worse and go away.'

I held up both of my hands. 'I'm sorry. I don't mean to cause more angst.'

I jumped down into the grass and, as Francois squatted on his haunches punching the ground, I reassembled the trestle, retrieved the plans, spread them out and placed a stone on each corner. I looked at them, but I had about as much chance of interpreting them as I would a text on string theory.

'Francois, in complete humility,' I said, 'can you explain the problem to me?'

Slowly, Francois raised his great head. The mass of fur on his face parted and from the gap therein sound emanated.

'Ve problem is vat ve fokken oke who was employed to build vis camp has fokked off, leaving vis mess. Vere is no uvver builder who can come fix it in six weeks so now we are fokked. Vat Kelly-Anne is made vis my problem, but I am not a builder. And I can't be fired. I got two kids.'

'And you, Mayan? What, pray, are you offering to the situation other than a certain amount of elegance?'

She shook her head. 'I am supposed to be managing Hogan Camp when it is built – *if* it is built.' She looked at the plans and shook her head. 'To be frank, I think I'd be better off just going home to India. This is a disaster.'

'Has Nicolette been appraised of the situation?' I asked.

'Kelly-Anne has told her that there is a major problem but that she has it under control. Nicolette will be here in two weeks and expects to see progress.'

'Why don't you just tell her that Kelly-Anne clearly doesn't know what the hell is going on?'

Mayan sighed, and then sat in the grass next to Francois.

'The short version is that my father and Nicolette go way back. I have a complicated relationship with my father, and let's just say that it would be very difficult for me to face him or my family if Nicolette were to let him know that I was part of this disaster. There is a much longer version, but I am not about to share that with you.'

Despite myself, I began to feel sympathy for the two people sitting in the new green grass, staring out at the river.

'Here's what I suggest,' I said after a few minutes. 'Meet me in the Tamboti Camp wine cellar at 17h00. Top secret. Bring those plans with you.'

'What ve fok is drinking wine going to do for us?' asked Francois.

'Nothing but ease the pain. However, that is not what I have in mind. Meet me there in an hour, and we'll see if we can solve this problem – even if it is temporary. You have nothing to lose.'

28

'Angus, I really do not have time for this,' String Bean said as I led him down the stairs to the wine cellar he had so lovingly helped create all those years ago. The glass-fronted bunker beneath the Tamboti Camp deck was excised from the bank of the river. Sitting in one of the old leather Chesterfields, looking out over the river and surrounded on three sides by fine wine, malt whisky and cognac was a profoundly wonderful experience. The space was dimly lit with a yellow glow emanating from vintage lamps on small antique tables. 'Seriously, what the hell do you want down here? I need to go and help Redman set the tables – we're doing a wine pairing tonight.'

'I'd like to know the same thing,' Mayan said from the depths of the cellar. She was sitting on a swivelling red-leather chair lit by the glow of a standard lamp.

Near the massive glass front wall, Francois lay on a low divan, his massive boots (mud bespattered) resting on the wooden armrest.

'Sorry to be late!' Bertie rushed in from behind us. 'What's going on? What's the secret?'

Our little group was complete – although they didn't realise they were a little group.

'There is no emergency – well, there is, but not an immediate one,' I said. 'I just needed you all in one place without the knowledge of what passes for a brains trust here.'

'Waddafok is vat soutpiel talking about?' Francois sat up and squinted into the room.

'Everyone, please sit down and give me ten minutes. After that, you're welcome to tell me to get knotted and carry on with your lives.'

Mayan leant back in her chair, Francois didn't move, SB slumped into a chair and Bertie sat on the end of a big sofa.

'Come on, Angus, get on with it,' said Hugh.

'As you are all aware, there is a problem at what is supposed to be the continent's top safari camp. If it is ever going to be built on time, then this room has the collective skill to make it happen.' I looked around. So far there were nothing but blank stares verging on aggression.

'Why the hell do you care?' asked SB.

'This is a good question,' said Mayan. 'You are not someone who has given the impression of having a deep affection for Sasekile and our guests.'

'I care because, contrary to popular belief, I am extremely fond of this place and I think it's being run by a sociopathic Cleopatra. While I may not have built the ranging team that I left here, I did maintain what was handed to me – all that is gone. And yes, I can see that my general attitude about guests could perhaps improve, but I have been deeply committed to the trainees and their training. And I think I've done a pretty good job with the time and resources at my disposal.'

There was silence as the group considered my words.

Then Hugh leant forward, head in his hands. 'Well, great Baldrick of the Lowveld, what is your cunning plan?'

'Hugh, you understand the building plans of the new camp better than anyone else. Francois and Mayan don't have a clue – no offence.' They both shrugged. 'Bertie has a vast history of making a plan with minimal resources in the most trying of circumstances. I'd strongly suggest that you, String Bean, explain all you can to Mayan, Francois and Bertie, and that you then enlist the not inconsiderable skills of Jacob Mkhonto to aid in the completion of the building.'

They considered me in silence for what seemed like an interminable period.

Mayan stood up eventually. 'Francois, please bring that plan over here, and roll it out on the table.'

A minute later, we were all gathered as String Bean took us through what was supposed to happen – obviously with a great deal of moaning about the criminal shortcomings of the previous builder and his contribution to the demise of the former GM's illustrious career.

'If you chaps get this right, I suspect your fortunes will improve rather rapidly.'

And so the team set to work, almost behind the scenes and certainly without the approval of the powers that be. Bertie brokered a meeting between Jacob and Francois (neither of whom spoke a mutually intelligible language), and SB secretly advised – going past the building site twice a day and updating Mayan on what needed to be done. In two weeks, the site was starting to show progress – walls were leaping towards the sky. With four weeks to go, it looked like the task might actually be completed.

I left them to it – my ability to contribute exhausted.

During this period, the remaining trainees and I spent just about every morning and afternoon doing training drives, fine-tuning techniques and studying. They were not yet totally despondent about their chances of becoming Sasekile rangers and they set to learning with the same joyful application they always had.

Obviously, there is always more to learn in the wilderness – especially after the first rains, when everything is fresh and new. We had one particularly adventurous afternoon after I'd decided that my backside could take no more beating from the Land Rover, so we headed out on foot. We crossed the Tsessebe River in front of Tamboti Camp. The water levels were up a bit after the first storm and some other rain in the catchment but we managed to ford without wetting our feet – well, most of us did. Jasper fell into the water where the river widened over a bed of coarse sand.

He sat for a while, allowing the cool water to flow over his thighs. Then he sat back, leaning on his wrists. The transformation from pot-headed wastrel was almost impossible to contemplate. Gone was the little potbelly and the flushed alcoholic pallor. His hair had grown back and although untidy, was relatively clean. With his mouth closed, Jasper Henderson was almost presentable. More than that, he seemed to have found purpose.

As Franci, Solomon and Donald laughed at the oxygen thief-cum-plant expert who'd become their comrade, I became quite emotional. Affection and respect for my charges combined with a growing sense of rage that their futures should be hanging in the balance – subject to the whims of the halfwits running Sasekile. I became determined to do everything in my power to make sure that when I left at the end of the year, these four fine human beings would be rangers.

We continued onto the northern bank, Jasper complaining that his undercarriage was chaffed from the walk. At the top of the next ridge crest, we climbed a small koppie to appreciate the view. Off to the west another storm was brewing over the mountains, but the sky was clear above our heads.

'There's a tree up here that I don't think any of you know yet,' I said. 'Just behind this boulder.' I tapped on the massive stone my back was resting on.

Jasper perked up immediately but then looked quite panicked at the thought of a plant that had escaped his notice. He leapt to his feet and the others followed more slowly.

'Here it is!' he said with childish excitement.

Two fat, squat stems grew out of the rocks and spread into a small, round tree. It had deliciously cracked but smooth yellow bark of the sort that made my hands tingle when I ran them over the surface. The branches were heavy with new foliage and the rocks beneath the stunted plant were littered with old star-shaped pods. Jasper picked one up and examined it closely, then a smile spread across his face.

'Bru, I know what this is!' he said. 'I've seen it in the book hundreds of times – it's a common star chestnut, right?'

'Shit, you really are good at this,' said Franci.

'That's the one,' I said. 'Let's carry on.'

We climbed down off the koppie and continued west along the ridge. At the foot of the Drakensberg mountains the storm was dumping a fearful volume of water onto the villages. Then, off to the north and down the slope, we heard an impala alarming. We froze and peered down through the woodland, now glowing gold and green with new foliage in the late afternoon. There was no longer any need to explain: the trainees' binoculars came up and they took care to make no sound from standing on dry vegetation.

The rest of the impala herd started to snort, fast and loud. We couldn't see them through the trees about 200 metres away. I looked at my four companions and raised my eyebrows in a question.

'Leopard,' whispered Solomon. 'I think he is walking west along the drainage line.'

'Why west and why male?' I asked.

'I saw one impala looking that way,' he explained. 'It may be male or female, maybe.'

'Lead on, Solly. Let's go find it.'

I slotted in at the back of the group and we made our way down the slope at an angle, estimating where we might catch a glimpse of the leopard. We had to move quickly but with great control – not wanting to frighten the predator but needing to find it before it disappeared. The impala continued with their agitated snorting. A few minutes later we saw a ram and a ewe looking down towards the thick trees lining the drainage line at the bottom of the slope. They saw us, snorted again and then took off in the opposite direction. The rest of the herd ceased their alarm call. Satisfied that the threat had moved off, they trotted off through the woodland.

'There's a game path that runs along the top of the drainage,' I whispered.

Solomon gave a thumbs-up and began to move again, quickly but carefully, all the while scanning the landscape ahead for the prince of cat's spotted pelage.

On the game path, we checked for tracks but found none. Around us, the summer-evening bird chorus was tuning up – red-chested cuckoo, white-browed scrub robin and a black-headed oriole exchanged a complicated, melodic counterpoint. Then, a hundred metres or so further west, a squirrel went ballistic – chee che che che che che – and all of its friends began to do the same.

'Come,' whispered Solomon and we moved.

The squirrels kept squeaking their heads off. Fifty metres later, Solomon put up his hand and we stopped.

'There,' I said, pointing to the gnarled trunk of a dead leadwood tree resting on the bank. 'The squirrels are up there.'

The aggrieved little rodents were sitting at the entrance to a hole in the tree, staring into the bush below, their tails quivering each time they alarmed.

'What do we need to remember about trying to follow squirrels to predators?' I whispered.

'They lie like politicians,' Donald quoted me.

'Correct. What else?'

'Their field of view is much greater than ours, which means it's hard to tell where they are actually looking,' said Franci.

'And we don't know how far away the thing is that has pissed them off,' said Jasper.

Step by step we moved slowly forward, peering into the bushes on both sides of the path, listening out for further alarm calls. Eventually, we were under the squirrels' tree, but the terrified rodents had absconded, leaving us to decipher what was going on without their help. We continued slowly along the thickening game path, breathing as quietly as possible.

It is astounding how noisy human beings are when they move. It never ceases to amaze me that no matter how hard a person might try, our long, flat, inflexible feet make it impossible to move quietly when the ground is littered with dead sticks and disintegrating leaves.

It is equally astonishing how fast a lion is able to fall into a deep sleep.

We didn't see him lying under a tangled red spike-thorn bush until Solomon, leading our little group, nearly kicked him in the bollocks.

Assuming that we were making enough noise to alert any predator in the vicinity, we had all failed to look under the spike-thorn bush. When Jasper trod on a dry stick, an almighty crack woke the lion, hitherto fast asleep five metres from us. The lack of regal bearing displayed by the huge cat made me wonder how his kind have maintained their reputation as 'king of the jungle'.

'Lion!' I shouted as the great head came out of the shade, smashing into a branch above.

We all froze. The king of the jungle stood up in a blind panic, his body twisting, legs whirring beneath him like a cartoon. He made no attempt to come at us, but devoted every fibre of his being to escape. Unfortunately for him, the bush he'd chosen to sleep under was brilliant for shade but dreadful for effecting speedy retreat – his entire body became ensnared by the thorns but such was the immense strength of his slashing limbs that he managed to escape out of the back. If you looked at the bush carefully enough, it was possible to see a lion-shaped path of destruction through it. And that was the last we saw of him.

I took the radio from my belt.

'Katie, come in.' I knew she had planned to drive north of the river.

'Go ahead, Angus,' she said.

'We have located a male lion on the southern side of the drainage line, northwest of Eland Koppie. Animal was highly mobile northeast. My guess is he'll fetch up on Mangawana Road North.'

'Copy, thanks,' she said. 'But we've all been told to come south of the river. There's a massive storm in the catchment and the river is coming up. We didn't want to be stuck on that side.'

I considered this for a second and looked up. There was a very distant rumble of thunder, but the sky was still clear above.

'Copy that.' I replaced the radio on my belt. 'Sounds odd, but it is getting a little late so let's head for the river.'

We turned due south and began to walk with some speed. Up on the ridge, just north of the Tsessebe, we could see the massive storm making its way towards us from the west. I didn't harbour any great fear, but this impression changed as we made our way down the final slope towards the crossing closest to the camp.

'Jirre, bru,' observed Jasper. 'That sounds like the sea!'

He wasn't wrong – the roar of rushing water seemed completely out of place. When we reached the bank, it was obvious that attempting to cross the wide ford would result in our being washed most of the way to Mozambique before being able to call for help. The river churned brown and frothy, like an angry cappuccino. Flotsam from the upstream villages and the reserve bobbed violently in the torrent – logs, litter, a plastic chair and a very dead goat being pursued by a tiny but brave crocodile.

'We can't cross here,' said Donald.

'Donald, Michael Phelps couldn't cross here,' I replied. 'We'd better run to Enock's Crossing and see if we can get across the concrete causeway. We'll have to get someone to pick us up on the other side because we're running out of light.'

'That's three kilometres east of here!' said Jasper, alarmed. 'I haven't run three kilometres since … I've never run three kilometres.'

'No choice,' I said, 'and everyone keep your eyes peeled.'

We set off at a pace that Franci and Solomon found entirely comfortable, Donald found tiring and Jasper found impossible, his lungs destroyed from years of abuse. After fifteen minutes, we arrived at the causeway and Jasper collapsed at the base of a jackalberry tree.

Even before I had taken two tentative steps onto the concrete, I knew that trying to cross would be suicide. In the middle of river, the water was at least chest-deep. Dusk was falling and the clouds were gathering overhead.

I took the radio from my belt.

'Katie, come in.'

'Go ahead. Are you guys back over the river yet?'

'Negative, there is no way we can cross this evening, so we will have to spend the night on this side of the river. Please tell Kelly-Anne and Brad.'

'Oh, um, okay, copy. Are you all okay?'

'Yes, no problem – we'll spend the night in the cave on Black Mane Koppie.'

I replaced the radio while Franci and Solomon dragged Jasper to his feet.

'We have to get to Black Mane Koppie before dark,' I said. 'It'll easily take 20 minutes, and we have roughly that amount of light left.'

Off we set at a brisk walk, cutting through the block towards the northwest, the shadows evoking an ominous feeling. The clouds swirled above as the wind kicked up sand and leaves around us. By the time we were three-quarters of the way to the cave, we could hardly see a few metres in front of us, the black clouds obscuring what little light the embers of the day provided.

'Stick close together,' I said. 'Solomon, you walk behind. I'll go in front.'

Then the rain started to fall – huge, heavy drops. In a few seconds we were soused. I knew the game path we were on so I wasn't afraid we'd get lost. I *was* afraid that we might blunder into an elephant, rhino, buffalo or lion. Ten minutes after the rain had started, we reached the koppie and felt our way around the western side to the cave. I hoped to goodness there wasn't a lion or leopardess nursing her wee cubs inside it – then we'd really be in for it.

When we arrived at the entrance – a pitch-black hole about two metres across, the same height and twice as deep – on an almost pitch-black night, I flung a stone in and waited for a reaction. It was difficult to see or hear anything in the storm, but as far as I could make out, the cave was empty. We crawled in gingerly, also hoping not to stand on a snake.

Out of the rain, it felt a little less eerie, but we were cold and blind.

'We need to make a fire,' I said. 'There is a dead milkberry tree to the left of the entrance – I'll see if I can get some dry wood off it. I don't suppose anyone is carrying firelighters and dry matches?'

'I have a lighter in my bag, I think,' said Jasper.

I crawled to the edge of the cave and found, to my great relief, that there was a stack of fallen wood of all sizes. A few minutes later we had a little fire going near the entrance as the storm raged around the cave. We warmed up slowly, trying to ration the wood. The only thing we had to eat was two ancient rusks Solomon had found at the bottom of his bag. Still, being rusks, they were edible.

As the fire crackled and the rain continued to fall, we laughed at memories of the training. Jasper teased Donald about the lack of time he was spending at the BC given Katie's more salubrious digs. I marvelled at how close the group had become. Even hard-arsed Franci, who was even more sparing with kindness than I was, had some gentle words for Jasper after I asked him if he thought he'd get through the second round.

'Bru, I can't see these dudes ever passing me – I'm just not their vibe.' He looked sadly into the flames.

'I imagine fear of Dennis will see to that,' I said.

He snorted. 'I sent him a message a few weeks back – just to make sure he had my back. His reply went something like: "Who is this? Don't send me junk messages. Fuck off."'

'Ouch,' I said.

'Jasper.' Franci sat up. 'You need to back yourself, man. You're actually good at this stuff. We've all said it. You were fucking useless a few months ago and we all hated you, but we rate you now. And we also like you.'

Jasper got a bit sniffy and wiped his nose on his skinny, hairy arm. 'Thanks, Frans, that's, um ...' He swallowed hard. 'That's really sweet.'

'She is right,' said Solomon in his sonorous voice.

'Fuck em,' said Donald as he lay back onto his day pack. 'We know what we can do.'

Having made a watch roster, we drifted off to sleep. It wasn't comfortable but it was warm and strangely pleasant to be in the wilderness all night.

The morning dawned, clear and bright. When I sat up at first light, Solomon and Franci were sitting at the entrance to the small cave, legs hanging over the lip, her head resting on his shoulders. Ah, I thought, my Padawans pairing off – although it was difficult to see Jasper and Jerome becoming romantically attached.

As soon as it was light enough, we walked slowly back towards the causeway. If anything, the raging torrent was worse than the night before, so there was no chance of crossing on foot (or in a vehicle). One of the properties about ten kilometres downstream had a steel bridge and this, I reasoned, was our only way across. I turned on the radio.

'Sasekile reception, come in.' I hoped rather desperately that Rhi-randzu would be on duty – but my wishes were not to come true. After repeating the call to no avail, I tried String Bean – who seemed to have taken on a new lease of life since his clandestine involvement in the building of Hogan Camp.

'Go ahead,' he said.

'Ah, String Bean, there was no one with a brain in the reception yet, so I have been forced to call you.'

This precipitated a stream of vitriol on the shared channel: 'Angus, this is Kelly-Anne. That is inappropriate radio language and you will not use it again, do you understand!'

'Good morning, Your Grace.'

'Stop calling me that!'

'We are currently – that is to say, I and the four trainees – on the northern bank at the causeway after a rather uncomfortable night in the wilderness. I wondered if you might prevail upon the good people of Shimpala Lodge to come and fetch us and then take us across their bridge – perhaps someone from Sasekile could fetch us that side.'

There was a silence – no doubt Kelly-Anne was considering her options. Five minutes later, she replied: 'Angus, come back.' I could hear the smugness in her voice. 'I have phoned Shimpala and they have granted permission for you to use the bridge and traverse their reserve on the river road. But they do not have any vehicles to come and fetch you.'

'Oh, fuck dammit to kak,' said Jasper.

A 20-kilometre walk awaited us.

'She really doesn't like us,' said Solomon.

'She really doesn't like *me*,' I corrected. 'I suspect she is rather indifferent to the rest of you.'

I clicked the radio and spoke into it.

'Our profound thanks, Your Grace, for your immense efforts on our behalf.' I turned it off before she could reply.

In the end, the ten kilometres to the bridge was as bad as it got. The head ranger from Shimpala found our bedraggled, thirsty and smelly group not far from the bridge.

'Angus MacNaughton!' he exclaimed, the honeymoon couple on his Land Rover looking rather alarmed by our sudden appearance. 'Back in the bush, I see – they didn't tell me it was *you* walking through the reserve.' He considered our group. 'Or that you were in this condition.'

'What ho, George,' I replied.

George Madsen and I had developed a friendly relationship over the short period I was his opposite number at Sasekile. He was a career guide, ten years older than me, and while he spoke too much, he was a convivial sort – so convivial that he barked some orders into his radio and a few minutes later we found ourselves in the staff canteen at Shimpala Lodge enjoying a slap-up breakfast of oatmeal porridge, toast and coffee. It was just what we needed to fortify ourselves for the long walk home.

Across the bridge, however, there was another surprise waiting. Bertie, in a Sasekile Land Rover, was parked in the shade. Scandalised at our treatment, he had simply absconded from the camp with a vehicle, no one in the brains trust being any the wiser.

We arrived home around 11h00 to find a letter pinned to the BC door – the second round of assessment drives would begin that evening.

29

'Three strikes and you're out' was the general rule. As expected, I was not invited to attend any of the trainees' second assessments. Equally, when three of them failed again, I wasn't provided with a written report, a time frame for remedy or anything else. Solomon was the only one to make it through this time, and I had a nasty suspicion he would be the last. The other three would be given a final chance for show and then booted.

On the dawn of Solomon's success, I went down to the building site to see how things were progressing. There I found Francois, String Bean, Mayan and a crew of builders, with Jacob barking orders at them. This, apparently, was how all mornings of the last few weeks had progressed. They'd all arrive before dawn – before the rest of the lodge had stirred. SB, Mayan and Francois would do a quick inspection with Jacob, who would then assign the day's tasks to the contractors. SB and Jacob would then return to their normal posts.

'Hello, Angus. How are you?" said Mayan, as I wandered into what was fast becoming Hogan Camp's Room 3. The roof was on, and the walls were being plastered with apparent skill by four young men and a sharp-tongued older woman.

Francois and SB looked around – they may have both actually smiled at me.

I was shocked on both accounts.

'Mayan, that is the first time you have indicated any concern for my wellbeing – another new phase in our relationship!'

'I was merely being polite.' Just the corner of her eyes twitched as she quickly turned back to the others.

'How are things going here?' I asked.

'Very well, actually,' said String Bean, 'although we are horribly over budget.'

'Perhaps the Pink Flute will make budgetary considerations disappear,' I suggested.

'There is still a problem wiff ve foundation at ve main area – and we don't know what to do about it. I hope it can hold up ve deck wiff people on it.'

'I am sure Nicolette harbours the same wish,' said String Bean.

'How are things with the trainees?' asked Mayan.

'Solomon took his drive last night and we're waiting to hear about it.'

String Bean stepped away from where he'd been inspecting some newly laid tiling in the bathroom.

'No need to wait – I'll tell you what's going to happen.' He rubbed his face, sighed and looked at me while the gentle sound of plaster being applied mingled with the dawn chorus. 'Simone was at Main Camp last night and she overheard a conversation between Jason and Brad. Seems they're going to pass Solomon this morning and then give the other three another go for show before firing them. With that, your purpose for being here will end.'

'I see, but don't they need all of the trainees – especially with Jackie gone?'

'PJ and I thought so, but they reckon three will be fine. Jason is bringing in his mate from Majombana Camp in the Klaserie.' String Bean looked genuinely perplexed. 'I'm not sure there's anything we can do about it – Nicolette is hardly going to listen to us.'

'That's for sure,' I said. 'Any idea when the next assessments will be? They refuse to tell me anything.'

'They want the BC cleared by the time Condé Nast arrives,' said String Bean. 'Kelly-Anne wants to remove the ceiling and turn it into a storeroom.'

For some unknown reason, I suddenly felt sorry for the bats.

'Who knows what will happen in the next few weeks,' I said, my mind trying, and failing, to find an obvious solution. 'By the way, where is Nicolette anyway? I'd have expected her to have been back by now.'

Mayan shook her head and began to giggle – I'd never seen her laugh before.

'Nicolette is in Australia. Dennis has moved into a hippie ashram on the Gold Coast.'

'Sounds like a perfect solution. Why didn't she leave him there?'

'Because he has discovered social media – and is posting photographs of himself with nubile young women, and tagging Sasekile,' said Mayan. 'He's created quite an online presence.'

'And,' said Hugh, 'it's almost certain the foul old bastard is funding their lifestyle of drugs, surfing, yoga and sex.'

I decided not to share what I had learnt about the fates of my three remaining charges, but if I'd had any inkling of the mayhem that was to unfold, I would have packed my bags, told them to do the same and headed for that Gold Coast ashram. Clichés exist because they have a ring of truth about them, and the adage 'It never rains, it pours' came to pass three weeks after Solomon passed his assessment drive.

I had yet to come up with a plan for the futures of Jasper, Franci and Donald. I was particularly concerned for the latter, given his rather sweet relationship with Katie, and for the former, who I feared would return to the Eastern Cape a broken man. I had no such qualms about Franci – I knew she'd survive no matter what.

And so it was that they were assigned a slot for their final drives three days before the Condé Nast group was due to arrive.

We had absolutely no time to do any last-minute preparations. In the week leading up to their arrival, every able-bodied person in the lodge (when not on drive) was enlisted to carry beds, lights, tools, ottomans, sofas, chairs, tables, paintings, sculptures, trays, fridges, books, shelving and an array of incredibly impractical-looking ornaments, fittings and whatever else goes into finishing a five-star game camp. The decorating process was led by an interior designer friend of Nicolette's – Angela

Hollard – who jetted in from Johannesburg smelling strongly of large invoices and luxury brands.

Three days before D-Day, and the day of Franci's final assessment drive, a specially commissioned and, in my opinion, entirely pointless construction was erected on the Hogan Camp deck at the behest of Angela Hollard. It was a giant sculpture of God-knows-what, fashioned from white faux-kudu horns. The artist himself came to assemble his magnum opus. He was from Cape Town and, therefore, a complete prat who thought his value to the art world equivalent to that of Michelangelo. The trainees and I spent hours carting boxes of resin kudu horns from a truck to the camp so that Sebastian Vantage Merino (surely his parents hadn't actually given him that name?) could assemble his creation.

Sebastian Vantage Merino wore the obligatory man bun, a pair of Birkenstock sandals and bits of ill-matched baggie clothing covered in paint stains (I'm not sure if these were added on purpose). The scent of onion and dried apricots, reminiscent of Jasper circa four months previously, permeated the air around him. I arrived with the umpteenth box to find him attempting to have a conversation with Jacob Mkhonto.

'Are you the builder?' he asked. Without waiting for an answer, he continued: 'This really isn't the sort of space I was expecting, you know – it doesn't have the ideal energy. This deck needs more light, so that tree' – he pointed at an ancient sausage tree – 'will have to go.'

Jacob looked the fellow up and down, clicked his teeth, shook his head and departed without a word.

'Hey!' said Sebastian. Then he saw me. 'Put those down there.' He wafted his hand towards the massive pile of boxes I'd already brought in. 'You can start carefully unloading the cuedoo horns from the boxes.'

'The *what*, bru?' said Jasper arriving with the last box.

'He means kudu,' I said.

While we set about unpacking the horns, Sebastian Vantage Merino retrieved four large crystals from a black tog bag and placed them around where his creation would stand. He then lit enough incense for a service at St Paul's Cathedral.

'I need this space now,' he said. 'Leave me.'

As the two of us exited the deck, Jasper said, 'What a poes.'

I couldn't have agreed more.

Later, while Franci was out on her final assessment, Jasper, Donald and I wandered onto the Hogan deck with a few boxes of wine, which Mayan needed to stack. Sebastian Vantage Merino had apparently just finished reassembling his creation. Standing behind it, right hand on his hip, left held out to the side, he looked like a teapot dressed in rags.

To me, the piece looked like a precarious pile of faux kudu horns. Still, it was an impressive height – standing around 2.5 metres with a diameter of around 1.5 metres. It was certainly the first thing anyone arriving on the deck at Hogan Camp would see, enhanced by shafts of sunlight intermingling with the beams cast by specially fitted down-lighters from above. If I squinted my eyes, the effect was impressive, if confusing.

Jasper put his wine box on the bar counter and with no compunction sought clarification from the great artist: 'Howzit, bru. So, like, are you done?'

Sebastian looked slowly around. 'Done?' he asked, head cocked. 'Done what?'

'Finished. Like, have you finished this?' Jasper waved dismissively at the pile.

Sebastian rolled his eyes heavenward and turned back to his creation, adjusting a piece slightly.

'I am now ... *done* ... as you put it.'

'Cool. So, like, what is it?'

I couldn't help snorting.

Sebastian swung around again. 'This,' he said testily, '*work* combines the savagery of Africa with her beauty. The anger of her people with their ubuntu. It is a culmination of African expression, years in the making.'

Jasper scratched his head. 'So, is this, like, what they call a art installation, bru, or is it a sculpture?'

'It is a sculpture!' said Sebastian. 'With elements of installation art!'

'If you say so, bru.'

'I do say so!' Sebastian returned his attention to the pile.

We unpacked the wine, much of which I could imagine Boris greatly approving. I handed the bottles to Mayan as she selected locations in the specially cooled rack. 'Rack' is not an accurate description – it was actually like a giant corkscrew of around six feet tall, varying in width and made of some composite material with holes for the wine bottles. The entire thing was specially refrigerated to keep its residents at the optimum temperature even in the height of the lowveld summer, and I suspected its carbon footprint was equivalent to that of Manhattan Island.

'Happy with the progress?' I asked, examining a bottle of De Toren Fusion V.

She took it from me and stretched up to a curving piece of the rack above her head. I was momentarily mesmerised as I glimpsed the gentle curve of her hips and a tattoo of the Buddha in the small of her back.

'So far, yes – I think we'll be okay,' she said, and then: 'That was a youthful mistake.' She settled back onto her heels, her shirt dropped and she turned back to me.

'What was?' I handed her another two bottles.

'The Buddha.' She looked me in the eye, defying me to deny that I'd seen it.

I shrugged.

'I never got a tattoo,' commented Donald.

'Bru, you should get Katie's name tattooed across your chest!'

At that, Donald went bright red.

With the wine stored, we all collected the empty boxes and left Sebastian to continue adjusting his pile of horns. It was a beautiful dusk, the sun just set, the puffy cumulus tinged with gold and the sky a glorious shade of ginger. All around was the smell of the bush coming to life after the dry season – new grass, wet soil, subtle blossom from the num-num bushes and *Jasminum* creepers. We dropped the boxes at the recycling centre.

'What a lekka evening,' said Jasper, facing the western horizon over the lodge soccer field, where a game between the butlers and maintenance crew was coming to an end.

'Quite stunning,' said Mayan.

'Moments like these make it all worth it.' This from the ill-treated Donald.

We stood there in silence for a while, not wanting the evening to end.

'I could use a drink,' I said.

'Me too,' said Donald.

'That would be a good way to end a hard day,' sighed Mayan.

'I'll get some beers from the staff shop and bring them to the Bat Cave,' said Jasper, disappearing at a run (or the nearest thing he was capable of).

'I hope you like beer,' I said to Mayan.

She shrugged. 'It's the company that makes the drink.'

A few minutes later we had pulled the chairs out from under the BC veranda and were enjoying some icy Heinekens beneath the canopy of bushwillow, a few stars twinkling through the gaps in the leaves. A fiery-necked nightjar called in the undergrowth nearby and a scops owl prrp-prrped high in the boughs of a leadwood down near the kitchen.

After a few minutes, Franci arrived, unsmiling.

We didn't need to ask. I pulled out another chair, cracked open a bottle and handed it to her.

'Thanks.' She sat down and took a long draw.

'Not good?' said Donald.

'Fuck, no. They literally didn't ask me a single question – just yakked amongst themselves the whole afternoon and told me to move on from every sighting except one of the Djuma female. We stayed there long enough for Jason to tell about the time she charged him on foot.' She took another sip. 'I don't think they were even trying to test me.'

'When do you find out?' I asked.

'Well, that's the other thing. They're only going to tell us the morning after Jasper takes his – as a group – which makes no fucking sense at all.'

'It does if the result is a forgone conclusion,' said Donald.

'... and if the head ranger is a coward,' I added.

'Fuck em,' said Jasper,

'I'm sorry about this,' I said. 'Really – for whatever part I have played in bringing about this sad conclusion.'

After a few minutes of listening to the far-off chorus of a cicada group, Mayan spoke: 'Well, I think your approach has been correct,' she said, standing. 'I must go. Thank you all very much for your amazing work today. Would someone walk me back to my room, please?'

'Let me get a torch,' I said.

The path to Mayan's quarters took us past the block where Katie and Jerome had found themselves as neighbours. (Of course, Solomon had yet to be given any quarters.) Katie was out on drive, but Jerome had just returned from leave. His Golf GTI with low-profile tyres was parked outside, some club anthem blaring from the speakers as he carried box-es of his belongings into his room. The undercut had been accessorised with a finely trimmed beard that made a thin line from his ears down to an equally narrow goatee. He looked like a Viking hybridised with a Portuguese gangster.

'Hello, Jerome,' I shouted as we walked past.

'Howzit, bud, Mayan.' He put his arms behind his head and stretched. 'Good to be back in the bush.' He picked up another bag and we contin-ued on our way.

Mayan's home was in a block of two, much like the accommodations I had occupied during those halcyon days as Sasekile's head ranger. We stopped at a gap in the hedge of Cape honeysuckle that grew on a low wooden fence.

'This hovel cannot be of the standard you're used to at home,' I said.

'You have no idea how I live in India,' she replied, pausing at the little gate. 'You have never asked me.'

'To be fair, you have never invited conversation with me,' I said.

A hippo grunted down in the river and Mayan said nothing.

'Okay, well, where do you live in India?'

'None of your bloody business,' she shot back. Then she laughed – very slightly mind. 'Mostly I live in Mumbai, but I spend a lot of time in Bandhavgarh and Pench, where we have lodges. Also up in Kaziranga. Know where that is?'

'Up in the north in, um ...'

'Assam,' she completed.

'That's it.'

We stood again in silence for a while. She made no move to go inside, and I made no move to leave.

'For what it's worth,' she said eventually, 'I do not know if your remaining trainees – or any of the people you have trained – are able to take good game drives or not. But it is easy to see what a tight group of hardworking, passionate people they are. That must have something to do with you.'

I felt myself flush. 'Well, coming from you, that's high praise. I appreciate it.'

I looked towards her, the gold in her hair catching the soft light coming from her house. She was looking out towards the river, arms folded. Then she looked into my eyes and smiled.

'Good night, Angus. And thank you for your help today.'

I felt a strange combination of elation and depression as I walked alone back to the BC.

Two nights later, Jasper took his final assessment drive. Just before that, I returned to the BC from Bertie's office – he'd needed some help sorting out his budgets for the next year and Kelly-Anne was either incapable or unwilling to help him. On my bed was a letter on an official letterhead. I sat down and opened it, jaw clenching.

To Angus MacNaughton,

Re: Departure from Sasekile Private Game Reserve

The training of the new guides is now complete. As such, there are no further tasks for you to complete and your contract is thus terminated with immediate effect. Please vacate the reserve by 11am tomorrow. The maintenance team will arrive at 10am to remove all the furniture, dismantle the outside roof and collect

the tents (except for Solomon's). Please make sure everything is
out of the building by then and the tents neatly folded and packed
away.
Sasekile thanks you for your service.

Yours sincerely,
Kelly-Anne Jenkins-Pringle
General Manager

If she thought I was going to prevail upon the spurned trainees to pack
up their tents, she had another thing coming.

I was not invited to attend Jasper's assessment drive. We made sure he
was spruced and ready by returning him to Zebulon the village barber
to receive a number four all round. He bought a new razor from the
staff shop and even prevailed on Minah in the laundry to iron his clothes
for him. The teeth we could unfortunately do nothing about but for the
rest, he looked (and smelt) presentable. He cleaned his Land Rover and
begged O'Reilly to make him some special snacks and cocktails for his
drinks stop.

When he emerged from his tent, ready for drive, we were all waiting
for him. Donald, Franci, Katie and Solomon shook his hand (well, Katie
through her arms around him) and wished him luck.

'Whatever happens tonight and in the meeting tomorrow, you
should be proud of yourself, Jasper,' I said to him. 'You've achieved what
very few Wild Coast wastrels could ever have hoped for, and for what it's
worth, I would consider it a great honour to work with you in any team.'

Jasper's eyes brimmed with tears and so did mine. The next moment
we were in a huddle of six, all feeling bereft. Katie sniffed and a tiny tear
made its way down Franci's face.

Then Jasper was off down the dappled path to meet his fate.

I went back into the BC as Katie and Solomon headed to Main Camp
for their game drives, and Franci and Donald returned to their tents. I
felt heavy, sad and angry. I imagined my father's face as he contemplat-

ed his eldest son (aged 33) and what manner of hopeless future awaited him. I thought about Jasper and how I could possibly help him find
somewhere to apply his new skills. Then, realising it would be my final
opportunity, I took my quarter-bottle of Talisker, popped it in my backpack, and headed west out of camp, along the northern bank of the river.

Twenty minutes later, I settled myself in the massive fork of Anna's
mahogany tree. As had become my tradition, I poured two glasses and
rested one on a flat piece of branch. Down on the bank, the mournful
call of the black cuckoo mingled with the gentle burbling of the river and
added to the sombre atmosphere, as did the piping of a water dikkop in
a shaded pool just visible from where I was sitting. Through the dark
leaves, the sky was impossibly deep, punctuated by building thunder-
heads. Somewhere to the south, a kudu barked in alarm and I hoped he
wouldn't meet his death that afternoon.

'Anna,' I began, feeling like a fool as I always did when I addressed
her, 'what am I going to do?'

I have never been someone who goes in for signs or messages from
the beyond. In fact, my attitude to people who derive meaning from
coincidence, ascribing it to a universal plan or benevolent deity, is generally one of contempt. But when, just after my imagined words with the
long-dead love of my life, a one-tusked elephant bull stepped into the
little clearing in which the mahogany stood, the hair on my neck stood
on end. I'm still not convinced the bull was Mitchell – but it did look like
him, bigger and more relaxed perhaps.

The elephant walked past the far side of the mahogany over to a
sausage tree growing slightly further up the bank. He reached into the
canopy and pulled down one of the enormous fruits, popped it into his
mouth and dropped his trunk to the ground as a loud crunch came from
his jaws. Then a light breeze blew up from the river – just for a few seconds. The elephant froze, the end of his trunk turning towards Anna's
mahogany. Slowly, he turned and looked towards the tree. I took a silent
sip from my glass, feeling no fear. It is often possible to sense if an animal – particularly an elephant – is bent on violence. I felt calm.

The bull took two steps forward and exhaled loudly. A huge volume of dust rose off the ground, catching a shaft of light from the setting sun and enveloping the elephant in a golden cloud. He raised his trunk in my direction, ears gently flapping, then he released a long, low rumble.

I don't know what it meant. Perhaps he was responding to another elephant miles away. Maybe he was singing to himself. Or maybe – just maybe – he was greeting the familiar observer in the tree. His trunk dropped back to the ground and he turned slowly before walking back to the sausage tree, picking up a fruit off the ground and melting into the woodland.

Tears rolled down my cheeks.

'Cheers, old boy,' I croaked, before tossing back the remainder of my drink and gently pouring Anna's over the bark.

I walked slowly back to camp, encouraged to take whatever was to come in life with courage, calm and no self-pity.

When I strolled up to the BC for my final night, I smelt smoke. Initially, I panicked. Then the sound of happy chatter touched my ears and I was astounded to find the space between the tents transformed into a fairyland. Lanterns hung from the trees and in the middle a table was set with a white tablecloth, a candelabrum, crystal glasses and silver (in colour at least) cutlery. Around the table, sipping from glasses or beer bottles stood Franci, Jasper, Donald, O'Reilly, Bertie, Craig, Simone, Jacob, Elvis and Mayan.

'Angus!' shouted O'Reilly. 'Welcome ta ya farewell dinner! We tought ya chaps could use a little send-off!'

'So you've been appraised of the predicament faced by the remaining members of the BC university,' I said. 'I'm assuming that word has come from on high that Jasper, Franci and Donald have not passed their drives?'

'Correct,' said Jasper, taking a long draw on the quart in his hands. 'We were back from drive by six o'clock, in the office fifteen minutes later and told to go home.'

'More accurately,' Franci drained her beer and pushed the thick blonde hair from her eyes, 'the fuckwits informed us that we don't fit the Sasekile guiding culture and values, but that we shouldn't be too despondent because Sasekile has the *best* guiding team in Africa, blah fucking blah, and we might be better suited to lesser lodges.'

'I'm sorry, chaps, I really am,' I said.

'It's not your fault – we're grateful to you,' said Donald.

'Come on!' said O'Reilly. 'Let's have a drink.' He handed me a bitterly cold Heineken, and chinged my glass.

I took a great swig as people began to chat again.

'O'Reilly,' I said, 'how have you managed to find the time and resources to put all this together? Surely you're required in the camps?'

'We're only about tirty per cent full tonight – de lodge is emptying tomorrow before de big arrival of de Condé Nast fekkers.' I nodded. 'But dis wasn't moi idea. It was hers.'

He pointed to Mayan, who was chatting to Franci. In her right hand she held a glass of champagne, arms folded across her torso. Unusually, her hair was loose, falling over her right shoulder; her left ear and its Fort Knox-worth of gold glinted in the lamplight. Her lips were touched up with deep red.

Katie and Solomon joined us after their game drives and so began a rip-snorting evening, delicious food and an obscene volume of booze supplied by O'Reilly's budget in lieu of 'staff welfare'. We laughed, some cried and we all shared happy stories of our lives in this special piece of Africa. String Bean came through after his guests went to bed, bringing a bottle of delicious Ardmore Single Malt that he insisted everyone round the table try. The only ones to refuse were Jacob and Craig – the former didn't explain why, the latter was asleep on the table, giant white Afro resting in a plate of chocolate mousse.

Slowly, people began to drift off to bed and eventually those who remained were residents of the BC, String Bean, Simone and Mayan. O'Reilly was technically there, but he'd passed out under the table after a fervent and moving rendering of 'The Parting Glass' in his delightful tenor.

'This time I don't blame you,' said String Bean as he stood to leave. 'You've been done up here, and it makes me very angry.'

'Me too,' agreed Simone.

'Come say cheers before you leave,' said String Bean, eyes brimming.

We roused O'Reilly and he staggered off with them, muttering about there being too many arseholes in the world who don't get what they deserve. Franci and Solomon disappeared to his tent, Jasper passed out in his, and Donald and Katie decided on one more night in his tent for old-time's sake.

Finally, Mayan rose to leave.

'Walk you back?' I said as we drained our glasses. We looked at each other across the table as the candles sputtered out.

She reached out and took my hand in both of hers. She turned it over and ran a long nail down the centre, then she looked up.

'I am sorry we will not have time to get to know each other better,' she said.

'Yes, me too.'

'Perhaps in another time and place.'

'Perhaps.' I smiled wanly.

She stood and I did the same, hoping she'd simply decide to stay but unable to invite her to do so. I retrieved my torch and she followed me down the path towards her room. At the gap in her hedge, I stopped and shone the light onto her veranda.

'Good night, Mayan Kholi.'

She was standing very close to me, so I tentatively put my hands on her hips. She put her arms round my waist and rested her head on my shoulder. I inhaled the scent of jasmine – unfamiliar and intoxicating at the same time. We stayed like that for what could have been an hour but was more likely ten seconds. Then she turned and walked into her cottage.

As I strolled back to the BC, it became apparent that ours was not the only party going on that night. With so few guests in camp, the rest of the staff were having an impromptu soiree at the Twin Palms – loud music and the sound of wassailing humans touched the night air.

Well, I thought, they'll need this blow-out before the Condé Nast group. Not dealing with that was the one positive of my departure.

30

I woke late the next morning with a pounding head, feeling lonely and bereft. I was in no rush to vacate the BC or to move back to Johannesburg, where my father's frustration would permeate my parents' house. I made my morning coffee for the last time and went outside to sit on the veranda. A covey of Natal spurfowls pecked at morsels of the previous evening's dinner. They were joined presently by a troop of dwarf mongooses.

The little carnivores were totally unfazed by my presence, and before long they were scurrying around the veranda, chirruping softly at each other. They'd become something of a fixture around our university, frequenting it at least three or four times a week, their den being in a large, disused termite mound between the kitchen and the BC.

The peaceful scene was shattered by Jasper emerging from his tent. The spurfowl squawked so loudly that Jasper levitated, shouted 'Fuuuuck!' and dived back in through the flap. The little mongooses shot off in all directions like turbocharged clockwork mice.

Slowly Jasper re-emerged.

'Sorry, bru, but geez, I'm a bit edgy when I'm hanging.'

'No problem, Jasper. There's some coffee left if you want it.'

The others appeared presently (bar Solomon and Katie, who were already on game drive and must have been having a torrid time).

The next time the peace of the morning was shattered came just as I was about to start packing. A small aircraft on final approach screamed in over the northern side of the lodge. This was unusual for nine o'clock in the morning – normally the planes came in around midday and the arrival of the Condé Nast group was set for around 13h00, by which time I'd be well away.

'That must be Nicolette,' said Donald from behind a mug and his rusk.

'Well, chaps' – I stood, draining my mug – 'they're coming to strip the place in about 30 minutes, so we'd better pack up.'

At 10h00, I was still at it and no one had come with a wrecking ball. By 10h30 I had all my kit outside waiting. Bertie had agreed to take the four of us to Hoedspruit, where we would hire a car – the shuttle being too awful to contemplate.

By 11h00, there was still no Bertie and no maintenance crew. I went inside to phone Bertie's office but there was no answer, so I walked up to the office to see what was going on.

It was eerily quiet as I approached the herb garden between the main office and the rangers' room. I poked my head into the office where Candice should have been manning the phones. There was no sign of her, but Hilda was there, tapping away at her computer, seemingly oblivious to the virtual tumbleweed blowing through the place.

'Morning, Hilda.'

She didn't look up. 'Hullo.'

'Um, any idea where everyone is?'

'It's month end, I got no time to be fokken worrying about where is everyone.'

'Right, well, thanks.'

I crossed the courtyard and poked my head into the rangers' room, where a few dust motes were being kicked up by a pair of skinks having a fight over a piece of muck.

Then I heard the sound of feet approaching and poked my head out of the door. Striding along towards the office came Nicolette Hogan, her waif of a PA two steps behind. She stopped in the middle of the herb garden, hands on hips, and looked from side to side. It took her two seconds to clock me. I was no longer employed by her, but I snapped to attention immediately.

'Good morning, Nicolette.'

'Hello, Angus. Where is everybody? What on earth is going on here?'

'Ma'am, I am afraid I am as much in the dark as you are – and I cannot find a soul able to tell me anything either.'

She scowled.

'Have you seen the new camp?' I asked by way of conversation.

'Of course I have. Kelly-Anne has done a miraculous job of getting it all together in time.'

This irritated me immensely and I was suddenly no longer inclined to ingratiate myself to the owner of Sasekile. I stepped down into the courtyard and said, 'I think you'll find there were a lot more people than Kelly-Anne involved. Anyway, I must be off – as decreed by your miraculous GM.' I lifted my hat. 'All the best with your Pink Flute. And, Mary,' I said, pausing briefly, 'might I just say that you look sexy as hell today.'

Mary turned the colour of a pomegranate.

Just then the whine of a golf cart approaching its limits of speed and endurance arrested our attention. Its driver, O'Reilly, grossly misjudged the brakes. He hit them hard, the wheels locked and he skidded off the road next to the courtyard and into a ditch.

'Fek, fek, fek!' he shouted. 'Dis place has gone fekkin mad!' He didn't even acknowledge Nicolette, so distressed was he. 'Angus, dere's a massive fek-up behind Rhino Camp at de GM's house. Help me wit dis fekkin golf cart. Hello, Nicolette. Shit, fek.'

Seeing that sense from the Munsterman would not be forthcoming, Nicolette got into the driver's seat while O'Reilly and I pushed the cart from the front. She then executed a 180-degree turn that would have shamed the stunt drivers in Fast & Furious.

'Get in,' she instructed and moments later we were speeding towards the residence of Kelly-Anne Jenkins-Pringle and Bradley Pringle.

'Dere was a party last noight,' explained O'Reilly. 'Tings got a bit outta control, dey tell me.'

And that's all we got by way of explanation before Nicolette slammed on the brakes at the GM's front door.

It was clear that much was amiss. Bits of clothing, an upturned sofa, cutlery, smashed plates and a duvet littered the ground. There was a great deal of shouting and banging coming from inside. I hopped off as the cart came to a halt.

The scene in the open-plan kitchen-lounge area was arresting. In one corner, on the only piece of furniture still upright – a La-Z-Boy – Brad lay with a cigarette in one hand and a half-empty bottle of Jack Daniel's in the other. He watched sleepily as Kelly-Anne ducked a missile in the form of a coffee mug. It hit the wall behind her head, bits of china raining down into her hair. Next to her, one Jerome le Roux was cowering like an impala lamb, a nasty welt coming up under his left eye.

The person holding them hostage was none other than the lioness of Brakpan herself. Candice, standing at the little bar counter, was screaming, flinging bits of crockery as soon as the two in the corner looked like they might move. Her aim, like her invective, was vicious.

'You slut!' she screamed (apparently without irony). 'You fucking slut! He was *mine!*'

Crash went another glass.

'How could you fucking do this to me, bitch – we were friends!'

Crash.

'And you're a fucking coward, Jerome. No one does this to me – who the fuck do you think you are!'

Jerome then made a profoundly stupid error by speaking.

'But I don't wanna break up, babes,' he slurred and stood up, apparently under the delusion that this revelation would rectify the situation.

When the bottle of Iona Sauvignon blanc hit him in the nose, he went down like a sack of old beetroot. I ran for Candice and grabbed her right arm as she aimed another bottle at Kelly-Anne, this time a Beyerskloof Pinotage. I copped one on the forehead for my troubles on the backswing.

'You don't wanna break up?' she screamed at the top of her lungs, tugging back her arm. 'I find you up to your balls in this hooker and you don't wanna break up? I'm gonna break you up!'

'O'Reilly, get those two out of here!' I grabbed Candice's flailing left arm and pulled it behind her back with the other one.

'Let me go! Let me the fuck go – I'm going to kill that hooker and …

her ...' Her brain failed to find the equivalent insult for Jerome, who was now sniffling and trying to stand, blood leaking from under the hand that covered his nose.

'It's not what you think,' said Jerome.

'I find her bent over that coach and you thrusting like an animal – and it's not what I *think*?'

This rather graphic description caused a loud groan to emanate from the La-Z-Boy. Tears streamed down Brad's face. He wiped it with the cigarette-bearing hand, burning himself in the process.

'Ow, fuck,' he drawled. 'You didn't have to do this, Kelly.' He took a swig.

Just as it looked like things were calming down, Bertie came charging through the door at a run.

'Where is management?' he yelled and then saw Nicolette, who had stood immobile, taking in the scene. 'Oh, sorry, Nicolette –'

'There's management,' I said, pointing at the snivelling head ranger and his dishevelled wife.

Nicolette cut through the impasse. 'What is the matter, Bertie?'

'Sipho and Jason,' he said, 'they are fighting in the gym.'

Between the frontline staff housing blocks was a corrugated roof roughly five by five metres. Beneath it was a concrete floor surrounded by a split-pole fence. Inside was a collection of gym equipment that the more health-conscious staff used. It was also used by rangers who wanted to 'get big' or 'bulk up' in order to impress. Now that Bertie had mentioned it, a clanging of equipment was audible.

Nicolette pointed at me.

'Get down there and see what's going on.' She looked at her watch, and then back up at me.

I felt disinclined to take any further instructions from anyone at Sasekile, so I made no move. Then, for the first time ever, a note of pleading entered Mrs Hogan's voice.

'Angus, Condé Nast is arriving in just over an hour – please help me!'

'Please is such a helpful word,' I said. Besides, it wasn't like I had much else pressing to do.

'Come, Angus!' said Bertie, grabbing me by the arm.

We ran round the side of the house, past the staff quarters and down towards the gym. The clanging of metal became louder, and I feared we might arrive to a horrific scene – strong men going at each other with heavy iron could not but result in trauma. As we came around one of the housing blocks, there stood Sipho and Jason, well-built young fellows, charged up on testosterone and jealousy. They were squared up, both bleeding from cuts around the face. Jason's left eye was almost swollen shut and Sipho was missing a front incisor. Both were shirtless and sporting wounds from collisions with the gym equipment. The fight had brought the old lat-pulldown machine crashing onto the rowing machine, which had split in two.

As we arrived at the fence, Jason took another swing – a wild haymaker. Sipho ducked out of the way and grabbed his opponent. In a second they were on the ground, grappling and throwing wild punches. I would happily have let them kill each other but Bertie, being a man of courage and integrity, leapt through the fence.

'Help me!' he shouted, so I climbed in.

Neither Bertie nor I were a physical match for the two combatants, but they were exhausted, injured and drunk. As Jason climbed on top of Sipho, I grabbed him round the neck in a choke hold. Sipho rolled onto his hands and knees and made to stand, but Bertie kicked his wrists from under him and he collapsed.

'Stop!' I shouted.

Separated and spent, both fighters relaxed. I slowly released Jason and he fell to the ground.

'What the hell is going on here?' I said. 'Jackie left ages ago!'

'It is *my* baby,' said Sipho with a wry smile. 'They told me yesterday.'

'Fuck you,' said Jason, head hanging. 'She was mine.'

I chuckled at the thought of Nicolette's Condé Nast guests meeting their bloodied, toothless and swollen-eyed rangers at the airstrip.

'Right, Bertie, do you think you might be able to take us to town now?' I asked, standing up.

'Yebo,' he said sadly. 'I meet you in ten minutes at the cave for bats.'

I wandered back towards the BC, my hangover subsiding slightly. I had just sat down next to Franci, Donald, Jasper, Solomon and Katie – the latter two there to bid their lovers farewell – when the sound of running feet once again disturbed the peace. This time String Bean came haring down the path.

'Anguuuus!' he yelled, waving his arms. He arrived and then doubled over, hands on his knees.

'What is the matter?'

'They're,' he gasped, 'they're coming.'

'Who is coming?'

'Condé' – he coughed – 'Condé Nast.'

'I am aware of that,' I said, 'and so is everyone else.'

Hugh banged his hand against his thigh, finally managing to suck in enough oxygen to make some sense. 'No, they're early – they land in 20 minutes.'

Katie and Solomon stood up immediately and made to leave.

'There you go, SB, my ex-charges are fully capable.'

'No!' Hugh finally managed to stand up. 'Angus, the head ranger is drunk, Jerome is bleeding from the forehead, Jason can't see out of his left eye and Sipho says he's leaving immediately to go and be with Jackie.'

My hungover brain began to compute. 'You want *us* to fill in? We, the despised and rejected of Sasekile?' I felt nervous energy flicker between the other five.

'Please,' he said. 'There's just enough time to get some uniform from the office and get to the airstrip, but we have to go right now.'

'We don't have to go anywhere, String Bean,' I said. 'We are not employed here any longer.'

'Oh, for fuck sake's, Angus. Do you really think Nicolette is going to send you away if you save this day for her?'

There was a stunned silence around the old BC. A brown-headed parrot alighted on the knobthorn tree above the roof and shouted metallically as a friend or lover flew by. He squawked again and took off, his green back flashing as he disappeared through the trees.

'Well?' Hugh was desperate.

Without a word, all five of us ran at top speed for the office.

It felt rather special to lead my group up onto the courtyard between the office and the rangers' room, the place suddenly a hive of panicked activity. Trackers were charging for the workshop to fetch vehicles; those rangers not maimed or drunk were emerging from the rangers' room at a run. Nicolette was standing next to the bird bath, radio in hand, directing operations.

'Get in the office for your uniforms!' she shouted as we arrived.

I stopped in front of her. 'Excuse me?' I glared at Sasekile's owner.

'Please!' she begged.

We darted for the door and found Hilda in front of the steel cabinet with the uniforms.

'Ah,' I said, 'Hilda's house of Haute Couture!'

'Shuddufokop,' she snapped and began flinging bits of clothing at us.

Seconds later we were standing in various states of undress as the first plane buzzed over the lodge.

'Hurry up, for God's sake!' came Nicolette's panicked voice from outside. 'They're bloody landing!'

A few seconds after that we emerged at a run and jumped onto the vehicles that the trackers had brought round. The new rangers (if that's what they were) froze, not knowing which cars to take.

'Jasper with Slumber, Franci with Joe, Donald with Vuvuzela,' I shouted. I then ran for the vehicle in which sat my old pal Elvis. 'Famba, General,' I said, leaping into the passenger seat.

He crushed the accelerator and a few minutes later executed a four-wheeled drift to bring us parallel with the airstrip on the northern end.

The first plane had stopped on the apron, and was disgorging around 20 guests. A few other rangers were there to greet them, although I feared for the Pink Flute given that their first impression of the Sasekile ranging team was Jeff Rhodes, the lovable village idiot. The rest of us brought our Land Rovers to a halt as the second of three planes turned onto the apron, shutting off its engine.

I jumped, running for the plane, and as the door opened I was standing at the base of the stairs smiling for all the world like this was the sort of thing I did every day. I was joined a few seconds later by Franci, Donald and Jasper, who was shaking with nerves.

'Jasper!' I snapped. 'You've got this – relax. They're people who make smelly poo just like yours.'

This had the desired effect on the waiting rangers such that when the guests emerged, they were met by four sets of grinning ivory.

By their very nature, the people who work for a group like Condé Nast are – how to put this politely – slightly detached from reality. More accurately, they are deluded. This is not to say that they are unpleasant people, just that they are constantly cosseted in a bubble of luxury accommodation, fine dining, exquisite booze and delicious perfumes as they travel from one swanky place to the next attending exclusive parties. Let's just say that the amount of contact the upper echelons have with poverty and deprivation is severely limited. Or that the people who arrived for the Condé Nast year-end conference had a grip on reality somewhere between impaired and nonexistent.

My first inkling of this came on the gentle drive back to the lodge.

In a nasal New York inflection, Stacy Johannson leant forward and tapped me on the shoulder.

'Driver, can you stop, please? I need to get my purse out of my suitcase.' This sounded like a simple request if you ignored the piles of luggage in the trailer we were pulling.

'We're just a few minutes from the lodge,' I suggested. 'Are you sure you need it at this minute?'

'I wouldn't ask if I didn't need it!' she snapped.

'Right,' I said, and brought the vehicle to a halt under a marula tree.

'Can you perhaps identify your bag?' I asked.

She stared at me like I'd just stepped out of a chocolate pudding.

'My bag has a tag on it. Surely you know where it is?' This was said more in a panic for lost luggage than as an accusation.

'I know it is in the trailer behind us, but where in the trailer, I cannot say.' I pointed behind us and her eyes went wide.

'You'll have to find it. I can't arrive like this! I'm a mess!' She looked perfectly well turned out to me.

The others – two couples in expensive bush-chic and Mr Johannson, who was wearing a khaki linen suit, head topped with a Panama hat – looked on impassively. One woman began fanning herself.

'Right,' I said, climbing out of the car and explaining to Elvis what needed to be done.

We spent the next ten minutes taking every item of luggage out of the trailer. Stacy's bag was, naturally, at the very bottom. When Elvis eventually brought it round to her she said, 'Oh yes, that's it.' Whereupon she removed a portable makeup kit and handed back the bag without so much as a glance.

Elvis and I then repacked the trailer.

We'd been in such a rush that no one had any clue which guests were supposed to go to which camps. I was pondering this when the radio crackled and Nicolette's voice came briefly over the airwaves: 'Angus, you need to bring your guests to Hogan Camp.'

I realised the head honchos were on the back of my car. I glanced back and came to the conclusion that they were led by Stacy Johannson, who, I was about to find out, hailed from a swanky part of New York City where she lived in a palatial apartment overlooking Central Park. Her husband, the downtrodden and depressed Dwight 'Johnny' Johannson, owned a hedge fund the complexities of which I was not capable of understanding (other than the fact that it had made him a stupid amount of money).

In front of Hogan Camp stood Nicolette Hogan, a smile pasted across her face. She was flanked by Mayan, and butlers Clifford and Bruno. All but Nicolette carried silver trays of champagne or warmed face towels. The guests had only flown for an hour from Johannesburg and then experienced a short drive to the lodge, but they leapt at the towels and champagne like alcoholic street urchins.

There were some preliminary greetings before Nicolette led the guests onto the new Hogan Camp deck. Elvis and I were left to unload the luggage (for the second time) and cart it off to the rooms, after which I made my way onto the deck to find out what was happening. By then the guests had occupied a small lounge suite on a sala that extended out from the main deck on stilts. Under the shade of a mahogany tree, it looked like the most gorgeous place to while away a lowveld afternoon.

Walking past the art installation at the centre of the deck, I half thought that it seemed to be listing slightly to port, but I gave it no further consideration as Mayan hailed me for an introduction.

'Angus is one of our most senior rangers and he'll be looking after you for the duration of your stay.'

This was news to me, of course, but there'd been a lot of surprises during the course of the day. I smiled toothily at the guests and felt Nicolette's eyes boring into my flesh.

'It is a great honour to be showing you the wonders of Sasekile. I would suggest that we meet here for tea at around three thirty and head out into the wilderness at four. Does that sound good?'

The guests looked at me as though I was speaking a foreign language. One of them grunted slightly and looked back at Mayan.

'Excellent,' I said. 'I am sure we will have a rip-snorting time out there!' I spun on my heel and departed.

The Avuxeni Eatery was abuzz as I wandered there for a bite of lunch. The new rangers – the least experienced had less than two hours on the job – were chatting animatedly amongst themselves. Jasper sat in front of a plate of lasagne but wasn't eating, still overawed by the thought of taking a game drive on his own. Mark, Sean, Sifiso and Johnno were seated at the far end of the long table talking quietly. When Mark saw me, he stood and pointed a finger.

'Why are you driving out of Hogan? You not even a proper ranger here – I should be doing it.'

I looked at the idiot for a few seconds as everyone's eyes rose from their meals and silence fell.

'Mark,' I said as I walked over to serve myself a meal, 'you are a complete prick.'

I noticed that, in a kind attempt to bring the new rangers into the fold, Jeff was sitting with them imparting what he considered to be good advice.

'So, ja, guys, awesome to have you on the team, just awesome. So don't be scared about taking this group out to the bush. They just like normal people, but very important ones, so like it's really hard that these are your first guests.' He shovelled a mound of lasagne into his mouth. Before swallowing, he continued, 'But ja, so I'll help you out there and also the other guys.' Jeff pointed towards the muttering group at the end of the table with his fork.

I helped myself to a small plate of lasagne and decided to have a little quiet time before the afternoon game drive. Halfway back to the BC, I met Mayan carrying an expensive-looking leather bag on her way to the office. We stopped and looked at each in the dappled shade of a russet bushwillow. She smiled and flushed slightly – I did the same.

'Good afternoon,' I said.

'Hello.' She pushed a piece of hair out of her left eye and tucked it behind her ear.

'Where are you going?'

'To the office – I need to put this stuff in the safe.'

'I shall accompany you – purely for the purpose of security.'

'That is too kind. I was very worried about highwaymen until this moment.'

'What's in the bag?' I asked as we walked.

'A collection of jewellery and cash,' she replied, 'and the famous Pink Flute. It's a crystal champagne flute with the Condé Nast logo on the front, created from a collection of fancy pink diamonds – twelve in all.'

'That makes it quite a valuable piece, does it?'

Mayan almost choked. 'Fancy vivid pink diamonds are the most valuable in the world.' She tapped the side of her nose.

'And you have one too.'

'My sixteenth birthday gift – a family tradition.'

In the office, Hilda was tapping away at her computer and Rhirandzu was manning the phones.

'Is vat the fokken flute?'

'It is,' said Mayan.

Hilda took a vast bunch of keys from her pocket and opened the door to an annex. Inside was a collection of filing cabinets and, in one corner, a large wall safe with a combination lock.

'Don't look at the fokken code, Angus MacNaughton,' she snapped.

The flute secured, Mayan and I wandered away from the office. Where the path to the BC split off from the camp track, we paused again.

'I'll be back in camp at three thirty,' I said.

She smiled, and pulled a leaf from a red ivory bush.

'See you then,' she said.

I returned to the BC to unpack my bags. The other residents were doing the same, and an excited energy pulsed through the university, though Jasper sat in quiet contemplation in his hammock. I have never been any good at pep talks but I thought I'd better try with him.

'Jasper, is there something bothering you?'

'Bru, I'm just so nervous – what if I get it wrong and say the wrong thing to these VIPs? I mean, I've never actually taken a game drive before.'

'Remember,' I suggested, 'that your guests know almost nothing about the bush, and you now know a huge amount. You have a blank canvas on which to create their experience and you have, against all expectation, absorbed all the knowledge and experience you need to deliver a great safari.'

He sighed. 'Thanks, bru.'

'I am also going to suggest – and I'll deny ever having said this – that you roll yourself a reefer, a very small one, to take the edge off.'

Jasper looked up sharply. 'Seriously?'

'For medicinal use only, and only for your first drive!'

I left Jasper to his rolling and went to lie down on my bed.

Back on duty, I realised that the only reason I was driving the head honchos out of exclusive Hogan Camp was because I'd happened to be the one who'd picked them up from the airstrip. Nicolette, not feeling particularly well disposed to any of her staff just then, had seen no reason to hand them over to anyone else.

My guests were the Johannsons, a Parisian couple called Claude and Jeanne and a Russian couple, Sergei and Olga. They were varying degrees of painful, although Sergei exhibited a deadpan humour that, combined with the accent and his limited English, proved rather amusing. Stacy Johannson was difficult to read or interact with. I was standing at the tea table before game drive when she arrived on deck looking like a cross between a sailing ship and a mummy, such was the volume of material fluttering about her person. Her husband was decked in a new linen khaki suit, with a bright-orange shirt.

'Hello, Stacy,' I said. 'May I get you some tea or coffee?'

'Oh God, don't make me decide,' she said, wafting up to the art installation.

It appeared to me that she felt about the pile of horns as I did, She said nothing, however, and glanced around nervously at her colleagues.

'Beautiful, isn't it?' said Nicolette, sweeping onto the deck from the kitchen.

Stacy obviously agreed, which in turn brought over the other guests, carrying their cups and saucers. They oohed and aahed at the monstrosity, except for Sergei who muttered, 'Vat een the sheet ees thees theeng?'

I decided Stacy should have coffee.

'Stacy,' I asked once I'd poured it, 'do you take sugar and milk in your coffee?'

She swung round to as if I'd slapped her in the face.

'Two sugars and cream!' she said. 'And one extra sugar.'

'So, three sugars?'

'That's *not* what I said!' she snapped and her eyes rolled heavenward as she turned back to the 'art'.

From a guest perspective, the game drive that afternoon went off without a hitch. Everyone saw at least one or two leopards, the first of which was tracked by Jasper and Slumber – a great confidence booster for the former, who was driving out of Main Camp with Solomon, Johnno and Sifiso. My guests seemed largely satisfied, although they did complain that the roads were a bit rough and Stacy warned me that if the heavens opened on her, she would be extremely upset.

It was all going swimmingly when Elvis spotted a herd of elephants emerging from a thicket just after our sundowner stop. It was a perfect, clear night with the almost-full moon just risen, the area bathed in a gentle blue light. I switched off the engine and Elvis killed the spotlight.

Twenty elephants of all shapes and sizes came wandering onto the clearing in front of us, the adults keeping themselves protectively between us and the youngsters. As they walked, they turned their trunks and lifted their heads to make sure we didn't pose a threat, and then they relaxed and began to feed. The moon was so bright I could make out the glint in the elephants' eyes as they moved their heads from side to side. The herd rumbled gently at one another, the only other sounds being that of fresh grass being torn by trunks and shaken free of soil. It was the most magical scene – made all the more so when a crèche of tiny calves lay down in the soft grass to sleep.

Trying to narrate what was going on would have ruined the mystical atmosphere, and some guests pick up on this. Olga was no such person.

'Why you no turn on the light to bright the elephants?' she asked loudly. 'My camera not see nicely the elephants. You must turn on a light for me to take picture!'

I gritted my teeth and whispered: 'We only shine on nocturnal animals, not animals normally active in the day. Try to just enjoy the sounds and smells of this magnificent herd – see how the moon lights them. Listen to the flapping of their ears. That rumbling sound is the herd communicating. Smell the different scents – the leathery scent is the elephants, and you can also smell wild basil and fresh grass. Isn't it magical?' I said this as softly as possible, trying not to break the spell.

'But it is night, and they eat grass now so they are night-time animal, yes? So you must put on the light, yes?'

'I'm afraid it will make them nervous,' I whispered again. 'This is an exceptional sighting – it is very rare to see them in the moonlight like this. See how the little ones are sleeping. We want to try and not disturb them.'

'This ridiculous,' said Olga, thumping down her camera on the seat next to her. Well, that's what she tried to do but Sergei's leg was in the way. When her 300-millimetre F2.8 cracked into his knee, he bellowed like a wounded hippo.

'Blyad!' he screeched, followed by a stream of what I assume was Russian invective.

This set her to shouting incomprehensibly. The main effect was that the elephants took fright and, trumpeting loudly, ran off into the night, tails extended and heads up.

I started the car and drove my charges towards their surprise bush dinner.

O'Reilly, with the help of the camp managers, had done a spectacular job. At around 19h00 all game drives converged on a clearing framed by three huge, dead knobthorn trees. From base to tip, the trees had been covered with paraffin lanterns. (How they'd got up to the top of the trees became apparent when I found Manfred of the maintenance team lying next to a step ladder under a bush nearby. He had a glazed look and a plastic bag of ice over his left eye.)

As we pulled up, the last to arrive, the camp managers and butlers made a guard of honour to either side of the entrance. They bore trays of cocktails, warm towels, cold towels and even mosquito spray. Right at the entrance stood Nicolette Hogan in a standard loose-fitting white shirt and khaki slacks, the proud owner and consummate hostess.

Inside the naturally formed arena, tables were decked with white cloths, silver cutlery and crystal glasses. Candles blazed in glimmering pewter candelabras. Instead of having the buffet to one side, the bush kitchen was the centrepiece. Within a circle of braai fires and tables overflowing with every deliciousness I could imagine, the chefs cooked, chopped, sautéed, mixed and did other chef-type things. The bar was at the base of the central knobthorn, and on it an array of profoundly expensive champagne, malt whisky, craft beer and bottles of exclusive South African wines made a dizzying display that succeeded in conveying a sense of luxurious abundance (what the barmen who lived on the smell of an oil rag felt was unclear).

My guests disappeared into the stunning setting and I headed to the bar – a strong Scotch was just the thing to ease my parched throat and irritated disposition. Phanuel, barman extraordinaire, was putting the finishing touches to a negroni when I arrived, and placed it on a waiting tray. Incredible the butler whisked the tray off the counter. Unfortunately, the glass of red cocktail flew off the tray and landed on Mark's shoulder as he arrived to order his umpteenth beer. Before the twat could complain, Incredible went for him.

'Why you are standing in my way?' he shouted. Then, with eyes so wide it looked like they'd pop out of his skull, he tapped the side of head with a flat hand and glared at Mark. I turned away giggling and Phanuel presented a glass of golden elixir without my having to ask.

'What have you chosen for me, Phanuel?' I asked.

'Tonight, a Balvenie with ice and a one water drop,' he explained. 'It is too hot for the neat one.'

'And why the Balvenie?'

'Ah! Angus!' he shook his head. 'On a hot summer night, you must drink the one from Speyside.' He clicked his tongue while effortlessly uncorking a bottle of Chenin blanc and handing it to Clifford.

I leant against the bar and observed String Bean bustling about, checking tables – straightening cutlery, adding the odd glass to settings and offering drinks to anyone without one. This was an environment in which he thrived.

The new rangers were standing off to one side chattering excitedly and I walked over to them.

'Cheers,' I said. 'You haven't really had a formal welcome into the fold, but well done to all of you on a somewhat more satisfactory end to the day than any of us expected.' We chinked our glasses. 'Are you all okay – any questions or concerns?'

We debriefed about the drives and talked through a few queries. On the whole, everyone seemed okay until Jasper, the great and reluctant leopard tracker, said, 'I have a small problem.' He grinned and looked at the ground.

We gave him our attention. 'I think … bru, I reckon one of my guests has, like, a crush on me.' This brought forth loud guffaws from the rest. Jasper looked slightly insulted. 'Bru, why's that so funny?'

'Why do you think she has a crush on you, Jasper and who is she?' I asked.

Jasper looked around conspiratorially and then pointed to a group of chatting guests. Before he could say anything, one of them turned and caught Jasper's eye. He paled, head swinging back.

'Shit, bru, she's coming over!'

I'm not sure if Jasper had a 'type' but I am fairly sure that the creature who approached us wasn't it. She was in her mid-fifties and not a woman who had spent a great deal of time honing her physique. She was as tall as Franci, she had a round face, a mop of curly blonde hair and a covering of flesh that suggested a great love of confectionery.

'Ah, look at ze rangers!' she said in a strong Austrian accent. 'Vat a lovely night is zis, so romantic!' She squished in between Jasper and Franci, turning her shoulder to the latter. 'So, little Jasper, vat are ve talking about?'

Jasper went the colour of pomegranate. 'Um, well, like, leopards and stuff,' he stammered.

She then slapped him hard on the backside. 'My little Jasper is such a funny little fellow, aren't you!' she giggled, and drained her glass.

We went to sit with our guests a short while later, Jasper arm in arm with his delightful conquest. My table included Nicolette Hogan, so I had to be on my best behaviour. The guests had no desire to talk to the garbage that was their driver so I contented myself with a good meal and going to fetch drinks for the bottomless well of hard liquor that was Sergei. Entertainment at my table came exclusively from the Russians, who bickered nonstop in their language, tossing in the odd bits of English swearing. Halfway through the pudding, Olga tossed her glass of Shiraz in her husband's face. He pounded the table and stormed off to the bar, where he remained for the rest of the evening, imbibing the best part of a bottle of Grey Goose.

At roughly 22h30 we rolled back into Hogan Camp, where Mayan was waiting for her well-oiled guests. They had no further desires so we handed them to the security team, who conveyed them to their rooms. Mayan hopped into the passenger seat of the Land Rover and I drove back to park it in the workshop. Then, on a whim, I took the road west out of camp and headed for the river. We stopped on the bank, about four metres above the strongly flowing ribbon of water.

We sat in silence, listening to the Tsessebe and watching the moonlight dance on its surface. Far to the north a lion roared and a little way downstream a hippo grunted. All around, the sound of summer cicadas, crickets and other insects bent on seduction buzzed, hummed and whirred. A water thick-knee joined the chorus and then fell silent.

'If I didn't know better,' Mayan eventually whispered, 'I'd think you were trying to seduce or at the very least court me.'

'Don't be ridiculous,' I replied softly. 'I just had to check the river was flowing before turning in.'

'I told you, I don't appreciate sarcasm.'

'That's because you haven't given it a proper chance.' I climbed out of the car, walked to the passenger side and opened the door. Then I walked to the rim of the precipitous bank and sat down, my legs hanging over the edge. A moment later, I felt her sit next to me, her legs touching mine. The faint hint of jasmine intertwined with the scent of the water and the chocolatey smell of *Hemizygia* flowers.

She was leaning back on her hands, head back, looking at the moon. She flicked her head slightly and her hair, unusually free of its plait, fell back revealing her long neck. My eyes followed its line down over her shoulders to where her shirt was stretched over her chest, down to her flat stomach and over her hips. I looked back to her face to find her eyes on me, right brow cocked.

By that stage, there was no force in the universe capable of stopping me kissing her full lips. I leant over and saw her eyes gently close before mine did the same. I inhaled the exquisite scent of her and prepared for the wondrous, full-body sensation that comes with kissing a beautiful woman on a perfect moonlit night in the African wild.

I say no force in the universe, but the universe is crafty ... And at this lusty juncture, two forces combined. The first was the force of the water undercutting the sandy bank, and the second was that old favourite, gravity. The piece of bank on which I sat gave way when my lips were but a millimetre from their goal.

'Aaargh!' I yelled, as the bank beneath me gave way and my lips began accelerating away from Mayan's at an alarming rate. They did not miss her entirely, and in fact made very close contact with her right knee, which reflexively came up as my head went down. I kissed her patella with hammer force and went over the edge, scrabbling frantically for something to arrest my fall. There was nothing, and my backside hit the water below with a colossal splash. The river wasn't deep – about a metre or so – but it was flowing strongly enough to carry me downstream about 50 metres before the bank flattened enough for me to grab an overhanging tree and haul myself out.

'Angus?' I heard Mayan calling. 'Are you alright?'

'Yesh!' I shouted back, my split and swelling lip giving me a lisp. 'Justht wait there!' I could taste blood so I spat, extricated myself from the tree that had saved me and made my way up to the point where Mayan stood looking down, her arresting figure silhouetted by the moon behind her.

'Was it something I said?' she asked with amused concern as I stood up next to her. 'Oh, your lip! What happened?!' Her hands held my face as she examined my injuries.

'You kneed me in the fathe,' I replied. 'We'd better get back.'

A few moments later we drove into the workshop. I noticed that the maintenance vehicle was absent, but assumed it must have been elsewhere on account of the bush dinner. We walked back to Mayan's place, where she examined my now horribly swollen split lip and applied an ointment that stung like hell. I then bade her goodnight – the possibility of staying the night out of the question given my muddy and injured condition.

The way back to the BC took me past the office. The camp was beautifully quiet, bathed in moonlight and sleeping easily after the first superbly handled night for the Condé Nast group. Quite suddenly, as I passed the herb garden between the rangers' room and office, an engine roared to life. At roughly the same time, a loud banging emanated from somewhere in the office. The lights were off, but a flickering of torchlight was visible through the window. Heart pounding, I ran for the office and tore open the door.

Through the opening that led to Hilda's annex, I saw two men wielding four-pound hammers, beating the wall next to the safe. It took a moment for me to realise that two heavy chains were wrapped around the safe and extending through two holes in the wall. With each rev of the vehicle on the other side of the wall, the chains tensed over the safe.

'Hey!' I shouted and rushed towards them.

As I reached the annex, the safe came clear of its moorings in the concrete floor and the wall gave way. One of the hammer wielders made it out of the hole but I grabbed the second one before he could make his escape. This was a mistake in many respects: I was unarmed and have never been much of a fighter. The man dropped his hammer (thankfully), grabbed my throat and the last thing I remember was a burn-scarred forehead coming towards the bridge of my nose with alarming speed.

31

When I opened my eyes, it was pitch black and I had no idea where I was. My head pounded and there was a strong taste of blood in my mouth. Eventually, my rattled brain rebooted and I looked around. The desk against which I was lying coalesced into something recognisable and I hauled myself upright. Then I sat down again rather quickly as stars appeared in my vision and the dark world began to swim. Eventually, I opened my eyes and looked at my watch: 01h15, so I'd been asleep/unconscious for about 90 minutes. Dim moonlight fell through the open office door.

I had to report this but to whom? I decided String Bean was the best option, so I picked up the phone on Hilda's desk and dialled the Tamboti Camp manager's cottage. It rang six times before he answered.

'Hello. Hugh speaking,' said the groggy voice.

'String Bean, it's me. You need to come to the office as fast as you can. Don't ask, just come.'

'Fuck, Angus, but what –'

I cut him off. 'Just come, quickly.'

A few moments later he arrived, walked through the door and switched on the light. The blinding brightness drove daggers through my brain. He saw the destroyed wall of the office next door and then he saw me.

'Jesus Christ, what the fuck happened here?'

'As far as I could tell before receiving a forehead to my eyebrow ... persons unknown have made off with the safe using the maintenance vehicle and some hammers. Agricultural methods to be sure, but effective, as you can see.' I rubbed my eyes as they slowly adjusted to the light. 'I saw a torch flickering in here and came to see what was going on – the last thing I remember is being headbutted by a bandit.'

'But, who, how, I mean *when*? Christ, that fucking priceless Pink Flute is in the safe! Fuck me, what are we going to do?'

'The very, very first thing you are going to do is wake Nicolette and tell her. Trying to deal with this on your own would be the worst possible plan.'

A few minutes later, Nicolette arrived – perfectly dressed, as if she'd not even considered being asleep when Enock 'The Fist' Mhlongo, head of security, banged on her door. I briefed her while String Bean listened. Enock also listened with great care, shaking his head and grunting at crucial points in the story. In Enock's mind, there was no connection between his department's responsibilities and the fact that a band of at least three desperados had absconded with a six-foot safe leaving a Francois-sized hole in the main office wall.

'Is very bad,' he said, clicking his teeth and rubbing his chin.

Nicolette cast her icy glare on him.

'I assume you are not asking a question, Enock? I assume you are making a statement – a statement that does not need to be made given *how bleeding fucking obvious it is!*' She took a deep breath, closed her eyes and composed herself. 'Enock, go and find the rest of your security team and get them in here within the next five minutes.'

Enock scuttled out, clicking his teeth miserably. Nicolette sighed and looked around the room.

'This is the Sasekile brains trust – the MacNaughton brothers and me. I find it disconcerting that this is how things have come to pass. Any bright ideas for how we can recover a priceless French antique from the bowels of Gazankulu?'

My head was still pounding but at least my lip seemed to have gone down slightly. 'Nicolette,' I said, taking my head out of my hands, 'in case it has escaped your notice, the so-called security team at this lodge –

and all others for that matter – are the least trained, most junior and most poorly paid staff. Do you really think they have the skills or interest required to pull off a Poirot-level investigation? In five minutes you are going to have ten of the most baffled and frightened residents of Gazankulu in here and they are going to be, to quote a good friend, as useless as tits on a fish. It is entirely possible that some of them know who has perpetrated this heist, but ratting out the brigands is simply not in their interests.'

String Bean gasped. Nicolette regarded me for a moment and then looked at my brother, who managed to find his balls.

'He's right,' SB said, shrugging. 'They're hopeless and it's really not their fault.'

'Get the trackers,' I said. 'Get Elvis and Slumber to follow the tracks. If you do that now, before anyone else drives the road, they'll follow that car to wherever those miscreants are trying to open the safe … assuming they're already not halfway to Johannesburg or Maputo.'

'And get Jacob on board to provide a bit of muscle,' said String Bean.

Nicolette looked from SB to me, hands on her hips. Then she exhaled.

'Right,' she said. 'And I'll call the police to join them on the outside.'

'That,' said String Bean, 'is a dreadful idea. They make our security team look like a SWAT unit. Just let Jacob deal with it and don't ask questions.'

'Finally, some bloody leadership,' she said. 'Make it happen, Hugh. Tomorrow night' – she looked at her watch – 'correction, *tonight*, they have the awards ceremony – that Pink Flute must be back here by then.'

String Bean nodded and looked at me. 'Angus, go to bed. You have to take a drive in three hours' time and pretend that nothing's wrong.'

'Yes, my lord,' I said as I stood, wobbled slightly, and departed for the BC, hoping fervently that this would be the last I had to do with the recovery of the bloody Pink Flute.

I arrived on the Hogan deck at 05h00 for 30 minutes of silent coffee. The pleasant aroma of freshly brewing grounds greeted my nostrils as I walked through the back entrance to the kitchen. There, standing over a steaming plunger, was Mayan, perfectly spruced, the gold-entwined plait back in place.

'Here to check I don't cock things up again?' I asked.

'If I was here for that, I can assure you I wouldn't be making you coffee.' She looked up, smiled and began to depress the plunger.

'How do you look like that at this time of the morning?'

'Like what?'

'Like you've been up making yourself presentable for hours.'

'Maybe I have.' She poured a cup and handed me the saucer. 'You, on the other hand, look a bit like you've been hit by a buffalo. Why do you look like you've been hit by a buffalo?'

We walked onto the deck, past the horn pile – still looking like it was listing to the left. We sat on a sofa in the sala beneath the mahogany and as I sipped the delicious arabica, I explained the events of the previous night. Mayan's large eyes widened with the telling.

'This would explain why you have an egg on your forehead and bloodshot eyes. At least your lip is a bit better.'

'Quite.'

We sat in comfortable silence as the dawn chorus filled our ears – crested francolins trumpeted down in the river, a flock of cape white-eyes swizzled in the leaves above us, a white-browed robin-chat sang an aria in the thicket below. Then a woodland kingfisher flitted up onto a thin limb a few metres from us, carrying a large centipede in its bill. It proceeded to bash the life out of the beastly looking invertebrate and, after a minute or two, swallowed its breakfast before looking around, cleaning its beak on the branch and then calling, 'chip prrrrrrrrrrrrrrr'.

Mayan looked at her gold watch, turned and touched my hand. 'Time to take a drive, Angus.' She took the cup out of my hand and I stood wearily.

'Here we go,' I said.

The drive was spectacular, half because the Russians chose to stay in bed and half because Franci, driving out of Kingfisher Camp, managed to find a pack of wild dogs hunting on Black Mane Clearings. We happened to be in the area when she found them, so Jasper, Franci and I spent a marvellous hour leapfrogging each other as we followed them on the hunt, with four thieving hyenas bringing up the rear.

I forgot entirely about my heavy head as the pack coursed over the clearing and through the thickets. We lost and found the twelve hunting hounds four times as they rushed through the combretum woodland – a white tail darting here, a contact call there and five times a scrub hare or duiker bursting from cover, running for its life. Then, as they came to the clearings below a spot called Klipspringer Koppies, a steenbok stupidly chose flight over freeze. The little antelope sprang from the grass and ran, giving the dogs way too much space and time.

As the first bleat escaped the hapless thing's mouth, the hyenas charged in from the northern side of the clearings. The dogs momentarily forgot their hunger as they fanned to defend their breakfast. The ensuing melee was deafening as the predators howled, cackled, twittered and growled at each other. Eventually the dogs lost patience and charged the bigger scavengers. Three of them got hold of a young hyena, nipping at its backside. With its ears flat back, braying like a donkey, it spun around to bring its formidable jaws to bear. The dogs released the hyena as one of its colleagues tried to make off with the carcass. The enraged hounds went back for their kill and another standoff ensued.

As the cacophony reached another crescendo, a young male leopard exploded from the cover of a raisin bush. He grabbed the carcass and in less than three seconds was in the boughs of a marula tree with his prize, the dogs and hyenas left to watch, helpless, from below.

Africa showing off in breath-taking fashion.

Back in the Hogan Camp kitchen, I was enjoying a cup of coffee with a croissant filled with camembert and berry coulis, thinking about a good long snooze back at the BC, when the camp manager burst in from the deck.

'Hugh is calling for you.' She handed me her radio and headed back out onto the deck.

'My lord String Bean, come in,' I said.

'Angus, come to the office ASAP.'

The path from Hogan Camp took me past Katie and Jerome's block.

He was sitting on the patio outside and it was immediately apparent that all was not well in the land of Jerome le Roux. His hair was out of place, falling lank on his large head in the manner of a dark, greasy bowl. Uneven stubble sprouted in patches around his face and neck, and he was wearing a shirt – unusual given his propensity to remove his top when the temperature went above freezing.

'Hello, Jerome,' I said.

He sniffed, and I was immediately irritated by his pathetic state, especially when he didn't reply.

'Have you lost the power of speech?'

'Shame, he's had a rough time,' said the ever-kind Katie, emerging from her room.

'You mean your, um – I learnt this word recently – *schtoomping* session with Kelly-Anne has brought about unintended consequences?'

He looked up like a sick puppy.

'Did you learn this sort of behaviour from your oupa?'

'Angus!' said Katie.

'Don't talk about my oupa like that,' snivelled Jerome.

'Jerome, I know you have studiously ignored everything I've said ever since you got here, perhaps considering your oupa a better trainer of game rangers at high-end lodges. With this in mind, I offer you a piece of advice now – use it or don't.'

He looked up and wiped his nose, snot catching in the matted hair of his scraggly moustache.

'I suggest you get up from where you're sitting, clean yourself up, take responsibility for your shitty behaviour and then, when everything has calmed down, seek forgiveness. But for fuck sake's don't sit there wasting oxygen.'

And with that I departed.

A few minutes later, I arrived at the office, fearful that my snooze was about to go for a ball of chalk. There I found Nicolette, String Bean and Bertie. There was no preamble.

'Angus, you need to go and help with the Pink Flute,' said Nicolette.

'The trackers are on the trail in Boxa Huku Village, but they need more manpower. They are pretty sure that it's still there, but the trail's gone cold. Take whoever you need and get out there immediately – you speak the language and you might recognise someone. Take your crew.'

Five minutes after that, six of us were bouncing along at an indecent speed towards the reserve gate in an unmarked double cab. Solomon was driving and I was in the back seat, being squashed against the door by Franci. Jasper was in the load bin singing Bob Marley's 'Jamming' very badly through the open window. It took about 60 minutes to get to the village of Boxa Huku (which literally means 'stab the chicken'). The ex-trainees thought this enormous entertainment. All I could think of was my bed and Mayan's luscious and as-yet-unkissed lips, sometimes in the same proximity.

It should be noted that the initial job of following the brigands did not require an enormously skilled tracking team. The criminals had continued with their agricultural approach and, possibly in a panic and possibly because of the safe's mass, the three of them had simply dragged the safe down Sasekile's main road, leaving a gouge that a blind man could have followed. They had then, in order to avoid the reserve's security gate (a wise choice if you are bent on successful crime), driven the vehicle through and over the game fence. Somewhere just outside the reserve, they'd press-ganged a group of local villagers, hitherto stumbling home after a big night at the local watering hole, into helping them load the safe into the back of the Sasekile maintenance vehicle. It was from here that the tracking became more difficult.

By the time we joined the other car's search at around 11h30, the tracking team (with some intimidatory tactics from Jacob) had followed the gang some ten kilometres from where the fence was originally broken. Once at Boxa Huku, we met Elvis and the others at a local spaza shop owned by a Bangladeshi man who spoke about three words of English and no Shangane. How he conducted his business was quite beyond me and he was of no help to our investigation. It was here that Elvis and Slumber had lost the trail because of the amount of morning traffic.

The village was hot and dusty. Listless donkeys wandered the eroded streets with industrious goats and the odd emaciated cow. Skinny dogs lay in what shade there was while people went about whatever business they could to bring in another meal for their families. Elvis suggested we drive around the village to see if anything looked suspicious. The vehicle we drove had been specifically chosen for the fact that it was unmarked and therefore unlikely to arouse interest.

We drove around with Donald prodding me in the ribs when I fell asleep (roughly every three minutes). It was hopeless – there was nothing to see, hardly anyone about and no sign of the Sasekile maintenance vehicle. No doubt many in the village knew about the crime – these things tend not to go unnoticed – but simply asking around would most likely have resulted in a warning going out to the criminals.

After an hour we met back at the spaza shop. Flute or no flute, we had to leave the village within ten minutes to make it back for the game drive. I went inside to buy a Coke, a true reflection of how utterly stuffed I felt.

I ordered my drink and some no-name-brand analgesic (which I hoped wouldn't blind me) from the proprietor, who had clearly not seen many white people in his shop.

'I don't suppose you've seen three buccaneers driving about with a large safe in the back of their vehicle, have you?' I asked.

'Oh, good day,' he said, nodding pleasantly and handing me my change.

I then noticed a fascinating and completely out-of-place collection of exotic condoms off to one side, behind a palate of maize-meal sacks. I opened my Coke, wandered over to the glass cabinet and peered into it absently while swallowing my pills. As I was considering how on earth a gold condom would find a user in Boxa Huku Village, I heard the proprietor greet another customer as he slapped his money on the counter. I turned around. The man had paused to consider a rack of contraband cigarettes.

The burn mark on the man's head was unmistakable – it was this fellow's forehead that had rendered me unconscious.

I ducked behind the maize meal and waited for him to leave, not wishing to spend the afternoon dead or knocked out on a bag of maize. Through the door, I noted that the criminal had climbed into a Toyota Tazz of astounding decrepitude.

Outside, the others were chatting and paying no attention to the scarred man making his second getaway of the day.

'Guys!' I hissed, the Coke, excitement and whatever pill I'd taken driving my heart rate to dangerous levels. No one heard me. 'Guys!' I shouted as the car rattled off down the track.

Finally they looked around.

'That's him!' I pointed frantically as the car turned a corner and disappeared. 'That's the guy who hit me!'

In two seconds, everyone was back in the vehicles. Our car took the lead, trying to keep our distance on the badly rutted roads, but not lose the Tazz – not wanting to put the man to flight. Jacob felt no such compunction. As we rounded a corner, the Tazz some 100 metres ahead, he overtook us.

I'm not sure if the criminal registered the chase vehicle – probably not given the lack of rear-view mirrors – but I imagine he registered alarm when Jacob rammed his tin can into a ditch. In seconds, Jacob had the man out of the driver's seat, up against the vehicle and had slapped him hard.

The man began to sing, point and gesticulate. A few minutes after that, we pulled up outside a collection of dilapidated buildings surrounded by a tumble-down fence. Jacob had the scarred man by the scruff of his neck, half dragging him from the car, and everyone else piled out and made it through a gap in the fence, heedless of any dangers there might be.

Some single-room buildings opened onto a central area out of which a tremendous whining emanated from an overworked grinder. The scarred fellow tried to shout a warning to his compadres but was prevented from doing so by a combination of the grinder noise and a cuff over the head from Jacob. In the middle of the central area lay the safe, on its back. There were two men, one armed with a grinder whose rapidly diminishing blade was producing a spray of sparks, and one trying to light an acetylene torch. As we arrived, the latter's flint finally sparked but he had his mixture wrong. A flame leapt from the end of the ancient piece of equipment and caught his mate with the grinder on the backside.

Until that point, I had never seen a human being fly, but I swear the heat sent Grinder-man three feet up and four feet across before gravity reasserted its authority. Grinder-man hit the opposite wall with a dull thud. Torch-man looked up, saw us and leapt over a low wall between two buildings and scarpered into the bush. Slumber ran over to the dangerous-looking cylinders of welding gas and switched them off. Elvis kicked Grinder-man in the knee as he tried to repeat his flying antics, and he went quiet – but for a bit of groaning.

It was all rather pathetic. The three men were not exactly sophisticated criminal masterminds, and they hadn't a spare shirt to share between them. The safe was a bit scratched but nowhere near being opened. Leaning against the buildings were bits and pieces of mismatched, endlessly repaired furniture. Just inside one of the doors, an old woman lay on a broken camp bed next to a glass of dirty water.

'Who is this?' I asked Grinder-man, who was now sitting up against a wall.

'My mother,' he said. 'She is sick and we have no food.'

There was no conceivable way this lot could have planned and executed the theft without inside help from Sasekile. I actually felt sorry for them.

'Let's just take the safe and leave them,' said Katie.

'No,' said Jacob. 'He must tell us who made him do this.'

I looked at my watch. 'Shit, we're not going to make the drive unless we leave now – we have 60 minutes to arrive on deck.' I turned back to Grinder-man. 'We'll send someone to take your mother to the hospital and bring you some food.'

Everyone spontaneously emptied the little cash they had from their pockets and handed it to the morose-looking fellow.

'What about the cops?' said Franci, slightly scandalised.

'Waste of time,' said Solomon sadly. 'They'll do nothing or else they'll hurt these people.'

A minute later we were speeding back along the road at breakneck speed. There was obviously no chance of catching up on any sleep and my headache was worse than ever. We sped into camp with two minutes to spare, and no time to shower and beautify ourselves.

At the appointed time I sauntered as casually as possible onto the Hogan Camp deck to where the guests, along with Mayan and Nicolette, were sitting in the sala. On seeing me, Mayan came striding along the little walkway, concern mixed with relief on her normally implacable visage.

I stopped at the horn installation and waited for her. One of the horns – the top one, as far as I could tell, had fallen to the left of the piece.

'Did you get it?' she said.

'I'd love a piece of cake and a cup of coffee, thank you so much!' I said. 'Been a helluva day so far.'

Her eyes rolled in exasperation. 'Well?'

'The safe is on its way back. I have no idea what state the flute is in, given that the safe was dragged most of the way to Boxa Huku during the course of last night.'

'Thank God,' she sighed.

'I don't mean to cause undue alarm,' I said, 'but are you sure this deck is still level? Either this piece of so-called art is not very steady – quite possible – or the western side of the deck is subsiding.'

Further consideration of the deck wasn't possible as Nicolette was already ushering the guests towards me for game drive. None of the guests bothered to greet me using the method of voice. Three of them nodded vaguely in my direction as they made their way out towards the car park where Jackson, a nineteen-year-old security guard, was deputising for Elvis, who was hopefully on his way back with the safe, no doubt looking forward to a good long sleep.

'Enjoy your drive! The deck will be set for the broadcast at eight – we are so looking forward to it!' said Nicolette. But as I made to follow them, she grabbed my elbow.

'Angus, tell me you have the safe,' she hissed.

I looked at her, raised my eyebrows and then put my hands in my pockets, pulling out the empty lining.

'Not with me, no.'

'This is *not* the time!' she snapped.

'No, quite. Nicolette, I suspect that if you hurry up to the office, you may be just in time to find the safe arriving with Jacob, Elvis and Slumber. The thieves didn't manage to open it, so the flute, or pieces thereof, must still be inside.'

For the second time in one day, I saw a human fly. One moment Nicolette was there and the next there was just the vague smell of her perfume.

As we departed the camp, I saw a small van arrive with a collapsible satellite dish on its roof. Craig followed with an army of maintenance crew carrying all sorts of technical equipment and cameras. I had no idea how the evening's broadcast was even technically feasible, but I was sure that if anyone could do it, Craig could.

While preparations were made for the evening's entertainment – the Condé Nast broadcast from Hogan Camp would be followed by a black-tie affair on the Main Camp deck – our game drive proceeded. Although not recommended by the textbook of great guiding, I had decided that my guests needed a bush experience that would either make them uncomfortable or knock some exuberant appreciation into them. This, I knew, would be best achieved on foot.

Normally, I would have had Elvis to help me on a walk instead of a green security guard with absolutely no big-game experience. Nevertheless we spotted the fresh tracks of a rhino cow and calf at the bottom of a shady drainage line, which provided the perfect opportunity to try and connect my complacent guests with the wilderness.

I stopped the car and climbed out. 'Everyone, if I might have your attention.'

Stacy looked up from where she'd been tapping something on her smartphone, and the Russians scowled. Bobby Johannson looked at me and said, 'Whatta you got there, driver?'

I ignored his referring to my occupation as 'driver' rather than guide, ranger or bush genius, and continued: 'We have some very fresh rhino tracks. The animals are heading towards a mud wallow not too far from here. I would like you to all come down from the vehicle – we are going to approach these animals on foot.'

One of the things you learn as a ranger is that telling guests what to do is far better than asking them what they'd like to do. (The last thing you want is guests making up their own minds and attempting a debate.) While they are often leaders in whatever industry they happen to be destroying the planet with, the African wild is unfamiliar and intimidating for most people. I have found that if you give firm, confident instructions, they normally just obey.

Soon six people in various shades of khaki-chic were standing in the sand next to me as I pointed out the rhino tracks. They didn't ask questions. I began to speak in hushed tones.

'See, here is the mother, and here is the calf.' I indicated the tracks. 'That game path up on the bank leads to a pan – or mud wallow – nearby. We are going to approach the pan very quietly on foot in the hopes of viewing the cow and calf in the mud.'

The guests eyed me without a great deal of interest. I then gave a brief safety talk culminating in the immortal safari words: 'If we should surprise an animal, whatever you do, don't run.'

I took the rifle from the rack and then instructed Jackson to walk at the back of the group, making sure that no one was left behind. My assumption that Jackson would react rationally in the face of a fast-moving pachyderm would turn out to be ill-considered.

We set off along the path, the tracks clear in the moist ground. I'm not an expert tracker by any stretch, but rhino post-rain on a hot afternoon were well within my capabilities. The game path led through some thick guinea grass on the bank of the drainage line. Some of the plants were just forming their distinctive inflorescences but most were just thick tufts of emerald. The path was littered with bits of grass where the rhino had grazed and then discarded or dropped half a mouthful here and there.

At one such patch, I knelt down and beckoned the guests. Jeanne-the-Parisian was starting to show a bit of excitement.

'What 'ave we 'ere?' she asked rather loudly.

'Let's try and talk quietly,' I said. 'Look here – you can still see the rhino's saliva glistening in the light.'

'Can I touch it?' she whispered.

'Yes, of course.'

She knelt down and felt the wet grass.

It is amazing to watch as the final barrier between human and wilderness breaks down. She knelt and touched the slimy tips of the grass leaves, and then a huge smile spread across her face.

'This rhino is eating this now?' she asked, still whispering – the need for quiet finally taking hold.

'Indeed, just a few minutes ago.'

We proceeded with caution on the game path, which turned into an avenue of tamboti trees. The light filtered through the young, tannin-rich leaves, burnishing the late afternoon in copper and bronze. About 50 metres later we came to a steaming pile of dung. It was so fresh that the flies had yet to settle on it. Once again, I gathered them all around.

'Why ve have stopped?' said Sergei.

'Can you not see ze shit of ze rhino?' hissed Jeanne, France's latest and greatest tracker. She then reached down and stuck her finger into the middle of the black dung. 'Zis is still ot!' she proclaimed. 'Zis rhino iz close!'

'Why you fingyer the shyeet?' said Olga. 'Thyet is disgyusting!'

'Please be as quiet as possible,' I whispered. 'This animal is very close – probably near the pan. We need to walk very carefully.'

At that moment, a dung beetle landed with a gentle thud and set to work scraping off bits of dung to make its little honeymoon ball.

'Lyook at little byeetle!' cooed Sergei.

Thin shafts of brassy sunlight filtered through the tamboti branches, spotlighting the industrious beetle. The Russian looked like he might cry – such is the power of nature. His voice also dropped to a whisper as he looked up. 'Thyet rhino is nyear, yes?'

'Yes, I whispered. 'Let's carry on.'

We continued slowly along the path towards a grove of splendid thorn and tamboti next to the pan. The next to fall to the spell of the glorious afternoon was Stacy Johannson: when Bobby stood on a twig that made a loud crack, Stacy rounded on him.

'Bobby!' she hissed. 'What the hell is wrong with you? Watch where you walk, you asshole!'

We were about 50 metres from the pan. I checked the wind and it was blowing towards us – perfect for an approach. I turned to the group and pointed at a fallen knobthorn tree.

'We're going to approach that fallen tree. From there, we'll be able to see into the pan where I think the rhino are wallowing in the mud. We must be *very quiet*.' I gave a thumbs-up to Jackson, who, looking like the least interested person in the Lowveld, half-heartedly returned the gesture.

About 20 metres from the tree, Claude stepped into a hole and had no compunction whatsoever about shouting at the top of his lungs: 'Putain, merde!'

'Shhh!' I admonished, turning to see what the problem was.

It was then that the rhinos stood, snorting loudly. I swung back to see the cow with her little calf running around in confusion next to her, uttering panicked squeaks.

In the manner of all rhinos who are afraid and unable to see or smell what is threatening them, they chose the most convenient escape – and unfortunately for us, the avenue of tamboti on which we had approached was exactly that. The terrified animals – calf in front and mother behind in the classic manner of the white rhino – came thundering down the path straight towards us.

I was about to instruct my guests to get behind a tree quickly when Jackson, hitherto mute, uttered his first words of the afternoon, and they were not helpful.

'Fuck-shit-dammit-fuck!' he shouted. 'Run!'

I'm not quite sure what he expected the six out-of-shape business-people in their early sixties to do, but he – being lithe, supple and terrified

– took off into the woodland like a turbocharged scrub hare. Before I could shout, 'Get behind a tree and stand still,' the guests attempted to follow their 'tracker's' example, with varying degrees of success.

Claude, foot still in the hole, simply fell over. His wife turned and ran into the trees, but tripped on a root and sprawled into last-season's leaf litter. Olga, wisely, picked a relatively easy tree and was about to climb it when Sergei, full of Russian chivalry, attempted to use her as a ladder. She, unsurprisingly, wasn't remotely able to take his weight and the two of them ended up on top of each other in the dirt. Stacy just stood still, hands covering her face, and uttered a mournful howl a bit like a drunk and depressed wolf. Bobby Johannson, blessed with the Rock of Gibraltar's shape and athleticism, began what he must have considered evasive action, but managed only two steps before the rhinos drew level.

I, meanwhile, was shouting, 'Hey! Voetsek!' on repeat and waving my arms about. Thankfully, I happened to be standing next to a tamboti tree and stepped behind this as the terrified animals thundered past.

As the sound of breaking vegetation receded, I came out to examine the damage.

Claude, leg beginning to swell, wore an expression of pain mixed with hatred – I'm sure he'd have tried to kill me if he'd been less injured. Jeanne looked confused and suspicious. Sergei rose from his prone position (atop his wife) to one knee. He was covered in dust and sporting a nasty graze from the tamboti bark. Olga, apparently stunned, rolled onto her back.

'Are you alright, Olga?' I asked tentatively.

'Blyad,' she muttered, sitting up, her bright-red cotton blouse now much more brown than red.

I didn't understand what that meant, but figured it was a good thing she was able to speak.

'Sweet-Lord-baby-Jesus-mother-of-God!' exclaimed Bobby, executing a turn with the speed of a stricken aircraft carrier.

'Oh my God!' yelled Stacy, dusting herself off, pulling leaves from her head and examining a tear in her slacks. What came out of her mouth next shocked me to my core. 'That was the greatest experience of my *life!* Did you *see* how close those rhinos came to us?'

I was so incredulous at this ridiculous utterance that I almost attempted to persuade her that she'd actually come damn close to death. Then I stopped myself. Hell, if Sasekile's most important guest of the last 20 years thought that eating dirt and tearing her clothes while avoiding a rampaging pachyderm bent on skewering her was an excellent experience, then so be it.

'Nicolette told us you were something special!' Stacy grabbed my left hand – the right one still held my rifle – and shook it. Then she threw her arms around my neck. 'The last time I felt this exhilarated was when I first made love to Bobby on the back of his daddy's pickup in the summer of '74!'

It wasn't until that moment that I realised the thrall in which Stacy held the rest of her party. Their expressions of distress, anger and pain softened to smiles and nodding as they beheld their matriarch fawning over me. All but one, that is – her husband.

'Stacy, you gone mad? We nearly just died here – you think this fool *meant* to make those dinosaurs charge us?'

I sensed a return of the hostile atmosphere.

'Oh, you're always so dramatic, Bobby.' Stacy rolled her eyes theatrically. 'You think he wouldna shot those things to hell if he'd thought they were gonna hurt us? You think he doesn't understand how important we are? Nicolette told me this is "Sasekile's most unforgettable ranger" – and I can see why!'

Before Bobby could object, the rest had gathered around to shake my hand and thank me for the experience of a lifetime.

'You know,' Stacy continued philosophically, 'we have to travel from hotel to hotel all over the world – it gets really tiring being wined and dined nonstop all the time. I mean, there's only so much foie gras, caviar and Bollinger a person can take! Am I *really* supposed to be impressed by yet another spacious shower and heated toilet seat?' She reached for her top lip and dabbed at some blood with her finger. 'No, *this* – this takes the cake!'

'I agree there,' I muttered.

We finished off the game drive with a stunning sundowner on a ridge crest overlooking the northern Drakensberg. The air was crystal clear as I served powerful gin and tonics to all the guests except Bobby, who grunted a request for an Elijah Craig twelve-year-old bourbon while eyeing me suspiciously. I was about to suggest he was mad if he thought I carried around such a thing, but then I spotted an odd-shaped bottle in the cooler box. Mayan had found out precisely what brand he liked and made sure we had it. Bobby was somewhat mollified after his second tumblerful.

As the cicadas trilled on the slope below and an African cuckoo piped gently from a marula tree nearby, we watched our star gently slip behind the ancient mountains. The guests went quiet without prompting, instinctively ending their conversations as dusk fell. Finally, they had tapped into the magic of Africa ...

I should state at this stage that Jackson was nowhere to be found – indeed, his tracks back at the pan had indicated that he'd run in the direction of the lodge, so I'd simply carried on without him. As I took the last sip of my sparkling water, the radio crackled with my brother's panicked voice.

'Angus, do you copy?'

It took me a little while to get to the radio as I'd been sitting on a low termite mound, enjoying the moment.

'Angus, Angus, Angus, do you copy?' he said urgently.

'Go ahead, String Bean,' I said.

'Angus, what the hell is going on there – Jackson has just arrived back at camp and swears that he saw you and the guests gored to death by an enraged rhino!'

'Jackson should be employed to operate a boom-gate at a Fourways complex where the most dangerous thing he'll come up against is the faux-Tuscan architecture.'

'Are the guests alright, Angus? This is Nicolette speaking, over.'

'No, I have buried them in shallow graves lining the ridge crest off Mamba Road. Rest assured that their mortal remains have an excellent view of the mountains.'

There was no reply on the radio but I could feel the ice coming from Nicolette. I found myself not giving a hoot.

32

We drove through the Hogan Camp gates promptly at 18h30 – allowing the guests an hour to dress in their finery and then a have a drink before the live broadcast at 20h00. The little satellite van was the only other vehicle in the car park, dish erect. Along with a blue glow, a strong smell of marijuana emanated from the open door, through which I could see the two dishevelled technicians in front of a bank of blinking lights and switches.

Unsurprisingly, Nicolette and Mayan were waiting tentatively in the car park – the former bearing a tray of warm refresher towels and the latter a silver tray of Bollinger-filled flutes (not pink). I have no doubt that the laughter emanating from the Land Rover must have come as a surprise for the anxious pair. Stacy was regaling her devotees with a lavatorial story about the time she'd imbibed salmonella on a yacht in the Caribbean. Before Nicolette could utter a word, Stacy – now quite drunk after two of my G&Ts – fell off the running board as she climbed from the car, righted herself and then kissed the owner of Sasekile on both cheeks.

'Delightful and profound!' was all she said before taking a glass and wafting down to her room, Bobby grumbling behind her.

'Good evening, ladies,' I said to the bewildered women before reversing the Land Rover and taking it back to the workshop.

I returned to the BC to change – we'd been instructed to wear the smartest clothes we owned. I had one level of clothing and there is no one who would have described my torn khakis, holey running shirt and collection of disintegrating underpants as 'smart'. I would have to make do.

The bathroom was occupied and there was a queue consisting of Franci, Solomon and Donald waiting to access the shower.

'Jasper, for fuck sake's, what the hell are you doing in there?' Franci was banging on the door. 'I have to wash my hair for this thing tonight!'

Jasper had, not unusually, been in there for some time.

'Bru, I'm just having a shit, shower and shave – I've done the first two but, yoh, I might have to go back for another of the first one. I tried some lowveld milkberry fruits today but I rate I ate too many ...'

Donald wisely headed to wash at Katie's new digs, and I went to my room.

On my bed was a surprise: a neatly folded black Sasekile-uniform shirt and a pair of khaki trousers. On the pile was a handwritten note.

Dear Angus,
This uniform is to be worn to this evening's events. I have made
sure that all your rangers have the same. Please make sure they
arrive looking as smart as possible – especially the one who looks
like a tramp.
Thank you,
Nicolette

This was significant – yes, Nicolette had written the note herself, but mainly it referred to my charges as rangers and not as trainees. I put it in the front of my copy of *Ornithology for Africa* for safekeeping. If there was any mention of the BC's residents (past and present) having to leave post the Condé Nast group, then this little missive would be evidence that the owner herself had decreed them rangers.

As I lay smiling on my bed, Jasper eventually emerged from the loo, followed by a cloud of steam and the odour of a thousand sewage farms.

'Oh, for fuck sake's!' said Franci.

'Sorry, bru!' I heard Jasper say, 'but, jissus, those berries are explosive.'

'No shit!' shouted Franci.

Around 30 minutes later, we were spruced and ready in our Sasekile finery. I'd polished my boots to a sheen, Franci had donned a pair of expensive-looking earrings and applied some makeup. Jasper, Solomon and I were waiting at the trestles when she emerged from her tent. Jasper's attention was drawn from his flower guide and his jaw fell open.

'Bru! Wow, you look hot. If you and Solly weren't hitting it off, I'd make a move for sure!'

For the first time since I'd known her, Franci flushed. Solomon's eyes grew wide and he uttered a single syllable: 'Yoh.'

I arrived at Hogan Camp 30 minutes before the broadcast. The other rangers had headed down to the Main Camp boma, where String Bean was making final preparations for the black-tie gala that was to take place after the awards ceremony. I, as Stacy & Co's personal-change architect, had to be at Hogan Camp for the whole awards-ceremony palaver, but I didn't mind – indeed, I was rather looking forward to seeing Mayan dressed up for the occasion.

All seemed to be quiet efficiency – the butlers were polishing glasses and pouring champagne, and off to one side September was overseeing a snack table while O'Reilly, Rufina, Hayley and Sam periodically emerged from the kitchen bearing trays of delicacies.

Craig had installed himself at a temporary desk near the fireplace. On this were a number of computer screens, and he was tapping away at a keyboard in typically ferocious fashion. Craig January's idea of black tie did not, I was fairly certain, conform to the designation as envisaged by Stacy Johannson or Nicolette Hogan. On his bottom he wore a pair of black tracksuit pants. These were far too short, such that his calves were completely exposed. On his feet he wore some brown sandals (polished), under which were a pair of Mickey Mouse socks that extended halfway to the black pant-bottoms. His top was mostly black – a long sleeved T-shirt with a white bowtie printed at the neck and a pair of white braces printed over the shoulders.

I turned my attention to the centre of the deck where the kudu-horn installation would form the backdrop for the awards. The pile was gorgeously lit from all angles and in front stood an elaborate lectern made of an old leadwood stump. From here, Stacy would deliver her address and then unveil the winner of the year's Pink Flute award. The maintenance team had strung two large spotlights from one of the roof beams, and these cast two bright beams onto the lectern with two cameras on tripods aimed at the scene.

It looked rather professional but for the fact that the pile was now most definitely leaning to the left. In fact, as I considered it, Clifford the butler walked past and the topmost horn slipped and fell to the deck with a soft thud, cracking into two pieces.

Utterly unconcerned, Clifford scooped up the broken pieces and tossed them over the deck before wiping the dust from the ground and carrying on with lighting the candles. I thought how amusing it would be should the entire edifice come crashing down mid Stacy's speech.

'What do you find so amusing?' asked Mayan.

I turned to look at the Hogan Camp manager and the breath caught in my throat. She was standing behind the bar next to the elaborate corkscrew wine rack, having just removed a bottle of chilled white. Her hair was up in a design of intimidating complexity, the golden thread woven throughout. A few strands hung over her face, which just then was softly lit by a flickering candelabrum. Unless the light was playing tricks with my eyes, there were gold flecks on her eyelids. Her dress was a black and strapless affair that defied gravity.

Mayan came out from behind the bar, a shapely leg escaping momentarily from a slit in the dress. On her feet she wore a pair of flat sandals with leather thongs that tied somewhere above the ankles. Being slightly at a loss for words I said, 'Um, no heels for the occasion?'

And regretted it immediately.

'No – I'll be walking around on decking and boma sand all evening.'

As if to illustrate the wisdom of her choice, Melitha came out of the kitchen just then, carrying a tray of martini glasses filled with some sort of pink cocktail. She was wearing a bright-red evening dress and a clicking noise indicated sharp stiletto footwear.

'Hi, guyth!' she said, breezily stepping onto the decking. She made it four steps before her right heel slipped between two planks. 'Oh, thit!' She tried to correct as cocktails flew in all directions.

Clifford rushed over with a mop, Mayan helped Melitha to her feet and I tried to wedge the shoe out from between the planks. As I tugged and twisted, I noticed something that in retrospect should have set off alarm bells: what pink cocktail hadn't yet been mopped was flowing west across the deck.

'I think you might have sprained the ankle.' Mayan was kneeling, somehow managing to maintain her elegance while ministering to Melitha's rapidly swelling ankle.

'Thit, thit thit! I thould have worn flat thoes like you!'

Mayan radioed for Jeff at the Main Camp and prevailed upon him to come and fetch his beloved. Mayan and I walked the patient out to the car park and lingered as Jeff and Melitha departed.

The moon had risen, casting its ghostly glow over the scene. We said nothing, just letting the atmosphere fizz, me watching the light paint Mayan's cheek as she looked at the dim stars. Slowly she turned to face me.

'You know I'm supposed to be engaged to someone at home.'

'Oh.' I didn't really know what else to say but realised I felt suddenly nauseous. 'That's, um ...'

I was about to comment further, but we heard the sound of approaching voices. I checked my watch – fifteen minutes to showtime.

'We'd better get back,' I said.

Without speaking we walked through the entrance and onto the deck, me feeling like a million bucks to be seen next to her. A few minutes later, the place was packed as 66 guests crowded into the exclusive Hogan Camp. Filling just about every space except that occupied by Craig and the two cameramen, people were sitting on sofa arms, ottomans, tables and one lithe fellow was perched on the bar. Most people, however, occupied the deck from which dining tables and chairs had been cleared. The railings had been decorated with fairy lights and three tall tables bore snacks, champagne and pink cocktails that were constantly refreshed by the butlers.

At 19h55, Stacy made her way to the lectern. The cameramen trained their lenses on her, spotlights came up and a minion – a small, mousy woman in a green cocktail dress – rushed over to touch up the Condé Nast chairman's makeup.

The guests went silent.

At 19h55 and 30 seconds, a dreadful groaning emanated from somewhere beneath the deck.

A horn detached from the installation and Clifford, on his way past with a tray, simply kicked it over the edge. At the lectern, Stacy removed her glasses and looked at her feet.

At 19h56, the kitchen swing door opened and I turned to see a silverback-grizzly hybrid silhouetted in the doorway. I stood protectively in front of Mayan until I realised it was Francois.

'Fok. Get everyone off ve deck now!' he wheezed, too out of breath to shout.

What Nicolette did next suggested she might have succeeded in professional rugby. She ran at Francois and drove him back through the kitchen door like he was a small tackling bag.

'Testing, testing, one, two, three,' Stacy said into the microphone, leaning forward to tap it.

With three minutes to go until showtime there was another groan from somewhere beneath the deck, but it was drowned out by Stacy, who had managed to hook her long beaded necklace on a protruding piece of the lectern's driftwood. She bellowed – her face but an inch from the microphone.

I put two and two together at the same time as Mayan, and we charged through the swing doors. In the kitchen, Francois stood backed against a serving counter like a buffalo facing a lioness.

'It's fokken collapsing!' he was saying to Nicolette. 'I been worried about it since we started ve building and I went to check. Ve foundations is collapsing wiff all vose people standing on it – vat deck is going to collapse!'

'You will *not* move anyone off that deck,' Nicolette snarled. 'She is about to make her address and – quite possibly – hand us the Pink Flute!'

The big man was close to tears. 'Waddafok is a floot?'

'She'll give no one a flute if your guests are lying impaled by timber in the Tsessebe River,' I said.

Nicolette had turned into something that resembled a rabid pit bull.

'No one is leaving this deck until I am holding that Pink fucking Flute!' she growled, pointing a finger at Francois and then at me. 'And that deck had better stay upright. So make a fucking plan!' She plastered a winning smile onto her face and swept back through the kitchen doors.

'Francois,' I said, 'what exactly is happening?'

The huge man shook his head, clutching at his hair.

'Ve pillars of ve fokken deck is sinking into ve earf!'

'Francois,' Mayan commanded. 'Just try and stay calm and tell us: with all the time in the world, how would you make it stop?'

'You have to take down ve deck!' he wailed.

'No, just temporarily,' said Mayan. 'How would you do it *temporarily*?'

Francois sniffed. 'You have to put somefing underneaf vose crossbeams – somfing wide and big.'

I poked my head out of the kitchen doors.

Cameras were rolling and Stacy was in full flow, blathering on about Condé Nast and all it had achieved. There was another groan from beneath the deck and this time it also shook. One or two guests uttered gasps of alarm and, behind Stacy, another kudu horn toppled. This time Clifford caught it with one hand before tossing it over his shoulder into the bush.

Then I had a bit of a brain wave ... something big and wide about the height of the crossbeams. I pulled my head back in through the kitchen doors.

'Give me your radio,' I said to Mayan. 'String Bean,' I called, 'come in for Angus – post-fucking-haste!'

'Go ahead,' said my brother. 'Are the results in? Did we win the flute?'

'Listen, and don't ask questions – I'll explain when you get here. Get every available Land Rover to Hogan Camp as fast as you can – by fast, I mean in the next three minutes. Lives might depend on it!'

There was a time (just a few weeks previously – and indeed for most of his years on Planet Earth) when String Bean would have simply refused. But not that night.

'Copy,' he said.

I turned to Francois, whose face was still in his hands.

'Francois, we're going to park the Land Rovers under the crossbeams.' I had no idea if this would work but we'd all know soon enough.

He looked up, eyes wide. 'But what about ve Land Rovers? Vey will break!'

'Don't worry about that – if we park a few cars under the deck with the seat frames under the crossbeams, will that work?'

'Ja.'

Mayan, who'd been through the swing doors to check on proceedings, reported: 'Another horn just came off that installation and one of the guests has lost a glass over the edge of the deck.'

'Come!' I said – I could already hear the fast approach of roaring engines, and we ran out into the car park as Jeff, String Bean and Solomon pulled up with three others behind them.

Francois wasted no time.

'Move!' he shouted, as he ran to SB's car, opened the door, and shoved SB onto the centre console. In a second, Francois was driving onto the golf-cart track that would give him access to the river and the deck just above it.

'Follow him,' I shouted at Jeff, jumping onto his car and then at Mayan: 'Get them to follow us!'

We drove off as fast as practicable in the darkness, threading our way past rocks and trees. After what felt like an age, during which my mind filled with images of guests plummeting into the river to be mauled by pissed-off buffalo, we found a space between suite 1 and the deck where we could get down to the river.

I looked up to the right as we drove down the bank. The glow of the festivities above cast a gentle light in front of us, but things were getting more raucous up top – Stacy, having completed her address, was beginning to hand out the various smaller awards. With each there was a toast, and with each toast there was a lot of clapping and cheering as the progressively soaked audience shuffled about on the subsiding deck.

Francois's car made it around to the front of the deck and Jeff and I followed. Something smashed onto the bonnet of the Land Rover: pieces of shattered kudu horn. I looked up to see Clifford, four metres above, dusting his hands.

The creaking and groaning noise coming from under the deck was disturbing in the extreme. Jeff drew level with Francois, who had executed a three-point turn and was about to reverse under the deck.

'What the fuck is going on?' said String Bean from the passenger seat.

'The deck is about to collapse with all those people on it!' I said.

'Shit,' said SB as the timbers groaned again.

This time, like watching a ship being hit by a wave in slow motion, we saw the whole deck shudder. There was a cry of alarm from above – the champagne glass belonging to a woman perched on the railing plummeted over the edge and landed with a smash between the two vehicles.

'Fok!' said Francois. He shoved the Land Rover into low range and reversed up under the deck, until, with a dull clang, the back-seat frame hit one of the crossbeams. This happened at the same time as another cheer came from above. Almost immediately, the car's front wheels rose off the ground as the deck bore down.

'Bring anover fokken car!' yelled Francois as another cheer came from above.

Jeff, who had a brain far too slow for this operation, just stared. I ran around the car, shoved him out of the driver's seat, leapt in and reversed under the deck, narrowly missing decapitation by a beam. There was a nasty crunching sound as a diagonal beam made contact with the steel bull bar. Like with Francois's car, the vehicle came off its rear wheels as the front began to bear weight.

'Stop there!' beckoned Francois. 'Bring ve next one, Solly!'

My work done, I left my vehicle and ran back up the bank, passing the three other vehicles making their way down towards the base.

'What's going on?' said Franci as I ran up past her car.

'The deck is sinking!' I shouted and carried on running.

'Of course it is,' said Donald easing past in another soon-to-be destroyed Land Rover.

I hoped they'd be able to wedge all six Land Rovers in place before the whole thing came down.

Back at the ceremony, things were reaching fever pitch. With each of the 20 or so awards that Stacy was doling out, guests took ever-larger swigs – this was, after all, not a group of people with an understanding of the word 'abstemious'.

Mayan was standing nervously at the railing just behind the horn pile, peering over as Stacy began to announce the next award. Next to Mayan, and ogling her with lascivious intent, was Bobby Johannson, umpteenth bourbon in hand.

A muffled shout from below momentarily distracted me from Mayan's gravity-defying dress, and I followed her gaze. Four metres down, the last three Land Rovers were in line, waiting to be wedged in place. Francois was frantically gesticulating, and almost managing to keep his voice down. The guests above, enrapt by the alcohol, festive spirit and accolades, seemed hardly aware of the sloshing drinks in their glasses and the shifting ground beneath their feet.

'Is this going to work?' asked Mayan.

'I have no idea,' I replied.

'What the hell is goin on down there?' Bobby drained his glass and glared at me. 'That doesn't look safe!' he added, indicating the activity below as another vehicle reversed under the deck and thudded into a crossbeam.

'And the award for best breakfast shervice ...' Stacy gripped the side of the lectern for support, blinked and ripped open the envelope she was holding. Out came a pink card at which she squinted. 'Sheen Fallsh Hotel in Knockdur ... Knockdoo ... shomewhere in Ireland!'

Another cheer erupted from the deck.

This time, as the crowd roared, the deck actually shifted. Mayan let out a little gasp and reached for the nearest solid thing: me.

As we caught each other, a selection of glasses that had been resting on the deck's railing went over. I heard a loud shout from below and looked down to see the dimly lit figure of Donald holding his head.

The deck shifted again.

Startled shouts came from the few people not too sozzled to notice. A tall table of snacks wobbled but was too surrounded by people to actually fall over.

Tempting as it was to remain staring into Mayan's bottomless eyes as the world ended, a yelp behind her distracted me and I swung round in time to see the falling figure of Bobby Johannson. The man had been leaning over the railing trying to figure out what was going on when the subsiding decking and his state of inebriation had combined with devastating effect. As he overbalanced, I shoved Mayan aside and lunged, catching his left foot as he went over the edge. There was little chance of my mass counteracting his – he was a big man with far too many years of fine dining in the bank – but thankfully Clifford the butler was once again on hand. This time, instead of priceless bits of art he threw his tray of champagne into the wilderness and lunged for Bobby's right foot.

There hung the head of Condé Nast's husband, his personal effects raining down from his dinner jacket onto the Land Rovers and rangers below. Almost entirely hidden in the shadow of the great kudu-horn pile, the kerfuffle went almost unnoticed.

'And the award for most eco-friendly boutique hotel goes to ... Le Nuku Hiva in French Polyneesh ... Polynee ... a French Island!'

Another loud toast commenced, Bobby flailing below us in the darkness, as the final Land Rover rammed up under the deck. As the deck jolted, Bobby's right foot slipped from Clifford's grip – only to be grabbed by the massive hams of Hanyani. Together we hauled until Bobby was close enough for Clifford to grab the lapels of his velvet jacket. We finally slid him back over the railing and he sat down heavily, leaning against one of the pillars. He waved a finger at me and looked like he might be about to speak but then slumped forward – either dead or passed out.

'And finally, the moment you've all been waiting for ...' said Stacy.

At this point, the mousy minion brought forth the wooden box containing the revered Pink Flute. For the first time since the ceremony began, silence fell over the crowd. Everyone turned their attention on

Stacy. Standing at the bar, Nicolette was the colour of a milk – her sharp eyes darting from Stacy to the comatose figure of Stacy's husband just discernible in the shadows behind the rapidly diminishing art installation.

The head of Condé Nast then reached inside the front of her dress in what may have been an attempt at a seduction but looked more like she had a tick bite on her left breast. She giggled into the microphone. After an interminable period of scrabbling around between her large and enhanced cleavage, she withdrew a chain. On the end of this hung a little key. There was a collective gasp. The only sound was Bobby's ragged breathing indicating that the old boy had some life in him yet and the odd muffled 'Fok' from below, where Francois was apparently still examining the construction.

Stacy awkwardly detached the chain from her neck – but dropped it onto the slatted deck planks.

'Oh fuck!' she exclaimed, forgetting that she was broadcasting live to countless hotels around the world. She dropped to her knees and scrambled about on the floor. Thankfully the chain had caught between the planks and did not fall all the way through, so after a bit of coaxing she retrieved it, stood unsteadily, banged her head on the lectern, swore again and then refocused on the box containing the Pink Flute.

There were a few mutters from around the deck but this did nothing to diminish the fizzing atmosphere of expectation. Stacy wiped a piece of hair from her eye and then made a painful attempt to pin it back with its companions in the complicated arrangement on the back of her head. When about 3 000 bobby pins exploded in all directions – releasing Stacy's coiffure such that she began to resemble Sasekile's least-fashionable employee, Craig – Mayan and I began to giggle. At least we managed to keep it relatively quiet. Clifford had no such qualms and let out a loud guffaw before Mayan stomped on his foot.

Bleary-eyed, Stacy aimed the key at the slot in the ornate antique box. I felt Mayan tense next to me. The Condé Nast chairman, eyes of the world on her, pushed and prodded but no matter how she tried, the key simply wouldn't go into the locking mechanism.

Initially, I assumed her state of advanced pickling was to blame. This until the minion sidled up to the lectern and began to help. The two of them tried for an awkward few minutes, during which Stacy muttered bits of alarming invective. The minion, sensitive to the industrial-level tension that permeated the atmosphere, squinted into the glare of the lights and cameras that were trained on the scene.

'Um, sorry, everyone ... yes, well, we just, um, have a small problem here ... no need to panic!' she panicked.

By this stage, Stacy was leaning her whole body on the box, sweat forming on her brow, from which sprouted an alarming volume of un-constrained, bleached and hair-sprayed hair.

I looked across at Nicolette, whose pallor had turned from milky to troll. She was squeezing the bar counter, nostrils flared.

'It won't go inshide!' Stacy exclaimed loudly.

The minion whispered something into her boss's ear and then grinned idiotically into the cameras.

Stacy's head shot up and she looked around as if just realising she was in front of a very large audience. She wiped her nose, stared into one of the cameras and held up her right hand, index finger extended.

'It sheemsh the box ...' she pronounced, looking around, 'will not open.' Then she nodded as though she'd just delivered the Grand Unified Theory.

There were a few mutters from around the deck.

'We will therefore' – she took a deep breath and leant into the micro-phone – 'announsh the winner without the Pink Flute.' She nodded again and held out her left hand, into which the minion placed a pink envelope with gold embossing.

By this stage, even I was getting edgy. I still can't say I was worried about whether Sasekile's name was on the card, but the moment had become so cringy that my toes had begun to ache.

'Sweet Muruga,' said Mayan, 'please just get it over with.'

After more fumbling and some help from the minion, the wax seal was cracked and the envelope came open.

Stacy looked into the cameras as the card emerged. Nicolette gagged where she stood, unable to keep her eyes on the scene.

Stacy looked down, then up again. Then she cleared her throat ...

... and dropped the card.

It fell neatly through a gap in the planking. A deathly silence followed. Stacy stared into the camera, then she looked at her hands as if hoping the card would magically reappear.

The silence was broken by a thud – I looked up to see that Nicolette had fainted behind the bar.

Then, from far below the deck, String Bean's voice.

'Shit!' he shouted. 'We won! Sasekile won the fucking Pink Flute!'

A ragged cheer could be heard from below the deck – which must have been very confusing to those who had no idea that a group of people and Land Rovers were desperately propping up Hogan Camp.

'Sasekile' began to ripple over a sea of whispers on the deck.

When it reached Stacy, she looked into one of the cameras. 'Well, the winner of the Pink Flute this year is ... Sshash ... um ... Shhha ...' She cleared her throat as Nicolette reappeared behind the bar, leaning heavily on Hanyani and O'Reilly. 'Shashek ...'

The minion lost patience, elbowed her drunken boss out of the way and took the mic in her hand.

'Oh for God's sake, Stacy – it's *Sasekile*! The winner of the Pink Flute this year is Sasekile Private Game Reserve.'

Applause and cheering rang around the deck, from below and from next to me, where Clifford was doing his best Rumpelstiltskin impersonation.

'Fek, yes!' shouted O'Reilly before planting a kiss on the stunned visage of Nicolette Hogan and then on Hanyani for good measure.

I looked down at Bobby Johannson, who finally looked up.

'This is some bullshit,' he muttered before his head slumped forward again.

Nicolette made her way unsteadily to the lectern, where Stacy hugged her like a long-lost relative. She then presented the antique box to Mrs Hogan, the key still sticking out of the jammed keyhole. More applause followed and then another cheer as the deck crew from below arrived through the kitchen swing doors, delirious with happiness.

'Thank you, thank you,' said Nicolette, tears flowing down her cheeks for the first time in living memory. 'This means the world to me and to the team here.' She looked down and swallowed hard. 'I am particularly grateful to the people who helped make Hogan Camp – our flagship camp – Africa's premier safari destination!' She looked up at Hugh, who was grinning at her from behind the bar.

I nearly choked as I considered the dangers to which we'd just subjected the world's most discerning travellers.

Mayan squeezed my hand.

Then it was over. Nicolette, to more cheers and applause, lifted the box and walked out of the light. As the noise died down, Hugh tinged on a glass and shouted: 'Ladies and gentlemen, the security team is ready to escort you to the Main Camp boma, where a sumptuous feast awaits!'

Slowly the deck emptied and happy chatter disappeared into the darkness towards Main Camp. Bobby and Stacy were the last to stagger out, the former muttering incoherently, the latter demanding another glass of pink champagne.

Mayan and I wandered past the wine rack and through the kitchen swing doors. There, sitting on an upturned crate in one corner, we found Francois, tears flowing into his beard, massive hands shaking as he slid them away from his face. I quickly returned to the bar, found the biggest beer glass I could, filled it to halfway with brandy, topped it up with Coke and charged back into the kitchen. Mayan was squatting next to the maintenance manager who, I was sure, would become the very first maintenance manager in any hotel worldwide to win employee of the month.

I handed him the glass. Shoulders shuddering, he took it, sniffed once and downed the entire thing in one gulp.

'Come on, old boy,' I said. 'You did it.'

33

Dinner in the Main Camp boma that evening was a triumph. The guests, plastered to a human, could have been fed from a trough of pig swill for all they'd have noticed.

As it turned out, the meal that O'Reilly's team had prepared was an exquisite array of deliciousness, served buffet-style, that my palate was nowhere near sophisticated enough to appreciate. The starters consisted of springbok carpaccio, pear-and-blue-cheese salads and what I believe are 'microgreens' – as far as I can work out, the young children of bigger greens. The main course was an array of braaied flesh – spicy chicken with groundnut sauce, African sausage (aka boerewors), ribeye steaks and giant yellowtail swimming in a delicious-smelling combination of butter, lemon and dill. The desert consisted of multilayered cake stands full of tiny sponges, tarts, mousses and other sweet things for which I do not have the descriptive language. Obscenely expensive wine flowed like water, as did post-dinner cognac and malt whisky by the gallon.

String Bean had directed the creation of a stunning dining area in the boma with a gutsy South African theme – 'shebeen' (or illegal drinking house to the uninitiated). For this job, he'd leant heavily on Clifford's experience as an actual shebeen owner – his house of ill-repute being situated in Lilydale Village, not far from the Sasekile boundary. The front of the bar was dressed with corrugated-iron sheeting painted in cheerful colours. Overhead, coloured bulbs blinked while the round tables – although beautifully laid – each had elaborate centrepieces consisting of colourful candles poking out of beer bottles of all sizes and colours. Hundreds of lanterns lined the split-pole fence, fairy lights blinked from the red-ivory and gardenia trees at each end.

My brother was in his absolute element. Through the dinner, he walked around with a bottle of red in one hand and white in the other, topping up glasses, making jokes with guests and, when required, ordering about the other camp managers and butlers. From where I sat with my guests, I did not see him sit down even once. He was dressed in a blue overall, tailored (presumably by Jeffry the village tailor) to fit perfectly, a black bowtie at his neck.

As the desert was cleared, the staff choir came in to perform. I normally detested these performances – exhausted laundry ladies, maintenance crew and gardeners singing traditional songs for guests with expressions less cheerful than a bunch of condemned standing before the gallows. The songs at many lodges took the form of a sort of homage for the lodge, its beneficent owners or the bloody Big Five, and that always made me cringe. This time, however, the songs had been inspired by none other than Incredible the butler, who'd apparently acquiesced to coming out of retirement for 'just only one show after insoforth it cannot go on'.

Rather than the usual awful ditties, the choir engaged in a traditional Muchongolo dance. They brought in an array of drums – wooden and plastic barrels covered in animal skins, many of which, I suspect, were extra-legally acquired in the greater Kruger area. The booming drums, raucous singing and exuberant dancing conjured a captivating atmosphere. People stared in amazement as Incredible strode to the front to perform, flinging himself with such athleticism that it seemed as if the boma floor was made of springs instead of sand.

Incredible's costume was something to behold – paying equal homage to tradition, ingenuity and plastic Chinese imports. Around his ankles (and those of many performers) were two sets of rattles. These were shaped like fortune cookies and made, ingeniously, from sliced-up milk bottles filled with stones and sewed together with fishing line. Around his knees he'd tied strands of leather strung with what looked like a shredded sheepskin car-seat cover. His midriff sported a cow-hide kilt (beneath which Incredible had donned ... well, nothing – which may have contributed to the gasps from the audience at each leap). He was bare-chested but for two thick straps of colourful plastic beads that crisscrossed his chest. Possibly my favourite part of the outfit was his headdress, which looked (and smelt) like he had found an expired porcupine and fashioned its corpse into a hat.

As he finished his performance – leaping up, doing a backflip and then falling into the sand – the rest of the dancers, both men and women, came forward as one. In less than a minute they had all the guests up and dancing with them. It's always hilarious watching guests attempt to dance like the locals – awkwardly looking around and eventually resorting to some sort of muted can-can. This time, however, the boma quickly turned into the Shangane version of a mosh pit, with everyone caught up in the energy of booze, drumming and exuberant dancing.

I, not being much of a dancer, made my way to the bar, against which SB was leaning with Simone, huge smiles over their faces. As I arrived, SB executed an elegant vault over the counter. Three tumblers appeared and into them he poured generous measures of Ardmore 10 Year Old and then plopped two blocks of ice into each. I took one and we clinked glasses.

'Christ, we make things hard for ourselves,' he said, taking a long draw.

'It seems unavoidable,' I agreed.

'I think that's just how it is with you two,' said Simone.

We watched the dancing for a while and then saw something that made us eject our mouthfuls of precious elixir. Nicolette Hogan was arm in arm with Incredible. They had forsaken traditional Shangane dancing and were executing something between a line dance and the twist, both grinning inanely.

String Bean topped us up.

'By the way,' I asked, 'what did ye olde Pink Flute look like when the safe arrived back from Boxa Huku this afternoon?'

This made SB spit out a second mouthful.

'You have no idea,' he said, shaking his head. 'I arrived at the office at the same time as Nicolette. Hilda tried the combination lock but it wouldn't work, so we hauled the safe round to the workshop – actually, we just pushed it back through the hole in the wall. Then Douglas and Bennet set to it with the acetylene torch and after an hour – during which Nicolette had to sit down and have a stiff brandy – they finally managed to cut it open.' SB took a sip of his drink and shook his head again. 'I brought the box back to the office and put it on Hilda's desk. Then we realised we didn't have the key. There was a lot of swearing, but we all agreed we couldn't let Stacy open it *live* to the world before we'd checked the state of the flute. Bertie picked the lock in about 25 seconds and then we crowded round as Nicolette prized open the lid.'

String Bean began to laugh, tears leaking from his eyes.

'When we got the lid open, Nicolette screamed, ran out and was sick in the herb garden. Mayan, Bertie and I then looked into the box and saw why: the precious Pink Flute was in more pieces than there are grains of sand in this boma.'

He drained his glass and topped us all up again as the dancing continued unabated.

'It was Mayan who hatched the plan. Whatever happened tonight – whoever won – the box had to remain closed. So Bertie filled the lock with epoxy – it will never work again.'

'And what now?' I asked.

'Now? Well Condé Nast leaves it with us for six months and then it has to go back to the headquarters in New York. So Nicolette is going to have to find a forger-slash-jeweller to construct another one – she doesn't look very worried now, does she?'

He was correct. Sasekile's owner was line dancing with Solomon, who had added Zulu stamping to the raucous melee.

'And did Jacob find the mastermind – if a heist like this could be said to have such a thing?'

'I'm not sure you'll believe it when I tell you. Jacob arrived in the office carrying the culprit by the scruff of the neck: it was none other than your old friend Mishak. And he required no coercion to start singing like a white-browed robin-chat. Guess who his co-conspirator was?' SB shook his head. 'None other than Bradley Pringle.'

'Sweet Lord!' I said, genuinely surprised.

'The two of them are currently enjoying the government hotel in Hoedspruit.'

'I suppose Jerome's ravishing of his wife drove him insane.'

'Quite,' said String Bean. 'I don't think that Nicolette will press charges – he's such a hopeless fellow and seems to be in deep financial distress.'

Just then the dancing ended – or, more accurately, the drummers became so fatigued they simply rose and left the boma. As the noise died, some guests returned to their tables and others headed for their sumptuous suites. Nicolette approached the bar.

'Congratulations, Mrs Hogan,' I said to her, raising my glass.

She was out of breath, sweating and grinning from ear to ear. 'I'll have one of those please, Hugh,' she said, nodding at our glasses.

SB produced another tumbler, uncorked the glorious whisky and poured a measure for Nicolette. The four of us clinked glasses.

'Cheers to you,' she said. 'Really, I am not sure we could have pulled this off without you two.'

'One does what one can,' I said.

'We're just happy it all turned out okay,' said String Bean.

'Well, I am very grateful.'

'Excellent,' I said, slapping down my glass and turning to face her. 'While you are filled with this bonhomie, I would like to make a request.'

Nicolette eyed me, but our relationship had changed over the last while and I no longer felt intimidated. Not even SB was taken aback by my tone.

'And what is that?' she asked.

'I'd like you to guarantee all of my trainees full-time employment here. Except the one who was schtoomping Kelly-Anne – I don't give a flying whatsit what you do with him.'

She looked surprised. 'Of course, they have more than proved them-selves. Anything else?'

There was a sarcastic hint to her voice that I chose to ignore.

'I think you should reinstate my brother as the GM – and give him an operations manager and head ranger with a lot more gumption than the lot you had installed before.'

'Angus!' said String Bean, finally registering alarm.

'No, Hugh,' said Nicolette. 'He's right. Even if you did make some colossal errors of judgement, we didn't give you enough support.'

String Bean was silent, not daring to hope.

'We'll have a meeting tomorrow when we've all sobered up a bit.' Nicolette drained her glass. 'Thank you both again – you have no idea what this means to me. Good night.'

She took two steps and turned around.

'And you, Angus, what do you want to do? I need some rangers trained in Kenya if you have any interest. Give it some thought.'

With that, Sasekile's owner departed from the boma in a happy haze.

String Bean once again topped us up – I was feeling quite pissed but there was to be no game drive the following morning given that the group needed to catch a plane at 08h00.

Still smiling, her hair still perfectly in place, Mayan was standing at the entrance greeting the departing guests.

'You'd be a moron to let that one go,' said String Bean.

'What are you talking about?'

'Oh, piss off,' he said. 'The way you look at each other is almost sickening.'

'I think it's really sweet,' said Simone.

SB drained his glass and slapped it onto the bar counter. 'Come on, my dear, let us go to bed. Tomorrow there will no doubt be many new challenges in this madhouse – whether I am Tamboti Camp manager or the big boss.'

'Good night, Mr and Mrs MacNaughton,' I said.

Simone gave me a peck on the cheek and they wandered out through the back of the boma, arm in arm, swerving slightly.

Having bade their guests goodnight, Solomon, Franci, Katie, Donald and Jasper came over to the bar. I executed the same vault String Bean had, but as I am much shorter than him I clipped the counter with my left foot and fell onto the floor below – being well oiled and relaxed probably precluded any severe injury. I jumped up as though this is precisely what I'd intended, lifted a bottle of Balvenie from the rack behind me, lined up six tumblers and poured a measure into each. Everyone took a glass.

'To all of you,' I said, lifting my tumbler. 'What a way to start your ranging careers.'

'To us,' said Franci, and the rest lifted their drinks and took a sip.

'And to *you*,' said Donald, causing everyone to clink their glasses again. 'I mean it.' Donald's jaw clenched in an uncharacteristic show of emotion. 'You have made a huge difference to all of our lives.'

'Unorthodox for sure,' Katie said, 'but anyone who can turn Jasper into a ranger is a genius in my book.'

Jasper smiled and looked around the group. Tears welled and one dripped down his right cheek.

'Thank you for letting me be part of this team.' He sniffed. 'Dudes, I've never been anything but a hustler without purpose.' He took a sip. 'Now it's different. I dig you okes so much.'

Another tear escaped as Katie threw her arms around him and kissed his cheek.

'We love you, Jasper!' she said.

'You love everyone, Katie,' Solomon said cheerfully.

I looked up from my group and spotted Mark and Sean making their way out of the boma. Solomon must have seen them too.

'Hey, madoda!' he said. 'Come and drink with us.'

They stopped for an awkward few moments.

'Wozani,' said Solomon. Then he detached himself from the bar, walked over, put his large arms around each of their shoulders and drew them towards the bar.

I pulled two more tumblers from the rack and poured a measure into each. They appeared stunned by Solomon's magnanimity, as was I – there is no way I would have done the same in a hundred years. But it wasn't long before the rest of the rangers joined us too – awkwardly at first, but after a glass or two of neat malt whisky, everyone softened up. Perhaps there was hope for the team after all – and I wondered how long it would take before Solomon was ready to run it.

When all the guests had left, the rest of the service staff joined us for a final drink. Mayan eased behind the counter next to me as we poured for everyone, the subtle smell of jasmine combined with the amount of whisky I'd consumed making me tingle all over.

Eventually, the staff began to drift off to bed. I had managed to get myself into a lengthy chat with Mark, Sean, Franci and Solomon. All utterly sozzled, they were lamenting that they hadn't been friendlier to each other – bullshit as far as I was concerned but, hey, if this fostered a team, who was I to decree otherwise. Strictly speaking, I had no further role at Sasekile.

They were chatting about their backgrounds, Mark open-mouthed as Solomon described his homestead. Franci teased Sean about the moustache he was trying to grow – only she could have gotten away with telling him it looked like a crowd of starving ants had gathered on his top lip. We all laughed and when I looked up there were only rangers left – Mayan was nowhere to be seen.

The present and past residents of the Bat Cave soon found themselves wandering along the path towards the old BC – Katie had decided to eschew her new digs for one last night in the BC. Under the veranda, the coloured lights cast a cheerful lustre on the space in which we'd all learnt so much. We sat down at the trestles to wait as the bathroom procession began: girls first, then Solomon, Donald and finally Jasper.

At last it was only me left beneath the veranda. I went into the bathroom feeling rather bereft – unsure of the future, filled with the emotion of the evening and the indescribable sense of nostalgia and affection that only an early-summer night in the African wild can conjure. I came out a few minutes later to the sounds of a white-faced owl calling in the woodland – 'tookoo tookoo tooo' – against a background of cicadas and a fiery-necked nightjar who was piping somewhere near the kitchen.

The spell was broken by Jasper emerging from his tent, dressed only in a pair of underpants.

'Bru, can you kill the lights?'

He zipped himself back into his tent as I flipped the switches.

The darkness only amplified my emotion. Not knowing what else to do with myself, I stepped into the full-moonlight and started walking. Of course I should have carried a torch, but the moon was so bright that I could clearly see the path. Through the combretum woodland I walked as silently as possible – not because of fear but to keep intact the spell of the night.

Just past the kitchen I heard a water dikkop whistling near the camp waterhole and far to the north a leopard sawed.

In the camp there wasn't a human sound. I continued past Jerome and Katie's block, noticing that Jerome's GTI was no longer parked outside. Perhaps his shame was too great to bear. Perhaps he'd learnt a lesson – who knows.

Eventually I came within sight of the low Cape honeysuckle hedge that surrounded Mayan's cottage. The lights were off. I leant against a knobthorn tree and considered returning home.

'Is there something specific you're looking for?' Mayan's voice was soft.

And there she was, elbows resting nonchalantly on the rickety garden gate.

'I heard a scops owl in this tree.' I walked the final three metres to the gate and stood awkwardly in front of it. 'I like owls.'

'Me too.' She stood up. Her hair was free and she was dressed in a short white nightdress that glowed in the moonlight. She pushed her night-black locks behind her left ear and looked at me.

'I think I might need to search your garden for that owl,' I whispered, opening the little gate.

Then there was nothing separating us but a few charged inches of jasmine-scented air. She closed the gap, resting her face on my neck. We stood like this for blissful age until, finally, she turned her face to mine.

'How much longer must I wait before you –'

I planted my lips on hers.

Just as I was savouring her full, willing mouth on mine, her arms drawing me in tightly, a tremendous din arose from the direction of Hogan Camp. We weren't close to it, but the rending of timbers and crunching of metal indicated that the Hogan Camp deck – topped with its kudu-horn creation – was no longer.

'I don't think you'll have much of a camp to manage tomorrow,' I said.

She put her hands behind my neck and pulled my head to hers.

Far to the south, a lion roared. In the river, a bull hippo grunted and somewhere, ghosting across the moonlit wilderness, a hyena whooped its approval.

GLOSSARY OF GAME-DRIVE TERMS

bamba – verb or noun for kill, derived from the isiZulu verb 'bamba' meaning 'to catch'

gonnie – lion, derived from the word 'ingwenyama', a SiSwati honorific for 'lion'

ingwee – leopard, from the isiZulu 'ingwe' or Xitsonga 'yingwe'

khalering – crying, an English present participle of the isiZulu verb 'khala'; used to describe any kind of animal call

madush/madash – word to describe wild dogs; origin unclear

malungus – guests, derived from the isiZulu 'umlungu' (pl. abelungu) for European or white person

madoda – male, derived from the isiZulu 'amadoda' meaning 'men'

mafazi – female, derived from the isiZulu 'umfazi' meaning 'a married woman'

mova – vehicle, word of indeterminate origin, perhaps from the verb 'to move' as in 'mover'

munti – common duiker, from the Xitsonga word 'mhunti' phuza – drink or eat, derived from the isiZulu 'phuza' meaning 'to drink'

shlashla – tree, derived from the isiZulu 'isihlahla' meaning 'tree'

shteam – meaning 'a lot', 'very much', 'with strength'; derived from the English word 'steam' (presumably to do with powerful mining or railway equipment)

skankaan or skankie – cheetah, derived from the Xitsonga word 'xikan-kanka'

voetsek – an old Afrikaans word, loosely translated as 'piss off'

GENERAL GLOSSARY

choofs/choofing – South African slang for cigarettes/smoking

elie – short for elephant

jol – party

doos – Afrikaans for 'box', slang for feminine undercarriage

nkondzo – Shangane and Xitsonga for 'foot' or 'track'

sakabona – hello, derived from the isiZulu 'sawubona' meaning 'hello' or literally 'I see you'

S-bone – a nickname, in this case for Sean (short for 'Sean-bone')

veldskoen – Afrikaans for 'veld shoes', a particularly South African style of leather or suede shoe

zarms – short for 'sandwich' amongst the South African surfing fraternity

ACKNOWLEDGEMENTS

Phew. As I have said before, producing an actual book when you have my less-than-sterling ability to spell, see detail and concentrate is an extremely difficult task. I can safely say that before the advent of the word processor and the spell check, I wouldn't have gotten halfway to writing a street sign, let alone a novel.

I can also say that without the wonderful people at Pan Macmillan who have consistently backed, coaxed, advised and generally cajoled me, this work would never have seen the light of day. I am eternally grateful for their faith in me – particular thanks to Andrea Nattrass, Terry Morris, Eileen Bezemer, Veronica Napier and Sean Fraser. Equally important on these pages are the eyes and hands of Nicola Rijsdijk, editor extraordinaire. I find it amusing when I read acknowledgements in books where the author refers to 'my editor' and 'my publisher'. I am grateful to be counted as one of *their authors*.

Thank you to my mum and dad, who have read and gently advised on just about every piece of writing I have ever published. It means so very much to have you read (and I hope enjoy) my offerings. To my dear wife Kirsten, to whom this work is dedicated, thank you for allowing me to read the bits I thought were funny to you ... and then for laughing in all the right places – you make me feel like a comedic genius.

Lastly, thanks to the guests, rangers, trackers, housekeepers, security guards, laundry ladies, mechanics, butlers, hosts and managers with whom I have had the inestimable pleasure to work in the wilderness over the last two decades. Your efforts in the wild, even though you might not realise it, are helping to protect what is left of the fragile African wilderness on which the fate and history of humankind are so inextricably entwined.